THE DIRECTOR

By Henry Denker

PLAYS
Time Limit
A Case of Libel
A Far Country

NOVEL
The Director

THE
DIRECTOR

HENRY DENKER

♈

RICHARD W. BARON

NEW YORK

1970

Second Printing

Copyright © 1970 Henry Denker
Library of Congress Catalog Number: 77–108976
Published in the United States of America
by the Richard W. Baron Publishing Co., Inc.
Manufactured in the United States of America
Design by Vincent Torre

To Edith, my wife

THE DIRECTOR

... with a special brilliance no other American director has yet exhibited, Jock Finley has placed his personal signature on *Mustang!*

But more, Finley has thrust himself boldly and gloriously into the upper chamber of Europe's great auteurs of film—Fellini, Truffaut, Antonioni.

To have achieved that with a cast in which the two leading players are Preston Carr and Daisy Donnell is the measure of Finley's artistry and power.

As for Preston Carr, cinema king of another day, the artistic triumph of *Mustang!* places him among filmdom's immortals.

Jock Finley has provided Preston Carr with a fitting and loving epitaph. . . .

TIME Magazine, January 22, 1971

CHAPTER

1

GET Preston Carr to do the picture and you got a deal."

That was the way the president had ended their meeting, apologizing that he was in a hurry to catch the four-thirty jet back to New York.

Now, six minutes later, Jock Finley and his agent, Marty White, were standing in the studio's executive parking lot, between Marty's long, white Rolls Royce and Jock's red Ferrari roadster.

"It's a stall," Jock said, his light-blue eyes hard with anger, his lean, handsome face leaner because the muscles in his jaws were tense.

"It's no stall," Marty said.

"He doesn't like the script!" Jock persisted. "And he didn't want to say so, because the writer's a client of yours, too."

"It's no stall," Marty repeated thoughtfully.

"Then why did he say get Preston Carr?"

"Because when he asked you who could play the lead *you* mentioned Carr," Marty said. But he conceded, "Along with Lancaster, Douglas, Greg Peck, and Tony Quinn."

"Exactly! So why did he single out Carr? Who hasn't agreed to do a picture in over two years! Who probably won't do another one again as long as he lives! And why should he, he's loaded! So the easiest way to walk out on the deal was to say, get Preston Carr. I tell you, he doesn't like the script!"

3

"And I say, maybe it isn't the script," Marty said this cautiously, looking away, appearing troubled. It was a tactic with Marty White, when giving a client bad news, to look away, to stare into space, thoughtfully and concerned. Especially when he knew what the client's answer was going to be.

"I'm not the first director who's ever been replaced on a picture!" Jock exploded.

"But such an important picture? And in London? With world-wide publicity?" Marty asked.

"It was either his picture or mine! I wasn't going to be pushed around! Not by him! Fucking English queer!"

"Laddie," Marty reminded him, "that fucking English queer happens to be one of the great stars of our time. A directing credit on a picture with him would have done you a world of good. World of good," Marty repeated.

"Even if it turned out to be a lousy picture?" Jock challenged.

"He doesn't make lousy pictures. His flops are called artistic triumphs. He falls on his ass with more class than anybody in the world. It would have been an important picture," Marty said regretfully.

Across from the parking lot a black Cadillac limousine of the kind used by presidents and mourners at funerals was pulling up to the broad steps of the executive building. The president came hurrying out, followed by the studio head who caddied for him, carrying his New York topcoat and his black attaché case. The president slipped into the back seat of the limousine. As the studio head placed coat and case beside him, the president noticed Jock and Marty in the parking lot and waved to them through the tinted glass.

They waved back. They smiled warmly, too warmly, all the while trying to read the president's puffy face, his martini eyes. For with the president of a picture company, the manner of his saying something was more important than the words, the look on his face more significant than any gesture. But this man revealed nothing.

"What do you think?" Jock asked, still smiling toward the limousine and the president.

"With that prick, who can tell?" Marty said, smiling too.

4

The car started away, taking the president off to LA International Airport, back to New York, back to stockholders' fights, phone calls from Rome, London, Madrid, the places which had become the centers of American picture-making. Once the limousine turned the corner, the studio head drooped, visibly relieved, turned, started back up the steps, another day of executive crisis over.

Now Marty's smile disintegrated into a frown of deep concern, of obvious professional torment. With clients, Marty sometimes found it necessary to overact, in order to prepare them for what he was about to ask, suggest, or command.

"Laddie," a favourite term of address with Marty, "Laddie, it is not the script. And I would be doing you no favor to let you think it is. I'm afraid it is *you*."

"You said that was over!" Jock exploded. "You said, once Sol Steiber sold his studio *that* was over! You said now, after two good, independent pictures, now was the time to come back here."

"I wasn't referring to *that*," Marty said gravely. "I was referring to London. That's what it is. It is the fear that you can't control a big star, a big picture. And *this* is a big picture!" Marty tossed the disputed script onto the passenger seat of Jock's Ferrari. The title *Mustang!* was fakely branded into the imitation rawhide cover.

"I can't control an important picture?" Jock demanded fiercely. "Me? What about *Black, Man, Black*?"

"What about it?" Marty shot back. Then with the deliberate, indulgent patience that eloquently bespeaks impatience, he explained, "A budget of one million one. A gross of five million nine. Foreign and domestic. That's important? That's big?"

"It made money, didn't it?"

"Sure. But that's not a *big* picture. That's not *Mustang!*" Marty scoffed, staring toward the script. "This picture must have a budget bigger than your whole damn gross! If it's made right."

But Jock was too busy defending himself to hear. "And what about *Tell It Like It Is*? The reviews on my love scenes alone are the greatest any American director has ever—"

Marty interrupted sharply, "Look, laddie, do me a favor! Don't quote me any reviews! And do yourself a favor. Don't ever

5

mention those two pictures in public again! Unless, for the rest of your life, you want to be considered a bright young kid, a director of small artistic gems that are good only in art houses."

Jock's anger was clear and strong on his handsome face. His baby-blues were hard, almost vicious. So Marty knew he must talk fast.

"May I point out something else? Both those pictures were about *schwartzers*. You want to be known as a director who can only direct niggers? That fad will be over pretty soon. Then you can take your Sidney Poitiers, your Sammy Davises, your Diahann Carrolls, and shove 'em. You can take all those reviews from the slick magazines and *The New York Times* and shove them too. What you need, my boy, is one picture that grosses twenty million dollars, thirty million! A picture that plays the Music Hall! That kills them in the drive-ins! Then you're a director! And that's what I was hoping to accomplish for you with *Mustang!*"

"The past tense," Jock said sharply.

Marty White seemed puzzled, "What?"

"You just used the past tense. You said, 'That's what I *was* hoping to accomplish'..."

"Christ, with creative people you have to weigh every word so carefully," Marty lamented.

But the truth was, Marty White always weighed every word carefully. He was not called the Owl merely because he resembled one. True, he was short, round, bald, shiny red bald from weekends of exposure to the smog-diffused Beverly Hills sun. And all his features were exaggerated by the thick, black eyeglass frames which he wore perpetually, so that his total image was one of a larger-than-owl-size, but smaller-than-man-size, owl. Actually, he was called the Owl because he was shrewd, wise, and meticulously dishonest—all of which served to make him the most successful independent agent in the industry.

His use of the past tense had been intentional. For he had his own rules. There were certain times in dealing with clients when you had to give them courage, conviction, self-belief. But there were other times when you had to inflict pain, uneasiness, or plain, simple fear. And, in so doing, you could feel just as loving and self-righteous. As Marty was used to saying, "If a surgeon

6

could cure cancer by operating without an anesthetic, would he hesitate?"

In Marty's mind, an agent was all things to his clients; father, mother, confessor, procurer, psychiatrist, surgeon, marriage counselor, but mostly committee appointed by the Hollywood system to administer the affairs of an idiot whose sole possession of value was an accidental, if perverse, talent.

So every word Marty White had spoken since they left the president's office had been aimed at one thing. To soften up Jock Finley—to create in him that gnawing uneasiness that afflicts creative people when they are between projects. At thirty-one, Jock Finley was still too young to have suffered any permanent defeat. And those glowing reviews were too fresh in his mind, their dates too recent to permit him to feel real fear.

For many reasons of his own, what Marty had to do was imbue Jock Finley with a need, a desire, and if possible, an irresistible hunger to do *Mustang!* Fear was the beginning of it.

For whatever interest Marty White may have had in Jock Finley's career, it was minor compared with the whole. First, there was the script. If it was not the best script Marty would ever sell, it was not the worst. And if the writer, Irving Warfield, was not hot at the moment, he had an established price, a good price. It was Marty's technique, if he could find an acceptable script to build on, to add his own director, and his own star or two. Then if the budget were big enough, somehow the sheer pretentiousness of expensive production could sometimes make even a very bad story successful at the box office. And if he had ten percent of the writer, plus ten percent of the director, and a star or two, and ten percent of their share in the net, Marty had enough of an interest going for himself to make it worth his while.

If, in addition, this picture were to become the one picture out of twenty that made money, he was far ahead of the game. Because in the picture business they didn't remember your failures, if you had a hit every so often. So if Marty White hit the jackpot once every two or three years he became known as a magician. And when he asked for a meeting with the president of any film company, he got it.

These days, men like Marty White, who sold whole packages

7

instead of individual pieces of talent, had, in effect, become the producers.

Marty White had a reputation with packages. His average was far better than most. And it could just have been a fact that the homely little man knew more about pictures than anyone in Hollywood, London, or Rome.

Fact or not, one thing Marty White did know. How to handle talent. How to encourage it, put it down, entice it, dare it, beat it. He knew who among the talented were sadistic, who were masochistic, who needed uplifting, who needed a whip from time to time. He knew where the hunger was. Who had it. What they hungered for. Always he set out to solve any problem by asking himself, How am I going to make my client fight to do what I want him to do?

While the best starting place was fear, Marty knew that with Jock Finley, because of his past, there was a pressure in addition to fear, a stronger pressure. The need of a proud young man to go back and relive a lost opportunity. The desire and the drive to prove something to this town.

With all that going for him, Marty knew he need not risk being obvious. So he seemed to console and reassure Jock when he said, "Look, laddie, let me mull a little. Wait for my call."

Marty reached the door of his Rolls, paused as if on cue, then turned suddenly to add, "Meantime, whatever you do, don't worry."

The Owl climbed into the back of his Rolls. Sitting there, propped up on the high, specially upholstered seat, his round, bald, bespectacled head framed in the window, he waved to Jock. Jock waved back pleasantly, but said to himself, Bastard! Put a fez on him and he'd look like a Jewish King Farouk.

Jock vaulted into the seat of his Ferrari without opening the door. When the motor growled aggressively, he pulled out of the parking lot, and headed toward Beverly Hills, via Sunset.

The late afternoon traffic aggravated his normal impatience. With four hundred and fifty horsepower under the hood, stopping for two lights every block was bad enough. When you had the Owl's words to ponder, it became almost unbearable.

Marty's use of the past tense, perhaps that had been careless,

8

and without significance. But what about that parting shot, "Meantime, whatever you do, don't worry." Why should Marty have said that? Jock Finley was not worried. Angry, yes. But not worried. Yet Marty expected that he would be. Why?

Did Marty know something that he didn't? Had Marty submitted the package of *Mustang!* and Jock Finley to other studios and been turned down? Had Marty forgotten to tell him—or deliberately refrained from telling him—because Marty didn't want him to worry? Of course if the package had been to other studios and they passed on it, that meant they weren't interested enough in the script *or* Jock Finley to even have a meeting about it. That would be something to worry about. It might mean that old blacklist business had never really been resolved after all.

The light changed. Jock pulled ahead a little too precipitously, so that he had to bring all four hundred and fifty horses under control with the sudden application of the special disk brakes, causing a tire screech that made other drivers turn to see who the overanxious jerk was. Screw 'em, Jock said to himself.

Of course, some of the things Marty had said did have truth in them. His two hits had been *succès d'estime*, winning brilliant reviews from the very "*in*," very neurotic critics of the New Wave who wrote for small circulation magazines such as *New York* and *The Saturday Review*.

But Jock himself had said recently in a speech to a class in motion picture technique at UCLA, "Films have become Rorschach tests in which critics see their own tortured and tragic psyches."

And it was true. True, too, however, was the fact that both of Jock's hits had had modest budgets, and modest grosses. Both were non-Hollywood independents. Both were mainly about Negroes. Sorry. Blacks.

Marty could have been right. It was possible, and dangerous, for a director to be typed. Cukor had been acclaimed as a woman's director and that was precisely why Clark Gable had had him fired off *Gone with the Wind*. And who would offer John Ford a picture with a dialogue scene that ran as much as a full page in length?

But the most persistent fact of all, the real worm in Jock's gut, was that since he returned from London ... okay, since he had been replaced in London ... he had not had a single offer good enough to make him say yes. There had been some offers. But only from independents, only pictures with modest budgets, without top stars, with odd-ball stories. "Realistic" films mainly, a word Jock had come to hate. Because it had become counterfeit currency, a euphemism of small indie producers who said "realistic" when they meant low-budget, cheap.

Nor had there been any offers from New York. Usually when a director of Jock's reputation, who had originally begun in the theater in New York, was announced to have finished a picture, or resigned from one, or even to have been replaced, he was bombarded with Broadway scripts of plays which had been held up in New York, like planes in a holding pattern, waiting for the right bright director who could become enthusiastic enough, salesman enough, to enlist the services of a star, so that the play could be floated financially, could get a theater, sell theater parties, etc., etc., through all the realistic etceteras of Broadway as it existed these days.

But this time no play had been offered. Besides Marty hadn't wanted him to do another play. "What's to gain, laddie?" he had asked. "You've proved you can do plays. What you need is a 'big' picture at a major studio."

And a "big" picture meant a big grosser, not necessarily a good one. Everyone in town was looking for another *Sound of Music*. Every agency, every studio, every producer, every director, forgetting all the while how long that property had gone begging before Fox finally bought it. Today it was the prime example of the "big" picture.

It was the example Marty had used in their very first discussion in his office, after Jock had read *Mustang!* "Christ, Marty," Jock had said, "you call this a big picture, a Western?"

Marty had stared back through his heavy-framed glasses, his eyes betraying a mother's hurt heart, as he said, "Laddie, you disappoint me. I thought you would see the potential, the possibilities."

Then Marty had been silent. The Owl had a way of using pauses,

10

playing them to the fraction of a second, to create the proper anticipation and anxiety for what he had to say.

"Sure, it's a Western. But that's the challenge. The great grossers of all time, did they have such great stories? No! Take *Sound of Music*. I mean how corny can you get? Is there anything special, fresh, or new about the story? Anything unusual? No! But it was what they did with it. The casting. The chemistry.

"Now, you take this," Marty said, fingering the imitation-rawhide-bound script of *Mustang!* "With a Western like this you got sure values. Action. Color. Conflict. Sex. All the elements of a big grossing picture for the masses. Then if, in addition, you give it the Jock Finley touch . . . the aura, the . . . what the hell's that word they're always using in those damned magazines . . . ?"

"Ambiance?" Jock had suggested helpfully.

"Yeah. Right! Give it your ambiance and you'll get the critics. And that means you get the way-out kids and the real movie buffs. Box office *and* prestige! You can't beat it. One picture like this and you can write your own ticket at any studio in this town for the rest of your life! And everything else will be forgotten. So, take it home. Read it again."

Then Marty White had shoved the script across the desk toward Jock. "What do you say, laddie?"

Because he hadn't known what to say, except possibly, "Screw you, Marty White," Jock hadn't answered directly. Instead, he smiled that boyish smile, which always dimpled his lean cheeks and lit up those disarming pale blue eyes of his.

"What's funny?" Marty had asked gingerly, almost resentfully.

"I was wondering why it is, Marty, that an agent originally named Morris Weiss keeps calling his client, originally named Jack Finestock, 'laddie'? Where the hell did you ever pick that up?"

"Look, Jock, I don't want any wisecracks! I don't want anything but serious thought about a serious problem. You're at the turning point right now. Either you make a *big* picture in the next twenty-four months or you'll wind up directing cheapies and half-hour television for the rest of your life! And that is nothing to joke about!"

It had had the ring of truth in it that day, too, Jock admitted

11

to himself now. Perhaps because Jock had never seen soft-spoken, imperturbable Marty White so close to anger before. Marty must have realized it too, because he had followed immediately with a more temperate explanation.

"Look ... uh ... " and he had almost used "laddie" again but settled for, "Look, kid, I have been in this town a long time. I have delivered scripts, carried briefcases for the best agents who ever lived. And I have seen this town change. In the old days, a studio would take time to build a star, a director, a writer, from shorts, to C pictures, to B's, to A's finally.

"But no more. Today, reputations are instant, like coffee or orange juice. It's become a nervous, impatient industry since you were here before. Today if a man takes his time, works his way up, learning his craft slowly, methodically, pretty soon they begin to say, 'He's been in the industry five years and he hasn't made it. That means he ain't got it.' And he's dead.

"So these days, you hit fast. Or forget it. Success comes in spray cans. Or it never comes. And you're still right at the age to make it all and make it big. But it has to be soon. Fast!"

By the time the Owl finished, Jock's smile had disappeared. His handsome face had become sober, almost grim. This time when the Owl shoved the script gently across the desk, Jock had taken it.

"Laddie, one big picture is all you need! And it'll last you the rest of your life! Then, if you want to make an occasional small art film, fine. But first, deliver me one big picture!"

As Jock had risen from the chair, script in hand, Marty stopped him with a suggestion that sounded kindly, fatherly.

"Take it home, kid. Reread it. If it isn't perfect, come up with ideas for a rewrite. But give it a chance to breathe in your brilliant imagination. Then, if you could honestly say to the head of a studio, or to the president of a production company ... "

Here Marty had paused, as if he were improvising, then he began again, "Well, *for example* ... if you could say you had this in your bag all the time you were in London. That you couldn't wait to get off that faggy picture so you could go to work on this. That you took the first plane home so you could start on this, because you simply have to do it! You know it's going to be a great picture, an epic! If you could say, *for example*, it'll have all the artistic merit of *Black, Man, Black* plus enormous box office besides. If you can say all that, let me know and I'll set up a meeting in thirty-six hours."

Marty White always used the words "for example" in exactly the same way a cautious, ethical lawyer carefully suborns perjury. Marty would never tell a client what to say. But if you listened closely to what Marty said after "for example," you would have it all. Word for word. Just as he wanted you to say it. And if you did say it later, in a meeting, or over lunch, deals generally worked out as Marty promised they would.

Except this time, Jock reminded himself, as he waited to turn his Ferrari left off Sunset and onto Rexford. This time, instead of "You got a deal" the president had said, "Get Preston Carr for the picture and you got a deal."

What the president had really been saying was that the story, even as told by Jock Finley, who had exhibited the required amount of enthusiasm, had not been enough. The reputation of Jock Finley, with two very good, but very small independent, non-Hollywood pictures to his credit, had not been enough. Whether it had been his being replaced in London, or not, the fact was clear—neither the script nor Jock Finley, alone or together, was enough to get the picture off the ground without Preston Carr.

Jock made his turn, accelerated his Ferrari up Rexford with a loud, angry, defiant roar of the powerful motor. Two blocks farther up Rexford, he slowed and pulled into the circular driveway of a huge house.

In any other community in America a house this large and pretentious would have been surrounded by several acres at least. But Beverly Hills real estate being as precious as it was, Jock's rented house was separated on each side from two other huge houses by a scant eight feet.

He pulled into his own driveway, put the four hundred and fifty horses at rest with a turn of the key, and leaped out without opening the door.

He was home. If he hadn't been talked into signing a long lease by Marty White, he would have lived in a small new apartment on

13

Sunset, but Marty had said, "Show 'em you're back in this town to stay!"

By the time Marty arrived at his office there had already been two calls from Irving Warfield, the author of the original screen-play *Mustang!* A long-established screenwriter, and one of Marty's oldest clients, Warfield was now suffering from the new and incessant hunger for youth in pictures. He hadn't worked in a year and a half. But since he and Marty were of the same genera-tion, shared the same secret resentment against youth, the same certain sexual predilections, they were friends. So Marty rarely kept Warfield waiting for a call back.

"Well, how did it go?" Warfield asked after the usual courte-sies. "Did they like the script?"

"Loved it!"

"And Finley?"

"Loved him, too."

"Then we got a deal!"

"Practically." Marty could sense the letdown, though Warfield had made no sound. "If we get Preston Carr, we got a deal."

"Preston Carr? He hasn't made a picture since *Blood Island!* And that was four years ago!"

"Three," Marty corrected.

"Okay, three! They didn't want Finley!" Warfield concluded. "Since he got taken off that picture in London, he's death!"

"Irving . . ." Marty interrupted.

"I told you it was a mistake to go with him in the package! A big mistake! That's a terrific script! I believe in that script, Marty!" Warfield said, in the way of Hollywood where a man can praise himself unashamedly, if he chooses the right words.

"Irving . . ." Marty finally interrupted. "Listen to me! We'll get the deal. But it'll take a little time."

"Time? Christ, Marty, I explained to you all about that land down in Palm Desert! It's a steal right now. But I need cash. I figured if we got a down payment in the form of an interest-free loan of a hundred thousand on the script, to be paid back out of deferments, I could maneuver the property without liquidating

14

any stock, and still have time to come up with my quarterly tax payment, without a bank loan. Money is tight these days, tight! And I'm up to my ass to the banks as it is, Marty. You know that. What's worse, I can't liquidate without incurring a capital gains tax. I'm land poor, Marty, land poor!"

"And I said, don't worry, Irving," Marty reassured him, always sensitive to the problems of his creative clients, especially writers.

"Marty, how are you going to get Preston Carr? Even if he likes the script, which he may not, before you can get the approval of his agent, his lawyer, and his tax man, it'll take two months, three!"

"Irving, sweetie, did I say it would be easy?"

"We should go for another director! Someone with big credits! And with no 'history' in this town," Warfield added euphemistically.

"Irving, Irving, take it easy. I promised you I'd get a quarter of a million dollars for the script and I will. But my way. I want that kid in there! He's good for the package! He's a hell of a director! *And he's young!* That's important! He knows what the kids like. What these new critics like. It's a new business, Irving, a new era. Kids run the world!"

"I know," Warfield said sadly. "Kids discover Preston Carr on the Late Show and suddenly he's hot again. If Bogie were alive today, he'd be the biggest thing in pictures all over again, because of those kids!"

"Exactly. Now don't worry. We'll get Preston Carr."

"How?"

"I'll think of something," Marty said.

"You know," Warfield reflected, "Carr would be terrific casting. It's a hell of an idea."

"That would really be a big picture!"

"Right!"

"You know, the first thing I'd do, Marty, I'd call Finley and . . ."

Marty interrupted, "*Shmuck!* That's the first thing I won't do."

"Okay, okay, handle it your own way." Then to make up for his gross error in strategy, Warfield offered, "Oh, Marty, you ever run into a kid named Dolly Evans?"

15

"Blonde? Little on the thin side? But good tits?"

"Yeah."

"What about her?"

"Put it down in your book. What a blow job! That girl has a tongue, drive you up the wall!"

Marty was studiously writing that note in his address book when his phone rang. It was a theatrical producer calling from New York about a playscript. Marty hesitated, then took the call.

"Mr. White, you remember me, David Frank, in New York. About five weeks ago I sent you the new Williams play for Jock Finley. Well, we were wondering . . . "

"Look, Frank, I could kid you but it's not my nature," Marty interrupted. "Jock read your script. Didn't like it. Not bad, but just not for him. You understand?"

"Maybe if he reread it and we had a chance to discuss it . . . "

Again Marty interrupted, "What would be the point? Jock Finley is not interested in doing a play. Not in the foreseeable future. Sorry. I don't want to be rude. But I find it's better to be honest in these things. Saves your time, saves my time."

When he hung up, Marty pressed down the intercom, "Evelyn, there's a Williams play we got from David Frank a few weeks ago. Find it. Send it back."

Almost fifteen minutes later, Evelyn called in to report that they couldn't find the script.

"It *has* to be some place in the office," Marty insisted indignantly. "I never sent it out."

It was almost six-thirty. The sun was a round, red ball, low in the sky, crisscrossed by the pink vapor trails of transcontinental jets. Behind a gauze of gaseous yellow smog, the Beverly Hills sky was a distinct early evening blue.

It had been two hours since Marty left Jock in the parking lot. There had been no call. Twice Jock had picked up the script of *Mustang!*, twice he had tossed it aside. Rereading it wouldn't help.

16

Once he had picked up the poolside phone to call Marty but changed his mind. Damn it, he never liked the damn script in the first place. Why did it burn him so that they had been turned down?

Or was it really Marty that burned him? For he had begun to strip away from Jock the "bright young man" image on which he so prided himself. Jock had a saying with which he consoled himself when he compared his few achievements with other, older and more successful directors. "One thing I've got, he hasn't. Future!"

But there was something to what Marty said, about quick success. Especially in this town, where timing was all. He was thinking and staring at the phone, when he suddenly realized that if he didn't take a swim right now, he was going to call Marty. And that was a tactical blunder. Never exhibit fear before a wild animal, or a Hollywood agent.

So, instead, Jock peeled off his French knit shirt, kicked off his custom-made English shoes, slipped out of his Italian corduroy slacks, pulled off his silk boxer shorts, custom-made for him by Sulka in Paris, then ass-naked, he moved to the side of the pool.

He stood there a moment, breathing deeply, tensing his muscles, especially those across his flat stomach, till they stood out in distinct ridges. A girl intern with whom he had had his last prolonged sex encounter in New York before coming back to the Coast had joked with him once, "They would teach Physiology One, Two, Three, and Four from your body. If you could just hold your breath long enough."

Then she had mounted him and done most of the work, as though she were conserving his body and his energies like some precious natural resource.

Since then, whenever he was naked, before diving into the pool, or after a shower, or just before getting dressed, he would tense his stomach muscles, especially if there were a mirror handy.

As he stood there naked, at the pool's edge, his mind made a jump from the Jewish lady doctor with the aggressive sexual tendencies to Marty White, and his disturbing "Don't worry." Jock suddenly said to himself, "When Marty calls, fuck him! Let him ring!" Then he dove into the clean, warm water, the taste of

17

chlorine assaulting his nose even though he held his breath on the way down.

Slowly, with easy strokes, Jock moved gracefully from one end of the pool to the other, then back, the warm water flowing over his lean body. When he was a very young actor, but not a very good one, he had made a fetish of keeping it in good shape. "Part of the actor's equipment," he used to say, a little pretentiously. The truth was, then, and now, Jock was as vain about his body as about his looks, although he always made it a point to appear resentful when people suggested he looked more like a leading man than a director. In truth he was flattered. And in dealing with actresses, he sometimes found his looks and his sexuality more of an asset than his knowledge of directing.

He had just turned over on his back, exposed, hard, erect, and was saying to himself, "Let the lady doctor work on that . . ." when he heard a car pull into his driveway. His first impulse was to climb out of the pool and slip into a terry robe. Although he knew it was not so, Jock always had the vague suspicion that Marty might be queer. He wasn't. Yet somehow Jock always felt slightly uncomfortable in Marty's company.

At this moment, strategy, if nothing else, dictated that Marty find him relaxed, in the pool, untroubled by the momentary defeat of the afternoon. So Jock rolled over and started stroking easily through the water, intending to seem surprised when he made his turn at the far end of the pool and spied Marty.

He made his turn, lifted his dripping head above the water and discovered he had no need to pretend surprise. For it was not Marty White, standing at the far end.

Louise was there. Smiling. Carrying her black script book, with her stopwatch still hanging from the silk cord around her neck, Louise was the model of a proper, efficient, script girl, though she was far from typical of script girls, being taller than most, and blonder, and far better built.

The way she was smiling made Jock call out, "What's so damn funny?" But he was smiling too. For he knew how he must look to her, floating on his back, his erection rising up out of the blue water. "Well, don't just stand there. Do something!" he called, laughing.

She put her script book down on the metal table and started to undress, slowly, neatly, methodically, as was her way, while she asked, "Well, how did it go? Tell me!"

"Not bad," Jock said, moving to the edge of the pool and raising himself so that his chin rested on the white tile and he could look up at her undressing.

"Did you get the deal?"

"Not exactly," Jock said.

Louise stopped, her sweater high over her head, her breasts standing out strongly. "What does that mean, not exactly?"

As he began to explain, she completed taking off her sweater and slipped out of her slacks, revealing her long, firm legs. Three years as a swimmer in a traveling aquacade, after she had failed as an actress, had left her with a body that was strong and sexually attractive. Unlike ballet dancers, swimmers have good, strong, beautiful legs, and when Louise locked hers around him, he felt a delicious, almost unbearable pain.

She had good hips too, and a stomach so flat that there were times after they had intercourse when Jock could count her rapid pulse rate by observing the rhythm of her aorta.

When she removed her panties it was pleasingly obvious that generally, in the sun, she wore only a very brief bikini. Two bold streaks of white served to emphasize the golden tan of the rest of her fine body and her blond pubic patch.

By the time Jock had finished telling her, in modified, self-flattering terms, what happened at the meeting, she was ready to dive into the pool. She did so by vaulting over his head, and going so deep her nipples made gentle contact with the slippery blue concrete bottom of the pool. She came up at the far end, just under the diving board, turned with a snap of her head to shake the water free from her blond hair, and asked suddenly, "Preston Carr?" as if she just now understood what he had said long seconds ago.

"If they really like the story, they'll settle for Lancaster. Or Holden. Or even Mitchum," Jock said confidently.

"I don't know," she answered thoughtfully and concerned. Then she shoved off. Her head raised above the water, she made her way across the pool with swift, small, deft kicks of her legs. When she reached the far end, she turned on her back and floated

19

toward the middle of the pool, her white breasts rising up out of the blue water, her nipples puckering in the early evening air which was cooler than the water of the heated pool. Then, gracefully, she let her body slip under the surface, so that she was treading water. Her breasts, more buoyant now, rode at water level, seeming even fuller, whiter.

"If he asked for Preston Carr he is not going to settle," she said very seriously.

Rather than pursue it, Jock shoved off from the side of the pool, ruddered down with his hands and came up out of the water, face to face with her, breast to breast with her, so she could already feel his erection between her thighs. That was the end of all conversation.

Between them, for some months now, it had been an affair devoid of verbal lovemaking.

For a girl who outwardly seemed so cool and poised and above sexual aggression, she had an enormous appetite for it, though she was not at all promiscuous. She pursued only one affair at a time, and it generally lasted for many months. But with the right man she was completely open and free, without the pretense, the petty tyrannies, and shams which most women exact in the name of courtship or false modesty.

Hers was a game in which all players were equal—where man was there to gratify her as much as she was there to gratify man. She was fortunate that her striking attractiveness made it possible for her to choose her man, most times.

That first time he had arrived in Hollywood, Jock resented the indulgence of heated swimming pools. He equated them with the kind of softness and decay that brought on the fall of the Roman Empire. But he could testify to one advantage now. The warm water did not inhibit, but actually encouraged, all sexual impulses. The ability to move freely and gracefully through its caressing warmth supplied a sensuality to sex that surpassed even the silk sheets of that hotel he once stayed at in Rome with that Italian star.

Twice they had each other in the pool, before he realized it had grown dark and cold. He was the one who got out of the pool to get the warm robes and turn on the pool lights while she swam back and forth as though performing her ablutions after the act. He held the red terry robe for her when she came up the steps out of the water. In just the few moments that took, her bronzed and white skin puckered in the cool air, her nipples became firm, tight. He wrapped her in the robe, turning her around at the same time so his warm hands could cup her breasts and press them hard. Before it could lead to more lovemaking she slipped free and went to lie down on the double chaise. He hesitated, then moved to the bar to make the drinks.

She lay on the chaise in the reflected bluish light of the pool. Her damp hair was close against her head, making her face stand out in relief. Though most times she was relaxed after such good sex, now she seemed troubled. He noticed.

"How's it going?" he probed.

"How does television ever go? Setup, setup, setup, shot, shot, shot. If they say all the words, in approximately the right sequence, it's a take."

"That's not what I mean, Lulu," which was his only pet name for her.

Instead of answering she discovered suddenly that her drink needed freshening. She started to get up. But he took her glass, preventing her from changing the subject. He was at the bar, his back to her, when she said suddenly, "There's something I have to tell you, Jock."

He turned sharply, "Oh, Christ, you're not pregnant?"

"Of course not. There is something I have to tell you about *you*," she said cautiously. He came back with two fresh drinks. She took a sip. "Too strong," and she started to rise to add some soda but he reached out, gripped her thigh firmly but not painfully.

"Okay, Lulu, what is it?"

Finally she said softly, referring to the pool and the events in the pool, "Tonight was the first time I've ever felt you afraid."

"What the hell are you talking about?" he demanded.

"Most times you're fun. Sex with you is good, enjoyable, strong. Without reservations or obligations. Sure, there are times when you kid and say 'Some day I got to marry you.' But you won't. You know it. More important, I know it. But that's okay.

21

"Other times you're all anger. Those times you make the love and I just happen to be there. It wouldn't matter who the woman was. You assault her. You use it as a weapon. And the woman is only a victim. The first week you were back from London, it was like that. It isn't as good as the other times. But I understand. And I try not to resent it. That's just the way you are.

"But this time. . ." she hesitated, "this time when you were in me I suddenly realized, by God, he's afraid." She used the long silence to take another sip of her drink. Then she dared to add, "It's the first time I've ever seen you that way. . ."

"I think you're out of your mind," he interrupted angrily.

"Is it because Marty hasn't called?"

"Marty will call!" he said dogmatically. To change the subject, he went on brusquely, "Get your clothes on, we'll go get something to eat."

Trying not to point up his own contradiction, she suggested gently, "If Marty is going to call maybe we'd better not go out. I'll fix something."

"I'll have something sent in!" Jock decided sharply. "Chinese! I'll call Ah Fong's on Beverly."

"Sure, good. Great," she agreed too quickly. For he was far more sensitive, far more uneasy than she had suspected.

It was almost an hour later. The night air was cool. Except for the pool lights, the entire place was dark. Overhead the fronds of the tall leaning palm were making an arid, crackling sound as the night breeze stirred them.

There had been no call, but it didn't matter so much right now. For he was making love to her again. On the double poolside chaise. Perhaps determined to prove that nothing she had said had inhibited or angered him. Yet he was aware, with some irritation, that he did not like the feel of the plastic against his knees. The things a man could think about when he was supposed to be in the throes of intercourse.

The front doorbell rang.

He went suddenly limp, apologized, disengaged, grabbed his robe and started for the door muttering, "Sonofabitch!"

22

Holding the robe around himself with one hand, clutching a hastily seized fistful of change and bills from Louise's purse in the other, he struggled to get the door open as the bell was ringing for the fourth time.

"I'm here! I'm here!" Jock called impatiently.

He managed the door. The delivery man was a boy of college age, slender, tall, smiling, and very knowing.

"Sorry, but you got to eat sometime," the boy said.

Jock took the large, warm, brown paper bag in one arm, shoved the money plus a dollar tip at the kid with his other hand, and was shouldering the door closed when the kid said, "Thanks. And that was a terrific speech you gave, Mr. Finley."

Directors, even the most famous, were generally not recognized by the public. Except for Hitchcock who had been on TV so much. Jock's surprise showed.

"I'm at UCLA. Motion picture technique."

"Oh, yeah. Thanks," Jock said, regretting now that he had only given the kid a dollar.

"Is it true?" the kid asked suddenly. Jock was puzzled, hesitated. "Your name. How you got it. We have two theories at school." Jock's reaction made him explain. "We discuss all the important New Wave directors. The guys say you got to be called 'Jock' because you can put more male sex appeal into a film than any American director going. More 'jock-sock,' as that critic said once in *The Tulane Drama Review*."

"That was Earl Wilson in *The New York Post*," Jock corrected.

"Yeah? Anyhow, the girls say it's because you're a stud in bed. That you get your best performances out of your female leads that way. Is that what a director must do to get a great performance? Become part of the actress, be in love with her, share her innermost uninhabited passions? They say you were carrying on an affair with the girl in *Tell It Like It Is*, all through the shooting. That's how you got those great love scenes. Is that true?"

From the darkness behind him, Jock heard Lulu's voice, mocking him in a clichéd imitation of a seductive impatient actress, "Jock, sweetie, Ah am waiting to rehearse that scene again with you."

The delivery boy smiled, shook his head, "Gee, sorry I interrupted," and departed for his delivery truck, thinking he had his answer.

Jock shouldered the door shut, turned to find Louise a naked silhouette with the pool lights behind her.

"Boy, you're very funny, aren't you? Well, if you were a better actress you wouldn't have had to become a script girl!"

Later when they were eating, Jock suddenly asked, "Christ Almighty, you think those wacky kids at UCLA really talk that way? About me?"

It was eight-thirty in the morning when the phone finally rang. On the third ring, Jock came awake enough to realize he was alone on the poolside chaise, and chilled. He had to go barefoot across the dew-damp concrete to get to the phone.

"Laddie," was Marty's cheerful greeting. "Did I wake you?"

"No," Jock lied unsuccessfully.

"We got to talk! Drive up and have breakfast with me! How long will it take?"

"Half hour?"

"Good. I'll wait!" Marty's enthusiasm held some promise.

Jock yawned, looked around. Louise had left, probably more than an hour ago, to go home, change clothes, and get to her studio by eight. Jock stood there yawning, scratching his head and pondering whether to shower or swim. Swimming was easier. So he dropped his terry robe, moved forward, dove in, and came up to realize that the pool lights had been on all night. He did a few laps, got out, dried himself, and with the towel wrapped around his flat hips, he started into the house to find fresh clothes.

Minutes later he was leaping into his red Ferrari. He found it damp, and reminded himself, goddamnit, either put the damn thing in the garage or remember to put the top up. He pulled out of the driveway.

Soon he was at the main gate of Trousdale Estates. He turned in and started up the steep wide road toward the crest, where Marty White had his huge bachelor house. When Jock realized that he would arrive before the agreed-upon time, he turned off onto a side street, sat there, motor idling, letting minutes go by.

If it were actually a fact, what Lulu had said last night, about detecting that he was fearful for the first time, then he must not get to Marty's house early and thereby exhibit any anxiety. So, when he knew that he would be late, he put the powerful machine into very slow motion, turned it about and resumed his climb.

He arrived ten minutes late. The Japanese houseman showed him in, through the elaborate, modernistic house and out onto the all-white concrete, marble, and stone terrace where the little round man was waiting breakfast for him.

Marty White was one of those plump people who, at Chasen's, Twenty-One, or any studio commissary or executive dining room, limited himself, ostentatiously and severely, to cottage cheese, fruit, and black coffee. And he never ceased to complain that for him, somehow, no diet seemed to work. In the privacy of his home, however, he ate without limit or discretion.

Right now, on the white enamel terrace table, shielded by the green sun umbrella, there was laid out a collection of cosmopolitan delights made possible only by the miracle of jet flight. *Fraises* flown in from France, with sour cream from Nate and Al's. Bagels flown in from New York, along with sturgeon from Barney Greengrass. And thinly sliced, delicately smoked salmon flown in from Scotland. Before he finished, Marty would have some of all of it, and all of some of it.

Despite Marty's urging, Jock took only coffee with some skimmed milk. He sipped that very slowly because he had come to listen, not to eat. The Owl talked and ate, using his butter knife or his fork to gesture and to score points. He paused only at those times when he took elaborate care to spread the cream cheese thickly but evenly on a toasted bagel.

"Laddie, I thought about it. All afternoon. All last night. Early this morning. I think I know."

He stopped to slide a large white and golden slice of sturgeon onto his bagel. When he resumed, it seemed a complete non-sequitur.

"You know, making a deal is like jujitsu. You got to put your

25

strength against the other guy's weakness. Now, in this case, what is our good president's weakness? Well, first, when he is saying, 'Get Preston Carr and you got a deal,' what is he really saying? Bottom line, he is saying, 'For this picture I am willing to pay Preston Carr one million dollars up front, plus a percentage of gross, which are his standard terms.' Now, if the bastard is willing to do that, he knows that with the extensive location shooting, the rest of the casting, and all the etceteras, this picture has got to cost seven million, maybe as much as eight. So, laddie, this *is* a big picture! But why, suddenly?

"So early this morning, nine o'clock New York time, I call a friend of mine in the eastern story department. And as I figure, there's an angle. Foxy sonofabitch, he *needs* a big picture. He is going to have stockholder trouble again this year and he needs a big flashy picture in production to hold out golden promises to them. That's his weakness! That's why he's got to have something as unusual as the return of Preston Carr!"

With surgical precision, Marty cut a slice of Scotch salmon in half, only to put both halves on the same slice of bagel.

"Now, what is our strength? He likes the script. He can see the potential. And he needs it. So I say to myself, if he needs the story so desperately, needs Preston Carr so desperately, *why* is he risking letting the deal slip through his foxy fingers? *Why?* Well . . .

"Now, laddie, don't get mad. Because I am about to show you how to fuck a fox. The *why* is, there is one element in this package he does *not* want."

Jock felt the anger rise in his throat, in his viscera, and in his groin as well. Except that it was not truly anger, but the fear Lulu had detected last night.

"Screw him! Take the package elsewhere!" Jock said.

"I thought of that, laddie. But there are two problems. First, we don't know what other studio wants such a big picture right now. Second, a picture package is like a girl. The very first time it's exposed, it loses its virginity. After that, like a girl who's lost it, she can explain forever how it happened, but she can't change the fact.

"Sure I could go to Warners. Or Fox. But by this morning they know already it was exposed yesterday. And I would have to ex-

26

plain how come that *shmuck* passed. What'll I tell them? He didn't want to put a seven-million-dollar picture into the hands of a young director, brilliant as he is? Then why should Fox or Warners take the risk? They have nervous stockholders, too, hovering over them like vultures. No, another studio is not the answer. There is only one answer. One good answer."

"Get Preston Carr?" Jock asked.

"That's only part of the answer. Because if Preston Carr reads the script, and likes it, what's his first question going to be? What's every star's first question?"

"Who's going to direct?"

"Exactly! So the answer is not to get Preston Carr to read the script, or even to like it. It is to get Preston Carr to say, 'I will do this picture only if Jock Finley directs it!' That's the answer, laddie! That's how we establish our strength and pit it against the studio's weakness. That's how we keep the package intact!"

"I wouldn't send the script to Carr through his agent," Jock suggested. "Send it to him direct."

"How can we make sure he'll even read it, a man who's turned down everything for three years now?" Marty intentionally specu- lated, hoping for a reaction.

"There's one way," Jock said suddenly. "I'll go see him my- self! I'll stay there till he does read it."

"Right! See him! Make him read it! Sell him the script! Sell him Jock Finley! And you can sell, laddie, I saw that yesterday."

"Where does Carr live?" Jock asked.

"He's a man who likes privacy. He could be at his place in Malibu. Or his ranch, more likely. Spends a lot of time at the ranch these days. I'll check it out."

"You check that out, Marty, and I'll do the rest."

"Good, laddie, and together we'll fuck the fox."

The sound of Jock's Ferrari had not faded away before Marty was on the phone to New York, to the president, on his private number.

"Bob? Marty White. Like I promised you, Finley's going after Carr."

"Great! You think he can get him?" the president asked.

"That kid's a killer where his work is concerned. He may not know it himself, but I spotted that the first time I ever saw him in New York. He'll get Carr."

"Marty, there's only one thing . . ." the president said hesitantly.

"Yeah, Bob?"

"Last night on the plane on the way home, I kept thinking. Finley *is* young. And it *is* a big picture. And I have my stockholders to account to."

"Well, Bob . . ." Marty said slowly, thoughtfully, and with seeming momentary inspiration. "If you have any doubts, tell you what I'll do . . . and I've never done this before . . . for anyone, Bob, you know that. But for you, I would be willing to act as executive producer on the picture. That's what I think of this package. And of my ability to control that kid!"

"In addition to your commissions, you want a fee as executive producer," the president evaluated.

"Bob! Please! We're friends! Forget any fee! I'll take my end from gross, after the picture's in the black. What the hell, I always did want to produce a picture," Marty said, trying to make it sound casual, unpremeditated, and extravagantly unselfish.

CHAPTER

2

T HE morning was fair and bright, for Beverly Hills. The yellow peril, as Jock had come to call that cloud of discolored, poisonous air, lay far below in the basin. Over Beverly Hills itself the sky was blue, the air cool and dry, with the promise of a strong sun. There would be no smog. Till about noon.

But by noon, Jock Finley would be far from Los Angeles, more than halfway to Preston Carr's ranch in Nevada. Alongside Jock, on the passenger seat of his Ferrari lay the imitation-rawhide-bound shooting script with the title *Mustang!* burned into it as if with a branding iron.

This was not the first presentation of a play or a picture script which Jock Finley had made, in person, to a star of consequence. But it was the most important. So his technique for approaching and handling stars, which was always expert, had been especially polished and sharpened for Preston Carr. Jock was dressed in old, faded, shrunk levis, a worn blue workshirt, and weatherbeaten, run-down-at-the-high-heels cowboy boots.

It made a world of difference how you finally brought a script to a star's attention. If you sent it, it could be intercepted by agents, managers, wives, mistresses, lawyers, accountants, any one of whom would dispose of it to his or her own personal advantage. So it was always possible that the star might never read it. Most likely he would remain completely unaware of its existence.

But if you took the script to him, if you talked about it first, praised it, romanced it, and then finally handed it over as if it were precious treasure instead of just another one hundred and thirty pages of description and dialogue, you could invest any script with the aura of a potential cinematic masterpiece. At least it would be read with anticipation instead of reluctance.

In addition, if you could possibly avoid it, you did not give the star any warning that you were coming. For most stars, given a choice, would ask you not to come. They disliked putting themselves in an embarrassing position by being under obligation to you when the odds were always great against their saying yes to any script.

So Jock had decided that even with Preston Carr, who was noted for valuing his own privacy, it was worth taking the risk of intruding, rather than the more serious and usual risk of his forbidding you to come.

In this instance, which was more fraught with personal risk, since the director as well as the script were not personally known to Carr, Jock had taken special care to prepare himself.

He had gathered as much information as he could about Carr. He decided it was not enough to screen his last half dozen pictures, which he had done. It was more important to know what motivated Carr, both personally and as an actor. What ambitions, if any, he had left which might be exploited to make him say yes to this particular picture after having said no to so many.

These days Carr spent most of his time at the ranch. He liked horses. That was to the good, Jock felt. But he liked avocados, too. And walnuts. For he raised all three at a good profit. But the main point was he liked to live close to the land when he could. He should like *Mustang!* and the character of Linc.

The challenge was how to make Carr like and respect Jock well enough to say yes to *Mustang!* provided Jock Finley directed it. So Jock had taken the past five days to get into character. *Being* a brilliant young director was not quite enough. *Seeming* to be one was more important. *Playing* one was most important right now. He had to look and sound and act like *the* right man to direct Preston Carr in a big Western!

Each day Jock had spent four hours at poolside, getting a deep,

30

rich, ruddy tan, which not only bespoke an affinity for the outdoors but which contrasted so well with those disarming blue eyes
that Jock used so effectively.

Each day during those four tanning hours, he had been reading
up on the breeding, training, and showing of Appaloosas. For he
had discovered, through a studio publicity man, that Carr's main
delight was breeding Appaloosas as a hobby and a business. He
was, in fact, one of the better breeders in the country.

Jock had spent his early mornings taking riding lessons, not that
he expected to master the art, but so that he could have a familiarity, at least, and an appreciation of the finer points of the various
skills required of horse and rider.

Through all of this, Jock had been bleaching and weathering a
pair of new levis. From dawn to dusk, into the pool and out, in
two-hour stretches, he had been alternately soaking them and sun-
fading them.

The levis had led to the trouble with Louise. Late one afternoon,
while he had been stretching out the levis on the hot concrete
alongside the pool, she drove in unexpectedly. Her TV series had
been doing exteriors up above Mulholland Drive. With daylight
beginning to fail, they had quit early. Since she was so close, she
stopped by without calling.

She was surprised, amused, and made no secret of it, to find Jock
tending a pair of fading levis with such care. She started to laugh.

"What the hell's the matter with you?" he asked.

"That's the kind of thing high school kids do," she said.

It could have been her unfortunate choice of comparisons, or
the fact that she caught him in the fraudulent act of getting into
costume to make a call on a movie star, but he felt demeaned and
exposed. One habit Jock Finley had developed since he first started
directing and which would stay with him all his life: when caught
off guard by anyone—an actor asking for a motivation, or a
designer, or an author—if Jock did not have a ready answer or
suggestion, he attacked.

"What's the big idea of dropping in without calling?" he demanded.

"We just finished shooting a little early and I . . ."

He interrupted, "What if there was some other dame here?" The

31

phrase "other dame" was unnecessary, unkind. Louise was not just another dame. And he knew that. Had he been less embarrassed and ashamed, he would have been less vindictive.

Hoping to pass it off, she said, joking, "Maybe you ought to have a red light blinking out front, and a sign, 'Quiet, Scene Shooting.'" She bent down to finger the levis, never suspecting that so casual an act would make him furious.

"Damn you, leave those alone!"

She pulled back, rose, started toward the bar. Though she had come here anticipating a refreshing swim, then sex, and a late dinner, now she made no effort to get out of her clothes. Instead, she made herself a drink and slipped into one of the wrought-iron armchairs, giving no sign that she intended to undress.

Apologies do not come easily to arrogant young men, especially not to young men like Jock Finley. So, in a gesture of conciliation, he stripped slowly, dived into the pool, swam lazily back and forth, fully expecting that she would join him. But she sat there till she finished her drink. Then she got up and started for her car in the driveway.

"Don't go!" he called out. Spoken as an order, it was a plea. She stopped, turned back. He was climbing out of the pool, reaching for a towel to dry and cover himself at the same time. He came toward her and finally was able to say, "Look, I . . . I didn't expect you. I didn't expect anybody. I didn't want anybody."

"I know. That's why I'm going."

"You don't understand. Wait. Please?" It was a highly unusual word, coming from him, and it made her wait. "Don't you understand? This is all a sell! A con! The biggest con job of my whole career!

"City-bred Jock Finley, from Brooklyn, is going to make a Western! Big enough switch? *But* I need Preston Carr. So I am going to have to con him every way I know. I am going to look as western as any cowhand. Sound like one. Be one. I know exactly the right things to say about Appaloosa mares, stallions, and colts. Because that is what Preston Carr is interested in. The king of pictures, the last of the great big stars, the great symbol of the American outdoorsman must be impressed. Well, Jock Finley is going to impress him!

32

"So levis that look just a little bit worn won't do. Merely talking a good game won't do. I have to look it, sound it, be it. A week ago I had never been on a horse in my life. Today I can ride. I'm not John Wayne. But I can ride, if I have to. Okay, it's a fraud. You caught me preparing for an interview, like a goddamned method actor prepares for a scene and I didn't like it. So I wigged out. I didn't resent *you*. I resented your seeing *me*. So, sorry. Sorry. Sorry. Sorry. Which is more times than I have said sorry to the whole human race in my entire life. Okay?"

"Okay," Louise said softly, but without forgiveness, still hurt.

He took her hand, drew her close, then reached playfully for her blouse. She remained rigid. He unbuttoned her top button, reached in to her full, bare breasts which needed no bra for support. He ran his finger over them, intending to arouse her, to lure her into the pool, into sex. She did not resist him, but neither did she respond. His finger circled her left nipple and he felt it rise and become hard. The desire for her leaped in him. She felt it and pulled back, "Please, Jock, no?"

They had had moments like this before and he had always prevailed. So he embraced her now, pressed against her to let her know the full size of his desire, but she broke free.

"Lulu?" It was a plea, in one word. But it said everything he wanted to ask her, what she felt and why, and why couldn't it be between them this night as it had been so many nights before?

She was still turned away from him when she said, "There's more sex and less love in this town than any place in the world."

He moved swiftly to confront her, fixed her face with both his hands, but gently. She stared back at him.

"I don't want to be used tonight. If you hate the world, or hate what you have to do to survive in it, say so. I can understand that. If you're afraid of tomorrow, or next month, or next picture, say that. I'll listen. But don't just use me physically."

That angered him, the color rising into his freshly sunburned cheeks. But she went on.

"I have never demanded love from you. I don't say I don't want it, but I have never insisted on it. I'm willing to trade passions. But not anything less. So don't take out your hates and your fears

33

on me. In this town, whores and psychoanalysts get fifty bucks an hour. I'm neither."

She started to leave but he reached out, seized her hand, pulled her to him, kissed her strongly on the mouth, his tongue trying to find its way into her but she was unyielding, though when he set her free he saw her nipples standing firm and hard against the silk of her blouse.

Still she turned and left him.

Driving down toward the desert on his way to Nevada and the Carr ranch now, he was not sure that Louise intended to come back, ever. He had phoned her twice last night and got no answer. He had left messages with her service both times. But she had not called back.

Well, to hell with her! he decreed angrily.

Right now, there was only one important thing in his life, one important person in his life. Preston Carr. Nothing, certainly no woman was going to get in his way. This time was not going to be like last time. This time he was not going to screw it up. Literally. Or in any other way.

Whatever he might dislike about Marty White, his personal habits, his odd expressions, his underhanded tactics, Marty was a sound show-business strategist, a veteran of the Hollywood wars. When Marty mapped a campaign, you followed it. When he gave you advice, you took it. Above all, when he gave you a warning, you listened.

If Jock had listened to Marty that first time, six years ago, his career would have been vastly different now.

Jock could still remember Marty's words precisely, "Laddie, you'll either fuck your way to fame or disaster out here."

Marty had warned him even before it happened. But Jock hadn't listened. And as a result, Jock had been forced to leave the Coast, go back to New York and do four more plays, off Broadway and on, those two, small-budget independent films and then sign to do that picture in England, when all the while he should have been a hot property for Marty White right here in LA.

In fact, Jock Finley should have been among the first and hottest of the new young breed of American film directors.

Instead, Marty White was being forced to create this entire strategy of tying Jock Finley into *Mustang!*, figuring that if he could also add enough star power to the production he would break down the six-year ban that had existed against Jock Finley in this town.

And even that was only possible because old Sol Steiber had finally sold his controlling interest in Steiber Bros. Studios, so he was no longer a power among company heads, and thus the other major studios did not owe him the allegiance they once had.

That was why Marty White figured that the time was finally right to get Jock Finley off that blacklist. Though in Jock's case being blacklisted had no connection with holding certain political convictions.

Contrary to popular belief, there was not one but two blacklists in Hollywood. Above and beyond the political, about which much had been said and written in the past twenty years, there was a second list of unemployables to which were consigned those who had committed some outrageous immoral act that subjected the entire industry to bad worldwide publicity or else, and worse, whose conduct constituted a grave personal affront to one of the powers at one of the major studios.

Of the former type, Fatty Arbuckle was the earliest case; Ingrid Bergman the most recent. In the Arbuckle case the rumors were worse than the facts, the girl's death having been caused by rupture of the vagina due to the abnormal size of his organ in erection instead of, as rumored, that on a drunken impulse he had used a Coke bottle which broke inside her, producing the fatal hemorrhage. What mattered was simply that no medium of family entertainment could abide anyone about whom such rumors circulated, true or false.

The Ingrid Bergman case was simpler, cleaner, in its way. She made no secret that she was carrying the child of one man, while married to another. The fact that the putative father was not an American seemed somehow to intensify the severity of her crime.

35

In both cases, for having subjected the picture industry to worldwide scandal and disfavor, each star had been barred from American picture-making—Arbuckle forever, Bergman for many years.

Cast into this same category were those unfortunate souls who had incurred the personal wrath and vengeance of some power in the industry.

When old Sol Steiber had a violent falling out with his son by his first wife and barred him from the studio as well as from his job as vice-president, every other studio in town followed his example. The young man could not get a job or a deal anywhere and was banished thereafter to the real estate business where he made a large but unsatisfying fortune.

There was another case, years before that, when a very famous director seduced a fourteen-year-old singer whom one of the majors had brought to the brink of stardom. That director was barred from that studio and all major studios for eight years there-after.

As the studio head had declared at the time, "You got to be some kind of pervert to fuck an underage star."

Jock Finley's offense had actually been a crime of ignorance. It could have happened to any very young, very attractive man unfamiliar with Hollywood sexual protocol.

You did not, under any conditions, no matter how young, handsome, or vigorous you were, you did not carry on an affair with the wife or the mistress of a company president or a studio head. You might bang her once or twice on the way back from a Beverly Hills party in the early hours of the morning, or even out on one of the back lawns in the dewy grass of the Racquet Club down at the Springs, or in a pool house, or on some dark pool patio. But it had to be a random event, unplanned, and without any more significance than a chance bang.

If it happened that way, it was quite acceptable for the lady to become your patron and to advance you at the studio by lauding your creative talents, or praising one of your pictures, or suggesting your name when picture packages were the table conversation of the evening.

But to bang her frequently, over a period of weeks or months,

36

with the regularity of an affair that got both of you talked about, that was a gross personal affront which no power in Hollywood would, or had to, abide from any young man no matter how talented. Or, in all fairness, from any young lesbian either.

But all this Jock Finley had not discovered till it was too late.

He had met Susan Steiber at a large party to which Marty White had taken him when he arrived in Hollywood that first time. This was Jock's initial look at some of the great stars of the industry, close up and in person. He found most of them to be less enchanting and less impressive than he had anticipated. Pretty faces had bad legs, and some photogenic faces were so hairy he had to look away when talking to them, lest they realize that he was staring. The male stars were mainly shorter and older than he had expected.

They were all pleasant enough, and some were actually effusive as soon as Marty introduced him as "the brilliant young stage director from New York." The Pavlovian syndrome in California operated on two bells. One labeled "Stage," the other "New York." Press either and the dogs salivated. Never press both unless you had a good supply of Kleenex.

It was very pleasant, very flattering for a young man just turned twenty-six. But one thing flattered him more: the one pretty, dark-haired woman who kept staring at him from the moment he walked into the huge white and fieldstone living room. Her stare was the kind that burned right between your shoulders even when you were turned away from her. She was tall, slim-hipped, with black penetrating eyes well set in her oval face. Her hair, glistening and black, was braided into a tiara, making an excellent frame for her delicate, precise profile.

Her lips were rich and red and always moist, though she never seemed to wet them. As Jock would discover, they stayed that way even after the lipstick had been roughly kissed away from them. And always they were slightly parted, showing white, even teeth, her own, not the laboratory-manufactured jackets which some future generation of archaeologists will find so indigenous to an area once known as Southern California.

That night she wore a black satin cocktail dress, somewhat formal for a Beverly Hills Sunday party, yet the simplicity of

37

the design was classic and understated. It set off her graceful white throat and her bare arms which were delicate almost to being thin, so that they made her round, full breasts enticingly surprising.

From the first she had looked familiar to Jock. One of the older stars, he assumed, who possibly had not made a picture in some time. Yet he knew that she was neither that old nor quite that familiar. But he had seen her picture somewhere. *Life*, *Look*, or possibly *Vogue*.

Now she was staring at him. When he stared back, she turned away abruptly to smile and speak to the man beside her, Marty White. Jock was tempted to laugh, for the poor, short bastard was just about breast-high to her, so that when he answered her it seemed as if she had a hearing aid parked between her breasts and he was talking into it, instead of just staring.

Smiling, Jock crossed from behind a fourteen-foot white couch to the high fieldstone fireplace where Marty and the woman stood.

"Jock-baby, I want you to meet Susie," Marty said. "Susie Steiber," he emphasized, though the emphasis was completely lost on Jock and would be till it was too late.

Because her full name was not familiar to him, Jock did not dwell on her surname but took her hand and held it, while he said, "Susie . . . hi." He was still holding her hand when she said to him, "Marty tells me you're the brilliant young stage director from New York who did Julie West's new hit."

"Good!" Jock answered. "That's what I told him to say."

They laughed uneasily, all three of them, till suddenly Susie dispatched Marty with her half-full glass, "Sweetie, refresh me? Marguerita. On rocks."

Reluctant to leave them, Marty had no choice but to go off. Now Susie turned her attention, her full, black-eyed, staring attention, to Jock Finley.

"I guess you're out here to get into the picture business," she said.

"Isn't everybody?"

Suddenly she asked, "Is it true?"

"True?"

"Your name."

38

"You mean, was it always Finley?"

"I mean, is it short for jock-sock, male sex appeal?"

"Oh," he answered, trying to appear shy. "That's something Earl Wilson made up."

"If there's one place modesty isn't becoming to a man, it's in bed," she said, and she laughed.

Marty was back. With her Marguerita, on rocks. She glanced at it and said, "Oh, sweetie, did I say rocks? I meant straight up. Be a doll and change it."

Marty glanced from Susie's intense, hungry, black eyes to Jock's mischievous blue ones, then he went off toward the bar again. This time he did not return, but had one of the uniformed butlers take Susie's drink to her.

It had been a hard choice Marty was forced to make. But between irritating Sol Steiber's wife and allowing a client to fall into serious error, the former was the more deadly in the intricate category of Hollywood offenses.

Marty knew what the inevitable outcome had to be when, late that evening, after the standard Chasen's buffet for Beverly Hills at-home parties had been served, devoured, or despoiled with cigarette butts, old Sol Steiber approached his wife and said, "Angel, I think we better go. It's late and I have exhibitors in from New York in the morning."

But by that time Susie Steiber had kicked off her shoes and was doing the Israeli folk dance that Jock had been teaching her. Her black hair, no longer a sleek tiara, was loose about her white shoulders. She smiled back at old Sol and called, pleasantly enough, "You go on, darling. I'll be home in a bit." Sol didn't move at first, so Susie added, "Please, don't worry. Mr. Finley will see me home, won't you?"

Jock, enthused and afire with his conquest, nodded enthusiastically and called out to old Sol, "Depend on me, Mr. Steiber. She'll be absolutely safe!"

Sol took a long, pessimistic look at Jock Finley, then at his beautiful dark-haired wife and said, "Okay, Finley."

There was something about the bland way Sol said it that sent a surge of acid through Marty White's stomach. But Jock had no sense of the offense he had just committed. Instead, he turned his attention back to full-breasted, slim, black-haired Susie Steiber and started to demonstrate the second part of the hora.

Somehow Susie's desire for dancing lasted only a very short time after old Sol departed. They were leaving, Susie and Jock, when Marty made his final effort to avoid catastrophe by offering to drive her home in his Rolls. But by that time Jock was so taken and afire with her that he only laughed. So they left alone. Marty turned to his host, an old-time producer on the Steiber lot, shrugged, and said, "Hal, you saw. I did what I could."

"I'm sure Sol will understand," the producer said, in an effort to console Marty.

They were driving back from Beverly Hills to Bel Air where the Steiber mansion was hidden high up in winding Stone Canyon Road. Since it was late and Jock was not yet familiar with LA geography, Susie kept telling him where to turn and how to proceed. Without knowing it, he drove farther and farther from Bel Air till finally he found himself climbing toward the crest of Mulholland Drive. When they reached the top she said softly, "Park here. Something I want you to see."

He pulled off the road into a lookout parking area. She took his hand and said, "Come!"

They got out, went to stand at the barrier that edged the parking area. Jock looked down and saw unrolled beneath him that luminous grid of green, blue, and red lights and streets, houses and huge buildings which was Los Angeles, Hollywood, and all the closely surrounding towns which comprise that huge, sprawling complex. Off in the distance, a jet blinking red and white made its turn over the black ocean and started to head east in the dark sky.

"This is the shot they always show in pictures in the scene where the producer or the agent takes the young starlet out and says, 'Honey, be good to me and all that is yours.' " Susie laughed at the cliché. It was a strange moment for Jock. For she was just provocative enough, and yet just amused enough, to keep him guessing. Was it a joke? Or a proposition? If she were a less attractive woman, he would have treated it as the former and laughed along

40

with her. But by now he had a hunger for her, for her delicate oval face, her surprising breasts. Those thin hips had made his hands eager.

He embraced her suddenly and kissed her hard on her moist lips, expecting they would part even further and she would open her mouth to him. But she remained aloof, though not angry.

"Uh uh. I'm no starlet, baby. Neither are you," she whispered. And he thought she was playing coy in order to invite further aggression from him. So he kissed her again, this time reaching for one of her breasts. But she broke free. "Don't! Don't ever!" He thought she was angry with him till she added, "Not here."

She started to the car and he followed. He backed the car out, and following her instructions, drove down from Mulholland to Sunrise and on out to Bel Air.

On the way, they said little. She smoked quite a lot, and he caught her staring at him from time to time. In his groin there was a sharp pain, for she had aroused him strongly before she rejected him. He was angry and she knew it.

They approached the huge iron gates of the Steiber mansion. The place was dark and seemed deserted. A little way from the gate she put her hand on his arm.

"You stop here," she said.

"I thought I stopped back there," Jock answered sullenly, as sullen as a young man with a bad, aching case of blue balls had every right to be.

"Don't be angry with me, baby," she said. "But I don't like quickies. And I don't have to settle for them." She got out of the car. He was about to explode in a fury when she said softly, "Now you save that. Till tomorrow. One o'clock. The Lodge. That's a motel you'll reach in the Valley if you just keep going on Mulholland. I was only showing you the way tonight."

She smiled at him and even in the dark he could see her oval face, her shiny lips, as she said, "One o'clock, baby."

She went to the huge iron gates and using her own key she let herself in through a small door cut into one of the gates. He waited till there was a light inside the palatial house. Then he turned the car about, started back toward the Beverly Hills Hotel along Sunset.

41

"Mr. Finley?" the clerk at the desk was asking the man who had entered just before him.

The other man was just saying no, when Jock interceded, "I'm Finley."

"There's a message. Very urgent. I'm to make sure you get it the minute you come back. Call Mr. White, at once, no matter what time!"

Jock went up to his room, got on the phone, gave the operator the number. Marty answered, interrupting the very first ring.

"Kid?"

"Yeah, Marty."

"What happened?"

"Nothing."

"Don't lie to me, laddie!"

"I give you my word, nothing!" Jock said irritated. But Marty was relieved.

"Okay. Keep it that way. Cool, laddie, nice and cool. You hear?"

"I didn't promise that. I just said nothing happened."

"Laddie, listen to me . . . this isn't New York. Here there is a whole code about fucking around, with who, and how and when. And the first rule is: Don't screw around with the wife or the girl friend of a studio president, studio head, or executive producer. Now that won't cramp you too much. There's too much other stuff around. Besides, most of the wives are ugly old coozes anyhow. You just happened to meet one of the outstanding exceptions. But don't get sucked in. We made lots of important headway tonight, till you got tangled up with her. Sol didn't like it. Didn't like it at all, kid. So I want your word, you won't see Susie Steiber again. Ever."

When Jock didn't promise or protest, Marty went on, half in anger, half in sadness, "I know, you got a date with her. You are already set to play a matinee with the Madonna of the Motel Circuit."

"Look, Marty . . ."

"Kid, don't bother to deny it. And don't lie to me. I'd rather you just never told me about it. I don't want to know. When I find out from Sol I want to be completely surprised."

42

Jock was silent another moment and that was when Marty said, "Laddie, you'll either fuck your way to fame or disaster out here." And he hung up.

When Jock arrived at the Lodge next afternoon, the clerk at the desk greeted him, "Mr. Finley?" Jock nodded. The clerk handed him a room key, saying, "Your secretary phoned and made the reservation."

Jock took the key, got back into his car, and followed the arrows till he pulled up at an isolated, single-unit motel bungalow, unattached to any other and secluded far back on the extensive grounds of the establishment. He opened the door and discovered a rather tasteful replica of a New England bedroom, in maple furniture, wallpaper with matching drapes in a tiny red and white nautical figure, and soft carpeting of a simulated hooked rug design. The room smelled fresh and clean and the air-conditioner hummed efficiently, almost drowning out the muffled roar of huge trucks on Ventura Boulevard.

He closed the door, threw the bolt for no reason at all except possibly Marty's warning of the night before. Then he heard a soft, cool voice from inside the bathroom.

"Baby?" It was her voice, it seemed just as calm as it had been last night, but somehow she managed to transmit to him the eagerness that was in her.

She opened the door and came out, dressed in a lace-edged negligee of light blue crepe, tied tightly around her slender waist, accenting her full breasts. Her shining black hair hung loose and she was brushing it, so that it glistened in its own natural oil. With her came a perfume so pungent that it reached Jock from across the room and set that feeling going again in his groin. It was so sudden, so sharp, that the pain of last night's frustration returned with it.

She moved to him and kissed him lightly, without interrupting her brushing. He held her face and stared into it. In the light of day she held up well. Those eyes were deep and dark and free of surrounding creases or wrinkles. Her cheekbones were high and cleanly prominent in her oval face. And her lips, moist, parted

43

somewhat, still revealed those even white teeth. His hand went from her face to her shoulders, pushing back the negligee which gave easily, the single looping knot offering little resistance. Yet she kept brushing her hair, even when he seized her and kissed his way from her lips down her delicate white throat to her breasts, which were not only round and full, but firmer than he had expected in a woman almost forty.

It was when she felt him hard against her that she whispered, "Uh uh." For a moment he thought the events of last night were going to be repeated. So he seized the hairbrush from her hand, hurled it against the wall. He heard it hit and drop to the carpeted floor. But he didn't look, because he was at her breasts, which were the source of that perfume, and the smell made her large, rigid, puckered nipples even more provocative to his lips and his tongue.

She turned away from him, taking his hand from under her left breast, and led him to the bed, saying softly, "Come, baby."

At the bed he tried to embrace her again, but she avoided him gracefully. She made him stand still, arms loose at his sides, and she said, "Let Mama." She proceeded to undress him, jacket, shirt, trousers, till he was completely naked. She did it with such care that it took on the precision of a ritual. He was being undressed as ceremoniosly as matadors were dressed.

It was during that procedure that Jock realized that with Susie the word "baby" was not merely an endearment or a form of expression but that she had to be mother, and dominant, in any sexual relationship.

When she had undressed him completely, she took his hands and pressed them against her breasts so hard he knew it must have hurt, but she seemed to want that. Then she pushed him so that he fell back onto the bed in a sitting position. She moved to him, forcing her narrow hips between his legs so that she was close to him and and she pressed his face against her breasts tightly till he had to move to find a place between them in order to breathe. But she held him there for what seemed a long time. All the while that burning part of him was pressing and probing against her white thighs, but she would not admit him.

Then she stretched him on the bed, knelt between his legs so that she was over him, her shiny black hair hanging down, the ends of

44

it just reaching the erect part of him. She began to sway, her long free hair sweeping back and forth, touching, titillating, arousing him till the pain returned. When he reached out for her, she shoved him back violently as though he had interrupted her in the throes of her orgasmic moment. When his natural instinct to thrust began to exert itself, she pressed her long, red fingernails into his thighs till he winced. She continued to sweep her hair across him, in faster and faster motions till finally he had achieved a full and complete climax and release. Only then did she hurl herself on him, press to him, and kiss him on his mouth, and in it, with a fever of great gratitude, as though he, not she, had carried out the whole act.

In a while, she rolled off him, turned on her back, and lit up a cigarette. She inhaled deeply and seemed to derive sustenance from the smoke, for it refreshed her.

"You are very good for me, baby. Very good. And I can be good for you," she promised. "But let Mama, always let Mama."

That afternoon Jock discovered what she meant, for in the entire six times, not once did she let him enter her. Yet she seemed more satisfied than many girls he had had in more usual ways.

And she prided herself that he did not tire but seemed as strong at the end as he had at the beginning. It was over suddenly when she said, "God, it's late. I have to run." She got up from their bed, dressed quickly but very meticulously, and in a matter of minutes she was the magnificently chic Beverly Hills matron he had met at the party the night before.

When she was ready to leave, she said, "You can't call me. Sol has all the phones tapped. So each time we have to make a date for next time. Or else I'll leave a message at the hotel, if Sol goes on any sudden trips. For now, Wednesday. The Riviera. In Burbank. Right off the Freeway. Same time."

She started for the door, stopped there to mention a business detail. "The room's paid for. You can just slip out, get into your car, and take off. Bye, baby."

She was gone. He lay on his back, hands under his head, saying to himself, "Christ Almighty! Weird!" And he promised himself that was the end of it. But by Wednesday he wanted her again. So he was at the Riviera.

As he was every time she set a place and time. For each time, within the demands of her need to be the aggressor and the dominant one, she employed what turned out to be a varied and fascinating arsenal of the sexual arts, to arouse, intensify, and satisfy his desires, which seemed boundless. But of them all, her hair was by far the most provocative and ultimately the most satisfying. Each time when he was empty he went away promising himself it was the end. But the next time he was at the spot she chose, at the hour she selected.

Each time as well, she allowed a little more of her past to emerge. She had arrived in Hollywood at the age of fifteen, already beautiful and determined to become a star. Slim, but with her breasts even then larger than might be expected for her age and figure, she passed herself off as being older. She became the mistress and then the wife of the art director of Steiber Studios. After much nagging on her part, her husband finally succeeded in arranging for her to have a screen test.

Sol Steiber himself saw the test while waiting for the rushes of an Errol Flynn picture. He was not so old in those days, and he was quite taken by her. Especially since her husband had dressed her in such a way as to reveal the best of her.

Sol sent for her, interviewed her alone in his huge office and kept calling her "young lady" though she was not yet sixteen. He seemed extremely distressed when he discovered that, too late. He was not about to run the risk of statutory rape even for this girl whom he wanted more desperately after that interview than he had before.

Under the pretext that she was a minor, he insisted she have an agent, at once, for her protection. Her husband's agent, it turned out, would do very nicely. Instead of the usual practice, which meant that a business affairs man would carry on the negotiation, in this instance Sol himself dealt directly with the agent, who secured a very favorable contract for Susie. And in addition a new and more favorable long-term contract for her husband as well.

Within the year, Susie and her designer husband were divorced. And by coincidence, so was Sol Steiber. Then Sol proposed and, since her career had not advanced very far during that year, a marriage to Sol Steiber seemed like a more favorable move, career-wise, as they say in Hollywood.

Her former husband continued to be employed at Steiber Studios. And at a huge salary for a designer. In effect, she had been passed from one hand to another in a transaction in which everyone profited. Except Susie. For in the end it turned out that old Sol wanted her for himself alone and never would let her become a star.

So now she justified her sexual infidelities as her revenge on Sol for destroying her career. And always she chose young men, younger and younger men.

Of course, the delicious irony of it was that now Sol could not divorce her, no matter how much she played around, because for tax reasons she owned almost as much Steiber stock as he did.

All these things Susie told Jock, a little each time, as they grew more and more intimate, familiar, and easy with each other. What amused Jock was that she never chose the same motel twice. Which in turn led him to wonder how many young men there had been, and how extensive was her acquaintanceship with motels and desk clerks.

But as long as she had that swinging, tantalizing black hair, those fabulous breasts so perfumed, those moist, moist lips, Jock didn't worry about peripheral details such as numbers.

If theirs had remained a matinee affair, it might possibly have run its course and ended naturally, without consequences. But after the first five weeks, each time that Sol had to fly to New York or London or Rome, Jock would find a note in his hotel box. It might say, "Tuesday, nine. The Sierra, Westwood." Or "Friday, ten. The Frontier, North Hollywood." Evening affairs were always after dinner, for Susie would not run the risk of having dinner with him in any public place. They arrived separately at the motel, departed separately. Risk was at an absolute minimum.

The only time they deviated from their meticulously safe routine was the one time when Sol was off on a ten-day trip to cover London, Rome, the Middle East, and the Orient. Once during that time, she dared to accept Jock's invitation to dinner at a restaurant out in Santa Monica. A dark, intimate place, it seemed quite safe. And it was.

47

Twice he picked her up near the Steiber mansion to drive her to the motel she had selected. So that twice he returned her to that huge, dark house, behind the high iron gates.

The second time, they sat in his car, the lights off, and kissed and whispered while her sharp nails were inside his shirt playing provocatively across his tan chest and raising welts where she dug in suddenly, although it still felt good to him. He kissed her at the same time, brusquely, and then pushed his way past her teeth and into her hot, moist mouth. She had begun to play with him, her nails digging into him so that the intense pain itself had become an aphrodisiac, when suddenly two sharp, blinding, penetrating lights turned the protective blackness into sudden daylight.

A voice called out in a fury such as Jock had never heard equaled before or since, "You bastard! You dirty bastard, I will kill you. Kill you!" The voice was old Sol Steiber's, but it was barely recognizable so intense was his fury and so shrill. His aged, angry face was glaring through the window of the car, and the anger in his eyes made them huge, maniacal.

Jock's first reaction was that that little old man was shouting at him, till he heard, "I'll kill you, you dirty whore! I'll teach you, you bitch!" He issued a command, "Get her out of there!"

Two men in studio security uniforms approached the car from behind the huge arc lights that almost blinded Jock and Susie. One of them approached the far door, opened it, and seized her hand, yanking her out of the car and pinning her by both arms. The other guard flung open Jock's door and seized him by the shirt in such a way as to imprison him and make it almost impossible for him to breathe.

Now the little old gnome, Sol Steiber, came at Susie, and using first the back of one hand then the other, smashed across her delicate oval face till blood ran from her exquisite lips and down her white face.

He kept shrilling, "You whore! I bought you. And I will sell you when *I* get ready. You do this to me again and I will kill you. You hear, kill you!"

When the old man was finally exhausted from shouting and flailing he stood breathing very hard. In a harsh whisper, which

48

he barely managed, he said to her, "Get inside! Whore! Fucking whore!"

When the guard freed her, she almost fell, but instead without a word or a tear, with her lovely face bloody and bruised, she started toward the dark house, walking nearly erect and with all the arrogance she could summon.

Once she disappeared, the old man turned his attention to Jock, who was still in the grip of the huge security guard.

"Get him out," the old man said, not nearly so furious now that he was spent. The guard pulled Jock from the car without loosening his hold. When Jock tried to strike back the other guard came around quickly and pinned his arms.

The old man walked up to him, stared up into Jock's face and said, "As for you, you *shmuck*, you have fixed yourself in this industry! I will teach you to fuck around with my wife! From tomorrow morning on, you are dead here. You will never work on any picture or in any studio in this town!"

Just when it seemed to Jock that he would be let off with threats alone, the old man said softly to one of the guards, "Okay."

As the one guard held him, the other struck out with a weapon that turned out to be a long nightstick. He caught Jock across the thighs at groin height, not once but time after time, till his thighs ached and the pain in his genitals was so fierce that he cried out in agony. But his outcry only seemed to invite more punishment, for the old gnome called out, "Teach him good!"

The guard kept flailing. Now the blows were striking higher, across his lean stomach, and then down across his thighs again, and his balls were shot through with such fierce pain that he fainted, finally.

When he came to, he was in his own car on a deserted side road in Westwood, just off the UCLA campus. It was the pain that had wakened him. He groaned, held himself, and brought his hands away seeking blood. There was none. He looked in the rear-view mirror, his face was unmarked, untouched. Only in his groin was there pain, unbearable pain. It was an expert job of beating, done by men who had obviously done the same kind of job before. It accomplished the result, left no visible outward marks, and was not the kind of assault one was likely to report to the police.

Despite the pain, he drove himself back to the hotel, parked on the street behind it, and made his way in through the rear patio entrance. At such an early hour, he could do that unseen except by a porter who was mopping the lobby floor. He had intended to walk up the two flights of stairs but couldn't make it. So he had to take the elevator. While he was waiting, one of the desk clerks called out, "Good morning, Mr. Finley," his voice sharing vicariously in what he assumed had been a delicious late-night sexual encounter.

Marty had got a doctor for him. The doctor's diagnosis was simple: no permanent damage, time would take care of things. The memory of it might inhibit Jock's sex life for a time, but there was no physical or organic damage involved.

By far the more serious matter was Marty's diagnosis. It was bad, very bad. Jock might wait it out and see what happened. But Marty held out no hope. The best advice he could give Jock was to go back to New York, immediately become involved in a play, and wait it out. After all, a man Sol Steiber's age couldn't live forever.

Once, by sheer accident, Jock met both of them in New York at an opening-night party at the Four Seasons. To observe them together, one would never have suspected that Sol and Susie were anything less than the happily married couple depicted in the Sunday supplements or in one of the national magazines.

Despite the events of that night, and Steiber's harsh words, his accusations, his physical brutality toward her, they treated each other with ostensible warmth, kindness, and respect.

When she was introduced to Jock by someone who did not know of their previous relationship, Susie handled the moment as though they were strangers and had never met. Nor did she linger in conversation with him but passed on to meet other people, other strangers.

Jock wondered, had that night been the end of her affairs or

50

did she still punish old Sol, but with greater care now? Jock never did find out.

All he knew was that Marty's warning had come true. He had fucked his way into disaster. And it was a long, tough road back. Talent was not enough. Time was not enough. It took old Sol's sale of his (and Susie's) interest in the studio to reopen the Hollywood doors to Jock Finley.

And this time, Jock promised himself, this time he was going to make it, make it big, make it all. Independents and cheapies and the hit-or-miss chances of Broadway were going to be a thing of the past for him.

But for that, for all of that, he needed Preston Carr. And he was going to get him.

The Carr ranch turned out to be a huge place, larger by far than Jock had anticipated. Once he passed through the open front gate under the big C he drove quite a distance before he finally came upon any buildings. When he did, they were in excellent condition, well kept, sturdy, mainly new. The entire place had the appearance and feel of a highly successful enterprise. To a Brooklyn boy like Jock Finley, it was vastly different from the simple, old-fashioned, weatherbeaten image the word "ranch" usually conjured.

So, too, it was different around the corral. For it was more than a corral. It had a grandstand at one end capable of accommodating several hundred spectators. No, this was no movie-set-of-a-corral, with hat-whipping cowboys in worn leather chaps busting broncos to the accompaniment of rebel yells.

Instead, several men were sitting on the top rail of the fence quietly watching a skilled rider put a graceful Appaloosa quarter horse through the precise and highly demanding exercises for a working breed of horse. When Jock's Ferrari pulled up to a respectful proximity, no man turned to notice. Jock jumped out without opening the door, considered taking the script but decided to leave it for the moment. He started for the corral in a rolling, rhythmic gait never cultivated on city sidewalks.

Even before he reached the rail, he was aware that the rider was Preston Carr. Astride the smallish horse, Carr seemed larger than Jock had expected. He handled the animal with ease, with sureness, and somehow Jock knew suddenly why during the last twenty years Carr had been called "the King" in the world of motion pictures. Handsome, rugged, sure, strong, browned from the sun, his hair and thin moustache still black, shiny, he seemed twenty years younger than he must have been.

Style was style. Good writers had it. Good directors had it. If you were sensitive, you could spot it in a man or a horse, or both. Even if you knew only a little about horses and riders. Jock knew Preston Carr had style.

Now Carr called out in the direction of the three men, "He's ready, Smitty. He's real ready." It was a compliment to the trainer as well as the horse. As Carr rode toward the rail, the trainer dropped to the ground to take charge of the animal. Carr slipped off, not in an abrupt dismount, but in a single, continuous, liquid movement with the same grace he had exhibited in pictures for years and which had made him so admired by men and women alike.

Even afoot, Carr was taller than Jock had expected. And broader in the shoulders. He was well put together, with hard biceps that stretched the short knit sleeves of his English polo shirt. Nothing hung loose or slack there. His forearms were brown, ridged with long muscles. He had the powerful hands and arms a good rider must have.

Jock started toward him, "Mr. Carr?"

Carr answered, pleasantly enough, with a not unfriendly, "Yeah, kid. What is it?"

It wasn't "kid" in an affectionate way. Nor was it hostile. It was what it was meant to be, a man talking to a kid. Jock resented that. No mature man would easily put himself into the hands of a kid. So Jock said firmly, "Finley. Jock Finley."

He expected his name would evoke a reaction. All he got from Carr was a cordial, "Hi, Finley. What can I do for you?"

Jock was beginning to burn now. For Carr said it exactly as he would have said it to a young farm-machinery salesman making his first visit. Or to a hay-and-feed man. Now, Jock knew, he had to check in, and check in fast and strong. Firmly, not nastily, he

52

said, "*Jock* Finley. And what you can do for me is ask why the hell I drove five hours all the way out to this place to see you."

If Jock hadn't said it with a smile, he wouldn't have got away with it. But it was his smile, the look of sheer innocence in his baby-blue eyes that got him by. Carr hesitated a moment, then he smiled, too.

"Okay, why the hell did you drive five hours all the way out to this place and could you tell me better over a drink, because you look like you need it."

Carr led him to the house which was beyond the corral. But it turned out not to be "the house" at all. It was a large bar-play-and-billiard room, done in luxurious fashion with redwood paneling and costly leather furniture which belied the simple exterior.

It was air-conditioned. And it offered a wide picture window, so that a man could sit in one of the huge chairs, drink in hand, perfectly cool and dry, and watch the action in the corral. Or else he could gaze at the distant Nevada mountains, purple, earth-brown, and dun-colored. And beyond them were mountains topped by snow, disappearing into friendly white clouds.

Air-conditioning, picture windows, huge leather chairs richly upholstered in New York, so that's the rugged frontier life of the day, Jock said to himself.

They both drank Scotch whiskey. Jock had his with soda. Carr drank his full strength, just cooled over ice. Jock noticed that it was an uncommon brand of eighteen-year-old-Scotch and that Carr drank it slowly, as a connoisseur would drink brandy, not in gulps like an alcoholic.

Jock's mind was still working on that phrase Carr had used . . . "could you tell me better over a drink because you look like you need it."

Had Carr referred to his long drive in the hot sun? Or to Jock's inner intensity? Or his insecurity? Was it showing? Was Carr saying the same thing Louise tried to say last evening?

If he had had any ulterior motive, Carr hadn't betrayed it. Not in the way he had poured or handed the drink to Jock or in the way he sipped at his own now. And certainly not in the casual way he waited for Jock to open up. It would have helped Jock if Carr had betrayed some feeling.

53

As it was, Jock was forced to make a few flattering pleasantries. How impressive the ranch. How magnificent the animals—and here Jock threw in a bit of the horseman's patois he had picked up in the past week. How great the view—one had to remark on the view, he felt. Carr accepted each banality pleasantly, with a smile. He responded, with answers he had given hundreds of times before, to visitors, to producers, to interviewers. It became demandingly obvious that the man was waiting, politely, but very clearly waiting for Jock.

Jock took the plunge, suddenly, precipitously. Not at all in the way he had planned. For he found himself blurting out, "Mr. Carr. I am a director. A picture director!" Carr continued smiling pleasantly. Jock pressed on, "*Black, Man, Black*." When that failed to bring any response from Carr, Jock went on, "*Tell It Like It Is?*"

"Oh," Carr finally said. "Oh, yes. Heard about that. Supposed to be a pretty good picture in New York." Then to soften the subtle slur, Carr explained, "I don't get to see many pictures these days. Except on television." He laughed, meaning that he saw himself frequently. But it had been said modestly and Jock could not take offense.

"I understand," Carr went on, "that your kind of pictures won't ever get to be shown on television." A gentle jibe at the *New Wave* school of utter frankness, nudity, and overt sexual perversion. Jock laughed at that. But it was a light laugh, merely a polite laugh. Because he did not like the way the whole meeting was going.

He thought now maybe it had been a mistake to drive out unannounced, uninvited. But if it had, this was the time to become bold.

"Mr. Carr, if you really want to know the truth, I'm here to find out if you're a phony or not."

The smile froze stiffly on Carr's brown face, but his eyes turned angry. Jock knew he had scored. How hard, how well he had scored, he didn't know yet. But he had the man's attention, his irritation, possibly even his respect.

"Let's get one thing straight, *Mr.* Carr," and now Jock was putting considerable bite into the "Mr." "I get a hundred and fifty thousand dollars a picture. That's a sixteen-thousand-dollar

54

Ferrari standing out there. I spent five hours of my valuable time driving down here. I'll spend the rest of the day here and five hours driving back. Tomorrow."

At the word "tomorrow" Carr's face started to redden. But Jock, having set out on that tack, didn't dare turn back now.

"However, before I leave, I am going to have an answer to that question, *Mr.* Carr. So if you're thinking of getting rid of me, you'd better call in the four strongest hands you have, get them to carry me out of here bodily, tie me into that Ferrari, and drive me to the edge of your property before they cut me loose. I'm not leaving here any other way! Not today!"

Carr sat quietly a moment. It was one of the longest moments Jock Finley would ever live through. Then Carr started to laugh. At first it was a small laugh, an "I've seen nerve but this beats all" laugh. Then a bigger laugh, a "kid, you've got more guts than I thought" laugh. And finally that hearty kind of laugh reserved for two men when they respect each other.

Now, finally, Carr was ready to talk. "Okay, Finley, what makes you think I'm a phony?"

"Because you sit here, dug in, in the midst of all the luxury that money and nature can afford. You hold yourself out to the world as being ready to go back into pictures as soon as the right script appears. But to me it looks like you're dug in forever. You've got everything you need. So the right script is never going to come along!

"Not for you. Because deep down inside, Mr. Carr, you have a gnawing fear. That this is a new day. That your kind of acting will show up pretty pale, pretty weak, alongside what we young guys have going these days. Or is it that my kind of director is too strong, too real, too powerful for the kind of pictures you were used to making? Now, if I'm right, say so. And I'll get into my Italian buggy, by myself, and ride off into the sunset. *A*-lone.

"*But* . . . if I'm wrong, and I hope to God I am, then I've got the damnedest part for Preston Carr that he's ever seen!"

Jock's director's instinct told him to shut up at that moment. Carr sat silent, rotating his heavy crystal old-fashioned glass, wiping the condensation from it with his thumb.

"Leave the script. I'll let you know."

55

Jock shook his head, quite firmly negative.

"I have to read it and think about it before I can make up my mind."

Jock nodded.

"Then leave it."

Jock shook his head again. Now anger was beginning to show in Carr's face. It was the most hopeful sign Jock had seen yet. He had struck the nerve for which he had been probing.

Feeling stronger, surer, Jock said simply, "I'll wait while you read it. I'll stay over while you think about it. Then whatever you say tomorrow, that'll be it. I won't argue with you. But at least I'll have my answer. Yes or no. But I'm not going to dangle for weeks, for months, the way you've kept other directors hanging before you said no. You're going to find out, Mr. Carr, that I am not like other directors!"

Carr hesitated, then asked, "Where's the script?"

"Out there. I'll get it." And Jock started out toward his Ferrari in that rolling cowboy walk he had adopted in the last few days.

Carr put him up in one of the guest cottages. But they had dinner together in the main house. After dinner they sat in the huge living room of bleached desert woods and rough native stone, before a great blazing fire, because it was a cold night. They were having brandy. Again, private brand, again the very best.

All through dinner Carr had not mentioned the script. His talk had been devoted to the old days in Hollywood, the fabulous characters, the great practical jokers, the prodigious drinkers, and finally, as it always had to, it turned to the great sexual exploits. Those had been the great days, before TV, before the competition of foreign films, before the influx of new critics, new picture-making, when Hollywood had still been a magic word, and Preston Carr had been the King.

But still no mention of the script. Not till Carr asked suddenly, almost irrelevantly, "Those scenes with the girl. After all, I'm old enough to be her father. How's that going to set with the audience?"

With that question, Jock knew finally that he had a prayer, a chance, an honest-to-God chance of getting Preston Carr, of get-

56

ting the deal, of getting that budget of eight million dollars, and that one *big* picture!

But he knew, too, that care, caution, was of the utmost importance now. For he had no clue as to how genuinely interested Carr was in the psychiatric approach to character or the deeper layers and meanings of sexual relationships. Jock knew one thing though, he had to make the explanation impressive, and also extremely flattering to Preston Carr. Jock smiled as he got to his feet and said, "You just said the magic word, Mr. Carr. Now I *know* that you and I are going to get along.

"Audience, Mr. Carr. Audience! That is the key. The key to everything I do and think! To every scene I envision and direct. That's what makes my new wave new! That's what makes me tick, a 'kid' named Jock Finley . . . that's right, Mr. Carr, it's practically the first word you ever spoke to me, 'kid.' But this 'kid' is world famous! *Where it counts!* In the very exclusive magazines, in the opinion of the finest critics, Jock Finley stands for something.

"Why? Partly because of me. But partly because I know something about them! The audience! Something they don't even know. We're living in a new world, Mr. Carr! Television did it. But not the way you think! Not by competing with pictures, but by changing the character of the audience. There was a time when people gathered together in theaters. They needed communion with each other to enjoy a movie. There used to be nothing as desolate as sitting alone in an empty movie house. You know that from sitting in empty projection rooms.

"But with television the whole world, the whole audience has gotten used to sitting alone, watching alone. Not only films. But news events. The most shattering, exciting, terrible, and wonderful events in the history of the world. And we watch them alone. Often with no one else to talk to, to share views with, or reactions, feelings."

Jock started to move about the huge room, talking, using his hands, his arms to make extravagant and dramatic gestures. He seemed in a world of his own. Carr watched, impressed. Jock was subtly, but fully, aware. As long as the King was impressed, Jock would keep talking.

"Suddenly, overnight, without word or warning, we became

solitary spectators of *everything!* But participants in *nothing!* The audience became fragmented into ones. Each human being suddenly became cut off, solitary. There was no group called an audience any longer. But great numbers of single human beings the world over, imprisoned in solitary, with eyes and ears and little else. Watching, watching, watching, but participating not at all.

"They have a strange thing going now, this new audience. They've been conditioned. They want to feel, be part of this world, hook up with other people. But only on the same basis as they do on television, with complete immunity from being truly involved, or truly hurt, or truly anything.

"We've become a world of voyeurs. Today people come to films to take part in lives they don't dare to live.

"Now I know that. So I know the audience better than they know themselves. I have to. Because each time I direct I live and feel for a hundred million individuals. I must have more sensitivity, more feeling, more everything. I have to be more demanding, too.

"Yes, Mr. Carr, I want to warn you now, there is no limit to what I ask of myself, or anyone else, in my need to fulfill the dreams, the desires, the terrible hunger of those poor individuals who have to live without running the risks of living, to love without loving, to kill without pulling a trigger, to be part of every feeling but no part of any reality.

"So I make films for that one person who is the audience. And I seduce him into putting his feelings, his innermost feelings, into my hands. Do I look down on him? No! Am I sorry for him? Yes! So I do my share to make his life more bearable, less dull, less solitary. Some experts say films are a narcotic for the audience. I say I won't let them be! So I hit them hard. Often. I grip them, hold them, change them! I batter down the aloneness that television has built up. I hold out my hand to them and say, 'Here, take it, let's experience this together!'"

Now Jock turned to face Carr fully, directly, seeming to apologize for having revealed so much of himself. Softly, as though spent, he said, "That's the way I feel about the audience. And that's why I was so relieved, so delighted, to hear that your first concern was about them.

"Now, what will they say about you and the affair with the

young girl? I can tell you what they'll say. Because *I* will make them say it!

"First, the sexual impetus comes from the girl. That alone relieves you of any resentment from the audience. But more, this is a girl who desperately needs your kind of man. Mature, handsome, sexual in an animal way, yes. But with the solid reassuring strength of a father. She needs the security that only an older man can provide. And intuitively you sense that. You know that girl needs you if she is ever to grow out of her confused and tortured state. And because you do, you finally give in to her and have the affair.

"Mind you, you are not seducing a young, immature girl. Till you meet her she is a tramp! Actually you are rescuing her from a lifetime of sexual searching, promiscuous sexual searching! So in reality you find a confused, beaten girl, used by many men, but you leave her a wiser, more mature woman, ready to marry and make a good life with a man of her own age. Even though you love her.

"The way I will do it, it will emerge as one of the most unselfish acts of love that has ever been seen in any film!"

Carr was silent a long time. Then he poured Jock another brandy. But Jock did not move toward his glass. He stayed on his feet, recalling, improvising, playing scene after scene from the script, ad-libbing, rewriting on the wing.

In each instance it was a scene to do with Carr's character, Linc. In each instance Linc emerged as a man of action, depth, sensitivity, or strength. Even Linc's scenes with the wild mustangs, Jock promised, would not be just the bare action scenes of old Carr pictures.

Oh, no. As Jock described them they would be much more than the conflict of man against beast. They would be symbolism of the new school. They would represent the clash of old world against new. Of individual against system. Linc was more than a middle-aged nomad cowman. He was the last of the great individualists, fighting against the whole overpowering system.

Then, turning from his description, which he had made to sound like a gallant, defiant challenge to the world, Jock moved close to Carr, talked low and soft, but with enormous conviction, "Do this picture, Mr. Carr. Do it my way. And I promise you that we'll rub the noses of those avant-garde critics in New York, London, and Paris in the dirt! After *Mustang!* whenever they call Preston Carr 'the King' it will mean more than merely your prestige at the box office. It will be because they finally accept you seriously as a great actor. They will find in the mature Preston Carr, in this picture of depth and meaning, a Preston Carr they never knew existed before!"

The great picture performances are not given by actors, but by directors. Not in front of cameras, but before a single foot of film is ever exposed. They are given by directors who desperately believe, correctly or not, that but for this one star there is never going to be any picture at all. The great performances are given by the Jock Finleys.

And now Jock had just given one of his greatest—despite the fact that all the while within him there was a strong resentment, a conscious hostility toward Carr, toward this whole charade. A great director, young or old, should not have to be dependent upon anyone, studio, star, or story. He should not have to argue, plead, beg, or humble himself by being a mountebank, a monkey on a string, performing for actors too vain or too stupid to understand, but who happen to be bankable names in "big" pictures, for one accidental reason or another.

Jock realized now that the anger he had vented on Louise last evening was what he dared not vent on Preston Carr.

But the performance was almost over. All that remained was to hear Carr say yes. The culmination of six hours of talking, enforced charm, performing, flattering, inventing, improvising.

Carr took one last sip of his expensive, exclusive brandy. "Sounds great!" Jock fought to control his smile of victory. Then Carr added, "I'll certainly think about it."

Think about it? Inside himself, Jock was burning: Why you arrogant sonofabitch! You let me go through this whole routine. Let me turn on every trick in my book, so that I have practically no ammunition left. And now, now, all you can say is "I'll think about it!"

But outwardly, Jock gave Carr an open baby-blue gaze, very big, very sincere.

60

"Carr, I'll say to you what I said to Paul Muni before I directed him."

Involuntarily, Carr's eyes glanced up from his glass and toward Jock, a gesture that asked skeptically, You directed Muni?

Jock was fully aware of it, but instead of answering Carr's doubts directly, he continued, "I said, 'Yes, Mr. Muni, I *want* you to think about it. Whatever you do, don't agree casually. Not if you're going to work with me. Because I don't do anything casual or trivial. I'm warning you now. I will be demanding, difficult. I'm a zealot about what I do because I don't choose to do anything unless *I* think it's important.'

"That's what I said to Muni. And that was before I'd had two hits on Broadway or done any pictures at all. That was for television. And it was one of my first jobs as a director. Because in those days they took a chance with anyone from the theater, and I had one off-Broadway credit to my name.

"I was the one who decided on Muni. The network, the author, they said, sure he'd be great in the part but you'll never get him. But I believed in that script and I wanted him, so I sent it to him. He was living out in Santa Barbara in those days. But I didn't hear from him. And time was running out. The network was getting very nervous. To say nothing of the sponsor. So I suggested I fly out and see him. They were sure it wouldn't work, and they agreed only because it was good publicity for the show. 'Jock Finley is flying out to confer with Paul Muni on their upcoming NBC dramatic special, etc., etc., etc.' I don't have to tell you, Carr, how they milk things that will never happen when they want publicity.

"I arrived in LA. Got into a rented car at the airport, with careful directions in my hand about how to drive to Santa Barbara, where to find Muni's house. All the way I rehearsed my opening line, 'Mr. Muni, I am so sure this script needs you that if you don't do it I am going to recommend to NBC that it should never be done.' How's that for an opening line to a great star? It had to intrigue him. Except I never got the chance to use it.

"When I arrived, his wife answered the door. She came out of the kitchen where she'd been supervising the cook who was preparing his dinner. When I introduced myself, she said, 'Muni's down by the water.' She said it with regret. As though I'd come to take him back to jail or to an asylum. I went through the lovely garden, found him sitting at the far end of it, looking out over the Pacific. It was early evening. The sun was almost touching the horizon. Huge and tired, it still laid a broad, bold streak of gold across the swelling, restless sea. That's the view Muni was looking at. When I approached, he put up his hand in that way he had of preventing you from talking till he was ready to listen. He motioned me to a chair beside him. He stared out at the water, till the sun was halfway down into the sea.

"Then he said, 'This is what you want to steal from me. You don't want me to enjoy this! Do you? Well, kid, you listen to me! I have worked long, hard, so I can spend the rest of my days watching that sun go down into that sea. And that's what I aim to do! Besides, you don't want me. You don't even need me. You think you do. Because I am Muni. But you want to know the truth? If you get an old man to play an old man you're not getting much. Get a young man, with plenty of vitality, and let him put all that into playing an old man then you'll have something! Besides, I'm too old to learn lines. And I'm hard of hearing. Did you know that? That thing I do, about keeping my head cocked so, while listening? What the fancy-shmancy critics say is such magnificent involvement in the scene, such artful listening to the other actors, you know what that really is? I *am* listening. Because if I don't look at them, as well as listen with every ounce of me, I won't know what the hell they are saying, and I'll miss my cue.'

"'You don't want an old dog like me. Old dogs can't learn new tricks. And old actors, surely not. I couldn't do a long scene. And I no longer have the patience for little bits and pieces like in pictures. I am missing one eye. My hearing is gone. And this'—he pointed to his heart—'and this is already not so perfect. Twice. So what do you want with me?' And he looked straight at me.

"The one thing I was not going to say was that presumptuous phony opening line I had prepared. So I said what seemed a stupid thing to me even as I said it, 'Did you at least read the script?'

"He stared at me impatiently and said, 'If I didn't read it would I feel so miserable? Idiot!! What kind of *shmuck* are you? For a director you have no *sechel* at all. You understand *mama-lushen*?'

62

Yes, yes, I told him, I understood Yiddish. I even spoke it. He challenged me. I spoke a few words to him. For the first time he smiled, 'You're not such a dope after all. Now, sonny, listen to me. Muni, the actor, would love to do this role. I like the script. I like the part. And television I have never tried, so it is a challenge. But Muni the man, the patient, is under strict orders not to do anything. If I didn't love this script, I would say my doctor forbids it. But because I love it, I don't know what to say.'

"He was quiet for a long time. Did he expect me to ask, beg, plead, argue, insist? I had no clue. So I just sat there. The sun had gone. It was getting dark. And, being California, damp, too.

"Suddenly he said, 'Lines. I can't remember lines any more ...'

"'We can feed you lines, through a headset. We can make your character hard of hearing in the script. And you'll wear a hearing aid, so we can prompt you that way.'

"'And move, who can move any more?' he asked.

"'With four cameras that move and intercut, I'll give it the movement,' I said, and I chose one of the key scenes and improvised how I would use the cameras, how little physical movement he'd be called on to do.

"It went that way, for about half an hour, despite the dampness that made him cough a bit, despite three calls to dinner that went unheeded. Without ever saying he wanted to do it, he was asking me, begging me to insist that he do it. Finally he said, 'I can't resist you. You talked me into it!'

"We walked up toward the house, through the garden. It was the first I noticed that he depended on a cane. I caught a glimpse of his wife standing with her face pressed against the glass of the dark sun porch. She had been watching all the time, her eyes sad, accusing. But she was silent. Even when we entered the sun porch, she said nothing till he announced, 'This kid is going to have dinner with us. And he's from Brooklyn, I have discovered, so I hope the fare is elegant enough for him. After all, once you have lived in Brooklyn you are used to the best.' He was joking, hoping to avoid her eyes, her accusations, her questions. But her expression had not changed. She watched him as he made his way toward the dining room, tossing behind him another attempt at lightness, another evasion.

"'You should hear this kid talk. To hear him tell it, he is a cockeyed genius with a camera. Tell him about some of the geniuses we have known! And not a talent in the bunch.'

"He was gone. When I started to follow after him she spoke for the first time.

"'Okay, so you did it. But don't you think you're so smart. He was going to say yes if you never got here. He wants to go, wants to do a part on television. He thinks that if he works in a new medium it'll give him new life, new youth. But you didn't do him any favor. He's too old. If you can think of some way to back out, please! Do it! Please!'"

"No young man, no young director with a chance to direct Paul Muni is going to back out. Ever! We went through dinner, his wife saying nothing, Muni doing all the talking. About his past, some of the great roles, some of the terrible ones. About his theories on acting, about his 'secret.' For years in the theater everyone talked about the 'secret' of Muni's great acting. He would say only, 'My secret is that I'm a little more careful than the next actor, that's all. Because I am more afraid than he is. So I come better prepared. And that's the whole secret.'

"I didn't get away from there till almost midnight, after turning down his four insistent invitations to spend the night. But when I did leave, Muni was no longer an old man. He was excited, alive again, vibrant. He wasn't leaning on his cane, he was using it. For magnificent dramatic gestures. Now, once more, he had a reason to get up the next morning.

"Of course, the rehearsals weren't easy. And she was always there. Taking care of him, seeing he was warm enough, or cool enough. That he had hot soup and warm tea at the breaks. That he lay down and rested at every opportunity. She kept staring at me, accusing me. I carried on, in spite of her, or maybe because of her. Twice, yes twice, during rehearsals he broke down and wanted to quit.

"Once he went dry in his lines, so even the prompts couldn't help him. He walked out of the scene, went back to his dressing room, broke down and cried. I tried to see him. She wouldn't let me. Till he insisted. So that he could plead.

"'Look, kiddo, I tried. You know that. I gave you everything I have. But I don't have enough any more. Now, please, do something for me. Go to them, whoever it is at the network, and tell them I can't do it. I'm too tired, too weak, whatever you have to say. Tell them I'm no good. That I'll louse up your show. That I'll disgrace the network. That I'll be terrible. Tell them anything, only get me out. Get me out? Please?'

"Carr, I was twenty-four years old at the time. I had a quarter of a million dollars of the network's money riding, as well as my reputation, my future. What can a kid do in a spot like that? How could a kid like me give confidence to the great Muni? How could I keep the whole cast, the whole show, from disintegrating right then and there? And worst of all, he was crying. Do you know what that means, to see a great man like Muni cry? Tears? Real honest tears, not because they were called for in a scene, but because inside, he was going to pieces. No kid twenty-four should have to see his idol crumble, ever.

"Whatever the hell it is I have, I dug deep down into it. Guts, *chutzpah*, fear, the desperate need never to lose, whatever made me do it, I turned on the monitor in his dressing room and went out. I assembled my cast. With camera one on me, as though by accident, I held a meeting right there. I explained to the cast and the crew that Mr. Muni was having trouble with this scene because the scene was wrong. That it was up to us to find out what was wrong with it and fix it before we could ask such a great actor to go on with a scene in which he had no faith. So I wanted to explore the scene myself, with their help.

"Then I, a bad young actor, a fairly good kid director, scared to death, not knowing the lines, having to carry the book, walked through that scene. With every other actor giving it everything and me giving it everything, too, except that my everything was pretty bad. When the scene was reaching its climax, I turned and played full into camera three the summation of his courtroom scene. If it was bad acting, it was at least sincere. When I finished I had tears in my eyes, my script book was on the counsel table, I was ad-libbing the words as I went.

"Then it was over. There was a silence in that studio. No one dared to move or talk, because no one knew whether I was very good or very bad. But across that huge studio, from the darkness, came a voice, loud and strong, with no tears in it, 'Did somebody

65

turn off the air-conditioning in here? What is that smell? Hey, kiddo, what are you doing to my part?'

"He was joking, of course. Muni would never hurt anybody's feelings, especially never anybody young. He loved young people. And when he stepped into the pool of light, he was smiling. He came to me, put both arms around me, then presented me to the cast, and said, 'This here kid will singlehanded destroy the whole art of acting if we give him the chance!' Then he turned me toward the control room door and, patting me on the behind as he would a child, he sent me off. 'Sonny, you go in there and watch. And we will do this scene as actors should do this scene. Though there were a few phrases you ad-libbed in the summation that I like. If we could use them . . .'

"After that he was magnificent. It wasn't easy for him. He had to fight age, loss of hearing, loss of memory, fear. But there were no more doubts about going on. And it was worth it. He won an Emmy for that show. So did I. I accepted mine in person. He was too ill, too tired, in Santa Barbara, to come even as far as Los Angeles for his.

"But he called me that night, Carr. He called me to say thanks. To say that in a long career of many many honors that one was the most important, because it was the last one. He knew then he'd never do another show of any kind, but he was glad that I'd made him do that one, that I'd insisted, persevered, that I'd done that desperate, laughable, outrageous thing of stepping into his role to do his big scene. How he laughed about that.

"Then he said softly, 'Kiddo, the day an actor finishes his last role, he is only waiting to die. I saw the sun set this evening, kid. Sitting out there, where we sat, I saw it set. I said to myself, Why can't actors go out the same way, silently, gracefully, beautifully like the sun setting into the sea? Why do we have to get old, lose our faculties, our organs, one by one? Why?'

"Then he said strangely, 'Because you are a young, mean, driving sonofabitch with enough *chutzpah* and courage for a whole cast of actors, you'll be a good director. And that's important. Always remember one thing, kid. Writers dream it. Actors live it. But directors make it happen. You made it happen, kiddo. That's a talent. God bless you!'"

Jock paused to let that register on Preston Carr. Then he said softly, tears filming his baby blues, "That is no small memory to have, that the last thing you ever heard Paul Muni say was, 'God bless you.' But it never would have happened if I hadn't insisted, dared, driven him, cruelly, even brutally, to get what I wanted. And, in the end, what he wanted too.

"When we're done with *Mustang!*, I hope you'll say the same thing to me."

It was the kind of clincher they had taught Jock to use during a short course he took once in insurance salesmanship before he went into the theater full-time. You maneuvered the prospect into a position where if he were going to say anything, he had to say yes.

But Carr didn't say anything. He thought a long while. Then he said thoughtfully, "That thing with the girl, you're sure that'll work."

The Muni story had done it, Jock reassured himself. To Carr, he said, "I give you my word. The way I handle it, the way I cast the girl and direct her, there won't be any adverse audience reaction."

He fully expected that now, finally, Carr would say yes. Instead, Carr said only, "Can't be too careful about a thing like that." With that Carr got up and left the room, with no good night, no commitment, no final answer.

Only when Carr was gone did Jock notice that dawn was creeping across the desert. It came out of the east, at first peering over the mountains, then unrolling slowly across the desert, overflowing everything that was sandy gray and turning it golden pink.

Jock watched, knowing he should respond to the beauty of it. But he was drained. Used. The way Louise had used the word "used." Carr had used him, as he might have used a girl, for a night, for flattery, for his own vanity, for a workout that let him relive his old glory. Then Carr had left him with no answer, nothing.

Whether he got Preston Carr for the picture or not, Jock knew he was going to hate him. Not that there was any evil in Carr. He was only being a star. In fact, for the King of motion pictures, he was extremely nice, considerate, pleasant. It wasn't Carr who was

evil, it was the star system. But Jock was too furious now, too tired
now, to draw distinctions. To him, Preston Carr was all stars. All
actors. All pricks.

It was four hours later. Jock was awake again. He had showered
and shaved in the most elegant bathroom he had ever seen. It was
completely equipped, with four kinds of razors, electric and steel-
blade, and with a twelve-headed shower which was indecently
erotic and had a touch more suggestive than most women he knew.
It was masturbation through the courtesy of gleaming hydra-
headed Standard Sanitary, which left no erogenous zone untouched.

Dressed in his costume, faded levis, worn workshirt, old boots,
but with his bronzed face shiny, his hair glistening damp, Jock
made his way to the main house, and to the dining room. The size
of the room, the overpowering effect of expanses of weathered
gray wood paneling and red native stone, all were magnified by
the contrasting presence of a single person, at the long, long table
set for only three.

She was a girl in her early twenties, possibly as much as twenty-
five, surely no older. She was dark, very pretty, in that particularly
Texas way that tall pretty girls are pretty. For she was fully developed, to judge from the way she enhanced her highly styled
hostess coat. Her smile was quick and warm, her voice soft, made
softer by the southern inflection of her speech, that tendency to
endow most syllables with two values rather than one.

"Good morning. You're Mr. Finley."

Jock smiled, giving her the easy, pleasant, ingratiatingly boyish
grin. "Yes, ma'am," he answered, wondering why he always said
"ma'am" to southern women, even tramps. Guys from Brooklyn,
he thought, are eternally at a disadvantage when talking to anyone
southern, especially girls—it was as if they'd won the Civil War
and were tolerating us.

"Breakfast?" she invited, as would any good hostess and lady
of the house. Before Jock could answer she reached the buzzer
with her foot. Before he could sit down, there was a Mexican
serving man in the doorway. In the Southwest, Mexicans are the

minority which serves, smiles, and seems ever anxious to please.

"Manuel," she said. "See what Mr. Finley will have for breakfast." To Jock, she suggested, "I recommend the *juevos rancheros*. No one makes them better than Dorita. Of course, we have anything else you might want. Not excluding blinis with caviar. If that's the way you're built."

Jock kept staring at her, but he spoke to Manuel, "The eggs'll do."

As he sat down opposite her, she told him, "Pres is taking his workout. Every morning. Like clockwork."

"It shows," Jock said, still looking for a clue to her. "He's in fantastic shape."

"For a man his age?" she finished resentfully. "Well, he's better than men half his age." She smiled, not ashamed, but proud to be able to say it. "You know his big secret?"

She caught Jock with his orange juice halfway to his lips. He paused, waited. "He's exactly what he seems to be. Just as nice, just as friendly, just as strong, just as vital, just as much Preston Carr as he is on the screen. He's not acting. That's him."

Jock drained his glass, thinking, Carr not only picked them young and beautiful, he turned them into a fan club. And that sonofabitch was worried about how the audience would react to him making love to a blond floozy because she was young enough to be his daughter? What did he call this young thing sitting across the table? How would his audience react to this, if they knew?

Jock had no way of knowing whether she was here for the night, the week, the month, or forever. Or what the other people in the house, on the ranch, thought about it. If Manuel was any example, they accepted her, respected her, and anything Preston Carr did was okay with them. Perhaps because he was as nice as the girl had said he was.

The eggs arrived. An omelet, flamboyant and promising, with red and green peppers, diced ham, glistening onion bits. It was huge enough to last a grown man a week in the desert.

Jock was eating, and asking probing questions, when Carr entered.

He was dressed in riding clothes, English-cut breeches, shiny

69

English boots, yellow polo shirt. Again the tanned biceps, the forearms strong, the muscles showing. Even when he merely lifted his glass of orange juice, those muscles responded, rippling.

"We're riding over to MacAllisters this morning," he said to the girl. Intended that way or not, it served to dismiss her. She rose, and Jock noticed that her hostess coat, artfully fitted at the bodice, did credit to her strong young breasts. Man, he said to himself, a lot of good eatin' there.

Once she was gone, Carr asked, "Eggs okay?"

"Fine. Great," Jock said with much obvious gusto, to please his host. To himself, he said, You fucking monkey-on-a-string, don't be so anxious to be nice!

"Kid, I'd like to talk more but I promised Mac we'd ride over and stay for lunch. Got to discuss an oil deal he has in mind."

"I understand," Jock said. "You were nice enough to give me all the time you did. After all, I wasn't expected."

Jock the affable, Jock the pleasant. As long as Preston Carr was even hinting that he might do the picture, affable and pleasant was what Jock Finley was going to be.

Carr turned to him and smiled suddenly. Jock smiled back but he was puzzled and it showed. Then Carr chuckled. "You weren't exactly unexpected. In fact, kid, you were a little overdue."

The last bite of that spicy omelet was still in Jock's throat. He almost choked on it. Which was all that prevented him from asking. But he didn't have to. Carr continued.

"Usually when a studio says to a smart, snotty young director, 'Get Preston Carr and you've got a deal' he's out here the next morning. Sometimes even that same afternoon. One young jerk flew out in a chartered plane, just to impress me. Stupid bastard didn't know I have three planes of my own.

"Tell you what I liked about you. You took a couple of days to think it over. Oh, I knew about that meeting at the studio the same afternoon it happened. My agent, Herman Parks, and Harry Klein, my attorney, between them, have more pipelines than the CIA. When Herman called me that afternoon and said, 'Get ready for another one' I expected you the next morning. When you didn't show up for five days that made you noteworthy.

"You weren't the usual, overanxious, undertalented, greedy,

half-assed young director who was looking to build his reputation on my track record."

Even though most of what Carr said was complimentary, Jock could feel the anger beginning to burn.

"And I know about that trouble over in London. But, hell, that can happen to any director. I've had plenty of directors bounced off pictures and I'm frank to admit I wasn't always right."

Jock knew the color was rising into his cheeks. He could feel the fury turning to a knot in his full stomach. But he listened.

"In a way I admire you for that. Some other young punk would have knuckled under to the star and said, 'Yessirree, sir' just to hold on to that important job and that important credit. But you didn't. Good! In fact I was interested to get a look at you when I heard about that.

"But when you showed up yesterday, pulled up in that red Ferrari, I said to myself, Oh-oh, here it comes. The usual chicken-shit director, with all his talent in an Italian car. You classy young bastards must stay home for days, practicing how to jump into and out of a Ferrari without opening the door."

The only thing that made it tolerable at all was that Carr was smiling now, pleasantly. Jock hated every word the man said but he was impressed by how well he could read character. And by the fact that Carr had a common-sense view of the craziest human activity in the world, the art and business of making motion pictures. In back of Jock's mind there was what the girl had said, that Carr was nice, frank, honest, and always what he seemed to be. Up to this highly uncomfortable minute Jock had no reason to doubt her. But Carr was not finished.

"The Ferrari was bad enough. But your wardrobe! Where the hell did you get that ranch hand's outfit, studio wardrobe? It's as phony as that plastic imitation-rawhide cover on that script! And branding on the title. Christ! Kid, there are ranchers. And there are gentlemen ranchers. Never, you hear me, never come to call on a gentleman rancher looking like that. What did you do, have those levis bleached in a laundromat? You're not a ranch hand. You're a director! Come here dressed like a director! The man who talked about making pictures the way you did last night, that man is no fraud. Why make him look like one?

71

"I bet if I'd asked you to get up on one of my Appaloosas and ride yesterday, you'd have done that too. Even though you don't know the first damn thing about riding. Do you?"

"I've ridden some. Had some lessons," Jock answered, which was truthful. Barely.

"I'm glad you're honest enough to admit you don't know everything there is to know about horses. Because I think what Westerns need, especially in these times in the history of the picture business, is a fresh eye. A kid from the city streets to whom every aspect of a horse, of the desert, of the wild, exciting life in that script, is fresh, new, and different.

"I won't downgrade the story. It's a good Western. Warfield is a good writer. But that's not enough."

Carr turned full on Jock. "Can you do this picture as though it's the only Western you're ever going to make?" Jock nodded, a small, cautious nod. "Good. Because it could be a masterpiece. But only if it's fresh and important for *you*. Then it'll be fresh for the audience. And important for the critics. But give it everything you've got. Do it like you'd make love to a wonderful girl you're only going to spend one single night with."

The way the man talked about pictures, and how to make them, gave him new standing, new respect in Jock's eyes. He wasn't just a star. Or a big star. Or even just the King. He was a picture man, a picture-maker, who loved and respected what he did. That girl had been right. This man was exactly what he appeared to be, as honest and as open.

Even the things he had said that made Jock squirm, that made the studio wardrobe boots tight on his feet, that made his arrival seem so transparently phony, all of that had been said in a feeling of friendship. He was asking Jock to have more dignity, more self-pride, not less. More self-love. Which was important to anyone in a creative field.

"Two things more, kid," Carr was saying, "then I have to go. First, I'd like to do your picture."

Jock hoped he had held still for that with the proper assurance, control, and cool.

"Second, I have to talk to my lawyer, my agent, and my doctor before I can agree to do any picture. My lawyer will probably have the last word. Because if he can figure out a way to handle my one million up front so I can use it in MacAllister's oil deal without giving up too much of a tax bite, that's half the reason to do this picture. Yes, kid, that's the way it is these days. Lawyers make pictures. Or break them."

Carr downed his coffee before he continued. "The doctor bit is a formality. For the last eleven years, before I sign for a picture, he reads the script and checks me out. I didn't work like a dog for years to get all this, only to give it up by dying a minute before my time.

"I want every taste of everything I worked for. I'm with Muni on sunsets and sunrises. But I want more. The best food, the best Scotch, the best brandy, the best horses and planes. And the best women.

"Young, well fleshed. And eager. I like the feel of a firm nipple on a young breast, pressing back against my hand. I like love-making, strong and intense. I like it with young girls who have long, embracing arms and legs. I like to be wanted as much as I want. As far as I'm concerned, there's no better way to end a day or start it. And I mean to have it that way till I die, which I plan to make a long, long way off.

"Laura"—and by his gesture he indicated she was the young girl Jock had found at the table—"Laura is like that. She's everything I want in a girl. And as long as she is, she's here. As long as I'm what she wants, she's here. The day either of us feels it's beginning to wear or wane, it's over. She knows it. I know it. Everybody here knows it. And there's no shame in it. So she's treated with the utmost respect. And treats herself that way too. Which is most important. I don't want to make love to a woman who doesn't respect herself. Because then she doesn't respect what I'm doing, she doesn't respect me.

"The old days, Hollywood, it was smart-alecky to talk about every girl as being a cunt. Not me. I never used that word about any girl. Not any girl I ever had anything to do with. To me, a bed is where two people meet because they love one another, not because they hate each other. And you don't apply nasty, degrading names to any woman you think well enough of to make love to. I've been married and divorced four times. And been unfaithful to every one of them. But never disrespectful. Never nasty. Not even at the end."

He stood up suddenly, held out his hand to Jock, "If my doctor approves, and Harry says I should, I'll probably do your picture, kid. I'll let you know." He started for the door saying, "The MacAllisters are waiting."

But at the door he stopped, turned, and asked, "By the way, those scenes with the mustang, we'll use a stunt man there, won't we?"

"Sure, sure," Jock said quickly.

Jock Finley's red Ferrari was sucking up a cloud of desert dust as it did ninety-four miles an hour, heading west, along the black two-lane highway. He was not aiming to do ninety-four. He was not even aware of it. For he was thinking of the man and what he had said. Of the promise he had given, yet held back.

What it really got down to was the tax angle. Vaguely in the back of his mind, Jock had some knowledge about oil depletion allowances. That made the deal possible. If he had to evaluate his chances right now, yes, he had a deal with Preston Carr.

And what that would mean! It would be wire service news the world over! Preston Carr was coming back! Under the direction of Jock Finley, that brilliant young director! The whole six years that Susie Steiber had cost him would be made up in one leap. The whole bitter aftertaste of London would be wiped out. Among the professionals at least, the blame would shift from him to that English fag star.

Oh, if only Carr would repeat in an interview what he had said about Jock's not knuckling under. About his choosing to walk out. If only . . .

Times in every man's life he knows there is some one thing he's got to have or die. A particular woman. A certain personal possession. A great opportunity. One object which to him, in that moment, signifies the be-all and end-all of his life. To Jock Finley, on that drive back to LA, Preston Carr in *Mustang!* was that one thing!

But what if Carr's lawyer said no? What if his doctor said no?

74

There were still a dozen different ways the deal could fall through. There were even ways that Great Big Casting Director in the Sky could thwart it. And how well Jock knew that.

One of the last plays Jock did on Broadway starred the greatest name it had been possible to have in the theater. And Jock had gone three years without a hit and needed one. It had been four years since his first big hit with Julie West, and he was getting desperate and beginning to doubt himself. But now he had a good script and the best name it was possible to have in the lead. There was even a good built-in advance and the theater parties because of the star's name.

Except that on the fifth day of rehearsal the star never woke up. That's all. Just never woke up. Died in his sleep in a suite on the fourth floor of the Algonquin Hotel.

The production was suddenly done, over, finished. They never replaced the star. They just forgot the whole thing. Leaving the author, the cast, and the brilliant young, twenty-nine-year-old director high and dry without a job. This after Jock had spent five months of his own time working on the script with the writer then casting and preparing.

Since that day, every time casting got too tight or sticky, or any particular star loomed too big, too obstinate, or too expensive, Jock had a nice, neat, personal formula. He would ask himself, Suppose this star died in his sleep tonight, who would I settle for? Then let's go after him and forget this arrogant prick!

No star would ever again be allowed to get that big in Jock Finley's mind! Except . . . except that in this case, the president had said, "Get Preston Carr to do the picture and you got a deal." Not, "someone like Preston Carr," or "there must be another Preston Carr around . . ."

The more he was dependent on anyone, the more Jock hated that person. By the time he got back to the hazy, smoggy edges of LA Jock Finley was ready to hate Preston Carr.

Unless, of course, Carr agreed to do *Mustang!*

When he pulled into his driveway, Jock expected that Louise's car would be there. It wasn't. He let himself into the house. It was empty. The cleaning woman had been there. But no one else. Out back at the pool patio there was no sign that Louise had been by.

He called his service. No message from her. All his messages were from Marty White, who had called twice last night, four times this morning, and three times within the last hour, leaving urgent instructions to call back at once.

Jock made himself a drink first at the pool bar, then settled down on the plastic lounge and dialed the Owl's private number.

There were three rings before the Owl's harried voice said, "Hold! I'll get right back to you!" For seven minutes, Jock could hear the Owl making frantic pleas to someone who was obviously intransigent about something. Finally, the Owl was back talking to him. "Hello? Who?"

"It's me, Marty."

"Jock, laddie! Sorry to make you hold. But I got trouble. Large trouble. You know Pat Knowles? I got her on a big picture in Rome. And she is six months pregnant! You hear me, six months. And not married. And this is a religious picture. So the studio is begging her to get married. And the guy, some wop bit actor, is willing. But *she* don't want to. Not till *after* the baby is born. It's a new kind of status symbol with actresses these days. Nonconformity! They fuck like conformists. It's only about getting married they don't conform.

"I haven't had such trouble with any broad since I had to talk Daisy Donnell into leaving the goddamn Actor's Studio and coming back to make a picture. I had to beg her, 'Please, Daisy-baby, please give up working in a loft and come make a picture with Sir Laurence Olivier!' Some world!

"But screw that! Why didn't you call me last night? Where the hell you been?"

Blandly, with enforced diffidence, Jock said, "I couldn't. I had to stay over at the ranch."

"He asked you to stay over?" Marty asked, but with not quite the degree of interest or excitement Jock had expected.

"We talked right through dinner, then half the night, and then at breakfast."

"Well? Is he going to do it?" Marty asked.

"Might, Marty. Might, was all he would say."

At which point Marty White began to laugh and Jock could envision the little man, his bald red head bobbing up and down in his huge, fan-shaped, black patent leather swivel chair.

"I'm not kidding, Marty! He would not commit."

"Come on, laddie, level with me!" Marty said, gasping from laughter.

"I told you what happened!" Jock was becoming steamed now.

"Laddie, laddie, laddie, don't play games with Uncle Marty. I'm not called the Owl for nothing," Marty chided pleasantly.

"I'm not playing games!"

"The director is always the last to know!" Marty laughed. "Laddie, listen to me. Listen real good. Less than an hour ago, New York got a call from Herman Parks. Carr asked him to 'investigate' the deal. Which means Carr will do the picture! If the terms are right! You heard me, laddie?"

"Yeah, Marty, I heard. I heard," Jock said, trying to control his surge of elation.

It was his diffidence which caused Marty to say, "Laddie, a Preston Carr picture! Do you know what that means? I can make this the basis of a three-picture deal. You know what we ought to do, form a company! You'll need it, laddie, as a tax shelter. Drop by in the morning. I'll have my accountant here and we'll discuss it. I have the same arrangement with a few of my people. We form a company, both of us become officers, which gives us all more latitude. I can act for you when you're away or tied up in shooting. I'll explain it all to you. A Preston Carr picture!" he ended up, the wonder of it pleasing him immensely.

"How long will it take?" Jock asked.

"To form a company? Week or two. Why?"

"I meant to know for sure about Carr."

"Oh. A few days. If Herman calls, they want to make the deal. If the studio called, it would have been tougher, taken longer. Carr needs cash, is the way I figure it."

"Yeah," Jock said, knowing that what happened at MacAllisters at lunch time was the determining factor. Not *Mustang!* Not Jock Finley. But what the hell, if it was a deal, that's all that counted. He was taking a gulp of his drink when he heard Marty.

"Laddie, there's only one trouble I can see."

"Yeah, Marty?" Jock asked, always alert to Marty's postscripts.

"He might ask for artistic control," Marty said, worried.

"Screw him! Artistic control is with the director on any picture I make! I walked out on that picture in London. And I'll walk out of this one, if there's any question about it!!"

"Laddie ... laddie ..." Marty tried to placate him. "I didn't say he *would* ask for it. I only said he might. We have to be prepared, that's all."

"You better be prepared for what *I* want!" Jock said.

"Laddie, I work for you. I protect your interests. I am only warning you of what may lie ahead. And I'll handle it. Laddie, don't worry about a thing," Marty seemed almost nervous, even tremulous as he said good-bye.

It amused Jock. He was smiling as he hung up the phone, his baby blues twinkling. So it was a deal. The King had said yes. Or as close to yes as it could be at the moment. He was still smiling as he slipped off the shabby, scuffed cowboy boots, which he despised. Then he peeled off the worn workshirt. He tore off the faded, shrunk levis which Carr had ridiculed.

Suddenly he rolled the levis into a ball, hurled them across the pool as far as he could. Then he followed with the shirt. And finally the boots, one at a time. They hit the ivied wall and dropped into the hedge, out of sight.

He stood there, in just his jockey shorts, a lean, strong, tan young man, with the world by the tail. Courtesy of Preston Carr, of course.

He could feel himself rising tight and big in the restraining crotch of his shorts. He ripped them off, dove into the pool. Right now, Jock Finley had the feeling that he could screw the whole world, literally. It was one of those moments of triumph when he could go right out into the street, find the first pretty girl, and rape her. Triumph to him was a strong, aggressive feeling. It was what love meant to him.

He rose up out of the water buoyantly, turned on his back and floated there, his erection rising up proudly out of the water. Oh, those warm-water California pools!

A Preston Carr picture! A Preston Carr picture! He was mimicking the Owl, aloud. That was when it struck him. And also

78

when the elation suddenly went out of him, when the pride and the firmness deserted him. And he was as limp as after an orgasm.

In everything the Owl had said, not a word about Jock Finley. No Jock Finley picture. A Preston Carr picture! And p.s., small p.s., there was a young kid director on the picture called Jock Finley. Or was it Laddie Finley?

Preston Carr could be a mixed blessing. Okay, so it assured the seven-million-dollar budget. But now Jock would have to fight for his own identity. And that little worm about "artistic control" that Marty had "just happened" to bring up. When you put that together with "don't worry about a thing," there was plenty to worry about.

Well, okay, Mr. Preston Carr, Mr. King, I am going to be a nice, agreeable, gentle kid, till the deal is firm. But the minute it is signed, watch out! On any picture, a Preston Carr picture or not, I am boss! And don't you forget it!

And now Jock realized that his erection had returned, harder, almost painful now. Triumph and hostility came to the same thing with Jock Finley.

The feeling made him suddenly lonely. It would be good to have Lulu here now. To share his triumph and his enormous sexual surge. He climbed out of the pool. Still wet, he seized the phone, dialed. There was no answer at first. Then the answering service picked up. She was not there. They had no word as to when she would be. They would take a message. Jock left his name, and "Call at once, important. Please?"

But Louise did not call. So after it was dark, and he was hungry and alone, he decided to hop into the Ferrari, drive down to La Scala, and eat. He was on his way to the door when the phone rang. Lulu!

He lifted the phone after the fourth ring, and trying to sound as casual and uninvolved as he could, he said, "Hello?"

But it was not Louise. "Laddie, I knew it! Everything's okay! Except one thing. The bastard did come up with artistic control."

"What did *you* say?" Jock asked, anger beginning to curl the edges of his voice.

"I said absolutely not!" Marty responded. "And that's when the deal fell apart."

79

"Sorry!" Jock said crisply. "But for a director to surrender artistic control is like having his balls cut off!"

"I know, laddie, I know. I'm not saying you should have agreed. It's just everything's blown."

"I told you he only said 'might.' You're the one said it was a deal!" Jock could hear himself shouting now.

"Laddie, laddie, take it easy. Because I am revolving a compromise around in my mind."

"Such as?" Jock asked suspiciously.

"Well, *for example*, what if you were to say you have the utmost respect for Preston Carr. For all his years in picture-making. For his ability. His talent. And you would not want to demean him. But still, it is highly risky to give any star artistic control over any picture. (And I can add about fifty examples of pictures where stars were also producers and which were disasters.) But you don't say that. You say, it is a risk to let a star make decisions, even such a star as Preston Carr. At the same time, you don't want to ram anything down his throat. You want to have a perfect working relationship with him. So you are ready to compromise . . ."

"Marty, there can't be any compromise on artistic control!" Jock interrupted.

"Laddie, hear me out! The compromise is, artistic control will reside in the hands of an executive producer."

"Executive producer?" Jock asked suspiciously.

"It's only a way of getting and keeping control for you without turning it into a make-or-break issue with Carr."

"How do we have an executive producer with control, and still keep control?" Jock asked gingerly.

"You just said it, laddie. The whole key is in the words, '*how do we.*' *We*. That's it. If I offer to be the executive producer we have control. You have control. And Preston Carr does not start off hating you and the picture and everything else."

There was a long pause from Jock. Marty felt a great urgency to fill the gap. Suddenly he said, "Jesus! *Shmuck* that I am, I forgot to tell you the whole deal. In exchange for backing down on the demand for artistic control, you want to be producer *and* director. And that's important, laddie, very important."

Marty gave that time to sink in.

80

"So what do you say, laddie? Would that be an acceptable compromise? Producer-director for you. Executive producer for me. That way we keep artistic control right in the company."

"Would . . . would Carr go for it?"

"Herman thinks he might," Marty said crisply, meaning it had all been talked over and the agents felt they could force their clients into it, and would, since the commissions could run into the hundreds of thousands.

Jock's first instinct was to say, "I'll think about it," as Preston Carr had said to him. But finally Jock said, "Okay. If you can work it out."

"I think I can," Marty said, making it seem still only a possibility.

Jock hung up, started out of the house, to where his red Ferrari stood. He moved to it, was about to leap into it, when he stopped self-consciously, opened the door, and eased himself in. He started up the motor with a roar and pulled out of the driveway, venting his hostility against Preston Carr on all of Rexford Drive.

Before Jock Finley reached La Scala, Marty White was on the phone with the president in New York.

"Bob, I spoke with Herman. I spoke with my boy. It's a deal."

"Terrific, Marty, terrific! I'll break it at the stockholders meeting on Thursday!"

"There's just one thing." There was a sudden silence on the New York end. For the president knew Coast agents like Marty White well enough to know that that phrase could include, would include, some outrageous demand.

"One thing?" the president asked cautiously. "What?"

"The kid and Carr have established such a beautiful relationship in such a short time, they are afraid the intrusion of another person, say a producer appointed by the studio, would create problems. So if you tell me right now that Finley is producer-director, you got the package."

The president was silent for a moment. "You'll be executive producer? You can control that kid?"

"I gave you my word, didn't I, Bob?"

81

"Yes. Yes, you did."

"All right then. Now, what do you say?"

"Okay!"

When Marty hung up, he glanced down at the doodle pad beside his private phone where he had absentmindedly printed, "Marty White, Executive producer . . . Martin White, Executive Producer . . . A Martin White Production, starring Preston Carr!"

CHAPTER

3

THE main thing now is to find the right girl! To protect the picture!"

The word was from New York. Passed on to Marty White, executive producer, by the studio head. And from Marty White to Jock Finley, producer-director.

Find the right girl! Protect the picture!, became a crusade.

The same president who had said he would risk the millions involved only if Jock could get Preston Carr was now turning timid in the face of stockholders' expectations and demands. The greater the promise, the more they would expect in the next stockholders' report, and at the next annual meeting. And stockholders have all the compassion of the French rabble at the guillotine. So the frantic word was out, protect the picture! Find the right girl!

That gave Jock only eight weeks, ten at the most. For the location shooting on *Mustang!* would have to be done soon, while the weather was most dependable in the Nevada desert. Thus, time had suddenly become extremely important.

Find the right girl!

The right girl was that girl whose name would add critical prestige to the picture, but whom the public would pay to see for attributes of a quite different nature. The right girl was a girl with obvious, even over-obvious sex appeal, measured in films by the

83

bounty of her bosom, the depth of her cleavage, the provocative curve of her behind. Sometimes these elements could be enhanced. They could never be completely faked. So the right girl must actually have them.

The right girl was also that girl who, in combination with Preston Carr, would have that mysterious thing Hollywood termed "the right chemistry."

The right chemistry meant those two stars from whose sexual encounter the voyeuristic sublimating public would anticipate and receive the utmost in vicarious sexual satisfaction. This was of crucial importance.

There was yet another demand in *Mustang!* Since it was only a cowboy picture, but of greater than usual pretensions, it would help if the right girl were also an actress whom the critics held in awe. So, if in addition to all else she possessed that mystique which defied arty critics to hate her, she was *the* right girl for *Mustang!*

For a time, the vice-president in charge of overseas distribution, an important power in these days of large foreign grosses, had been holding out for Sophia Loren. With Loren and Carr, he felt sure, they could clean up in Europe. But it was explained to him that the whole concept of the story would have to be changed, since the girl in the picture was an indigenously American character in a purely American locale.

He was quick to see the logic of it. So he suggested that they dub in another voice for Loren in the American prints. It took a flying trip to New York for Jock Finley to convince him that American audiences were accustomed to Loren's Italian accent, would expect it, and would resent her voice being dubbed. Besides she was too mature and knowing for the role, which demanded innocence. A dirty, used shabby kind of innocence.

The vice-president ended up nodding and agreeing to everything Jock said. However, once Jock was gone, he called the the president and said, "Okay, don't use Loren! But watch out for that kid. He's crazy! I know, I know, he's one of the new wave. But, Bob, you tell me, what the hell is 'dirty, used, shabby innocence'?"

But the president said, "Write that down! There may be an ad campaign for the picture in that."

The search for the right girl went on. Only stars of the first magnitude were discussed. And discarded. Featured girls and unknowns were not even mentioned. She had to be a top star. She had to protect the picture. She had to be an American girl. "With tits." As though very few women had them. But in Hollywood "with tits" meant thirty-six inches or better. Preferably better.

In his search for the right girl, Jock spent hours alone in dark, smoke-smelly projection rooms, watching films and clips of films which encompassed a whole range of female stars, each one—her agent swore—"the right girl to play opposite Preston Carr."

Finally, there was really no right girl. Or so it seemed. At least there was no right girl whose time schedule made her available for *Mustang!*

This was the conclusion they arrived at during one long discouraging afternoon in the office of the head of the studio. Jock, Marty, the studio head, and the casting director all knew it suddenly, when Jock turned to the casting director and asked, "Is there an unknown girl? Some girl we can *make* into a star? On Broadway, we find that sometimes that's even better. The public loves to discover new stars."

As the casting director was opening his huge folder of hopefuls, Marty White was forced to speak up.

"Wait! Let's not get desperate. I gave Bob my word we'd protect the picture. I am not taking any unknowns."

"What about Dustin Hoffman and Katherine Ross in *The Graduate*?" Jock asked crisply, almost angrily. "They were unknowns!"

"Laddie, laddie, don't fly off the handle. If I didn't have an idea, I wouldn't be sitting here saying no to unknowns."

"You mean you have someone?" Jock asked.

The studio head joined in, "For Christ sake, Marty, we are fighting shooting schedules and weather! And you're holding back?"

"If I said this a month ago, you'd all have jumped on me, said I am trying to push my own client. So I didn't want to say a word.

But if we're down to talking about unknowns, then I'm forced to."

"All right, then," the studio head demanded, pleaded. "Say it!"

Simply, softly, without emphasis or shadings, Marty White said, "Daisy Donnell."

There were long seconds of silence in the office. For the idea was both so brilliant and so terrible that neither Jock Finley nor the studio head dared react. The casting director said, "She's certainly the type." But since his opinion was of least consequence in the room no one acknowledged it.

The studio head spoke finally, "In terms of box office, there isn't any better protection than Daisy Donnell. But, oy, the headaches with that cunt! The wasted time! On top of her salary, which has got to be seven five plus a percentage . . ."

"One million!" Marty corrected at once, if there were to be a deal here. When the studio head looked at him sharply, Marty explained: "Daisy Donnell never takes second money or second billing to anyone!"

"All right! Suppose somebody was stupid enough to pay her a million dollars up front, it costs another million or more to shoot her because of the delays."

"You know what they say," the casting director supplied, seeking to support his boss. "If you have Daisy Donnell in your picture, don't hire a director. Hire a psychiatrist!"

Jock said nothing. For he was thinking. Marty's suggestion was completely logical and completely impossible, all at the same time. She was the type. Physically. And in every other way but one.

You did not cast Daisy Donnell in a part which demanded depth, perception, and that true and genuine flame which so few picture stars have. It is called, simply, a talent for acting.

Whether Marty sensed that Jock was not ready to speak up, or whether it was his own purely selfish motives which dictated it, the little man rose from his chair. With the same gravity Winston Churchill used when he addressed Commons during the war, Marty began, "You are going to tell me she is a strange girl. A weird girl. Who knows it better than the man who has represented her for eight years now? Who better than the man who has seen her through three marriages, three divorces? Through hysteria and suicide attempts? Through six, yes, six psychoanalysts? So, please, nobody in this room tell me what a strange girl she is. I could teach courses on that in any college. *But . . .*

"*But!*"—and here Marty turned from the casting director and the studio head toward Jock Finley—"Talk about 'innocence, used, shabby, dirty innocence,' who has it better? Ask yourselves, who has that quality more than Daisy Donnell?"

He had scored a point, for Jock knew that his own description of the character fit her precisely. But there was risk, terrible risk that she would break down in the course of shooting. And that was no way to protect a picture.

Or protect a director, Jock was thinking.

"Gentlemen, if gold was easy to find, easy to mine, it would be like manure in the streets. That girl has gold in her! But someone will have to mine it! Now, I have not said a word to her about *Mustang!* I don't even know if she wants to do a picture. Any picture. I am only saying this is the right girl. *If* we can get her."

The studio head looked at Jock, then offered, "I'll call New York. I'll check it out.

"Meantime," the studio head said, "think about it." This last he directed at Jock, who had to approve the casting before any decision could be made.

They were leaving the administration building, crossing to the parking lot, when Jock finally asked, "Marty, you're sure you're not doing it for the commission?"

Marty turned to him, not angry, but almost pathetic. "You mean why did I play it so cozy? Why didn't I mention her before?"

"Exactly."

"Laddie, you want to know the real truth? I didn't mention her before, because I haven't talked to her. And I haven't talked to her because I have been calling her half a dozen times a day for the last ten days. She does not answer. She does not call back, even though she picks up her messages. I don't know if I can get her for this picture. But for the sake of the picture we have to try. *You* have to try."

Jock looked down into the owl's round, upturned face. The little man stared back.

"Laddie, I am telling you the truth. If you want her, you'll have to get her. *If* you get her, *if* you handle her right, she'll be worth her weight in gold. But God knows, after what she's been through, if *anybody* can handle her right."

Jock was walking along the studio street, toward the art department to examine the watercolor sketches of the sets which the designer had prepared for his scrutiny. What, he wondered, did Marty know? Or was it just happenstance that had made him add that last bit, "But God knows, after what she's been through, if *anybody* can handle her right."

It was a warning. And a challenge. Precisely the kind of challenge Jock Finley loved. His first big step toward fame had come from taking a psychotic alcoholic actress and making her give the performance of her life in a Broadway play that would otherwise have been of small consequence. He had been warned against her, too: that she would be fine for a few days, but when her lines kept eluding her she would take to drinking and that would be the end of her. And it had happened in just that way. Except that Jock had moved in with her. Worked with her, prompted her on her lines, made sure she ate regularly. Even had an affair with her, though she was at least twenty years older than he was. But it had been worth it. For on that one night when it mattered, she had been great. It was she who had earned for Jock his reputation as that brilliant young director who could accomplish the impossible in the theater.

Daisy Donnell was the impossible. She was weird. She was strange. It was her strangeness that made her the pathetic gamin whom every man in the world wanted to protect. And lay. She was the ideal symbol for Hollywood films. Men could feel noble while having daydreams of screwing her and their wives didn't even mind. Half of Daisy's appeal was in that strange, helpless, pathetic quality. The other half was right where it should have been, in her breasts and in her behind.

She had been just another blond girl, looking to make it in Hollywood, till she had become the mistress of an assistant casting director at one of the major studios. He had finally been able to maneuver her into a small, undemanding part in what turned out to be a surprisingly "important" picture. That simply meant it had received more acclaim and had earned a larger gross than anyone expected.

In that picture, Daisy had been "discovered." The unusual, special quality which was hers and hers alone, which glowed more luminously before a camera than in real life, suddenly had come to the attention of the entire world.

At the first viewing of the rough cut by a company president, a producer, and a director, the president had stared in wonder and said, "Jesus! That's some girl! She deserves bigger parts!"

The director had wisecracked, "Her parts are big enough. What she needs are bigger roles."

"Yeah," the president said, grinning, "I'll have her in and have a talk with her. Who's her agent?"

"Marty White," the producer answered.

"Oy," the President groaned, envisioning all kinds of trouble.

Marty White knew when he had a good thing going. He knew Daisy was a precious commodity. He wanted her treated that way. Meticulous attention must be paid to her makeup, her hairdo, her costumes. But most important of all, no role was allowed to exceed her limited talent. Each role must capitalize on her gamin-like sexuality. With Daisy Donnell, one did not strive for Academy Awards, but for solid box office successes.

As usual, Marty had been perceptive and right. With the critics, worldwide, Daisy was a huge joke. A pleasant joke, an indulgent joke, but still a joke. No critic granted her any talent except sexuality. The phrase "sex symbol" began to haunt her from review to review. It distressed her. But to the studio and to Marty it was money in the bank. So every aspect of her every film had been worked on carefully to make the most of her status as the world's prime symbol of sex.

Special bras had been sewn into her dresses, as many as four different bras in the same dress, depending on how much breast was to be shown in the camera angle to be employed for the particular take. A clever homosexual designer had worked out a special Daisy Donnell tuck which was sewn into the back of every skirt, just below her delightful behind, making that curve more pronounced and sexy.

Footage of Daisy walking up a flight of stairs was run and rerun time and again in the projection room for slobbering executives and important visitors from the East. Jokes went around, of which the most truthful was, "Daisy Donnell is pound for pound the most valuable piece of meat in the world."

She had heard it said. More than once. She had resented it. But there was also reassurance in it. To be valuable was to be needed. Daisy was a girl who needed to be needed. Then. And now.

After the first flush of success, it had begun to worry her. Then it began to frighten her. The more inventive the things that were done for her by designers, and the more cinematographers had to favor her with gauzes, silks, diffusion lenses, filters, and special angles, the more the fact of eventual age began to impress itself on her. And to terrify her.

Her lateness on the set had originated with that. Her absences, unexplained, extending over days, were due to it. Most of the time she was late arriving. Or she slipped away early, to consult a psychoanalyst. When the first doctor had failed to still her fears, she tried another and another and yet another. Two of them had tried to lay her in the office. On the couch. The third had strongly hinted at it, veiling his approach with disturbing questions about whether she was unsure of her femininity and had a great need to prove it. Instead of trying to prove it, Daisy found another analyst.

This last one was in his late sixties and gave the impression that he was constantly in deep thought. He was not devoid of lecherous yearnings for Daisy, but age had made him less ardent and so more able to resist making an outright attempt at sex with her. That had given Daisy more confidence in him and made the transference possible. Actually, his particular form of sexual gratification would have required more effort, initiative, and ingenuity on her part than he could reasonably have expected. So he had contented himself with treating her merely as a patient.

The most important incident in her analysis occurred during one late Friday afternoon hour. The aged doctor was using his yellow pad not to make notes about the patient but rather about items to take down to his Palm Springs house. In the midst of making a note about the delicacies he was to pick up at Nate and Al's, he had paused suddenly, aware that there had been a long lull in the session. To keep her occupied while he finished his delicatessen shopping list, the doctor suggested that Daisy would never be at ease with her real enemy, her unconscious, unless and until, once and for all, she had tested herself against her inner insecurity which kept protesting that she was not really an actress at all.

Perhaps, he suggested, interrupting his note-making about a dozen kosher special frankfurters, perhaps in her next picture Daisy should not play the same clichéd sex symbol of a voluptuous girl, but should reach out instead for a role of depth and stature, perhaps a classic heroine or a historical one. Such a role would present her to the critics on a serious level at last and enable her to test herself as an actress rather than as the familiar caricature.

There was no harm, certainly no risk, in making such a suggestion. Any analyst whose patients were all in the motion picture industry knew very well that no studio was going to risk five million dollars on a serious picture starring Daisy Donnell. Nor was any studio head going to risk destroying her value through a serious effort which could end only in critical catastrophe.

So, he knew, there was no danger in tossing out the suggestion. Besides, it would give Daisy something to ponder until Monday's hour. It might even eliminate, for that weekend at least, those frantic phone calls from her while he was relaxing down at the Springs.

The good doctor had just finished making his shopping list. It struck him that Daisy had been quiet a long time.

"Vell, Miss Donnell, ve are very quiet today."

In addition to his age and his trim, white, pseudo-Freudian beard, a great source of comfort and confidence to Daisy and his other patients was his sometimes Viennese, sometimes middle-European Yiddish accent.

But by then the hour was over. So the doctor had no way of knowing the time bomb he had implanted in Daisy's terrified imagination with his idle suggestion.

A conscientious worker, Daisy had completed shooting her picture before she took any action. But on the very day that her last sequence was over, she had slipped quietly out of Hollywood.

91

"Disappeared" was the word the press, radio, and television had used. When she surfaced, it was in New York, at "the home of real acting."

"The home of real acting" was a euphemism that had been created by a handful of self-annointed "in" critics serving *The New York Times*, *The Nation*, *Time* magazine, *Newsweek*, *The Saturday Review*, and several avant-garde publications, all of whom had enshrined a certain school of Russian acting as the only "real American" acting.

Grace, charm, color, brilliance, versatility, design, even costume had fled the New York theater before the onslaught of that critical pogrom. Drabness and dirt took over. Sweat had become a sign of talent. Or a substitute for it. So pervasive and all-powerful had this cult become that those actors and actresses who did possess charm, grace, and the ability to articulate speech were scourged from the American theater and expelled like Jews with packs on their backs to become the homeless, wandering refugees of the theater. For a generation thereafter, America's finest actors would have to be imported from England.

Of all of this, Daisy Donnell knew only what all other critic-indoctrinated Americans had known, that the holy city of real acting was New York. And that in the holy city there existed one true shrine. Whoever would pursue the true religion of the theater must go there to worship and take holy orders in a sacred temple called the Studio.

Had Daisy been capable of conceiving such a deliberate publicity stunt it couldn't have worked better. World attention, which had first focused on her disappearance, was doubly aroused by her sudden reappearance in New York. When, finally, in her timid way Daisy had dared to appear at the temple of real acting, it was front-page news, with photographs, worldwide.

And whatever its fame had been before, the Studio became world-famous from that day forward.

In her first days, Daisy came quietly, to "observe," deeming it a great privilege to be allowed to "listen" as the high priest of "real" acting analyzed and diagnosed the attempts of actors to improvise scenes, during which they were acting out their own neuroses.

The patois of the high priest was special, unique, a confused and confusing jargon of psychoanalytic misinformation and acting technique. However, the terminology possessed a mystique the very obscurity and obfuscation of which endowed it with the same power that Latin ritual holds for Catholics or Hebrew incantations hold for Jews who do not understand their holy language either.

Daisy had been confused at first, numbed, frightened, a traveler lost in a strange land confronted by a strange language. But she had persevered, listening and pretending to absorb it all, while wearing that same expression of intensity she previously had adopted in her serious close-ups. Occasionally she was observed to make a note or two in a small black pad with a genuine crocodile leather cover, using a solid gold pencil.

But in the main, newspapermen and critics continued to treat her presence in New York and at the Studio as a stunt, or even worse, a bad joke.

The joke would have worn thin had not the high priest, for reasons of his own, tempted and coaxed Daisy into preparing and presenting a scene at the Studio. After days and nights of preparation and rehearsal with a young crude actor, after one whole week of nausea and vomiting during which she had lost eight pounds, Daisy Donnell was finally ready to do her scene at the Studio.

Every one of the seats on the unpainted wooden benches of the arena had been occupied that day. For a full forty minutes it had seemed there would be no audition after all. Finally, after considerable coaxing and reassurance, Daisy had said she was ready. Pale, thin, thinner than usual, her face ascetically white against the severe black of her sweater and slacks, Daisy entered.

Before her first line it appeared she might collapse, not once but twice. Yet her very fear and tension gave great impact to the moment. Once she began, she moved forward into the scene in fitful eruptions of dialogue, followed by long, unnerving silences. The young man playing opposite her, confronted by this performance, so vastly different than any rehearsal with her had been, remained constantly tense, attempting to anticipate her next word, his next cue, their next moment.

Her very terror invested the scene with electric uncertainty.

Her uncertainty evoked pity, even from those aspiring young actresses who had come resenting her, hating her, envying her because she had an opportunity with which they could have accomplished so much more. When she was through, each young aspiring actress and actor in that huge arena had the satisfaction of knowing that she or he was better, far far better, than the great Hollywood star. That satisfaction alone had been enough to insure a wave of sustained applause.

Daisy, excited, applause sounding in her ears, cramps gripping at her empty stomach like her worst menstrual pains, fled the arena. It took almost half an hour to coax her out of the ladies toilet to hear the high priest's evaluation of her interpretation.

He put her at ease with his first word, "Fascinating!" Then he continued: "In fact, never in my years in the theater have I seen such tension, such an interpretation of sheer terror in a performance. Did you notice the uneven rhythm of the scene? As though the words were erupting, impromptu, unrehearsed, a cry from a tormented soul rather than dialogue written with cold, precise intent by O'Neill. In a way the interpretation matches the very torment and self-reproach which O'Neill himself felt in his writing.

"I think I have just witnessed an honest emotion, not merely a performance. Realism. In the finest sense of the word. Truth. Yes, truth. We have just witnessed it. Literally felt it. Experienced it. Lived it. This has truly been one of the most remarkable performances I have ever seen." Then he took her hand and kissed her pale, thin cheek.

Thus it happened that weakness became strength, fear became emotion, hesitation became pace, and sheer terror became truth.

That afternoon and evening the word had spread along Forty-fourth Street and Forty-fifth Street and Shubert Alley, through Sardi's and Downey's. The high priest had spoken. And behold he found her very good.

Though Daisy would never be so rash as to appear in a play in public, from that day on, critics had begun to see new springs of talent in Daisy. From a sex joke, she had turned into a "fine actress" with "hidden reservoirs of talent" which Hollywood "in its crude, crass way had been too long hiding, abusing, perverting."

94

When her next picture appeared, the same critics to whom she had been a sex-symbol for so long suddenly discovered deep wells of enormous talent in her. Her body, which had been the subject of dirty jokes before, now reflected significant meanings and nuances. Her use of it was credited with subtleties that transcended performances by Lynn Fontanne. Monosyllabic speeches now achieved the power of poetry on her pouting lips.

With the approval of the high priest of real acting, Daisy Donnell had risen finally, and for all time, above that long, endless line of sexy Hollywood stars who are doomed to dumb-blonde roles from the first moment some picture company places an alliterative name on them.

Daisy Donnell had become an actress, a star of stature, admired, respected.

Daisy Donnell had finally become strongly enough entrenched to weather any professional storm. Except one.

The storm that raged within her own terrified mind. No matter what the film critics had said of her, despite their reassuring evaluation of her "realism" and her "truth"—two words which they had begun to use promiscuously about her in their reviews, she had never been able to accept herself as real.

The warmer, the more favorable the critical reaction, the worse her fears had become. As her legend grew greater, her own estimate of her abilities grew punier by comparison. She grew more frightened rather than less. Panic had become a constant state of mind with her.

She signed for fewer and fewer pictures. And never even started most of them. She withdrew from almost all social life. She made few phone calls and took none. Sporadically, she picked up her messages from the service but hardly ever acknowledged them, especially those which hinted at new films.

Fear of being unable to match her own new image had forced her, finally, to retire. Her retirement was neither announced nor proclaimed. It had simply become a fact.

She had become a frightened recluse in a city where she could have been queen.

As her agent, Marty White had grown accustomed to it. Occasionally, when a director or a studio pressed him very hard, he would send Daisy a script. But the result had always been the same. She kept it for a week, then sent it back with a brief, small, little-girl scrawl, "Thanks, Marty, but I don't think so."

Actually, the script was almost always unread. Marty could tell from the smooth, absolutely unwrinkled cover.

When the inspiration for her to do *Mustang!* had first come to Marty White, he pursued her by telephone but with no results. Several times he had gone to her apartment, had rung and rung but got no answer. Though he was sure she was there. After ten days, he had given up.

He knew that she had a habit of getting into her Ford convertible, tying a scarf around her head, driving north or south along the Pacific coast. She would stop at gas stations, lunch counters, the places where ordinary people stopped, to see what effect she had on people—meaning men—without the artificial aids of designers and their special supports, or cinematographers and their kindly filters and lenses, without five-thousand-dollar-a-week writers to write monosyllables for her.

Many times she was not even recognized, which led to long bouts with sleeping pills followed by hour upon hour with the white-bearded Viennese psychoanalyst, who was actually from Cracow.

Those times when she was recognized put different pressures on her. For she always felt that she disappointed them, which meant more panic, more pills.

What Marty White admitted so freely was true. Daisy Donnell was trouble. But she was more trouble to herself than to anyone else.

Jock was moving about the designer's office. Its walls were continuous easels for the designer's sketches, which Jock found brilliant. His excitement grew with each watercolor, for the designer had caught the color and the texture of *Mustang!* as Jock had envisioned it. But now Jock was interrupted by a phone call. The studio head had been searching for him all over the lot.

96

"Jock? Kid? I just talked to New York. Bob says if we can get Daisy, she's our girl! Even at Marty's price!"

The next day, instead of calling, Jock pulled up outside Daisy's garden apartment, sat in his red Ferrari and waited. She never appeared. He checked the basement garage. Her car was there. But she did not come out. So, too, it was on the second day, the third, and the fourth.

On the fifth day, thinking that perhaps the Ferrari was a tip-off, Jock rented a Chevy and parked at a discreet distance from the entrance. Sure enough, soon a yellow Ford convertible pulled up out of the steep driveway of the garage. The driver was a girl hidden behind sunglasses with a scarf over her head that concealed her blonde hair. She wore a camel's hair sports coat. She turned the car onto the street and pulled away.

Jock started after her. She drove toward the Pacific, and onto 101, heading north. He stayed far enough back so that he was not constantly in her rear-view mirror. When she stopped for gas, he drove on by to avoid being obvious, made an abrupt turn at the first feeder road, and drove into the gas station from the opposite direction.

She was not recognized while she bought the gas. She paid her bill and started up; it was only after she was gone that the attendant realized who she might have been. Jock had to hurry the surprised man, who would have liked to talk about it. With his tank half filled, Jock threw the man a folded five and took off, so as not to lose her.

It was long past lunch time. But Daisy had not stopped to eat. When she reached Big Sur country she forsook the main highway to descend by subsidiary roads to the level of the Pacific.

She stopped just off a deserted beach, hidden from the main road by huge, humped rock formations. She slipped out of the car, untied her scarf, shook free her blonde hair, stripped naked and, seizing her bright beach towel, she ran toward the ocean which was crashing onto the beach in high, thundering waves.

97

The sight of her thrusting against the water terrified Jock—as it always would anyone who remembered Frederic March walking out into the Pacific in *A Star is Born*. Somehow, from that picture onward, movie stars plus Pacific surf spelled suicide.

She disappeared from Jock's view a time or two but always she reappeared. Actually she swam well. After some minutes in the angry water, she started out, riding a wave to where the water was thigh-high. She rose up from the surf, naked, with the sun glistening on her white skin. Her hair, tousled and clinging wet, gave her a pathetic, waif-like appearance.

If a camera and crew had been standing by, Jock would have taken that shot no matter how it would cut into the film. The director's soul within him knew that this was the kind of shot you never get twice. Though he also knew that he would try for it somehow, in *Mustang!*, even though there was not such a scene in the script now.

He waited till she had almost dried herself but before she started to dress. He made his presence known by simply calling, "Daisy!" He expected his sudden voice would be a shock. He wanted it that way. With a star, any star, he wanted the insecurity on their side, if he could manage it.

At the sound of him, she turned, quickly draped the towel around herself as she had done in a dozen pictures, tight just above her breasts, and an exaggerated miniskirt just below mid-thigh. With her hair damp and clinging, she was the provocative little-girl gamin, worth her weight in gold in any picture, as Marty had said. If she was insecure, or caught off-guard, she was hiding it well.

Jock moved toward her to introduce himself. But she anticipated him. "What happened to your red Ferrari?" He smiled, that city boy's idea of a disarming, shy, country boy's smile, meantime giving her the maximum candlepower his innocent baby-blues could generate. He played it as though he were a naughty little boy caught with his hand in the cookie jar. Some cookie, he thought. Some jar.

"You had me figured all the time," he said, pleading guilty to his little charade.

"When you went by the gas station and came back on the opposite side, I almost burst out laughing," Daisy confessed. "I said to myself, I hope he directs better than he chases." She was smiling now too.

"Go on, burst! Laugh!" Jock said, pretending deep hurt. Actually he was encouraged, she did know he was a director. "Yes, Daisy, be my guest. I camp outside your door for days. Five straight days. Like a goddamn star-struck movie fan. Or a sex maniac who'll go home and play with himself after one look at you! Pardon me, lady, for speaking so brusquely and straight out. But I am hurt. Deeply hurt. Yes, I am a director. And I drive a red Ferrari. And I have a fine part for you in a fine and truthful film. And I can't even make contact with you. When I finally do, you think it's very funny. Why shouldn't I be hurt?"

Certain basic things about human nature Jock Finley knew. People who are most sensitive are most susceptible to being black-mailed by the sensitivity of others. If humiliating himself was the way to win her confidence and compassion, then he would do it.

And it was working. She began to search his eyes for signs of the hurt she had inflicted. Being a fair actor, he could simulate it well enough. Being an unprincipled sonofabitch, he could project enough hurt to pick up on a wide-angle cinemascope lens.

"I'm sorry," she said softly, that same almost-whisper she used so effectively in tight, intimate scenes in pictures. It was not acting, he discovered. It was the way she was. "I didn't mean to make fun of you, Mr. Finley."

That threw him. He had never met her. But she knew him. His surprise was evident.

"When I was observing in New York at the Studio, your group did a scene. I watched you watching your actors. I never forgot it. The way you were part of them. Of every syllable, every move. You were like a father to them. It must be great, I thought, to have a director be that much with you. To care for you that much, be part of you."

She spoke softly, as though she were alone with him in a small, quiet room, instead of on a sandy, windy beach within sound of a roaring ocean. Quite unconsciously, he took on that same softness when he spoke.

99

"If you felt that way, why didn't you answer our calls? Two weeks we've been trying. Marty. Me."

"Because I knew you'd be asking about a picture. And I won't be able to answer you."

"Why not?" he asked gently.

She shrugged. She turned away to stare out at the ocean. He studied her. A waif on a beach. Being pursued by a man who wanted to offer her one million dollars-plus to appear opposite Preston Carr. And she was too frightened to make a decision. A decent man, a truly sensitive man, would have said, "Daisy, get dressed. Go home. Don't torture yourself. Above all, don't let me torture you."

But the stakes were too high, the chance too promising, the need to guarantee the picture too strong. Above all else, the need to produce that one big picture was too demanding.

"Daisy, I'm going to start up there. You get dressed. I'll wait for you at the top of the hill," he said modestly.

He turned, started away. From the top of the hill, looking down at the beach, one could see the late sun lying long on the water. And a girl slipping off her towel to be naked for as long as it took to slip into her brief panties and dress. Walking away from it all, as though he were a man of sensitivity and honor, was Jock Finley.

But from a closer angle one could have seen Jock Finley, his eyes revealing his calculated anticipation, fully aware of what was going on behind him.

If one could have gotten a close angle on Daisy Donnell, one would have seen her watch Jock Finley walking away from her. On her face was a look of respect, awe, and fear for a man who was accepted as a director in the New York shrine of "real acting."

She didn't want a drink. So they sat in her convertible and talked till the sun went down into the Pacific. When it was dark, he remembered she hadn't even had lunch. In their separate cars they drove to a small restaurant at the end of a long pier off 101. A mediocre restaurant, it would protect them from the crowd which would have given them no peace at Chasen's or La Scala.

100

During dinner they talked pictures. And life. And finally *the* picture.

Daisy brought it up herself, because she knew it was inevitable. "All right, tell me about your picture," she ventured with a tone of resignation which indicated her inner tension, and her need to have it out of the way, finally.

The way she asked made Jock know that he must be very careful in his answer, more subtle and low key than he had been, or needed to be, with Preston Carr. Carr was a man motivated to make pictures. Provided two things were right. The story. And the money.

With this girl, too frightened to know self-interest, who did not respect money but feared it, he had to be extremely cautious. Or extremely daring.

Ever since he had first started to direct, Jock had an intuition which became a rule. When confronted by a clichéd situation or scene, in order to impress a critic or arrest an audience, do the most usual thing in the most unusual way.

What does a director usually say to a star he covets? I have a great part for you in a great film! I have the greatest part for you in the greatest film!! Daisy Donnell had heard that as often as she had permitted directors to talk to her in the past few years. Jock knew there had to be another way, a different way.

So he didn't answer at once, but continued to eat, as though he were troubled or reluctant to launch into the subject. Finally, seeming to make a very private admission, he said, "The girl in my script is not right. And she worries the hell out of me!"

This was not a director talking to a star. This was a director talking to his wife. Or a director talking to his agent. Or a producer talking to a studio head. It had an innate plea in it: I'm in trouble. Help me.

"It bugs me! Drives me crazy! I can't sleep nights because of it. And I'll be perfectly honest with you, Daisy, that's the real reason I want you. The studio may want your name power. Not me. I want something that you can do for the picture, for me."

Daisy, who had heard them all, had never heard this approach before. She tensed a little. It was bad enough being involved in a film where she had been assured the script was brilliant, the part perfect. But to be told at the outset the script was in trouble, and it was her part which was the trouble, that was cause for alarm. Jock sensed the tension, saw it on her face when she stared out at the darkness and the ocean, rather than looking into his eyes. But he would bring her back.

"I have been trying, for weeks, to get it through that writer's head that he doesn't know women. Sure, the old-style, clichéd Hollywood concept of women, yes, he knows that. Too damn well. But a real woman. This woman. Oh no! But he won't admit it. He won't let me call in help. Believe me, if this wasn't his original story I'd fire him off the picture in a minute! But my hands are tied. Which is bad enough. But my ... my soul is tied, too ..."

He glanced at her to see if the word "soul" had any impact. It had.

"I should walk away from this story. And I would. If I didn't believe with every instinct in me that this has the makings of a great picture. This picture has to be made. And I have to make it. I know that. If only I could cure the girl. This will be the greatest film in Preston Carr's career but only if the relationship between him and the girl is right. It could also be the greatest thing that ever happened to the girl who plays the girl. If the part is written right. And that's where I need you. You're the only one who can help me. That's right. You!"

She half turned to look into his face. Close as she was to him he could feel her reaching out to be told.

"My girl is as lost as you are. As frightened. As hurt. Yes, Daisy, there it is. Straight out. On the line. What I want is the *inside* of you. Not the outside. I don't want the blond hair, the pink-and-white pretty face. The beautiful, mouth-watering tits. The provocative ass. I want you. The inside. On paper. And then on film. So what I am saying to you is this, if you can't promise to work with me on the script, then please, for your sake and mine, say no to the picture when Marty calls again tomorrow. Or better still just don't answer his calls. That'll save you the trouble and the pain of refusing, explaining, avoiding."

She didn't answer. He didn't press her.

Almost two hours later, in a dark corner of a hippie coffeehouse,

102

high over Malibu, Jock and Daisy sat unrecognized, sipping *Cappucino* and staring at the flickering candle in the empty, wax-encrusted bottle. They had not said much, either of them, since Jock had asked for her help. The flickering candlelight added sadness to his baby-blues. Whether it was compassion for him, or because of her own inner conflict, Daisy started to weep suddenly and softly. He reached out to touch the tears with his fingertips.

"I'm sorry, Daisy. I didn't mean to make it your problem. And it isn't. Unless *you* make it yours. But I promise you, if you do, it'll be an acting experience you'll never forget or regret. You'll be proud of it for the rest of your life."

She sat there, eyes wet, quite touched. She was being wanted, implored, this time not for her body but for her own inner self.

After a long moment, she nodded.

"You'll do it?"

"I'll do it."

He took her small, cold, tense hand, kissed the fingertips, then held it warmly in both his hands.

"For once, just for once, I'd like the world to know the real Daisy Donnell. They will love her even more than the one they know now. We'll start working on the script tomorrow afternoon. I'll come over to your place and read it to you as it is now. Then we'll go to work!"

He followed her yellow convertible home, saw her to her apartment door. There was a moment when she might have asked him in and he would have accepted but she didn't. They stood there and stared at each other. She was seeking to believe him. He was giving her the full, compassionate power of his eyes, which said trust me, trust me, trust me. She had her key out. He took it, unlocked her door, pushed it open, put on the light, and when he was sure she was safe, he handed back the key. She reached for it. He held her hand, brought it to his lips, and kissed it. Then he let her slip into the apartment and waited till she locked the door.

He started out of the foyer, into the garden area and across it, to his own car, sensing that she was watching him every step of the way, through the slightly parted curtains of the picture window, and she was.

It was after midnight when he arrived back at his house. Despite the lateness of the hour he phoned Marty. Marty was just falling asleep but became sharply alert when Jock spoke.

"Marty! You can call New York! She said yes!!"

"Tonight!" Marty said. "Tonight she said yes. Wait till tomorrow. Or just wait a few hours. In fact the minute you hang up she could call and say she's changed her mind. I'm not calling New York till I'm sure."

"She won't change her mind," Jock said firmly.

"Look, laddie, I know her. You don't."

"I'm telling you this time she won't change her mind! You can call New York first thing in the morning!"

"If I had a dollar for every time I have heard a producer or director say that about her."

"Because she's been afraid, Marty. Afraid. I won't give her a chance to be afraid. From now till we start shooting I'm not going to give her enough time to herself to think! She'll be too busy to be afraid. Marty, take my word for one thing, she won't be afraid any more!"

Starting the next day and during every day thereafter, Jock followed a crowded but meticulous schedule.

Each morning from eight till noon he was at his office in the studio, planning the shooting schedule, discussing and approving costumes, the style of production design, the cinematography, how much shooting was to be on location, how much back at the studio, plans for capture and handling of the mustangs.

As to the cinematographer, Jock had been most fortunate. Joe Goldenberg was available, and as a favor to Preston Carr, he agreed to do the picture. That was important. For Joe was a veteran who had been nominated five times for Academy Awards—three times for color cinematography—and he had won twice.

The mustangs required for the shooting would have to be found on location or close by, which necessitated professional union wranglers to capture them, handle them, doctor them, and keep them fit and ready to meet the demands of the schedule.

But endless as the detailed decisions were, they were never allowed to prevent Jock from leaving the studio precisely at noon every day. From the first day when for the first time he read the script aloud to Daisy, and every day thereafter, till the script was in final shooting draft, Jock spent his afternoons with her, seven days a week.

On the first day he suspected that her apartment was inhibiting. Pleasant enough, large enough, bright enough, it was in some way as stifling as a prison cell. He thought it was the effect on him alone. But then he realized that she was not the same as she had been on that first night. It could have been her sudden, capricious moods which Marty had warned him about. But, after two days, Jock decided it was the apartment.

So from the third day on, he made it a point to stop on his way, pick up some picnic food, San Francisco sourdough bread, cheese, wine, and fruit. Then they would drive out of LA either far to the north along the ocean, or south toward La Jolla or Palm Springs. There they found some beach or hilltop, deserted and hidden away from people and cities. And only then did Daisy seem to come alive and relax and breathe freely without tension. She became the girl on the beach again. So finally Jock knew. It was not the apartment. It was the city, the studio, picture business and its burdens from which she sought to escape.

Secluded, alone, they could talk of the script, the individual scenes, the bits and pieces of dialogue that troubled her or puzzled her or eluded her altogether. Gently, carefully, subtly, he gave her line readings which most actresses would resent. Slowly he led her into the character and into the story and into the relationship with Linc, the Preston Carr character. They talked, they discussed, she questioned, she even argued, something she had not felt strong enough to do before.

They laughed, too. And they ate, they drank. In those moments when the script was put aside, Jock sought to probe into her past, hoping, as all amateur analysts always do, that he could unearth

105

that one fact, that one wound or scar that might change her completely into what she could have been. He never did, of course. But he kept hoping, trying.

One thing he knew. She was at ease with him, finally. He could tell. Her hands, which that first night had been icy cold, were cold no longer. Her body, small actually for one considered so voluptuous, was no longer tense. She breathed more easily, almost deeply, something she had never dared do on those first days.

She no longer seemed only a single reaction away from panic. Now her insecurity was evidenced in only two ways.

Occasionally, with no motive Jock could discern, she would grasp his hand and hold it, as a little girl might have grasped her father's hand. It might happen when she was listening to him explain a scene, or when they were driving, or when she was merely staring out at the ocean far below them. She held his hand, then seemed to become conscious of doing so, and surrendered it awkwardly.

The other evidence of tension was more directly related to the script and the picture. She lapsed into long, thoughtful moments while Jock was talking. Then suddenly she would suggest a camera angle or a line of dialogue or a move which had worked so well for her in a previous picture.

This was not an uncommon thing for actors or actresses who were uncertain of their talent. Jock had run into it before, mainly with comics doing a play for the first time and not getting the kind of laughs they were accustomed to in nightclubs or at Las Vegas.

If patriotism was the last refuge of a scoundrel, familiarity was the first refuge of a frightened comic or actor. The desire to escape to their own personal, long-standing clichés was sometimes overpowering. Only confidence in the director could wean them away from it.

It was the same with Daisy. But since Jock knew the syndrome well, each time she suggested some past bit of business or a familiar camera angle or a clichéd reaction shot, Jock explained gently and with great care, "Daisy . . . Daisy . . . no. If there is one thing we're striving for, you, me, Pres Carr, it is to avoid all the clichés of picture-making. The fact that something worked before is the best reason we have for *not* doing it in this picture. We are going to

106

make this the most *un*clichéd Western of all time! We are going to make *you* the most different, touching, inspiring Daisy Donnell that anyone has ever seen!

"Remember what I told you that first night. Even if you want to change that, I won't let you. Don't be frightened. Just trust me. Have confidence in me. Believe in me half as much as I believe in you and you will be great!"

Times like those, she took his hand, held it against her soft cashmere sweater, pressed it against her breasts, fiercely.

It had begun that way. Their affair. During the sixteenth of their meetings. Near the edge of a seaside cliff which thrust out over the Pacific far below.

She was holding his hand, frightened again. The coldness had returned to her fingers. Even as it happened, Jock was wondering what had brought it on. All he had said was, "Two weeks from today, we start."

She reached for his hand, held it close to her, began to tremble. He had not seen that since the very first night. Quickly he moved to embrace her, hold her, as though the strength of his arms could still her trembling. But it could not.

She burrowed into his shoulder, into his neck, seeking to hide there, to be protected there. Gently, he forced her face to turn to him. He kissed her to give courage to her trembling lips. Once he did, she opened completely, lips, mouth, body. She embraced him, fiercely, desperately.

Almost any woman at certain moments on certain days will be one complete erogenous zone. The slightest touch will do it. Nor need it be flesh on flesh, or even skin against skin. A completely clothed contact can cause it. Or mere proximity. Even a thought can do it. Can cause her to open to a man. Almost any man. On certain days.

She allowed him to undress her as she clung to him. When he stared at her body, she turned away shyly. When he kissed her breasts, she held him there tightly, straining against him. But her hands were still icy cold against his warm back, her body was still tense against his.

She wanted him, needed him, desperately, yet strangely. Through it all, the embracing, the thrusting, to her moment of orgasmic

107

spasm and whimpering, he was part of it and yet he was apart from it.

When it was over, he lay there, cn his side, still between her soft, white thighs, and looked down at her face. Her eyes were closed. Her rhythmic breathing was slower than he had expected. When he touched her body, she was calm, soothed, completely without tension for the first time.

Eyes closed, she searched for his hand. She found it and he discovered that her hand was warm now, relaxed now. She brought his hand to her face, held it against her cheek. And she smiled.

Her eyes were still closed when she spoke for the first time. "We'll do the locations first, won't we? We don't have to go to the studio for a long time, do we?"

"Not for a long time," he said. He moved forward to lie close to her. Her arm went around his neck, her hand pressed his face close to hers.

He made love to her again. And every day thereafter. From it he learned one thing. It was the only sure way to allay her fears, to free her of tension. As long as she was dependent on him for confidence, for security, for sexuality, he would be able to get a great performance out of her.

108

CHAPTER

4

"Shoot the whole picture on location?" Marty asked, his round face growing red. "Do you realize what that means? Cost-wise? And every other wise? The lighting is never dependable! You have a short shooting day! Vapor trails in the sky from the jets, if you want to match shots. No, laddie! Not a whole picture on location! It's too much of a risk!"

"But, Marty . . ." Jock pleaded, "take my word for it, it'll be better this way. And maybe cheaper in the long run."

"How could it be?" the little man demanded. "Just take the dailies! How are you going to see your dailies on location?"

"Fly them in. By helicopter. Show them in a projection truck," Jock answered quickly, for he had investigated all the details.

"You know what it costs to rent a truck like that for sixty days? You don't shoot a whole picture out in the desert. You don't even mention it. Not now, when the whole mess in London is finally forgotten. Why it could cost another million, million and a half!" Marty speculated. "To say nothing of Preston Carr. He didn't sign to do a picture on location. He won't like being away that long. And under those conditions. He likes to live, that *boychick.* And I don't blame him. So, forget it, laddie."

"Marty . . . Marty, what if I told you that I am not sure I can get her through the picture if we shoot in the studio?" Jock said that very slowly, for the full, unsettling effect he knew it must have.

It did. Marty looked up, speechless. Then he began breathing again, demanding, "All right, what happened? Tell me!"

"Nothing happened. Yet. But she's terrified. Of this town. Of studios. They give her claustrophobia. She is the most frightened human being I know. Away from here I can control her, get a performance, a great performance out of her. Here, with the studio, the pressure, gossip, demands, guilts, sense of responsibility, I can't guarantee anything. Please, Marty, not for me. For her!"

'New York'll have to approve. Carr will have to agree. It won't be easy, laddie."

"I'll go to New York myself. I'll go see Carr. I'll get his okay."

"If it's okay with New York . . ." Marty began to relent. "If Carr has no objection . . . okay with me."

Jock started for the door. Marty's voice reached him, stopped him, "Laddie, you're not in love with that girl, are you?"

Jock spun around, angry. "What kind of question is that?"

"You fucking her?" Marty asked, with merely clinical interest.

"None of your goddamn business!" Jock exploded.

Marty nodded, relieved, for he knew now. "That's okay then. Because she never marries a guy she screws. So you're safe. You better go to New York now."

It took almost all of a whole day in New York, from eleven o'clock in a meeting that started in the president's office through lunch upstairs at Twenty-One and back to the office again, till four-thirty. Only when Jock ended up threatening that this was the only way to protect the picture did the president finally concede. "Okay, shoot the whole thing on location if you want!"

Jock did not even get to the ground floor of the building before the president was on the phone to Marty White. Marty was prepared for him, "Bob, sweetie, if you want that girl in this picture, let him have his way."

"Christ, all the publicity! And the stockholders, when I announced her. We got to have that girl!"

"Then do what I say. Say okay," Marty insisted.

110

"I already said okay. I'm worried, that's all."

Jock found Preston Carr at an Appaloosa horse show in Houston at which Big C horses had already taken four ribbons.

They discussed it as Carr had his prideful eye on several of his horses which were being groomed to enter the show ring. Carr did not like the idea of spending all that time on location in the heat and the dust. And it would add shooting days, no doubt about that. Jock tried to bribe him with word about a special air-conditioned trailer, larger than any previous model, more than a huge dressing room it was a one-room suite on wheels, with the latest and utmost in electronic comforts.

But Carr only watched his horses and seemed detached, uncooperative, until Jock asked with sudden sincerity, "Please, Pres? As a favor to me? I've never asked you for a favor before."

"Sure, kid, if it means that much. And if you can get that trailer. Okay!"

When he told Daisy that he had arranged to shoot the entire film away from Hollywood she was openly relieved, obviously happy. She seemed relaxed suddenly, in a way exceeding even those times when he had just made love to her. She kissed him impulsively, laughing with joy. She lapsed into herself, smiling.

Then she reached for him. It was not the icy-handed tremulous reaching of those times when she verged on panic, but the enticing reaching way she had when she let him know she wanted him inside her where it was moist and warm. He kissed her and her lips opened to him, her tongue began to slowly pry and seek the inner reaches of his mouth.

With as much curiosity as he could manage despite the fact that he wanted her fiercely, he let her have her way and for the first time in all the times he had had her, she was the aggressor completely, totally. Hands, mouth, legs, all of her came alive, all of her was involved in it.

He had spent himself in her and lay gasping, his face against hers, so close he could feel the pounding of her blood even above his own. He moved his head slightly to gaze at her. She lay face up, eyes closed, a small, satisfied smile on her full lips. It pleased

111

him, till he thought suddenly, It's nothing I did to her, it's because she's relieved she doesn't have to shoot in the studio. This is her way of saying thank you. Like you toss a buck to a parking attendant who's brought you your car. She had no other way of saying thanks.

The day arrived. The day to move out to the location in Nevada.

The exodus of the Jews from Egypt was a modest expedition compared to the logistics of moving a first-class shooting company from Hollywood. Armies have moved with less trouble. And locusts with lesser appetites.

Aside from a few days in a carefully selected, nondescript town on the California border, *Mustang!* was to be shot in the semi-arid foothills of mountainous country indigenous to Nevada, where small herds of wild horses still roam.

Of course, there would also be the water scene at Lake Mead which Jock had been trying to convince Irving Warfield to write in, to "protect" the picture by getting the most of Daisy Donnell. God knows, they were paying her an enormous salary, so they had better get all the mileage, or footage, out of her that they could, was Jock's argument.

Finally it was agreed that a scene originally conceived to take place at night, in the small-town bar, would be moved to the shore of Lake Mead, in broad daylight. Warfield had resisted, arguing that dialogue that would sound good in a bar, muted by shadows, accented by garish neon lights, would not sound right in the bright, sunny outdoors. But Jock had already begun to rewrite the scene in his own way, in his own mind, because he had never liked the damned dialogue anyhow. Warfield suspected that. So, since the property in Palm Desert demanded development at once, he did the rewrite himself and at least avoided the inconvenience of having to go out to location.

When Jock arrived on the location in his red Ferrari, it was already a city in building. Generator trucks, tank trucks, trailers for living purposes, a fully equipped prefabricated commissary,

112

THE DIRECTOR

cameras, sound booms, camera cranes, helicopters, a crew that
ran into hundreds when one included the wranglers who were to
supervise the preparation of a corral for the wild mustangs, all
had been brought together to become a sudden city where before
there had been only desert.

For the next eight weeks, ten, fourteen, fifteen, for as long as
it took, this place would live, would function, would support life
in insulated, air-conditioned comfort, and then would disappear.

Jock Finley stood in the center of all this activity and realized
that he was responsible for it and it was responsible to him. All
of it.

Jock Finley, thirty-one, a kid from Brooklyn, lean, handsome,
blue-eyed, was putting down on the Nevada earth a city larger
and more complete by far than the first encampment Caesar
caused to be established when he invaded the islands of Britain.

His satisfaction was interrupted, as well as enhanced, by the
endless torrent of hundreds of details of construction, dispersal,
and disposition brought to him for his final approval as he walked
out amid his own private city.

Three days after Jock arrived, Daisy arrived. The next day
Preston Carr arrived. Two days later shooting was scheduled to
begin.

The first shots of any picture are always important. Shots of even
trivial scenes sometimes are crucial if they are first shots. For the
morale, expectations, and receptivity of a number of key people
can be shaped or destroyed in those first few days.

This is especially true of location pictures. One marvelous bit
of film flown back in the first day or two, no matter how small,
if it pleases the executives at the studio, means New York will
hear about it at once, which, in turn means they will not be looking over the director's shoulder, and money will not be a problem
if later he goes over budget.

That first bit of film can also breed a surge of vital confidence in
the cast. If the actors see rushes which excite them, they feel they
are in the hands of a fine director, that the picture will look good,
will be important and successful, will further their careers, their

113

reputations, their price. Hence, it makes them more cooperative, more amenable, allows the director to make greater demands on them, on their talent.

The attitude of cast, crew, studio, even of the director himself, his own confidence, all of it can be shaped, or warped, by the scenes shot in the first few days.

With *Mustang!* this was especially true. Largely because of Daisy. Jock knew that no matter how he contrived it, her first scene must give her enormous confidence in the picture, and in him, but mainly in herself. It must be a scene which aroused in everyone, on location and at the studio, a sense of excitement about her return to pictures, and about the chemistry of Preston Carr and Daisy Donnell. Consequently, her first scene could not be *the* first scene. Jock knew the risk was too great.

Nor should the first shots involve Preston Carr. For Jock needed to establish more respect, more dependence on him from Carr before they could try any important scenes. Carr still called him "kid" in that nice, pleasant, even affectionate way. But there was not the core of respect that very good actors must have for a very good director when the going gets rough and the differences heated. Jock knew it, resented it, and meant to win his respect at any cost.

A great first scene would be one way.

An ideal first scene would also give everyone a clear, strong sense of the level of realism Jock envisioned for the entire film. It must prove that *Mustang!* was not just another Western—or even another good Western, but a story about real people with deep psychological motivations, honest conflicts, a story with universality of application, making a comment on life in our time. If its conflicts were real, its dangers must also be genuine, believable, powerful.

For days before he arrived, Jock had known this first scene must be all good things to all men. And to one particular woman. Most of all, it must instill in everyone a deep, genuine respect and loyalty for the director, his talent, and for the work they were all about to do for him.

So Jock arrived with a decision already made, but kept completely to himself, that his first takes would be camouflaged by

114

calling them color tests. Ostensibly they were only to be sent back to the lab at the studio to determine what results they were getting from the raw stock they planned on using, and from the desert lighting at various times of day. Thus he would be protecting himself from adverse reaction in the event that the first shots failed to live up to expectations.

So the first slate was chalked to read:

> *MUSTANG!*
> JAN. 4
> DIRECTOR: FINLEY
> CAMERA: GOLDENBERG
> COLOR TESTS: TAKE ONE

Since much of the picture would be panorama views in wide, wide screen, Jock decided his "test" shots would be the wild-horse sequences. They could be impressive, exciting, could establish the scope and texture of the desert and of the entire film.

The first "test" shots would be the helicopter shots from the air, in which the camera would sweep down into the deep crevices and canyons where wild horses grazed, rousing them, frightening them into stampeding flight across the stony mountain ground, through the canyons, down into arroyos, across patches of desert stubble, sand, earth.

In line with his general rule, when you must do the ordinary do it in an *un*ordinary way, Jock was not content to have Joe Goldenberg's assistant, Dave Graham or his camera operator handle the Mitchell up in the copter. He asked Joe to do that himself. And Joe, an amenable man at most times, and especially when dealing with young directors, most of whom he regarded as brash scared kids, consented to go along, though it had been years since he touched the controls of a camera.

The Mitchell was tightly bolted alongside the open bubble. Joe Goldenberg and Jock were lashed inside loosely enough so that they could lean far out and see what the camera was getting. The copter made one probing pass after another, seeking its subjects.

Desert and foothills passed beneath them, a haphazard patch-work of sunlight, shadows, earth, brown, green, dun. On the third pass they spotted a small herd of wild horses grazing just within the protective shadows of the foothills. At Jock's signal, the pilot swept down till the noisy, throbbing machine was only fifty feet from the ground. With the mountain a wall on their left, they moved up behind the grazing mustangs. The animals stopped feed-ing, came alert. Then their terrible, angry whinny of alarm cut through the whisking sound of the blades, and the animals ex-ploded into swift, terrified flight.

The copter pursued, keeping the main band below and before it, always in camera range. Joe Goldenberg leaned far out, with Jock just over his shoulder, his naked eye seeing what the camera would get. Beneath them, fierce, frightened animals raised a ter-rified screaming, a thumping clatter of hooves, and a trailing cloud of desert dust. Above them, the blades were whirring, whipping the air in steady, cutting sweeps.

The excitement of it all was to Jock what the first blows are for a prizefighter in an important bout: the impact which dissolved all nervousness and created instead a drive, a desire to fight this war he had come here to fight.

The feeling of power, or sheer sadistic impulse, whichever it was, the terror of the animals became a game from which Jock derived enormous enjoyment, sweeping down, watching these magnificent beasts exert every fierce bit of energy and muscle to escape the inescapable mechanical pursuer.

Joe Goldenberg, a small, quiet, bearded man, whom one would take to be an accountant or a dentist before learning that he was one of the finest motion-picture photographers in the world, was the first to call it quits. If this was a color test, he had enough foot-age. If it was more than that, it would be wiser to get into the action of the story before piling up expensive footage of scenic beauty and terrified animals which might never find its way into the picture or onto any screen, except as rushes and eventual out-takes.

When Jock insisted on yet another run, Joe prevailed only by pointing out that the slant of the afternoon sun was such that the copter shadow would show up in the shot and destroy all illusion.

That alone forced Jock to give the sign to the pilot to start back to location.

They landed. Jock leaped out of the bubble and walked away even before the blades ceased their slow, dying sweeps. His legs felt weak, trembling, vibrating almost in rhythm with the copter when it had made its intrusive sweeps at low heights. But it was not copter rhythm, Jock discovered. It was excitement, the sheer excitement of what he had seen and participated in. If only it were possible to transmit that to an audience. True, you could give them the omnipotent feeling of flying so close to the earth and yet being immune to gravity, so close to the mountains as to be in actual danger, so close to the wild pack that the sight and sounds of their terror, even the terror itself seemed to reach up to you. Yet all of that would not be as real as if one were in that herd, actually, literally.

From above, even if it were only as little as fifty feet, there was still the sense of being in a controlled situation, above the danger, aloof from the raw fear of wild beasts, sealed off, antiseptically safe somehow.

There should be a way, a more dramatic way . . . and suddenly, as the temptation began to flood his mind, Jock knew there *was* a way to give the audience, and the avant-garde critics in this country and abroad, the total feeling of having been immersed in, having lived a picture which was real and not the elegantly faked reality of scenes shot by a traditional camera and crew, in which almost every inch of movement is figured out, every change of focus of every lens is meticulously planned to the split second.

Yes, there was a way! And it was that inspiration which made him come away from the copter, his legs, his entire body trembling with expectation, excitement. The way was one he had used before. With great success. He had captured sex with it, a city with it, relived a riot with it, and had made it so real that his two successful pictures had the urgency and honesty of newsreels instead of carefully plotted films. And he would use it here.

The matching shots for intercutting with the copter shots of the herd in flight, those shots of the racing herd on the ground, would be made with a hand-held camera.

117

That was the only way to capture the jerky, staccato, abrupt movements and imperfections which let critic know, and audience feel, that the event they were witnessing was real. That the danger was real, that it was life, unrehearsed, unguarded. Let the dust obscure the shot, let the hooves beat against the lens if chance made it happen that way. But get that total feeling of terror, flight, hooves, whinnies. Let the audience be in it, of it, trampled by it.

With its bed concealed as a studio couch, Jock's trailer looked like a well-furnished den in a good Beverly Hills home. Its long, narrow contour was overcome by lush green carpeting, large, comfortable chairs, subdued, tasteful lighting. One could forget completely it was only a location trailer.

The leather-paneled bar at the far end was fully stocked, as though for eternity. Jock stood at it now, holding up a huge, crystal old-fashioned glass with two inches of Scotch in it, asking, "Enough, Joe?"

"Enough," Joe Goldenberg said.

"Rocks?"

"Straight up will do me."

Jock handed the glass to Joe and was making his own Scotch and soda when he broached the idea of hand-held shots of the herd in flight. Joe never even brought his glass to his lips, but listened to Jock expound on how he wanted the audience to be "in it and of it and trampled by it" and how hand-held shots were the only way to achieve that.

Joe stared at Jock, wondering, Does this kid mean it, and if he does, is it merely out of ignorance? So, calmly, thoughtfully, as was Joe's way with the new breed of young directors, he said, "I know what you want. And I can get it for you without any physical danger. I'll use a one-fifty millimeter lens with a zoom and you get me within forty feet of the action and nobody, no critic, no audience will be able to tell he's not right in with that herd. Believe me."

Joe took his first sip of Scotch. When Jock did not accept the suggestion, or even answer, Joe brought his glass down and ex-

118

plained patiently that the trick was in setting the camera platform expertly over a small, confined pass so that it straddled the opening and became a funnel into which the herd was driven by the pursuing copter. With the camera at the right angle, and with a one-fifty, you would swear they were coming right at you, into you, through you. And yet no one was as close as forty feet to any of the dangerous wild beasts.

Joe went even further. With two cameras hitched in tandem, they would get all the footage they could ever need in one pass, all highly effective, very real, and, most of all, very safe. But Jock still hadn't answered.

As his final, and what he hoped would be his convincing argument, Joe said, "Believe me, Finley, that's what any good director would settle for."

"I am not any good director," Jock said in a soft but deadly serious voice. "And this is not any picture. And if I'd wanted photography as done by 'any good cinematographer' I wouldn't have held out for you. Or paid you your price!" So said thirty-one-year-old Jock Finley to sixty-three-year-old, two-time Academy Award winner Joe Goldenberg. Joe reddened a bit under his neat, trim white beard.

"I want . . . and I mean to get . . . right into the midst of that thundering pack. I want the dust and grit. The frightened eyes. Nostrils that seem to breathe fire. I want their open mouths, gasping, revealing foam, their slobbering red tongues, their dangerous, huge, white teeth. I want every detail. And then when I combine that with the sound track, I am going to give every human being with the price of a ticket the most thrilling few minutes of film ever made! That's all I want."

There are no secrets on any location. Loves, hates, differences, and disputes, all have a way of becoming common knowledge almost at once. The disagreement between Jock and Joe Goldenberg was no exception.

It was already well known by dinner time in the commissary. As Jock ate at the long executive table, his assistant, a spectacled, undistinguished-looking young man named Lester Ansell, pulled up a chair to go over the shots for the morning. Joe Goldenberg, and his own assistant, Dave Graham, Preston Carr, the copter

119

pilot, the chief wrangler, all continued eating, but conversation had ceased, for they all waited to hear Jock's decision after the argument with Joe.

Jock sensed it. He could almost feel that Carr was waiting, listening, though he went through the motions of eating. Carr it was who had first suggested Joe Goldenberg for this picture. Carr it was who was of Joe's generation of picture-makers, which created a certain loyalty and solidarity. So Jock knew well that, given a choice, Preston Carr would vote for taking the best you could get without running any outlandish risks.

As he ate, Jock studied the map of the terrain held for him by his assistant. A few glances and he turned to the pilot, "What do you think, Walter? If we want a natural funnel, so all you have to do is start them up and they can only come toward us, toward the camera platform, where would you choose?"

At the words "camera platform," Carr, Joe, Dave Graham, the chief wrangler, who was called Tex, all of them resumed eating in earnest. The issue had been decided Joe's way. The pilot wanted to restudy his own aerial photos again before making his decision final, so he left the table.

Jock finished eating hastily and joined the pilot in the production trailer. Together they pored over the aerial stills the pilot had shot during location scouting. They were joined by Joe, Dave Graham, and in a few moments, by Preston Carr. Around the map and the photos the decision was made, precisely where to erect the platform, fifteen feet high, twenty feet by thirty feet, of sturdy iron structural pipe and thick planking, strong enough to support two Mitchells, two camera crews, director, a total of some twenty-five people.

It would directly straddle the path of the stampede, with the terrain providing a natural funnel, sucking in the mustangs at one end and spewing them out in frenzied flight at the other.

Everyone agreed on the proper place for the platform. Jock gave the order to his assistant, Lester Ansell. Construction was to start at once; by dawn the morning after next, two Mitchells were to be in place and ready. Jock's assistant started on his way out to give the orders for the construction.

However, as he reached the door of the trailer, Jock added,

"And remind me to make sure there are two Reflex hand-helds ready and loaded, too."

Everyone turned sharply toward Jock—Joe Goldenberg, Preston Carr, the pilot, Jock's assistant. Whether it was bravado, or anger, or a sadistic need to humble Joe Goldenberg, Jock said calmly, "As long as they're stampeding toward the platform we don't lose anything by having a hand-held on the spot, cranking away. Do we?"

"If you can get someone to go out there and hold it," Joe said, his face growing redder against his short, white beard.

"The assignment carries hazardous pay," Jock offered.

"I'm not asking any man in my crew to do it!" Joe said with a kind of firmness that should have closed the matter.

But Jock turned back to his assistant. "I want those two Mitchell Reflexes ready. Each loaded with a thousand-foot magazine. Got it?"

"Just who do you think is crazy enough to go out there and hold one of them?" Joe demanded, staring straight at Jock, but conscious of Preston Carr and inviting his intercession.

"I am," Jock said softly, deliberately, playing for contrast to Joe's angry question.

"You're not a member of the Guild!" Joe shot back.

"That doesn't prevent me from knowing the rules. When a Guild member refuses, as he has a right to refuse, to do any job he considers too hazardous, then the director or the producer has a right to do it and is not breaking any Guild rule. Right?"

"The Guild has said in the past . . ." Joe started to explain.

"I am not asking any Guild member to take any risk! *I* am taking the risk! I am doing so after a Guild member refused to! Now if you want to report that to the Guild, go right ahead. Get on the radiophone now and do it!" Jock said, without raising his voice, but his eyes were steel-blue.

Joe turned, said to his own assistant, "Dave, I'll give you the list of what I want on that platform." He walked out of the trailer.

But Jock knew what pride will make a man do. Any good director knows, because the pride of others is the most effective instrument he has.

Within the hour, as Jock expected, Joe Goldenberg was back.

He had talked to his crew. Dave Graham, an excellent man on focus and zooming, had volunteered to go out there with the hand-held.

Nothing was said, but Jock was sure that Joe had discussed it with Preston Carr first. Which was all to the good, as far as Jock was concerned. It was important to let the whole company know, stars included, that Jock Finley was a tough, firm, hard man on all artistic questions. He would get plenty of mileage out of this, in more ways than one.

Location City was a military camp the night before an attack. Conversation was too loud or too soft. The smallest events became the source of too much laughter or not enough. Tension was everywhere.

In the commissary, those not actually involved in the construction sat in little groups, talking routinely about their assignments for the next morning. Others had started playing gin or poker by the time Jock Finley walked in to get a late-night cup of coffee.

He sat at a table by himself, sipped his hot coffee slowly. From time to time, everyone in the commissary stole a look at him, then indulged in more deliberate stares. No one in this dining room had been in that meeting, but every man knew word for word what had taken place. And every man in this room felt he was in the presence of a genius or a madman. Or a thirty-one-year-old kid who would risk anything or anybody to get what he wanted on film.

Before he had finished his coffee, Jock felt there was a gulf miles wide between him and every other person in that company. Well, the hell with them! He'd get what he wanted! He'd prove himself right! That's what pictures were all about these days, someone daring to do what had never been done before. At least that's what Jock Finley was all about. Let them know it! Let the whole fucking world know it!

He slammed his white mug down so hard the remaining coffee splashed over the rim.

He decided to stop by at Daisy's trailer before going to sleep. She was not there. It frightened him. He burst out, but as soon as

122

he got past the far end of the trailer, he found her, staring up at the moon, rising over the far-off, shadowy mountains, against the star-filled, deep blue, night sky.

He was relieved to find her so safely, so pleasantly occupied. She asked again about her first scene, when it would be shot. He soothed her by saying, "I want your relationship with Pres in the picture to start up naturally, to develop naturally. That way your performance will grow the same way relationships grow in real life. So your first sequence will be the one where you two meet. We'll get to it in a few days."

She nodded, smiling, but he could sense the trembling underneath. This girl was frightened of everything, even of those things she did best.

"Don't work on your lines," he asked softly. "Okay?" She turned to look up at him, her eyes puzzled. Most directors would have said just the opposite. The moonlight on her face softened and flattered her more than any gauze, lens, or lighting effect that man could produce. "Remember what I told you. What I want, when we get around to it, is *you*. Not lines written by someone else, not acting preached by someone else, not a performance. I want you."

What he really meant was, I want me. I want that well-intended terribly troubled little mind of yours to leave my scenes alone, till I get to them with you, teach you, shape you, take what you have to offer, and turn it into acting by my sheer will and talent.

"Do you believe me, believe in me?" he asked seductively.

She kissed him tenderly. It was answer enough. All those afternoons of working with her, making love to her were paying off. She believed him, trusted him. If he said, wait, don't worry, she would wait. Asking her not to worry might be too much, though.

"I hope nothing goes wrong tomorrow,' she said.

"Thanks." His eyes were ultra-sincere as they reflected the strong, clear moonlight. He reached out playfully to tap her pert nose. He reached for her hand, ostensibly to kiss the palm of it, but actually to touch her fingers. Icy. Painfully icy. She was more tense than he had ever known her to be. Using her hand, he drew her close, held her tightly. She tried to embrace him but it was a desperate clutching, a child drowning, not a woman impassioned.

He kissed her and would have done more but as if she sensed what it would lead to and what it really would be, she slipped from his embrace, ran quickly to the stairs, up them, and into her trailer. She closed the door. He waited to hear the lock snap into place.

He turned, starting for his own trailer, saying to himself, No one, no one, should ever be that afraid of anything. Sitting on his own bunk, he kicked off his desert boots, slipped out of his shirt as he studied his copy of the map which outlined tomorrow's work.

Inside her trailer, Daisy sat before her dressing-table mirror, taking off her clothes, inspecting herself, searching as she did every night for facial changes, betrayals of age. She pressed under her breasts for telltale sagging. Finally she put out the light, slipped into bed. In the dark, she felt for the lower drawer of her table, sought out a bottle of sleeping pills. She was able to take them now without water. She swallowed one. Then, because she sensed she would need it, she opened the bottle again and took another and then placed a third in the unused ashtray, just in case.

The next morning, dawn rose up behind the mountains, discovered the camp, painted it pink and gold as it came awake. The pilot and his mechanic checked the copter. The work crew started off to finish the camera platform. Joe Goldenberg and his camera crew met to plan their day. Numberless electricians and lighting men made ready the giant aluminum foil reflectors which might be needed. As in an army, each corps of specialists was working on its own, yet all were readying for a concerted assault on reality.

Joe Goldenberg and Dave Graham, his assistant, faced a special problem: how to lash that hand-held camera to Dave so that it would withstand any shock, while still allowing him to retain the control and mobility he would need to secure the most advantageous footage. An ordinary harness for a hand-held wouldn't make it. But Joe devised a way.

By the time Jock appeared for breakfast, things were almost ready. He was finishing his coffee when Preston Carr joined him. As Carr sat down, Jock said, "You're not in the shot. There's no need to be up so early."

"I wouldn't miss this for the world, kid." That might mean, this is going to be historic and I want to see it for myself. Or,

124

this is going to be a monumental fiasco and I want to be able to talk about it from firsthand experience.

Jock's smile was fixed, cool, measured, almost frozen. He put down his cup. He rose to go. Carr asked, "Can I ride the platform with you, boss?" Again that slight, subtle stab. Had he really meant boss? Or had he meant kid-trying-to-play-boss?

"Be my guest," Jock said, starting away.

Within an hour they were out on the shooting location and up on the platform, Carr, Joe Goldenberg, his operator, and the other men needed to crew the two cameras which were lashed together to move in tandem. Joe was busy with light meters, lens settings, reassuring himself on the mobility and speed of the two Mitchells.

Beneath the platform, equally busy, was Dave Graham; the hand-held, fully loaded, was now being strapped to him, fixed in Joe's improvised shoulder brace. Jock was down there too, checking it. Dave's nervousness was obvious. Jock's deliberate desire to avoid Dave's accusing eyes was obvious too. When he was satisfied with the camera and the brace, and when the two helpers had the battery belt that would power the camera strapped around Dave's waist, Jock patted Dave on the shoulder, then climbed to the top of the platform.

Up top, silent looks passed between Jock and Joe Goldenberg. Joe, the craftsman, worked away at his job. Now the radio contact man reported the copter pilot had sighted a herd. He was laying out his pass to drive them down from the foothills, into the arroyo, toward the platform. When he had worked it out, the pilot called in again. He estimated the herd would be thundering toward them in about six to seven minutes from the time he got Jock's signal to make his pass.

Jock surveyed the situation, uncomfortably conscious of Carr's silent but critical eyes. He took the radiophone from the chief, spoke into it, "Okay! Let 'em come!"

From the air the pilot could see the action below. The horses, at first grazing, were startled, then began to race against the whipping monster above.

From the platform Jock followed the action through his

125

binoculars. On the platform, they waited. Ready, Joe, his operator, Preston Carr, the rest of the crew.

Below the platform, Dave Graham, ready, nervous, frightened, was suddenly made more so by Jock's shouted warning from above, "Get ready down there!"

The sound of the horses and the copter was loud now. The faces on the platform were grim with danger, yet intense with anticipation. For Jock it was a mixture of elation and terror. Sound, dust, surging animals, faces, fear, hatred all came together, a great sexual experience, it would be like an orgasm.

The herd came charging at them. Joe gave the order, cool as a surgeon; an assistant at his side, gave the routine responses. Speed! Picture!

Horses, copter, crew on platform, crew below platform, all working together now. And in command, Jock Finley, with a feeling of power, great power. He cupped his hands to his mouth, dropped to one knee to shout the order below, "Go, man, go!"

Joe Goldenberg, at his own delicate work, was aware of Jock's order. Carr, as well as every man in the crew, was aware of it, too. But most of all, below, Dave Graham was aware of it. He hesitated momentarily, was shoved forward by two men whom Jock had secretly primed for just this moment. Dave was catapulted clear of the platform, thrusting out to meet the tide of terrified wild horseflesh that was surging at him from across the flat, dusty desert with the destructive inevitability of a flood of molten lava.

More terrified than the stampeding horses, yet with the automatic reflexes of a professional, Dave Graham was grinding away, till the moment when the horses surged against him, around him, to finally obscure him.

From the platform, they could see Dave go down, suddenly buried somewhere in the dust as the herd trampled over him. Every man on the platform had the impulse to stop, to cry out. But Jock shouted above it all, "Damn it, keep turning!" It was the only thing that prevented panic from erupting. The herd thundered by. The tandem cameras followed the mustangs to the limit of their angle of movement, then stopped filming.

The animals were gone. Their noise was fading into the distance.

126

Now, grim, sweaty, fearful, angry faces turned back to where Dave Graham had been.

Jock was first to move, hurtling down the platform, two rungs at a time, jumping the last four to the ground. He raced across the dry earth, through dust still suspended in air. The others followed him. Jock was the first to arrive. The first to see.

Dave Graham lay still, face down, inert, possibly lifeless. His clothes were ripped and stained with oozing blood. The camera still harnessed to him was badly damaged but not shattered. Jock turned him over. Dave's face was shattered, one cheekbone seemed smashed. Some teeth were gone. Possibly an eye.

In only moments, they had all gathered. When Jock rose from Dave's side he had to face Joe, Preston Carr, the crew. He shouted hoarsely, "Get the copter! We'll fly him into Vegas!"

In a matter of minutes, the copter was hovering over them. The men cleared to give it landing ground. It descended, whipping air and earth. Jock himself helped load Dave into the machine. He gave a single order, "Make sure nothing happens to that footage!" and climbed in. The copter rose, soared, turned to head for Vegas as swiftly as it could.

Holding bloody, wounded Dave Graham in his arms, Jock knew that for once he was having it real. Realer than he had ever hoped. Life and death, literally, were cradled in his arms. Suddenly, he was aware, the picture was too. And perhaps his career as well.

Long before the copter landed in Vegas, radiophones between location and LA carried the news. In minutes, New York knew. The wire services knew. They didn't know the details. Or if Dave Graham would live or die.

Orders had been radioed on ahead, so at the Vegas airport all takeoffs and landings were halted and an ambulance and two doctors were waiting. The copter set down. As Jock surrendered Dave Graham to the waiting doctors, he sought to read their faces, their instinctive reactions. But he got no indication as to whether Dave Graham was alive or dead. After that, it was sirens, swinging doors, hushed hospital corridors, the operating room.

Jock waited outside with the pilot. Jock became aware of Dave's blood, encrusted on his clothes, on his hands. He kept wiping his hands on his chino pants, but dried blood does not come off that way, he discovered. A nurse who noticed brought some towels, some ether. As she started to dissolve away the crusty blood, there was a call for Jock. Long distance. LA. He hesitated, decided not to duck it, went to the phone.

"Finley speaking."

"Jock? Jock?! Marty! What the hell happened?" the usually placid, calm, wise Owl was screaming. "I already got two calls from New York! What happened?"

Calmly, in deliberate contrast to the Owl's hysteria, Jock said, "We were shooting one of the wild-horses sequences. We had an accident. But I don't think it's too bad."

The nurse, who was using the ethered towel on the mass of dried blood, glanced up on hearing that obvious lie, but Jock avoided her stare.

"There has to be more to it!" the Owl was screaming. "New York already knows! That's bad! How did it happen? What's this about some crazy shot you wanted? Is that guy really dead? Are you lying to me? Your own agent?"

"He is not dead," Jock said firmly, though he did not know. For inside the operating room they were right now discussing Dave Graham's chances of recovery, and if he did recover, how much of him would be left to function. Would his eyesight be intact, including that left eye that seemed so bad? And his brain, would there be brain damage?

"Don't *do* a thing! Don't *say* a thing! Don't take any calls! Till you hear from me!" was the Owl's final advice.

The medical questions about Dave Graham were not resolved, could not be resolved in the first twelve hours. What was resolved, and very quickly, was that Jock Finley had been summoned back to LA for a meeting at the studio, at once! But he refused to leave till Dave was out of surgery. Twice he hung up when the president called from New York.

In the picture business it is suicide to hang up on a president. But it could be suicide, too, for a president to have such a tragic episode on his hands, especially with a stockholder's suit coming up. Not seven minutes later Marty was on the phone again. The president had called him, berated him, and Marty had to promise

128

that he would personally guarantee that Jock Finley would be in LA by two o'clock this afternoon!

Jock would not leave the hospital till he knew Dave Graham had survived the operation. The doctors' first assessment of injury included possible serious damage to the left eye, a shattered cheekbone, some hint of, though no definite proof of, brain damage. Also a right arm shattered in three places. However, it had been set, wired into place, with a fair chance of seventy percent mobility if it healed properly.

When Jock arrived at the studio in the Owl's Rolls-Royce, still wearing his dusty boots, dirty chinos, weatherbeaten jacket, he was an object of awe, curiosity, pity, vindictiveness, and relief. The relief was shared among those producers and directors who had now written him off, and could tell each other his career as an *enfant terrible* of the New Wave had ended for all practical purposes, and exactly as they had expected it would.

The Owl was at his side, a criminal lawyer shepherding a client into the courthouse. Jock moved briskly up the steps of the administration building. There were even a few press photographers and newspapermen trying to interview him. But there were no stops. Jock moved at a pace that made little Marty hurry at a half-trot to keep up with him.

Into the building, past the reception desk, not waiting for the elevator, Jock bounded up the two flights of stairs to the executive floor. Marty, short, stout, sweaty Owl, raced breathlessly to keep up with him.

When they reached the executive waiting room, the special, private, personal waiting room of the studio head, a secretary was ready for him. "Come right in, Mr. Finley."

Jock followed her. The Owl followed Jock. They burst into the office of the studio head. But he was not alone. As he stood behind his huge desk, he was flanked by two lawyers, the executive manager of the studio, and the chief of public relations.

The studio head snapped at the secretary who was just closing the door, "No calls! I don't care who!" Then the studio head started to attack Jock at once. From the way he related by oblique glances to his assistants, it was obvious to Jock that what he was saying had been approved in advance by the lawyers, the public relations man, the executive manager, and "New York."

"Young man, what are you trying to do? Destroy this studio? We never gave you permission for any such wild stunt. It was never mentioned in any discussion we ever had about the story, the script, the shooting schedule!"

That's right, you yellow bastard, Jock was saying to himself, get off the hook. Get the studio off the hook. Disclaim liability. Cut down the damages. Don't ask about Graham, you dirty bastards. Don't do anything but what the lawyers cautioned, and what the public relations man advised.

"We will have to issue a denial! A complete and total denial of this whole terrible tragedy! We pride ourselves on making good pictures! But also on taking care of our people first of all! We do not ask men, family men, to go out and risk their lives! We are as concerned about the families of the men who work for us as we are about the families who come to see our pictures!

"In fact, we have already called on Graham's family and promised all the help they need, medical, financial, everything! Everything!" the studio head proclaimed righteously.

Jock said softly, "Everything that is covered by insurance, you mean. Everything that you will be liable for in any event, you mean."

Jock had never seen such rage, such indignation. But then neither had he ever seen a studio head fearful of losing a two hundred-thousand-dollar-a-year job. The attack which followed would have destroyed any lesser man. But Jock held his ground firmly, his eyes fixed, unblinking, defiant. Even Marty, standing alongside him, grew paler, damper, seemed to shrink with every vile, abusive name the studio head shouted.

Finally, he came to the end of his tirade. He was breathing heavily from the sheer physical exertion involved in shouting so loud, so long.

He finished with, "Two million dollars this could cost the company in damages! Two million!"

130

So they've gone that far, Jock said to himself, right down to figuring liability, damages, all the nice sentimental details. But his own
inner reflections, bitter and sardonic as they were, didn't last long.
Because now the studio head got to the real business of the meeting.

"For taking this outrageous, unauthorized step, uncalled for by
the script, without previous notice to or knowledge of the
studio . . ."

It sounded so much like a document written by lawyers that Jock
said in a low, tough voice, "Why don't you read the fucking statement right from the paper? What are you trying to ad-lib it for?"

But the studio head, in the presence of his own assembled witnesses, continued, as he had to, "For exceeding your authority,
you are off the picture! You are off this lot! And we are moving
to have you expelled from the Directors' Guild! You are finished
in the picture business!"

At that, the Owl sagged into a chair. He was pale, his bald head
damp, glistening. To Jock, this meant that what the studio head
was threatening to do, he could do and he would do. It was not
only possible, it was positive.

Turning to the publicity chief, the studio head said, "Draw up a
press release to that effect, at once!" The publicity head nodded,
a single nod, but enough. The two attorneys, using their eyes alone,
reassured the studio head that he had said everything, done everything legally required to minimize the emergency in which the
studio found itself.

"The picture," Jock asked slowly. "What's going to happen to
the picture?"

"We'll probably close it down and forget about it."

"Somebody . . . somehow ought to make that picture," Jock
said softly. "It could be great."

The studio head looked at the Owl, at his own attorneys, at the
publicity chief. What kind of crazy kid was this? One man was
dead or dying. The kid himself had just been fired, disgraced,
destroyed. And all he kept asking about was the picture. The
studio head exploded, "For your information, young man, that
picture belongs to the studio! And the studio will decide when, and
if, the picture is ever to resume shooting! But that is no concern
of yours! And never will be again!"

131

"I've got a lot of my ideas in that script . . . I worked with the writer . . . with Carr . . . with Daisy Donnell . . . half that script is mine! Half that dialogue!" Jock protested.

"You've been paid for the work you did! The script belongs to the studio. So it is ridiculous to talk about it any longer!" the studio head said, closing the subject and the meeting.

"I want it on record that before Graham went out with that camera, *I* offered to do it myself! Do you bastards hear that? I offered to do it myself! And I will do it! Now even after what's happened!" If the studio head had been shouting before, it was a whisper compared with Jock Finley's outburst now. "So I'm going back there! I'm going to continue on that picture! If only to prove that I don't ask any man to do anything I won't do myself!"

"The subject is closed!" the studio head shouted, trying desperately to close it.

"God damn it, don't you think I am sorry for Graham? For his family? Don't you think *I* know what it can cost. But I do not sit around measuring costs! I make pictures! Because I believe in pictures. To me they are not something to be figured in terms of costs, box office, gross, net! To me they are living things. Experiences. Experiences you share with the world. Men who can't speak my language, or any language, can experience one of my pictures. People who never in their lives will own a share of stock, get a dividend, or care whether this company makes or loses money, will see my films and never forget them! They'll carry them around in their memory forever! Forever! Do you hear that? I, Jock Finley, am alive in the minds of millions of people! Not you! Not your studio, not your liability insurance, your assets, your real estate, your lawyers, your publicity men! Me! I! I have a love affair with an audience of millions of people of every race and color on this earth! That's what matters! That this picture gets made is what matters!"

When he finished, there was a silence in the room which was only broken when the phone rang. The studio head answered. "I told you, no calls! Not even New York! Vegas? Oh? Yeah?" Everyone turned to watch, to listen. "Yeah? I see. I see. If that's the way it is, what can I say?"

132

He hung up. "Graham's taken a turn for the worse." He turned to the publicity head, "Fly his wife and kids out there."

"They're already on the way," the publicity head said. "I took the liberty of sending a photographer along with them," he added.

Nice, cozy, Jock was saying to himself. Everyone is being so nice that I can hear them on the stand testifying under oath now, how nice, helpful, solicitous, careful, legal, nonliable they all were when it happened.

Jock stood there, alert, cocky, ready to attack. But the studio head spoke to the Owl. "And as for you, Mr. Executive Producer, my advice is get your client a lawyer! A very good lawyer. We do not accept any responsibility for any of this! It was all his idea! In excess of any authority he had under his contract."

That closed the meeting. Jock didn't move. Not till Marty put a firm hand on his arm and forced him to go. They started out, headed for the stairs and down. As they descended the Owl warned, "Those reporters out there, don't you say one goddamn word to them, you hear!"

Jock nodded. They started toward the doors. Through the glass they could see the reporters waiting. "You hear!" Marty repeated.

They opened the door. A torrent of questions engulfed them. Marty said loudly, aggressively, "My client has nothing to say! Except he's sorry the whole thing happened. He's very sorry!"

"Do you know the man's condition?"

"No," the Owl lied.

"They say he won't live out the day, is that true?"

"We don't know any such thing!" Marty countered.

"Is it true they're shutting down?"

"If it is, they haven't told us," Marty lied again.

"We understand Joe Goldenberg didn't want Graham to take that risk. Is that true?"

"Goldenberg is a professional cinematographer, a damn good one. He would never refuse to do anything that would help a picture along. He did not tell the man not to do it," the Owl said, playing the avoid-the-liability game himself now.

"That's a lie," Jock said softly, straight out, but in such a way that instantly everyone else grew very very quiet.

"Jock, baby, listen to me," Marty started to say.

"It was my idea. Joe Goldenberg was against it. I offered to do it myself. And if the picture starts up again, I *will* do it!"

"You would go out there with a hand-held camera and take those shots yourself?" a reporter asked precisely.

"Yes, I will," Jock answered just as precisely.

"You mean to say, after what happened . . ."

Jock interrupted, "I don't 'mean to say.' I just said it! Loud and clear! Not subject to interpretation! Or correction! Or further comment! Or explanation! I will do it myself!"

With that Jock ripped free of the Owl's restraining hand, started down the street, away from the parking lot, away from the Owl's Rolls. Reporters followed, clustering around, leeching like pilot fish to a shark. But Jock said no more. To anyone. Finally they gave up pursuing him.

The Owl stood watching, saying to himself, Crazy kid! If he kept his mouth shut, I could have got him another picture. For less money. But another picture. Somewhere.

"Burn the goddamn film!" was the order from the studio head. But such orders have been given before in the face of lawsuits. Once a noted and notorious South American beauty had done a long dance sequence without remembering to put on her panties under her dress. So there she was pubically and publicly exposed, on film, every detail of her, in full color. Her lawyers had threatened to sue unless the negative was burned. And it had been burned. Yet the next morning, frames from the printed film were circulating all over Hollywood.

So not every order of every studio head was carried out exactly as given, or when given. To make sure that this one was, the studio head called Robbie Roberts, who was in charge of the lab, called him at home, late that night. At dawn the next morning Robbie arrived at the studio to personally supervise the destruction. One of his assistants who had worked all night was waiting for him. Instead of eyes weary and red from a night of work, the man was bright, intense, highly excited.

"Robbie! You got to see this!" the assistant said. Robbie slipped into a small darkroom where the disputed, possibly fatal

134

film was run for him. It was a brief sequence, only seconds long. The color and focus were not precise. But the imprecision was powerful. The trembling of the hand-held camera, the dust which partially obscured the frightened eyes of the wild beasts in flight, the flaring nostrils, the noble heads, plus the hooves crashing in, shattering the lens, all this was not film of something which happened. This was the thing itself happening. Unadorned, even without sound, music, editing, story, anything, it was an experience on film. Once Robbie had seen it he knew he would never forget it.

When his assistant moved to put on the light, Robbie interrupted: "Run that again." The assistant rewound it, ran it again. It was more powerful the second time than the first.

Only twenty-four seconds of film. But it was amazingly powerful. What it lacked in precision it made up for, by far, in reality. The very awkwardness, the trembling, the inability to keep the action properly centered in frame, all of it said, this is not elegant fake, this is not careful, precise make-believe, this is real!

The assistant put on the light. Robbie was thinking. Protocol was involved here. Studio politics. Diplomacy. And jobs, his job. How do you let the studio head know what you know and at the same time not let him know you disobeyed orders? How do you do one other thing? Let Jock Finley know. There was some reluctance on that score. Finley was one of those brash, smart-ass, young, upstart directors who seemed more interested in being different, revolutionary, than in making the usual, fine, commercial, bread-and-butter features that keep huge studios alive, that keep people employed.

But Finley was a craftsman, Robbie conceded in his mind; maybe Finley believed that only by being different could you make great films these days. Whatever Finley's rationale or purpose, Robbie was faced with the fact that here was this bit of magnificent film, and Finley had made it. So he was a talented young man. And in big trouble.

Still there was that order, "Burn the goddamn film!" Undoubtedly an order emanating from New York, conceived by corps of lawyers and publicity men. Robbie hesitated, thoughtful,

135

as a man should be who was contemplating risking twenty-two years of tenure in an important job, risking it for a kid he hardly knew. Robbie reached for the phone, but interrupted himself to say, "Get out, Charlie."

Charlie started out, but not without saying, "I never saw any film, Robbie. I couldn't burn what I didn't see, could I?"

Robbie dialed for an outside line, meantime looking up Jock's house on Rexford. He dialed the number. It rang. No answer. Robbie considered a moment whether Finley was back on location; if he called out there that would mean the radiophone, the radio operator, and no more secrecy. Everyone on the damn location would know. That was too much risk. But suddenly the phone was picked up, answered, by a breathless Jock Finley.

"You just get in?" Robbie asked, assuming Jock had heard the phone from his own front door and raced to answer it and so was breathless.

"What the hell kind of crack is that?" demanded Jock, who was naked, in the dark, on his side, in bed and having a lit cigarette placed between his fingers by Louise.

But Robbie ignored that, talked briskly, directly.

"Finley, this is Roberts. At the lab. I have just screened about the greatest twenty-four seconds of film I have ever seen. Made by a director some people say is the biggest prick in the business. Now, if there is any way you can get this footage without getting any of us in trouble, I'll help you. Or if there is any way I can let it be known that the film exists, without getting everybody in trouble, I'll do that. But I have an order to burn that film. What do you suggest?"

Jock sat up swiftly on the side of the bed, spitting out smoke, holding the phone, thinking. Then he asked, "Do you have the can the footage came in?"

"Sure."

"What is it marked?"

"Color tests. Why?"

"Right! Now I'll tell you why! Nobody did anything but follow strict studio routine. We flew in our color tests. The lab had to give us a fast answer. Some night man on duty in the lab when the film arrived followed the routine, rushed the test through,

136

flew it right back to location so I could see it before I went on with my shooting this morning. That's what you'd do for any director of any picture shooting exteriors on location, right?"

"Right."

"Then do that! I'll leave now and fly back. And if there's any question, all your people did was receive the exposed film of a test and follow studio routine. The order to burn it never caught up with the film."

Robbie considered that briefly, then said, "Okay!"

"Robbie. I'll go to my grave before I admit I ever got any call from you. So don't worry. And thanks. Thanks a million! I'll never forget you!"

Coolly from the other end came Robbie's voice, "I'll never forget you either, Finley. Though that's not necessarily a compliment."

"Do *you* think I wanted Graham to get hurt?"

"I think you'd photograph your own mother having an abortion if you thought it would make good film." Robbie hung up.

Jock hung up, then shouted at the phone, "I'm a film-maker! Not a goddamned candidate for public office! I'm not running any popularity contest!"

Louise, not having heard what Robbie said, watched Jock as he started for the shower. From inside the shower, over the rushing water, he carried on a fierce monologue, giving her all the arguments and justifications he should have used on Robbie, and the rest of the town!

He came out of the shower, combing his wet hair, a towel covering the middle of him, and he was still talking, "Damn it, get some clothes on!"

Startled, Louise looked up angrily. "You haven't bought and paid for anything, Jocko. So don't order me around."

"Don't you want to come with me?" She was puzzled. "To the location. To see that footage!"

"Of course!"

"Then move your lovely behind out of that messy bed and get some clothes on! I'll go make the coffee!" He started toward the stairs, still in his towel.

Her first reaction was one of resentment. But she got out of the

137

bed and started for the bathroom, on the way picking up bits of clothing where she had dropped them hours earlier.

On location, inside the projector truck, the projectionist was waiting. The film was threaded up, ready to run. Jock burst into the room. Louise was following right behind.

"You got my color tests?" Jock asked, strictly playing the game.

"Color tests all threaded up and ready to go," the projectionist said playing the same game. But he was excited, expectant, interested, which projectionists never were. To them every foot of film was like every other foot of film, they never bothered to become involved. But this time it was different.

The door of the trailer opened. Pres Carr came in, in a beautiful vicuna robe, his hair still bedraggled. His 'Hi' to Jock was casual, reserved. But his "You had me waked up to see something" was to the projectionist. "It better be worth it."

Suddenly it was clear to Jock. The projectionist had not only run the film, but had asked Carr to come see it, not even knowing that Jock would be here.

"Okay! Run it!" Jock ordered.

The projectionist started the film. Jock, Carr, and Louise watched it. Jock gestured to run it again. Rewind and rerun took only sixty seconds. No one said a word. Till Carr said, "Once more!"

Rewind, rerun. Carr broke the long silence, softly, but with great feeling, "Man!" Louise reached out to touch Jock's hand. Not hold it. That would be too sentimental for Jock Finley. She just touched him, withdrew her hand, waited.

"Kid, you can make pictures for me anytime," Carr said. This was the first moment that Jock knew that Carr was using the word "kid" with genuine respect.

Suddenly Jock snapped at the projectionist, "Put that back in the can! They are not going to burn this film! They are not going to close down this picture! I'm going East to tell New York that. And I am going right now!"

Jock exploded out of there. With no apology, no farewells, he

138

deserted Louise in the early morning, hundreds of miles from home, in the company of a strange projectionist and the King of motion pictures. She was hurt and angry but had no chance to give vent to either feeling. That didn't have to be explained to Preston Carr.

"Making a picture with him is going to be exciting. But as for anything else . . . no, thank you," Carr said. "Come on, honey, I'll get you some coffee."

He opened the door for her. She smiled, because it was more graceful than crying before strangers, and she started out.

Copter to Vegas, commercial jet out of there, Kennedy Airport, time-zone changes, mid-afternoon, and Jock Finley, can of film in hand, was getting out of a cab in front of the new, tall, glass-cubicled building which was where "New York" lived, breathed, pulsated, and ran the world of motion pictures.

Up to the highest floor, past receptionist, private secretary, into the private conference room where the president of the company, fat, florid veteran of stockholders' suits, pawn of Wall Street manipulators, was conducting a conference with his legal staff, his publicity vice-president, and a doctor sent in by the insurance company for consultation on the medico-legal situation resulting from Dave Graham's injuries.

For any person to burst into that meeting against strict orders would have been an outrage. But for handsome, booted, jeaned, dirty-jacketed Jock Finley to enter was an abomination. When he slammed down the scratchy metal can of film on the highly polished walnut conference table, digging raw scars into the wood, the president turned on him violently, "How dare you come busting in here while we are trying to straighten out this terrible mess you've got yourself into!"

"Do me a favor, look at this film," Jock said softly.

"Young man, you have damaged this company severely, almost destroyed it! Our stock has dropped four points since the market opening."

"Just look at the film!"

"Well, young man, don't think we're going to take this lying

139

down! We are holding you personally responsible for every dollar of damage! It was unauthorized, the whole thing, and you know it."

"Look at the film!"

"We'll attach every dime you have! Every piece of property, every interest in every picture, every dollar you ever earn!"

"Look at the fucking film, will you?" Jock cried out, overriding the nervous, beefy president.

Nine minutes later, when the lights went on again, in the executive projection room the fat, florid man, no longer under the effect of three luncheon martinis, was staring. Just staring. So were the publicity chief, both lawyers, the man from the Wall Street banking house, and the insurance company doctor.

Before any word could be uttered, the president said to the doctor, "I'll ... I'll talk to the insurance company later. Tomorrow." The doctor knew he was being dismissed. He left.

"Well, well, well ..." the fat veteran of stockholders' suits said. He turned to Jock. "Kid ..." In the picture business, a negative answer is preceded by "Young man ..." But if the answer is going to be affirmative, it is preambled by "Kid ..." After that one word, Jock knew he had won. He could relax. He could afford to listen.

"Kid, that is one exciting piece of film," the president was saying. "It lives! It breathes!"

"Sure, because it's got Dave Graham's excited heartbeat pulsating through it. You can feel it."

"About Graham. You go back and make that picture. We'll do the right thing by Dave Graham. Maybe ... maybe ..." the fat, florid man began to daydream, "maybe we'll even get him a special Academy Award. For courage above and beyond ..."

The publicity chief was nodding, but at the same time protesting, "The Academy doesn't like to give special awards ..."

Undeterred, the fat man said, "So we'll find some other outfit. Must be somebody, some organization would give such a brave man an award just at the time the picture comes out. Anyhow,

140

we'll worry about it later. Kid, go back and make that picture! That's the main thing!"

Jock didn't move or answer. He was letting the man talk. Till the man said, "That . . . that is the most fantastic piece of film I have ever seen . . ."

"And right now the most famous," Jock added.

The fat man smiled. So did the publicity chief, who said, "People will pay to see the picture just to see that bit."

The president congratulated himself, "They'll love it at the stockholders' meeting."

He held out his hand to seal the moment. Jock didn't move to reciprocate. "Kid?" the man asked genially but puzzled.

"Mr. President, I don't have a picture to go back to. Or a job to go back to. Or a contract, either. They were all canceled. By your studio head. On your orders. In the presence of my agent, and two of your legal staff."

"I'm telling you everything is okay. Go back and make that picture." But Jock did not move. "Isn't my word good enough?"

Then Jock said the one thing that would make up for all the humiliating threats, accusations, and foul curses hurled at him in the past twenty-four hours.

"You better talk to Marty White. We're going to have to negotiate another contract to replace the one you canceled!" So saying, Jock Finley picked up his can of film and walked out.

Forty-eight hours later, with Dave Graham finally off the critical list, with the publicity department having thoroughly milked the first wave of worldwide coverage, Jock Finley returned to Nevada, his price per picture doubled.

He assembled the entire company, announced that despite any rumors the picture would go right on. Then, crowding groups of eight and ten into the projection truck, he ran the footage for them.

In full hearing of them all he instructed his assistant, "We'll start with the stampede sequence again, in the morning. Tandem Mitchells on the platform. One hand-held working out from under the platform."

Joe Goldenberg, his substitute assistant, Preston Carr, Daisy, Louise, all of them were stunned. Before anyone of them could question, protest, or ask, Jock continued, "That's right, we're going to do it all over again. Only this time there'll be one difference. I'm going to take that camera out myself! There'll be no cast calls tomorrow. Just the crew! And I want everything ready!"

Jock turned, started away. Louise and Daisy both looked to Joe Goldenberg to object. But Joe, when he was of a mind to, could be the least belligerent, most quietly stubborn of men. Only one other man in the company had the stature to argue with Jock, or convince him. Preston Carr.

Within the hour, Carr went to call on Jock, who was poring over his maps of terrain, studying the arroyo, the natural path of the herd. He did not look up when Carr came in. Or when Carr spoke to him in that straight, disarming Carr style that worked so well in pictures.

"Nobody's doubting you, kid. It took guts to conceive the scene that way. More to try it, to risk your career for it. You don't have to prove anything now."

"That footage isn't long enough to edit. You know that."

"So what! It's so famous now that just a flash of it will goose the picture. I figure that's worth an extra million to my share alone! Besides, what are you going to prove?"

"I said I would do it! And I will!"

"So you shot your mouth off to the newspapers. We all say things. Besides there's not a reporter here."

"*I* banned them. Now they'll be sure I did it because I want to cop out."

"Look, kid . . ."

"I'm going to do it!"

Carr hesitated, then closed the issue with, "Don't hurt yourself, kid." It was only a turn and a step to the door of Jock's trailer. As Pres opened the door he looked back and said, "Don't hurt *anybody*."

Louise hadn't spoken to Jock since he returned from New York. She stayed out of his way, avoided him, in fact. If she were not so frank and free, he would have suspected she was sensitive about what people might be saying about her being on location.

In late afternoon with the whole camp an army preparing for battle, and Jock, the commanding general, moving among them,

142

Louise did make her way to him. She knew how annoyed he could be with women, at a time when important things were going on. But she felt compelled to risk it.

"I have to talk to you," she said, asked, insisted.

"Look, I'm busy," but her hurt eyes made him add, "All right. Go to my trailer. I'll be there soon as I can."

She was no more successful in dissuading him than Carr had been. Jock listened, smiling all the while, that surface smile, with his eyes exuding indulgent and superior charm. When she was done, he kissed her on her good, full, red lips, and his hand went to her firm breast, fully expecting that he was going to have her there and then. But she broke loose.

"You don't care who you hurt, or how. Just so you can have whatever satisfaction you want, whenever you happen to want it or need it. Well, I need you now. I'm asking you not to get yourself killed. I can't stand it. I can't stand to be hurt. Not now. Not again."

Jock moved her back from him, gently, to look into her eyes. She was crying. She had never cried before. No matter his abuses or rudeness, no matter the jibes or jokes at her expense or about their relationship. Never tears. Till now. Nor had she ever made reference to any previous hurt, till now.

"You're really frightened for me."

"I'm frightened for me," she said softly. "I can't stand losing again."

He didn't relent. He only reached out to touch her face, to run his finger down her neck to her breast, to circle it. She remained unmoved, unaroused. She broke away, started out, stopped at the door long enough to say, "You're dangerous. You hurt people. But worse, you enjoy it."

In his anger over the rejection, he was glad she was gone. Till he remembered that only a little while before someone else had said almost the same thing—Preston Carr. "Don't hurt anybody . . ." Had the two of them been talking? Or perhaps doing more than talking?

It was more obvious at dinner as they all sat at the long executive table in the commissary—Jock, Pres, Louise, Joe Goldenberg. Daisy took her meals, all her meals, in her trailer.

Jock kept watching as he pretended to eat casually. First Pres. Then Louise. He kept watching, his suspicion building. There was something between them. He was convinced of it later, when he invited her to spend the night in his trailer. He did it in his most boyishly seductive way, the baby-blues as soft and entreating as possible. But she refused.

Jock Finley, dressed in his work clothes, chino pants, zipper jacket, came down the steps of his trailer, started across to the commissary for a first breakfast. The whole camp was coming awake early this morning. Crewmen who passed him with pieces of equipment said good morning as casually as they could. But nothing was casual this morning.

Everywhere he went to check, the loading room where he inspected the hand-held, the map room, the radio room, Joe's trailer, everywhere there were two prevailing moods: one, an enforced, business-as-usual attitude the moment Jock appeared; the other, the enormous tension that precedes inevitable disaster. No one spoke of it, no one asked or pleaded with him not to do it. It wouldn't have changed his mind. But at least it would have dispelled this uneasy undercurrent of silence.

He returned to the commissary for one last cup of coffee. Before he finished sipping the black coffee, which was too hot, Joe Goldenberg's new assistant, Eddie, came to the door to call, "Jock! Joe says the light'll be right in about forty-five minutes!"

All eating stopped, all drinking stopped. Even at the steam tables, all the chef's helpers stopped serving. Every man turned to watch Jock Finley get up, cross the commissary, and leave.

On the camera platform there was military coordination. The copter circled overhead, reporting in. Joe was in command at the cameras. Under the platform, when Jock appeared, three men stood ready to equip him with the camera, explain that it was loaded, ready to go at the touch of the button. As they strapped it onto him, a fourth man, one of the propmen, produced an object which resembled an old Roman shield except that the top had a V cut

144

into it, for easier, broader visibility. When he presented it, Jock stared questioningly.

"I thought if you use one hand to work the camera, you could hold this with the other. It could help," the propman said.

"Thanks, Albie. I'll need both hands for the camera. But thanks a million."

Albie, who had known all along it wouldn't work, yet couldn't let it happen without doing something, nodded, smiled, "We try, boss, we try."

Up on the platform, Joe Goldenberg was getting ready for his own shots with both Mitchells. In the background the pilot could be heard reporting in by radio on the position of the mustang herd, their probable path. It all seemed favorable. Now Pres and Louise climbed up to the platform to join Joe. No words were necessary. People gave way to both of them so they had a vantage point from which to watch the action.

The view from the platform was endless and impressive. Desert, pink mountains, white-hot sun. They looked out at it, Louise and Pres. Then he looked at her. She started to say, "God, I hope nothing . . ." But the pilot's voice interrupted, "Making my downward pass now."

They saw the copter in the distance starting down, seemingly toward the foothills, actually toward an unseen arroyo, hiding place of grazing mustangs. In a few moments a wave of dust began to rise, the copter pursuing it. Wave and copter moved across the desert, the dust rolling swiftly along the ground, growing in size. The copter, fifty feet above, rode herd on it. Then came an awareness, which grew into a sound, a low, thundering, rumbling, as the earth was beaten, pounded, set to vibrating by the fierce, angry hooves of a score of terrorized beasts in flight.

On the camera platform, Louise, Pres Carr, Joe Goldenberg and his assistant and crew, the radio man, all waited, ready, tense.

Beneath the platform, framed by the crisscrossing struts of iron pipe, Jock Finley waited. The loaded hand-held Reflex, which weighed only twenty-four pounds, felt like a hundred now, affixed to his body by the leather harness. The power belt around his waist seemed to inhibit his breathing. But even without it, he would have had difficulty.

Three grips stood by to catapult him forward if he should hesitate, this on his own order. Each man had a rifle cradled ready in the piping, should it be necessary, or in fact even possible, to rescue Jock. It was the kind of precaution that makes no sense, but that men take nevertheless.

Jock fingered the control button, repeating over and over to himself, Hands steady, body balanced. That was the secret of a hand-held shot. Right foot forward, left to the side somewhat. Weight on the left foot. That made the human body a virtual camera tripod with the greatest stability. For the rest, keep yourself cool. Because your heart rate and any abnormal throbbing would show up in the shot. So while some of the throbbing helped the shot breathe, made it more real and alive, too much pulsating made it jumpy and totally unusable.

So, cool was the word.

Now Jock could see it, as well as feel it under his feet. Rolling toward him, the dust wave, the thundering sound. There was a moment when he was suddenly frightened, when he must turn and try to run. But pride prevented it. His face grew tense. His eyes were hard, overdetermined. The moment was here. Proud, brave, scared to death, and determined, Jock Finley bolted from the protected area under the platform, moved out into the path of the surging, oncoming herd. Holding the camera firmly before him, he planted himself, looked down into his viewer, and started grinding.

Now they came at him!

Mustangs, fierce as they were frightened, hooves sharp, flailing, cutting deep scars in the hard desert floor, they bore down on him, around him, over him. It was a torrent of huge heads, wild eyes, foaming muzzles, great white teeth bare and sharp, muscular bodies, dust, sounds, frightened and frightening. It came at him, around him, seemingly through him.

From the top of the platform he could be seen one instant, then he was gone suddenly, out of sight, trampled beneath the herd. Dust hung thickly over everything so no eye could spot him.

146

Louise surged forward. Pres Carr held her tightly, more to still her trembling than to prevent her from moving. There was nothing anyone could do. The herd must pass. Once it was gone, once Joe had followed its flight to the furthest angle of his camera arc, an eruption of humanity took place from the platform and below. Everyone surged out, down, across the flat, dusty, hoof-beaten ground to where Jock Finley lay, crumpled, awkward, half on his side. And not moving.

Carr and Louise were among the first to reach him. The grips turned him over. If he was alive, he was unconscious, with both arms vise-tight across the camera, fists clenched. His last conscious thought, protect that footage!

Turned over, his face was bloody from one cut across his forehead, another along his cheek, clean cuts as though razors not hooves had made them.

Louise stared down. His one shoulder was twisted into a strange, awkward, unnatural position. She turned to Carr, who, having seen his share of injured men, was actually more concerned than she. She buried her face in his muscular shoulder. He patted her head in an instinctive but useless gesture of comfort.

A jeep pulled up. The company doctor leaped out, bent down over Jock. With one hand he sought a pulse, with the other he probed for the more obvious signs of skull fracture. He was tense, noncommittal, avoiding the demanding faces that crowded around and above him. To carry on his examination, he removed the camera from Jock's deathlike grasp and shoved it aside as if it were debris.

Joe Goldenberg picked it up, handed it to his assistant. "Unload it. Carefully. Fly the stuff right back to the lab!"

The doctor evaluated the situation in a long silence, then leaned down again. Chest, ribs, stomach, face, eyes, cheekbones, shoulders, including the oddly twisted one, he did a swift examination of them all before deciding, "Help me get him into the jeep. But careful!"

Tenderly, four men lifted Jock, placed him in the back seat of the jeep. As the vehicle pulled away slowly, a voice from the group said softly but sarcastically, "Thus cracks a noble heart."

Preston Carr turned, his face angry-white under his deep tan.

147

"You don't have to love him. But the bastard did have guts."

They pulled up to the first-aid trailer in a jeep, Carr and Louise. The man posted at the foot of the steps had orders not to let anyone in. But no one refused admittance to Preston Carr.

Inside the trailer, on the examining table, all clothing cut away, lay Jock Finley. A nurse assisted the doctor who continued to make his examination, carefully, very carefully, for fear of aggravating a hemorrhage if there was one, or starting one if there wasn't.

One thing that was reassuring, Jock's lean, tense chest showed he was breathing.

"Pulse?" Carr asked.

"Not too bad."

"Fractures?"

"No. Shoulder dislocation."

"Hemorrhages?"

"No evidence. Yet."

"Head?"

"Take a day or two, unless we fly him into Vegas for X-rays."

"Well?"

"Rather not move him."

The radio man, hat in hand, as though he were making a condolence call, entered to say softly but urgently, "LA's on one phone. New York's on the other."

"Tell them when I know something definite I'll call them," the doctor answered, without interrupting his work.

"I can't tell that to New York," the man protested.

"Then get somebody who can," the doctor said, unperturbed, cracking an ammonia capsule under Jock's nose. At first there was no reaction. Then Jock instinctively pulled away, slightly but enough to encourage the doctor. He pursued him with a fresh capsule, then a third one, each time with increasing responses from Jock.

Finally there was a flicker of consciousness, one eye opened. Then the second eye. But it was a vague, traumatized look, recognizing nothing, no one. Carr and the doctor exchanged flickers of looks. Neither said anything. The doctor pursued Jock, with more testing, lightly applied pressure, ammonia capsules. The nurse, meantime, was dabbing away blood from Jock's face with gauze sponges. The ooze of blood was slowing.

Suddenly the doctor put aside ammonia capsule and stethoscope. He moved around the table, took the oddly twisted shoulder, assayed it a moment. Then using great force and with no warning, he snapped it back into its normal position in the socket.

There was a scream from Jock so piercing that even those company members not immediately outside the trailer could hear it and came running. It was a terrifying scream. But it did prove that he was still alive.

Inside, pain had brought Jock back to a degree of consciousness that medication had not. He opened his eyes, wildly blinking, unfocused. He closed them. He began to breathe irregularly. Sweat covered his chest, erupting out of his pores in a visible flow, oozing, riveting down his chest. He was gasping more than breathing.

"What's your name?" the doctor asked. "Your name! Tell me your name!" He was holding Jock's eyes open with his fingers, staring into them, searching. He reached for an instrument. The nurse passed it. It was a probe light and magnifier. He held one of Jock's eyes open, used the instrument, looked long and deep into his pupil. He kept asking, "Your name?"

All the while Jock's chest was heaving with a combined gasping, breathing, sighing that made Louise turn away and seek comfort against Preston Carr's shoulder. But Carr was staring at the doctor, trying to read his reactions. "Your name. What's your name?" the doctor persisted.

"Finley?" Jock answered unsteadily. "Finley?"

"Where are you?"

"Here."

"Where's here?"

Jock seemed to drift off again. The doctor applied some pressure to the reset shoulder. The pain brought Jock back. He came to consciousness, saying over and over, "Finley . . . Finley . . . Jock Finley . . . Jock Finley . . ."

"Where are you?"

"Nevada . . . location . . . picture . . ."

149

"What happened to you? Do you remember?" Jock didn't respond, seemed to drift off. The young doctor applied more pressure to the shoulder. The pain brought Jock awake with a gasp.

"For God's sake, give him something!" Louise exploded.

The doctor snapped at Carr. "Get her out of here!" Louise left by herself, without any urging from Carr.

"What happened to you, do you remember?" the doctor repeated.

"Horses. Went out . . . wild . . . mustangs . . ." Jock said haltingly, but breathing a bit more smoothly now.

"Feel anything?"

"Pain. Hurts."

"Bad?"

"Oh-huh."

"Okay," the doctor said, continuing with his examination, still searching for signs of possible internal injuries. For some moments, Jock lay still, breathing unevenly, gasping from time to time, sweating, bleeding less and less, his face becoming cleaner under the tender, careful hands of the nurse.

Finally, he spoke on his own, unasked, "Pain . . . give me something . . . huh?"

The doctor neither responded nor interrupted his examination, which centered on Jock's head and eyes again.

"Doc?" Now it hurt even to utter one syllable at a time. "The pain," as though reminding him.

"I'd rather not. It might mask symptoms." That made sense, even to Jock. He tried to nod, though the pain was quite bad now.

Gradually, carefully, precisely, the doctor established the facts; no obvious skull fractures, no serious internal injuries, a dislocated shoulder which would heal, cuts and bruises, scars of which he would carry the rest of his life. He was at least in good enough condition to be flown to Vegas for extensive X-rays to confirm or refute the diagnosis.

The copter was standing by, refueled and ready to take off. When Jock was put aboard the small craft on a stretcher, it did not leave room enough for the doctor, so he was to follow in a second copter.

150

The first took off, leaving the doctor, Preston Carr, and Louise surrounded by the crew. As they waited for the second copter to touch down, Louise asked the doctor, "Shouldn't you have given him something for the pain?"

Carr explained to her, "He doesn't want a sedative to mask any symptoms."

But the doctor said angrily, "And I also wanted to teach that sonofabitch some respect for the human body."

Before anyone could answer, the copter was overhead, the whirring blades the only sound that could be heard.

X-rays, neurological tests, genito-urinary tract exams, all confirmed the young doctor's estimate of damage.

In three days, Jock was free to leave the hospital, one arm in a sling to protect the healing shoulder, two white patches on his lean, now-not-so-brown face. His photograph, as he left the hospital in Vegas, smiling, left arm raised in victory, was a wirephoto, worldwide; his grin, accented by the bandage patches, a symbol of inspiration to millions of loyal new generation kids who worshipped every deed of every New Wave director.

The footage which Jock had taken was better than Graham's. But the color could be matched and corrected so that all the footage, about one minute and four seconds now, could be cut together. It would make a short but magnificent sequence, probably the action high point of the entire film, certainly the most publicized scene of the entire film.

Both the studio and New York breathed easier, happier. Especially New York. What a saga of courage and inspired, dedicated picture-making to relate to the stockholders at the interim meeting, which was now only a few weeks away.

When Jock arrived back on location, he was greeted with a respect and loyalty that few directors achieve, even after winning an Academy Award.

Only Louise was not there. She had left, without a note, a phone call, or any message. Jock could not bring himself to ask Preston Carr about her. Carr never volunteered. She was just gone. Secretly, Jock assured himself he was better off. He should devote

151

himself totally and completely to the film. And Louise was a strange girl, he kept telling himself.

CHAPTER

5

WHAT fascinated me about this story from the very first time I read it," Jock Finley was saying, "was its pure and poetic symbolism."

They were having lunch in Jock's trailer. Daisy Donnell. Preston Carr. And Jock Finley.

"Of course, all the nuances, the existential components, the inner philosophical outlook, all these must be alive and implicit in every scene without intruding upon the action or slowing the pace."

Daisy hardly touched her food, so busy was she nodding, giving every evidence of being involved. Pres Carr listened too, silent, thoughtful, enigmatic, betraying neither rejection nor acceptance. Occasionally, he sipped his coffee, which had grown tepid and somewhat unpleasant.

"Of course, the prime symbol is the mustang itself. As it refuses to submit to being captured, caged, tamed, defeated, so you two, the last few, strong, daring human beings, the leading characters in this film, refuse to be caged, ground down, forced to conform to a mechanized, materialistic society."

Daisy listened, conveying every outward sign of deep thought. Her pretty face, plain of all cosmetics now, reflected her intense desire to understand and believe. But her soft, myopic eyes more truthfully betrayed great puzzlement. She needed to believe, needed to be involved, needed to be sure she was doing something more than merely another moving picture. This was a *film!* which was almost as holy as "real acting." She had to believe she was engaged in building a character deep from within herself, was becoming the actress she had failed to become in New York. And Jock Finley knew she needed that.

"Of course, we'll shoot in sequence, as nearly as possible..." Carr looked sharply toward Jock, for this was the first he had heard of that. Jock hastened to explain to Carr, by saying to Daisy, "Just as I promised you we would."

If originally it had been a rash promise made during courting time when he was wooing her to do the picture, Jock knew now that he could not lie to a girl as insecure as Daisy Donnell.

"We'll run through your opening scene this afternoon. Where you and Pres meet for the first time. We may not even go for a take. We'll just get used to each other. Okay?"

Daisy nodded. Pres Carr nodded.

"Whenever you're ready, dear," Jock said.

"I'll . . . I'll need a little time, alone. In my trailer. To prepare." It was a word she had learned in New York. It was pathetic, it was almost amusing. Pres Carr was quicker than Jock to say, "Take your time, honey. I'll be ready whenever you are."

She nodded thankfully and left Jock's trailer. When it seemed safe, because she was out of earshot, Jock rushed to explain, "I had to promise her we'd shoot in sequence otherwise . . ."

But Carr interrupted, as though no explanations were necessary, or else that none would suffice, "Look, kid, I'll be in my place with my tax man. Call me when she's ready."

There was an air of great expectation about this scene. It would be the first time that the King and the Sex Symbol had ever worked together. The entire company and crew enjoyed the same kind of vicarious, nervous participation that prevails at World Series time, at a Presidential convention or the coronation of a Queen of England.

Hundreds of requests to witness this shooting had poured in on Jock from newspapers, magazines, and syndicated columnists, who were famous personalities in their own right. All were turned down. All at Jock's firm insistence. The publicity chief himself flew out, sent by New York to beg, plead, threaten. Still Jock refused. Any piece of creative art should be allowed to live first and be exploited later, he decreed.

Inwardly, he was afraid, terribly afraid that Daisy would not be able to stand the pressure. So he was going to take much time, under the right, private circumstances to get her started securely, safely. For her first scene there was not to be a single outsider on location. No one who was without a specific job on this picture was permitted within miles of the location.

That turned out to be a coup. For the curiosity, the guessing game as to why, led to enormous space in the press. Most of it had to do with a possible romance between Carr and Daisy.

For the world's first view of Daisy Donnell in Jock Finley's first Western, he wanted an angle and a shot that would provoke and intrigue the critics.

Using Daisy's stand-in, he worked out the take for Joe Goldenberg and the crew. Although the film was in color, they would start tight on what seemed to be a big black-and-white shot of a bull's eye target, which filled the entire wide, wide screen. However, unlike the usual fixed target, this one would start to move. Actually, it undulated, it lived as the camera followed it, keeping it in full screen perspective. Then, on cue, the camera held and the target moved away. When it got far enough away it became clear that this was no target but a dress, on a girl. On a girl with a lovely, luscious behind which moved with tantalizing, sexy rhythm as she walked away on unsteady high heels down what turned out to be a dusty desert road. She carried a battered suitcase. And she was headed into the distance, which was nowhere, infinity!

That was the entire first take of Daisy Donnell. They walked through it several times with her stand-in. Then Jock described for Joe Daisy's reverse close-up, her reaction during which she was to be attracted by some object in the distance. Then in her point-of-view shot that object would turn out to be Preston Carr, as Linc, a hobo cowboy on horseback, riding toward her from the distance.

155

So they would meet. Two solitary souls, in the vastness of the great south western desert. A strange chance meeting.

From sheer curiosity, Preston Carr sat in his camp chair watching the scene get set up. If Carr liked it, he concealed that fact very well. Meantime, Jock moved about with an excitement of creativity which he hoped would infect the rest of the company. When they had walked it a few times for Joe's camera crew, and when Jock was finally ready to shoot, Lester Ansell, Jock's assistant, called out to his own assistant, "Get Miss Donnell! Stewie, get Miss . . ."

But Jock interrupted with protective concern and indignation, "Just a minute! *I'll* get Miss Donnell."

Carr's eyes, which accentuated that enigmatic smile so famous the world over, followed Jock as he went to her trailer, knocked, said something, waited. The door opened. Daisy came out, attired in a bull's-eye dress that matched the one her stand-in wore while they were lining up the shot. All eyes were on her now. Everyone on the set realized suddenly how very different two attractive blond girls could be, even when dressed exactly alike. For Daisy was vastly different from any other girl in the world of her shape, size, and dimensions.

People would always believe that the secret lay in her breasts or her behind or her parted lips or her blond hair. But one could duplicate those precise attributes, and sizes, and that hair color a hundred times over in one cast call in Hollywood yet never find another Daisy Donnell. Her uniqueness was something inside her, something indefinable.

Taking her hand, Jock led her to the place where the camera would pick her up. He explained meticulously what she would do, the way she would walk, on those run-over high heels. The way she would carry that battered bag. And precisely what the camera would be doing under Joe's expert guidance . . . all the while that she. . .

But the look on Daisy's face, the moistness that flooded her eyes, interrupted him. She turned suddenly, started away, running toward her trailer, deserting the King, Pres Carr, and the entire company. But most of all, worst of all, deserting Jock Finley in the middle of his explanation. He was speechless, gripped by that

156

sudden terror that can only attack a creative person when he suddenly realizes that he may have lost a crucial gamble, one that could ruin months of work, years of work, possibly damage his entire career.

He knew it was going to take a great and convincing performance on his part to jolt her out of her terror. He started after her, intercepted her, coming round between her and the trailer, her refuge.

"Honey . . . wait, listen to me!" She turned away. He darted to confront her. She was weeping. He put his good arm around her, using the hand to press her head comfortingly against his chest. Now Joe was here. Followed by Pres Carr. With a gesture of his eyes, Jock asked for privacy from Joe, who left. But he wanted Pres to remain. So he did.

"Honey, we discussed all this. Remember?"

"You said it was going to be different! You said this time they'd see the real Daisy Donnell!" She was crying now, a simple, hurt child. "And the very first shot is my ass close up!"

"Honey. Honey. Listen to me. Listen to Jock, will you, baby?" Whether she was crying too much to talk or was actually listening, her gasping sobs gave Jock the chance he needed.

"Daisy, darling, listen to Jock, will you? But I want *all* of you to listen! Daisy Donnell, picture star, woman, little girl, sex symbol, actress, all of you. Yes, the first shot is your behind. Deliberately, purposefully. Planned that way. There, right on screen, in a wide, wide close-up, sixty-two feet wide on the Music Hall screen, is the most famous ass in the world! Accented by the special bull's-eye dress that I had designed just for you. Just for your world-famous behind.

"Now you don't think I'm doing that just to get another shot of Daisy Donnell's behind? Do you? What the hell kind of director would I be, if that's all I aimed to do? First of all, no shot in any film of mine does only one thing. It should do many things, all at once. It should have meanings and values for the story, the character, the style of the film. It should make a comment on our times. *Every shot*.

"But most especially, the first shot of a leading character in an important film must do that. We have to reveal a whole lifetime in

157

a single shot. Arouse sympathy, pity, understanding, curiosity.
Who is she? What is this obviously attractive, sexy girl doing walking on out-of-place high heels in such a remote part of the world?
How did she get there? Where is she going? What's the story of her
battered suitcase?

"Is she lost? Abandoned? Or running away? It's all in that one
shot. And the reason we start close on your behind is very simple,
and dramatically very sound. To create anomaly. Who would expect that when we widen our perspective from your behind in
black and white we're going to show that you are walking all alone
along a desert road and there is a great, wide, color-rich vista
out there? They'll sit up and say, Hey, what's going on? What's
this all about? We have created curiosity! Suspense!

"But more than that, about your character, about you. Remember I told you I wanted *you* in this picture! Not the character Rosie,
but you! Daisy Donnell! Remember?"

She was crying less now, listening intently, nodding, the begin-
nings of belief started to appear in her eyes.

"Remember, honey? Well, this is where we start to do it to the
critics. The wise guys. The experts. Give them the finger, right
where they tingle. First we are going to make them sit back and
say, Oh-oh, here it comes, another of Daisy Donnell's 'performances' with the undulating behind, the low cleavage. And then ...
then as the film goes on we are going to show them the real Daisy
Donnell ... the talented Daisy Donnell. We are going to transform
Daisy Donnell from the world's most famous piece of ass into
Daisy Donnell, actress, real star, Academy Award winner!"

She heard. She listened. She seemed to believe. He took her
hand in his one useful one and said softly, almost crooning into her
ear, "We are going to make them apologize in print for every
snide, nasty thing they ever said about you, darling. We are going
to do it by disarming them at the outset, and then cutting their
balls off by what we show them before this film is over! That's what
we agreed! Remember?"

She nodded, feeling safer, surer, now that he had given her
a reason for doing the very thing she had never wanted to do
again.

"Now, go inside and let Stella make you up again. Then

158

whenever you're ready, you come out and say, I'm okay now, and we'll do the shot."

She thought a brief instant, she nodded, her wet eyes making her even more pathetic, more appealing than usual. She started into her trailer but he grasped her hand, held it, kissed her tenderly on the lips, then released her.

Jock turned away, the relaxed pitch of his body, the rhythm of his breathing, everything indicated the relief he felt at having overcome a moment of great crisis. Pres Carr was waiting.

"Kid, if there's an Academy Award in this picture, you'll get it." Jock's momentary swell of pride was quickly deflated when Carr added, "For acting."

The opening shot of Daisy was done. As was the reverse shot of Pres Carr on horseback. Then came the more intimate moments, with dialogue. The opening lines between Linc, hobo cowboy, and Rosie, runaway dance-hall girl, who was walking because she had gotten a lift, had had to fight off a horny ranch hand, and was stranded now in the middle of nowhere as a consequence.

Jock Finley learned what many directors, good and bad, had learned before him. With Daisy Donnell you lived from long stretches of insecurity, to brief moments of confidence, to stretches of insecurity. There was never an entire day during which she believed in herself or in what she could do.

Yet, through it all, Jock was patient, kind. He explained, motivated, did the scene himself, even having some fun with it, so the crew and Pres Carr would not grow too restive, too resentful of Daisy's frightened, dilatory peculiarities.

One bit, six lines, forty-seven words, they did over and over. She tried, dared, did it better certain times than others. Once she wished to try it her own way, and she was quite terrible. She knew it, ran away, had to be seduced back.

By the time Joe said they didn't have sufficient light to work with, there was enough footage so that Jock thought he could cut it into a scene. The exposed film was packed, coptered back to the lab to be processed that same night. Crew and company wrapped for the day.

An hour later, in Jock's trailer, he was inviting Carr, "Pour yourself something, Pres." Carr moved to the little bar to find his favorite brand, his private stock. He remarked on it. Which gave Jock a chance to polish an apple with, "I learned a lot about high-class booze as well as high-class picture-making that day at your ranch."

It was a compliment, but it didn't change the tenuous air. Carr poured, sipped, appreciated, then turned to Jock.

Before Carr could say a word, Jock anticipated him: "I know what you're going to say. Do I think she's going to make it? Yes! She's going to make it! But she's going to need more than my help. She's going to need your help. That's why I asked you to drop by."

"I did that scene nineteen times with her! I haven't done nineteen takes of anything in my entire career! Doesn't she study her lines? Why isn't she prepared when she gets there?"

"Prepared?" Jock countered "She's over prepared! She knows every word. And, unfortunately, five different ways to say it. It's her conflicts, her inner conflicts that do it. That's why I have to ask you, at the outset, please, please, Pres, be a little patient?"

Carr did not answer readily.

"After all, it's her first day. She'll get better, easier as she goes along."

"What if she doesn't?" Carr asked.

"She will! But you could help." Now Jock began to invent a little fable of his own. "You see . . . you see she told me that she thinks you don't like her . . . that you resent her."

"It's not her. It's the way she works," Carr said.

"Then let her know you don't dislike her," Jock pleaded "It'll help us all."

"Well . . ." Carr considered, "if it will help the picture . . ."

"It will!" Jock urged and secured Carr's nod of assent finally.

Behind his baby-blues Jock was saying: Actors are all alike. Give them a project, something to worry about, a problem to solve, and you can keep them out of trouble.

But the trouble, when it came, did not originate with Preston Carr. The next day, after lunch, they were setting up the first shot, a sequence in which Linc was explaining to Rosie what drove him to become a hobo cowboy. He was using the whole wide desert

160

panorama to do it. This was picture-making at its best; words—spare, colorful, expressive, Preston Carr's unique voice, his very sincere, understated delivery, Daisy Donnell's face with reactions subtle, wide-eyed, naïve, and, for intercutting, shots of the desert, its vast reaches, the far-off mountains, the sky, the sun. When this scene would be finally cut together, as Jock was cutting it in his fervent imagination, it would be poetry, touching and strong.

They had finished the master scene. They were doing Carr's close-ups, where he was looking out at the vast vista and speaking. There was silence all around, a silence of tribute from camera crew, grips, electricians, assistants, everyone, even after the scene ended.

Jock moved from behind the camera, past the men holding the reflectors, right up to Preston Carr. In front of the whole company he held out his hand, "There isn't another actor in the world could do that scene the way you just did it." Turning toward Joe Goldenberg, Jock called out, "That okay for you, Joe?"

Joe made an okay sign, adding, "We could do it again for protection."

Jock called back, "You can't protect a scene like that! That's a one-and-only, a once-in-a-lifetime! Man, that is history!"

Preston Carr, the King, the best there was and the most famous, blushed a little under his deep tan. Even though he suspected he was being conned, he liked it. Because, goddamnit, it had been a great take and he could feel it. And this arrogant, aggressive, grasping con-man of a kid *was* a director.

Carr was frank enough to admit to him, "You know when I first saw that dialogue, when we talked about that scene, I said to myself, I can't say that crap. Now, I understand what you meant, about poetry."

"Thanks, Pres, thanks."

Jock walked away. Inside himself he was seething with pride. He had won. Preston Carr had finally decided to put himself into Jock Finley's hands. But as he was riding that great wave of elation, the radiophone man came running toward him. "Jock . . . Jock!" It was an affectation, that all his crew call him Jock. It created an atmosphere of informality. It also sustained the boy-genius legend. Jock Finley, youngest man on the set, was boss.

161

"Jock ... Jock!" the man was saying, quite obviously perturbed. "The studio. Greenberg wants to talk to you. Urgent!"

It was unfortunate, a damaging blunder. No message of obvious urgency should ever be delivered within hearing of even one crew member of a picture set. It leads to a dozen rumors, none of them constructive. Jock joined the radio man, raced to the trailer. When Jock picked up the phone, he could hear Greenberg, studio head, bellowing, "Where is that arrogant young prick?"

So, as sweetly as he could, for the most acid affect, Jock said, "I'm sorry I kept you waiting, *sir*."

"Oh. Oh! Look, Jock, sweetie, I got to talk to you right away!"

"Well, by all means, talk, *sir*."

"Look, Jock baby, some of the guys here at the studio ..."

Jock Finley, and any picture director, knew that particular preamble even better than they knew, "We, the People of the United States." For whenever a studio head had a feeling but was afraid of going on record with it, which was most of the time, he started out saying, "Some of the guys ..." So that if he were wrong, which was most of the time, he could later disclaim the entire idea.

"If it was just one man's opinion, sweetie, I'd say screw it, I go along with Jock Finley. But they are unanimous, sweetie, *u-nan-i-mous*."

"What's the problem? *Sir*?"

"The girl, Jock! Everyone here in the projection room is terribly let down about the girl! We ran the stuff twice. It just isn't Daisy Donnell. And she looks awful!"

"I tried to tell you she would be different. That was the whole angle, for the critics, for the promotion. See the *new* Daisy Donnell. Remember?"

"New is new. But this is nothing."

"Let me worry about that."

"Seven million dollars ... maybe eight before we're done. That's without prints and advertising. You don't mind if *I* worry a little, too, do you?"

"Be my guest!" Jock said, his irritation beginning to erupt.

"We think, here at the studio ..." the head began.

"You think! You like to think you think! All studio executives

162

always want the female star to be lighted to look beautiful. Well, maybe the scene itself, the reality of the scene, demands that she be lit harshly. After all, she's out in the desert. She's been walking in the hot sun for hours. How could any woman in the world look beautiful?" Jock demanded.

"A star could," the studio head said, beginning to become irritated now. "A star should!" he added angrily. "Anyhow, that's all theoretical now. Because we think . . . here at the studio, we think you should replace the girl . . ."

It was said haltingly, which impressed Jock all the more. If it had been said forthrightly, overbearingly, he could have shouted it down. But said haltingly, with full knowledge of what it could mean to the picture to make such a radical cast change, that meant the studio head was serious. That he was suddenly fearful of the whole project and of its chances for success.

"Change the girl? You can't mean that!" Jock was saying.

"We mean it, we mean it! And do it right away, before we get in too deep. You shoot around her for a few days. We're finding out who's available who could be right for the part. We'll check with you every few hours."

"I'm not going to do it!" Jock Finley said.

"If you read your contract, you'll do it!" the studio head said firmly. So they had already checked that too, Jock realized. They must be panicky. But he had only one answer, "Don't worry! I'll get the performance out of her."

"If what we saw is any indication . . ."

"I said I'll get it! I'm the director!"

"Director? Based on what we saw, you couldn't direct traffic!" the studio head was bellowing.

"Look, mister, I am making a picture! I have a cast and crew waiting. I cannot stand here and listen to your old stupid cliché jokes about directors. Now, if you ever have anything of importance to say to me, do call. But till then, shut up!"

The stunned radio man heard it all. Jock could see the look on the man's face. So he seized him by the front of his zipper jacket, saying, "You're the only one who knew. So if a word of this gets out, I'll kill you! Mind you, I'm not just using the word. I will not beat the hell out of you. Or fire you. *I will kill you!*"

163

"Look, boss, I take an oath ..." the frightened man stammered, because he believed implicitly that Jock would kill, over a picture.

"Now, they'll be asking, all of them, what this was about. And I am telling you. It was about how great yesterday's stuff was. Got it?" The terrified man nodded.

Jock calmed down somewhat. One thing he hated was to lose his temper unintentionally. He considered it the prime sign of insecurity in a director. It was the equivalent of tears in a woman. So now he had to repair his image. "She's a great girl, but very sensitive. This would destroy her. We can't let that happen. Can we?"

"No, sir," the radio man promised.

"Good. I'm glad you understand." Jock felt free to leave the radio trailer now.

He walked back into the work area, saying, with a broad smile, "They loved yesterday's stuff! Loved it!" He went straight to Preston Carr, playfully punched at his chin, that sign of loving admiration which men use when they are too shy to overtly admire another man. Then he took Daisy's hand, kissed her fingertips. Thus the whole company was told that Daisy's first rushes must have been received with fantastic acclaim back at the studio.

The shooting went on. Daisy Donnell was secure, and quite good. For the next few hours.

When shooting wrapped for the day, and Preston Carr started back to his trailer, Jock caught up with him.

"Pres ... can I talk to you? Man to man? I'm in trouble."

Carr said simply, "I know. The rushes. They don't like them back at the studio." Jock would rather have said it in his own way, for the right effect.

"You guessed. How?"

"That phony bit," Carr imitated the jaw-punching. "Then the hand-kissing. Christ, kid, how obvious can you get?"

"You think she suspected?"

"I don't know. Now, kid, listen to me. You're in a spot. You're making an important picture. Maybe the most important of your life. You don't help it by trying to con me. You've got talent.

164

You're a good director. And I'll help. All I can. But just stop the horseshit. At least with me. Okay?"

There was nothing quite so difficult for Jock Finley as simple, plain talk unless it was a simple straightforward emotion. It was easy to handle lying, groveling, domineering studio heads. Or New York. That game Jock played and played well.

"Pres, I wasn't trying to pull anything on you. The jaw-punching was just to set it up, so she'd believe the hand-kissing bit. Because . . . well . . ."

"They're telling you to reshoot yesterday's stuff." Jock shook his head. "I think you should," Carr said. But Jock shook his head again. "Well, what is it then?"

"They want to replace her."

"Oh, God," Preston Carr said. It was a soft, compassionate, honest reaction.

"Exactly," Jock said.

"What I said yesterday, forget it. I'll do whatever I can. I don't want this to happen to her," Carr volunteered.

"I'm glad you feel that way. Because I'm going to need all the help I can get to fight them. If it comes to a showdown, if they ask for your opinion, what will you tell them?"

"I'll . . . I'll tell them I think she can make it," Preston Carr promised.

"Thanks, Pres. I'll never forget this!"

"Kid, I've made more pictures than you ever will. Good ones. And bad ones. Successes that deserved to be failures. And failures that deserved to be successes. But no one picture, no one anything, is worth a human life. That's why I won't let them replace that girl. Even if this picture goes down the drain. Eight million dollars? So what! She's made hundreds of millions for this industry. They owe her respect, kindness, indulgence. And a chance. You owe her a chance. Not because it will enhance *your* reputation. But because it might save her life. As I get on, I value that more and more. As things get bigger and people get smaller I value people more and more. We're going to keep her on this picture. And she is going to give a performance. And we'll walk away from this with a little respect for ourselves. Okay?"

Preston Carr held out his hand. Jock shook it. While their hands gripped, Carr asked suddenly, but softly, "Tell me, kid, you going to bed with her?" Jock reacted with what he thought was proper modesty. His eyes shyly announced, gentlemen-don't-talk-and-I-am-a-gentleman, thereby confirming precisely what was going on.

"Instead of that, maybe you should try making love to her." Before Jock could answer, Carr added quickly, "I got some papers on a complicated land deal and I have to give Harry an answer by midnight."

He started away, toward his own trailer.

The second day's footage of Daisy Donnell did nothing to re-assure the studio. By the end of the day, the rushes had been flown to New York by special courier, screened, returned. Now New York was backing up the studio, insisting on a replacement.

Under the guise of an inspection tour of all company films-in-production so that he could make a firsthand report to the stock-holders at the interim meeting the next week, the president himself arrived on location. Wearing new boots, new denims, new Stetson, he looked in all respects the florid, fat, over-alcoholed company president from New York trying to simulate a southwestern native. He was introduced all around, had his picture taken with Preston Carr, did all the things that big-city hicks do when they come to picture locations far away from home.

The shooting went on. Jock was working on the scenes he had lined up and intended to shoot. But the president's presence made Daisy even more tense, more uncertain; twice she broke down, rushed back to her trailer in tears.

At that point the president put his arm around Jock Finley, feigning fatherly fondness, and led the way to Jock's trailer. There he sat Jock down, refused his offer of a drink, and said, "Look, Finley, I came out here hoping to see for myself that we are wrong. That the girl can cut it. But it is obvious now ..."

"Showing up the way you did, you made her nervous."

"That girl was born nervous." He was closer to the truth than he knew, or cared to be. "But the point is, we are fools, all of us, to risk the company's money, or *our careers*"—and he injected that

166

phrase with all the deftness of a hostile nurse handling a rectal thermometer— "on a girl too nervous to remember her lines. Or to follow direction. You could be the greatest director in the world, no one would know it from what that girl is doing. For your own sake, don't be stubborn . . . "

Jock shook his head. "Tell you what," the president went on, "suppose, for a price, a fancy price, I could get Marty White to convince her to quit the picture. She is not fired, not replaced. She quits. She's quit pictures before."

"She's wanted to quit before. She doesn't want to quit now." He did not say, she can't quit now and survive.

"Kid, why're you protecting her?" the president asked.

"I am not protecting that girl for any reason except that I am protecting your picture, Mr. Wiseguy!"

"Are you screwing her?" he asked.

"You're the one who kept screaming, 'an eight-million-dollar picture, we need protection!' Remember the day I called you and said we finally had her, how you promised me the moon! Well, now that we got her we're going to stay with her," Jock persisted.

"So you *are* screwing her!"

At that point Preston Carr entered, without knocking, without a word of apology. It was obvious he had been listening.

The president turned to Carr, invited his help in dealing with this intransigent young director.

"Tell him! Tell our young genius she can't cut it! She'll never be able to cut it!"

Carr, cool, soft-spoken, not only ad-libbed the scene, but played it with impeccable conviction. "I think she *can* do it. And even if she couldn't, I'd still insist on having her in the picture. You see, she and I . . . well, we . . . ."

He never did finish that sentence. But the president made it unnecessary. "You mean, *you* are . . ." and he made a vague gesture indicating that Carr and Daisy were having an affair.

"It's both of us on the picture or neither of us. That's the way *I* want it."

It was the first time, and the only time, that Jock Finley ever saw Preston Carr use his weight as a star.

167

"Well, if that's ... uh ... the situation ... " the president fumbled, speechless, this man who snapped at waiters, barbers, shoe-shine men, secretaries, and unfortunate projectionists in darkrooms.

Carr closed the matter. "That's the situation."

"Then for God's sake," the president said, turning to attack Jock, "get a performance out of her!"

Carr interceded again quietly, "Look, Mr. President, around here we don't shout. Voices carry in the desert. If we have something to say, we say it softly. For example, 'Mr. Finley, do the best you can with that girl. Because she is overanxious. She is scared to death. She *has* to succeed, this time. She can't run away from another picture. Will you please?' That's what we say. Around here. Mr. President."

The president's florid face grew redder still. Now suddenly he wished he had that drink in hand. He needed it. Carr was staring at him. So he turned to Jock. "Look, kid ... Mr. Finley ... you know how important this picture is. To all of us. So do the best you can with that girl? Will you? Please?"

"I'll do my very best," Jock promised.

"Good ... good," the president said. "Now, I've taken up a lot of your time. You men have work to do. But it's been a very ... very helpful talk ... very enlightening. I'll tell the stockholders how devoted you are. To the picture. To the interests of the company. I'll tell them about the spirit of cooperation of the whole cast, the crew ... everybody."

"We'll appreciate it," Preston Carr closed the meeting.

The president left. Jock turned to express his appreciation to Preston Carr, but Carr cut him off.

"Kid, till I was an actor I was a roustabout. A day's work here, a few hours work there. For a meal, a night's sleep. It is not good for any man to be dependent on another man for his job, his next meal, his existence. I don't like men who take advantage of that. So I have an aversion to presidents. To bosses. To any man who can tell another man what to do, and make him do it. What I just did, I did for myself. And for her. And only a little bit for you. So don't thank me. Now what are we going to do about that girl?"

168

"If only she didn't try so hard," Jock said. "If she'd just be herself, I'd get enough out of her to create a performance in the editing room."

"You really believe that?"

"Yes."

Carr considered that a moment, then said, "Okay." Thoughtfully, a moment later he repeated, "Okay." As though he had made up his mind to something. But he didn't confide it to Jock.

They went back to shooting. But it was useless to try to get anything out of Daisy the rest of that afternoon. If she didn't know precisely why the president had been there, she could suspect. So they worked on Carr's part of the scene. And it was a pleasure to do, a pleasure just to watch. He was at his easy, skillful, convincing best. He was masculine, tough, gentle. He had a subtle way of moving, a way of using his eyes so that it all seemed accidental and natural. Yet their slightest move, flicker, or blink conveyed warmth, sensitivity, anger, whatever emotion the moment called for.

Best of all, it was all related. Related to the scene, the other characters, the plot, the entire film. Without any mystical ritual of acting principles, motivation, sense memories, he did all things with a thorough understanding of the total character, the entire film. There were no false moments with Carr, moments which later in the cutting room would not work without upsetting or defeating some other moment of the picture. Nor was he seduced into unrelated moments by those bright or inventive ideas that always crop up in the course of discussing or doing a scene, those ideas that seem so inspirationally creative one day, but are so terribly wrong in the rushes the next morning.

When Preston Carr walked away from the last setup that day, every man in the crew looked up from his particular job and watched him go. They had just seen the best. And most of them being old, experienced hands at this work, they knew it, they respected it. When an assistant started after Carr with the sweater

169

he had forgotten, Jock took it from the assistant to deliver it himself.

At the door of Carr's trailer, Jock caught up with him. "Pres, your sweater."

"I hope I wasn't going too fast for you," Carr said apologetically as he took the sweater.

"Too fast?"

"The time we lose with her, we have to make up for in the rest of the scenes. Only one way we're going to get this picture finished without running the budget so far over there'll be nothing in it for anybody. Right?"

"Right, Pres." Then Jock added, with a sense of premonition, "Only I don't want you overdoing. I'll plan it so you can have a half day off, a whole day off, occasionally."

"Don't worry about me, kid. I'm tougher than you think." He smiled, and excused himself with, "Got the papers on an electronics deal inside. Promised Harry I'd give him an answer by morning."

Later that evening, while Daisy was alone in her trailer, and about to take another pill, there was a knock on her door. Even so simple a thing could create indecision for Daisy. The door first? Or the pill? She said, "Come in," then took the pill, followed it with a gulp of Scotch and water. The door opened. It was Preston Carr.

"May I?" he asked, smiling.

Caught with the pill still in her throat, she couldn't answer at once. She made a pathetic gesture of welcome and smiled back. Carr sized up the glass in her hand, the little box on her dressing table.

"Mind if I join you in a drink?" he suggested. She shook her head tensely, trying to smile. It was not much of an invitation, but all she could manage under the circumstances.

When she swallowed the pill she was finally able to say, "Please. Make yourself something. Anything." She pulled her negligee together, not to protect herself, but to make herself more presentable.

170

Daisy was not a girl who had company often in her private life. Home to her was a place for escaping the world.

Her affairs were carried on elsewhere. In hotel suites, in men's apartments, almost anywhere except where she lived. Home was for hiding. For being alone, apart and away from the world. A place to be free, if only briefly, from the insupportable burden of being responsible for other people's jobs, multimillion-dollar pictures, and the price on the exchange of the stock of large motion-picture companies.

Each step forward, each surge in her importance had only served to make the responsibility, the burdens, more unbearable. And the pills less effective.

The slightest decision created great problems. Did you swallow the pill first or did you say come in? In a restaurant, did you order filet or lobster? Or sometimes did you just not eat at all because you couldn't make decisions? The tension was constant. Sometimes it grew worse, but never better. Many times she took deep painful breaths, hoping to shatter the fierce knot that kept growing, pressing within her, making it painful just to exist.

This was the girl to whom the world said, Be our symbol of sex, be glamorous, happy, gay, the seducer of all men, the escape of all of us who are tired of our drab lives.

Preston Carr made a drink, looked around in such a way that Daisy was forced to say, "Please . . . sit down . . ." As she snatched a dress from one chair. And from another, she took a stack of photos which were waiting to be autographed. But the slippery glossies slid to the floor, scattering, making her feel more inept. In the presence of her idol, Preston Carr, she knelt to gather them up. He put aside his glass to help her. Down on their hands and knees, the King and the Love Goddess gathered up the photographs. Till suddenly he laughed.

She stopped, looked at him. He reached out to brush back her loose blond hair.

"If they could see us now," he said, smiling. She felt encouraged to laugh. She tried. She did not quite succeed. Instead she turned away, letting her hair fall over her face again.

"What do you think they'll say when they see us in the picture?" she asked.

"They'll love us. It's going to be a great picture. You know how I know? The crew. That's where I like to win my wars. If the crew likes it, everybody'll like it. You'd find that out if you came into the commissary more often."

This was a generous euphemism, since she had not yet come into the commissary for a single meal in all eleven days on location.

"Just as you'd be more related to the whole picture if you gave yourself a chance to talk to people. For example, you did something the other day in a close-up that I thought was the greatest, most inventive bit of picture-acting I've seen in years! It was a small thing, but just great. Great!"

Now she turned to face him, gracefully pulling the hair back from her eyes, looking straight at him, instead of away from him or past him as she did most times with most people.

"Just great," he repeated. "And I wanted to tell you. But you ran right back here and never showed up the rest of the day. I was hoping you'd come in for dinner, but no. So I figured if I wanted to tell you, I'd better come in here."

"What was it?" she asked directly. "What I did that you liked?"

"Remember that reaction, the first time we meet and I say, 'Lady, just what the hell are you doing way out in the desert in those ridiculous shoes?' Then you looked up at me and did that funny little thing with your nose. The way you wrinkled it, told it all, your resentment, your annoyance, and yet it was appealing, appealing enough to make me, as Linc, say to myself, 'Hey, hold on. You don't want to lose this girl. She needs you, needs your help. But you sure need a girl like her, once in your life.' That's what it did to me."

"That one little bit?" she asked ingenuously.

"Pictures are made by the little bits. The littlest reaction, the slightest moistening of the eyes will leave an impression for a lifetime on millions of moviegoers. That'll do more to them than tears. That's why I'm like a prizefighter. I do my best work in the infighting. The little touches. I score there. And you do too. That's why you're a star."

Since it came from Preston Carr, she seemed to believe it.

"I have known some of the greatest actors in the world," he

172

continued, "men and women of talent who can handle big words and big emotions with enormous skill, but who will never get to be stars. Not picture stars. We're a special breed. Sometimes we wonder why"—and here he began to do some subtle in-fighting in a different cause—"We think we look the same as other people, we know we feel the same. So we ask ourselves, what's all the cheering about? I'm not the handsomest man in the world. In fact some people think I'm funny-looking from certain angles. Days I look at myself in the mirror and say, 'Christ, Carr, who the hell ever said you looked like an actor?'"

"You . . . you do that too?" she dared to ask.

"More often than I like. Then I say, I didn't ask for this. It was given to me. Somewhere in this world there's a guy who looks exactly like me and is selling hardware. So I'm lucky, very very lucky. Because whatever that thing is, I have it, and he doesn't. The same with you. You're a beautiful girl. But there are other beautiful girls. But they're not stars. You are. And there's nothing you can do about it, except *be* it. And it's fun. Not so much the money, which is good. Or the fame, the people following you everywhere. That's boring. And very annoying, painful sometimes."

"You too?" she asked.

"Well, men don't whistle at me, the way they do at you. But the way things are going in this country, they might . . ." He got her to laugh a little with that.

"That isn't the part that's fun. The fun is doing the scene, just for the crew, for the cast, the people who really know what good picture-acting is. The people who when they like you and respect you, do it honestly, with open hearts. I'd rather be in this business than any other I can think of, because of the pros. When you do a scene, everyone is working with you. They want you to be good. They're part of it, part of you. You're never alone out there. Not even in a close-up. Don't you feel that?"

She picked up her glass, which was almost empty. She turned to refill it but he didn't let her; he reached out to take her hand at the wrist, then he took the glass from her.

"Good God, you haven't been feeling you're out there all alone, have you? What a burden to carry. What an unnecessary burden. Because if you feel that way, you feel that the success of

173

the whole picture depends on you. Those people's jobs, the millions of dollars it takes, all depend on you."

"You never feel like that?" she asked.

"Never," he lied. "If I went around with a burden like that, I wouldn't be able to act worth a damn. No, the way I figure it, Preston Carr is only one element in any picture. Sure, he's going to do the best he can. But the success or failure depends on the director, the script, the editor, the music, a hundred different things for which Preston Carr is not responsible."

By now she was listening, nodding. She didn't need the drink, so he could release her hand, subtly, gently.

Suddenly he exclaimed: "There! There, you just did it! Fantastic!"

"Did what?"

"That bit with your nose. Your wrinkle. You just did it, instinctively, honestly, beautifully. Just . . . just . . ." as though words had failed him, he added, "just great! Great!" She was smiling, more confident now. "Do it again! Come on!"

And she did. He laughed. "Look, do me a favor? Please don't do that in my big scene? You know, where I'm going out to tame that one single mustang that just won't be tamed? That scene, give me. I need it. The whole scene. My way. Promise you won't use that bit in your reactions in that scene! Okay?"

"Okay!" she promised sincerely.

"Then I won't twitch my biceps in the scene we have on the lake shore. When we're lying there, making love."

"Is that what you do?" she asked.

"Look. I'll show you." He slipped off his tobacco brown cashmere jacket, unbuttoned his yellow silk-knit Italian polo shirt, pulled it over his head, at the same time tousling his black hair, exposing his deep tanned naked chest, his muscled arms.

Then, like a fifteen-year-old high school athlete, showing off for the pretty blond girl in geometry class, Preston Carr raised his right arm and tensed it, making the biceps dance. She laughed. He laughed, too, explaining, "That's not the one you have to worry about, though."

Now he dropped his arm, and while appearing casual, relaxed, unconcerned, he made the muscles of his right biceps pulsate

174

subtly. "That's the one. Women go wild about that. I have never been able to figure out why. They think it throbs. It has passion." He laughed. She laughed. "So if you upstage me with the nose bit, I'll murder you with the biceps."

They were both laughing. She was relaxed for the first time since they had come on location. But there was a knock on the door. It was the waiter from the commissary, with Daisy's supper on a tray. He entered, started setting up, as he had done for every meal of every day since they arrived. Preston Carr scanned the bland, nonirritating, low-residue diet and asked disparagingly, "What the hell is that?"

"Miss Donnell's dinner."

"You can't do that to me," he protested to Daisy. "You can't put me out now. What would people say? Tell you what! You and I, we go out to supper. To the commissary."

Before she could protest, Carr told the waiter, "Take that stuff back! And tell the chef I want something special tonight. Starting with caviar from my personal stock. I'll let him plan the rest of the meal. And we want a table just for two. Tonight, we have no time for anyone else. And if he can't arrange that, tell him we'll just get into my car and drive all the way to Vegas for supper! And tell him, I am still waiting for my first decent meal since we got to this godforsaken place!"

With a profusion of "yes, sirs" and "yes, Mr. Carrs," the waiter took Daisy's simple, stomach-soothing supper back, unserved. Then Carr turned to Daisy, "And you. I want *you* to be something special tonight, too. You have a date with Preston Carr. He deserves the best. He demands the best!"

It took her less time to dress than it had taken her in several years. There seemed to be no indecision. She selected a dress, put it on, swept her hair up into an impromptu arrangement which added to her genuine little-girl charm, instead of making her the obvious product of an expensive stylist. Tonight, she was as close to being relaxed, untense, uninhibited, and the girl she used to be as she had been since her name first appeared over the title of a film almost nine years before.

When she was ready, she was the most refreshing, most appealing young woman in America. When Carr looked at her, he reacted

175

with a look he had used with devastating effectiveness in many a close-up before in his life, but never had he tried to be so convincing.

"My God!" he said. Then he repeated it, softly, "My God." And he meant it. This girl was a special human being, special to all men, and right now, special to him.

He took her hand and wheeled her about slowly, gracefully, in a retarded ballroom dance step. "Who was it said . . . something about wasting sweetness on the desert air . . . that's you. Tonight instead of this desert, I'd love to walk you into the Savoy in London. Or the Ritz in Paris. The Plaza in New York. Or some big opening on Forty-fifth Street. Or best of all, down my old home street in Wilding, Montana.

"You know, till tonight, of all the thrills I've ever had the biggest one was the night of my high school prom. Walter Stamm, he was the school athlete, he and I were both dying to get Hazel Anson to go to the senior prom. Some prom. Twenty-six kids in the senior class. And most of them boys. So girls were at a premium. And Hazel was the very best. The only girl in class without buck teeth, and with two very nice bulges in front, just the right size to be in good taste on a seventeen-year-old girl in Montana. So Walter and I both asked her. If she had any brains she'd have picked Walter. He was the class athlete, taller than me, and nice-looking. But for some reason she picked me. I walked her right down Main Street that night to the dance, the proudest kid in that town. So everyone'd know she'd picked me.

"Till tonight that was the biggest moment in my life, believe it or not. Because it was the first time someone had confirmed it to me, that I had something, something that people liked, that women liked. Now, tonight, when I walk into that commissary with you on my arm, it's going to be Wilding, Montana, all over again. Except this time, it's going to be the most beautiful, the most famous girl in the world."

When they came out of Daisy's trailer, the big desert moon was just rising from behind the cleft in the distant mountains. It was not fully risen yet, but it was bright enough to light the whole desert, making clear and sharp every object for miles around. The camp stood out in distinct silhouette, each trailer, tent, and truck, each piece of equipment. Far off there were the dark shapes of rock formations and cactus. Farther away, the dark mountains rose up out of the desert floor.

They stood, staring at all that, at the night and the stars above them. He looked at her face, her delicate features made even softer by the moonlight.

Not by his design, she caught him staring. It was a compliment beyond any she had ever received. It seemed now that she would cry. He took her hand, drew her close, and kissed her on the nose. He smiled. She smiled back. Then hand in hand they walked toward the commissary.

When they entered, the rest of the company was at dinner, all at their accustomed places at the long community tables. Jock Finley was at the head of the executive table, fork poised, watching, as Preston Carr led Daisy into the room and toward the small table set at the far end of the room by a window. To Jock, to Joe, to the entire company it was the most important moment of this production thus far. It was as though a great battle of crucial importance to the entire war had been fought and won.

Jock knew two things. On the screen this couple were going to be dynamite. And this girl, with that look of confidence on her face, was going to be able to do it. The whole company knew that. Joe leaned in a little to whisper to Jock, "Oh, if I could put a camera on her now."

Each person in the commissary was delighted inwardly, and were it not too obvious they would have gotten up and applauded. If Daisy Donnell had come this far, the rest of the way looked very bright indeed.

The table at the window was set with a fresh white cloth. The stainless steel cutlery was polished to a silverlike gleam. There was a centerpiece, an impromptu clutch of desert flowers, mostly purples. Carr seated Daisy and was just slipping into his own chair when the assistant chef came out with a tray bearing a blue, fourteen-ounce tin of gray caviar, flanked by finely chopped hard-boiled eggs and tender, minced onion. He served it as well as he

177

knew how, which did very nicely amid the rugged surroundings.

The rest of the supper was exceptional. For the chef had done something with a sauce that started out to be béarnaise. It ended up being somewhat different but was still very tasty when put alongside two rare filets of beef.

They ate. They talked. Carr, intent on making sure that she ate enough, and of everything, did most of the talking. He poured the wine himself, discoursed on it since it was from his own stock and had been carefully brought out to the location in his own station wagon by his ranch steward.

Around the rest of the room, by chance or intention, other people slipped away from their tables and left as soon as they had finished, so that before Daisy and Carr finished their supper, they were the only two diners left in the large room.

The three hours between the time Preston Carr had entered her trailer and the time they started to walk back to it from the commissary were among the most relaxed, enjoyable, and fulfilling hours of Daisy's adult life.

At the door of her trailer, he reached for her hand, kissed it, then kissed her softly on the cheek. He smiled, the moonlight on his face. She asked softly, "What's funny?"

"That night of the prom when I took Hazel home, that's all I had the nerve to do. Then I walked home, kicking myself all the way, and wondering what she would have said if I'd tried to do more. And here I am tonight, kissing a girl on the cheek again, wanting to do more, and wondering. And I'll kick myself all the way back to my trailer."

He was smiling less, and more serious now.

"What happened to her? Hazel?"

"She married Walter Stamm." He laughed again. She laughed too. Then he kissed her on the cheek, opened her door, and she slipped inside. He closed the door, waited to hear her lock it, then started back to his own trailer.

From inside the dark trailer, Daisy peeked through the venetian blind to watch him, relieved, delighted, ecstatic. She started to undress and ended naked, sitting in front of her dressing table, looking at herself. She wrinkled her nose, a dozen different ways. Then she stared at her face, looked deep into her eyes. She felt good, strong, right. That night she went to bed and slept. Without a single pill.

The next morning she rose, ready to work, anxious to work, eager to work.

CHAPTER

6

FOR the next two days Daisy worked without difficulty. She was on time for every take. She knew her lines, not perfectly but certainly much better. For two days, shooting was practically on schedule.

For two days there were no frantic calls from the studio or from New York. Even Marty sounded optimistic and unconcerned in his usual nightly call to check on how it went that day.

But on the third day there were some few words in the dialogue that troubled Daisy. Simple words she couldn't say comfortably because she didn't understand their impact and relevance to the scene. Jock had to discuss her characterization all over again, endlessly, while Pres Carr and the entire crew waited patiently and shooting light was wasting.

The next morning the studio was on the radiophone again about "the girl." So was New York. So was Marty. It was all Jock could do to prevent Marty from flying down to see if he could help with "the girl."

The girl . . . the girl . . . the girl . . . Through the nights it kept Jock Finley awake and tormented. Even Pres Carr was awake and concerned. "The girl" herself was up as late as three-thirty or four, taking her fifth or sixth pill. But the pills bought no sleep. All they served to do was make her less certain the next day, more hesitant, duller.

Each take became agony. Each take was worse than the one before. No two takes would match to allow for intercutting, because her attack on the scene was never the same twice.

Jock kept saying "great" and "sensational" and "real" and "true." But she knew what was true. So after a while the more he enthused, the more shots he "loved," the more conviction he exhibited, the more uncertain she became.

It affected her feeling about him, too. There had been a time when she took courage, relief, peace, even some satisfaction from him in bed. It had not been sexual satisfaction. Only the feeling of being accepted. In their early days when he represented the East, the theater, the new approach to picture-making, he had been a figure of glamour to her. On sheer faith in him, she had bought the idea of doing the film. Of doing it his way, with his explanation of scenes, of lines. Lacking any judgment of her own, she had accepted his judgment because he had accepted her. Their sex was only her way of giving him something of herself that she thought he wanted.

All her affairs were never truly relationships. They were gifts. Since it was something that most men in the world could be proudest of, to be able to boast that they had been to bed with Daisy Donnell, she gave herself as some stars give out engraved cigarette boxes or lighters as mementos after shooting a picture was over.

Actually, she suffered her most serious sense of inadequacy in bed. Every man always found her less satisfying than she promised. But how could any woman live up to the image they had invented about her? She was the most desired, most sought-after, most voluptuous, best-breasted, most beautifully behinded girl in the world. Still there was nothing in that concept that should mean that she was also the most sexually voracious girl in the world. Yet somehow men expected it of her. So those who got into her bed, or into whose bed she came, were always disappointed. She was there, desired, available, willing to lend herself, give herself, willing to be used, delighted in, sought, loved, left, always the object, but never a participant. So she was always a disappointment.

For a time, a very short time, she had tried to be otherwise. She had tried to be the aggressor in bed, in every way, hands, mouth, breasts, but somehow the men had seemed to like that even

182

less. They were, if anything, frightened off by her aggression. Perhaps because they sensed that she never did enjoy it. Perhaps they had some idea of how many times she used three different brands of mouthwash for hours on end, after such encounters, trying to wash the whole concept out of mind and mouth.

So that phase of her sex life hadn't lasted long. Even though the phony Viennese analyst from Cracow, with a "doctorate" in psychiatric literature, not an MD at all, had discussed the whole thing with her quite thoroughly and tried to make her feel there was nothing abnormal or distasteful about it.

But only part of Daisy had ever gone to a psychoanalyst. Inside, there was always the unrevealed, secret part that made deductions, set down rules, operated with a shrewdness and an animal wisdom that came closer to reality than any other part of her mind.

Now it told her that Jock Finley was too worried about her to be attracted to her. That she had become to him, as she had ended up being to all men, including her three husbands, a danger, a destroyer of them and their professions. She was destroying Jock Finley, his picture, his career. And he finally realized it, she told herself.

There are people who live with a constant sense of doom. Who relate all manner of evil, accident, failure, and death to themselves. Who feel they are bearers of a curse, that whatever and whoever they touch must wither and die. There is no cure for it. Nor ever will be.

Daisy Donnell was one of those.

Yet she continued to search among men, though with the legend of her sexual attraction she could always make it appear that men came searching for her. She sought some men, that man, the man, who would love her and whom she could love back and to whom she could bring great good luck, fortune, success.

There was no such man. Nor ever would be.

For the man Daisy wanted, needed, and had to have to survive was her father. Ever since early childhood, Daisy had been under the impression that she it was who had frightened her father away.

Her mother, a poor demented woman, always said, "He used to love me till I had children. Then something happened. I don't know what it was, whether she cried too much or what, but he never cared for me the same, after that. I should have been more careful. I shouldn't a had no kids."

She would say "children" and "kids," though actually there had never been more than one and that one had been Daisy. So Daisy had grown up believing it all, blaming herself for the fact that she had been the cause of her mother's marriage failing, of her father's disappearing, and of the eventual sickness and dis-integration of her mother into a gray-haired, catatonic old woman who spent her days staring at the walls of the institution to which she had finally been committed.

Daisy had been born bringing destruction with her, destroying her mother, her mother's marriage and, since then, she had always had within her the power to destroy others. Sooner or later, they all discovered it, could see it in her eyes. Three husbands had seen it there. And countless lovers.

All this she fervently believed.

Now, during the nights she lay in her location trailer, awake despite all the pills, and convinced that Jock Finley had finally read it in her eyes. Once more she was going to bring disaster to a man who had made love to her. She would not permit Jock into her bed again, she decided.

If Daisy's panic was the result of a tortured imagination, Jock's was not. Like a general outmanned and outgunned, he fought a desperate battle under attack from all sides. No director can fool a crew or a cast forever. And there were the incessant calls from Marty, from the studio, from New York.

He had even overheard a grip observe, "That poor bastard Finley is giving a better performance walking from the set to the radio shack than Gary Gooper gave walking down that damn street in *High Noon.*"

There was only one person on location Jock could talk to. Preston Carr. Even there, he met unexpected anger.

"Kid, what do you think I'm going through? Take after take, and giving it everything I've got every time. Because I don't know which one will turn out to be her good one. Waiting for my cues, hanging on her every word and breath.

"Sure when she's great, she's very great. She does things no one can take away from her. Except she really doesn't do them.

184

They just happen to her. That may be how they act in New York these days, kid. But not in my day. We went out and did it intentionally, consciously. Acting was for the audience. Not for the actor. Acting was being what was written on the paper, not revealing what was sick inside yourself.

"And if I'm old-hat, over the hill, out of style with your arty-farty critics, well, screw them! About her? How can I feel about her? Doing the same scene over and over, the same words, till they lose all meaning. And then having to do it all again, when I'm empty, dry. Hoping all the while that she'll make it this time.

"Understand me. I'll do it. I'll keep on doing it. But it isn't easy. It's taking its toll. And you don't help me by coming to me and complaining about her."

Jock made no effort to answer or dispute Carr. And, as he expected it, it turned out to be the most effective reproach. After a few quiet moments, Carr asked softly, "What does she say?"

"Not much."

"Even when you're alone with her?"

"I'm not alone with her much."

"No?"

"She doesn't like my touch any more," Jock said simply, frankly.

"How long has that been?" Carr asked, with the sudden alertness of a physician confronted by a vital symptom.

"Since the night you took her to supper."

"Oh," was all Carr said. Then in a while, after a few sips of his iced Scotch, Carr observed, "She's like a gambler with a losing streak. She can't leave the table without winning. And she can't win for losing. She needs a winning hand. To give her courage. Can you find any sure scene for her?"

"She can't miss with the lake scene," Jock said.

"Then move it up. Let's get to it fast. Tomorrow!"

The next morning when Daisy came out of her trailer she discovered there had been a change in shooting plans. The scene on the lake shore, scheduled to be done four days from now, would be done today. The crew had been there before dawn, setting up. A jeep was waiting to drive her out. Jock Finley and Pres Carr had

185

already left. Only Daisy's hairdresser and her makeup man were waiting to accompany her.

As they drove to the shooting location, the hairdresser and the makeup man were both wondering the same thing: Good God, how do you overcome those eyes? For they betrayed quite clearly another night in which Daisy could not have had more than two hours of sleep.

When they arrived at the lakeside, an expanse of deep blue water ringed by mountains of red desert earth and rock, Daisy found everything already set up, everyone at work. Trailers, generator trucks, reflectors, chairs, cables, commissary wagon, portable comfort stations, cameras, tracks, sound booms all were there, ready, waiting.

At the water's edge, Jock, Joe Goldenberg, and Preston Carr were discussing Carr's first take. The panorama shots establishing the locale were already in the can, Joe wanting to capture the fresh, dewy feel of desert dawn on film in order to set the mood. And the wide shots of the lake, the mountains, the reflections of red mountains in blue water, which were best seen before any boat appeared to ripple the water, had been made too.

For the closer shots, the more intimate ones, Jock could cheat by limiting their range to that area which the crew could police so as to keep away the annoying, noisy, nosy speedboats. This dialogue could be dubbed later back at the studio, so boat and jet noises didn't matter.

When the assistant informed Jock that Daisy had just arrived, all three men went to greet her. There were the first-thing-in-the-morning kisses, an easy, sometimes graceful, and gracious gesture on motion-picture stages. But in times like this, when the going was rough, kisses became tenser, less natural, less easy, they made their own comment.

They kissed her, Jock, Pres, Joe, in that order. Each with a different purpose. Jock to see what her general condition was. Had the sudden change in shooting plan thrown her into a state of tension? He could feel that, from the slightest touch of her body. Carr to find in her some special, secret thing of his own. And he could sense it. Joe, to see how close to her eyes he dared to get today, and with what lens, what gauze, or what filter. The answer

186

was, not too close. Not today. Which was no promise at all that tomorrow would be better, or even as good. Just not today. With her, Joe worked along one day at a time, and did it without complaining.

Jock made a pretense at having to take Joe aside to confer with him about some distant shots of the mountains, which they had actually already taken and which were quite satisfactory. When they reached the water's edge, Jock pointed out the far mountains and the reflections, but he asked, "What do you think?"

"If they see those eyes back at the studio tomorrow they'll close down the picture."

"A telephoto lens could soften the wrinkles," Jock suggested.

"But not enough," Joe said, canceling out that possibility.

"What can we do?"

"We got water, mountains, Pres Carr's face, and the girl's body. Closer than that I don't dare go."

"Even with a diffusion lens?"

"I have gone back to using gauzes and silks, and it don't help!"

"What about more back-lighting?"

"I'm highlighting her hair and silhouetting her face so much, pretty soon you won't be able to tell she's a girl!" Joe said, impatient not with Jock, but with his own professional limitations, for he liked the girl, felt sorry for her, and wanted desperately to help.

Jock thought for a moment, then asked, "Do me one favor, Joe..."

"Look, kid, I'm a cinematographer, not a magician!" Joe protested sadly.

"All I want is time. Give me an hour or two. Shoot something, anything. Just give me some time by myself. Then no matter what I ask you to do, do it without argument or discussion, as though we had agreed on it weeks ago. Please?"

Joe Goldenberg nodded finally, then at once he started to call out orders to his assistant. Suddenly, there was a fresh angle of those mountains that Joe wanted, because the light had changed in the past half hour and was much more favorable.

Jock went back to his trailer, thumbed frantically through his script, the scenes before the water scene, the scenes following.

187

There must be a way to shoot around all those takes which required close-ups of Daisy. Of course, he could do the scenes and come back to her close-ups some other time, some other day when she looked better. But with her, that could be dangerous. She did not find or hold her performance too well, at best. It would be manufactured picture-making, close-ups in vacuum, cut together with the scene, the kind of fake picture-making Jock detested. It was a last resort. He must find some other way. He would find some other way!

This was the moment, Jock Finley told himself, to be brilliantly inventive, to save the picture, to save the girl, to save the picture by saving the girl. There is a time in any creative enterprise when it is too late to turn back and when going forward is sheer folly. Jock had seen it happen in plays, when the opening date was pressing on you and there was no time to do what needed doing, and no money to buy time. So it was in a motion picture when too much money has been spent to consider abandonment, yet when the future looks impossible. Jock was at that point now.

What could he have been thinking about when he agreed to her name to "guarantee" the picture? This girl who couldn't even guarantee herself a night's sleep! He should have had his head examined. Marty! It was all Marty White's fault! Conniving bastard! Getting himself another hundred thousand in commission in addition to his percentage as executive producer! It would be a just irony if Marty had screwed himself by trying to grab too much, if his percentage had turned out not to be worth a dime because of his own greed!

But even as Jock was indulging his silent rage, he knew that it had not been Marty. Not the studio. Not anyone but Jock Finley who really had chosen this girl. For good reason. Where she went, publicity went, worldwide, the best there was. Her whereabouts, her husbands, her love affairs were a prime concern to half the world.

So, if in the making of *Mustang!* some of that were to rub off on Jock Finley it would substantially help his career. If, in addition, he were to manage to get a performance out of her, it would have stamped him as *the* young genius in an industry of young geniuses.

Now it seemed the attempt must fail. And the feeling of failure would infect the whole company, and everyone in it. Picture-making is like war-making. There is a time when the battle can be won and everyone knows it and rises to it. Then, in some cases, there is a time when the battle is lost, not yet over but lost, and everyone knows that too. Morale disintegrates and the commander's toughest job is to cut losses, keep the outfit moving, even in retreat, to preserve some sense of unity, to emerge with some dignity.

But Jock Finley had been there before, and in a medium far more evanescent and treacherous than film. On film, at least you could store up an actress's best bits and pieces and manufacture her performance later. Jock had faced this same crisis in the theater, where you could store up nothing. And where everything had to work as if by magic on one given night, else you had created a disaster that was on your record forever,

They had told him, from the first interview, that Julie West was trouble. Brilliantly talented, but trouble. Not that they had to warn him. For he knew her work and her reputation.

It was tacitly understood by young Jack Finestock, by his agent, and by Kermit Klein, the producer, during that first meeting, that if Julie West were not such trouble they would not now be considering a kid director with only two off-Broadway credits to his name to direct her in her first play in several years.

Nor would any director welcome the chance to direct Julie West, with her reputation, unless he were young, eager, and still seeking his first credit in the only place in this whole world that really mattered in the theater, Broadway.

When Kermit Klein, a portly man in his fifties, who had had several big successes on Broadway, none in recent years, asked twenty-five-year-old Jack Finestock, "Have you ever met Julie? Seen her work? Know anything about her?" Jack assured him eagerly, "I've seen her. Onstage. And doing scenes at the Studio."

"*When?*" the wispy-haired, perspiring producer asked.

"Two years ago, three. Why?"

"Two years ago? Well . . ." Klein belittled, more to Jack's agent

189

than to Jack. The agent, a bulky woman with a bosom huge enough to qualify her as all Jewish mothers, made a sad gesture of her head which needed no words to explain, two years ago was *before*. This was *after*.

When anyone talked about Julie West in the days of Jock Finley's youth, *before* and *after* had special reference to only one event—her breakdown.

Jack Finestock understood this silent game, for he said, "Look, Mr. Klein, an actress doesn't lose talent! If she had it, she'll have it forever! It's a matter of bringing it out, that's all!"

"And what makes you think you can?" Klein asked, wondering how much of Jack's strong opinion was the conviction of youth and how much sheer ignorance. "Logan couldn't handle her finally. And Kazan damn near went out of his mind. She's not easy."

"I didn't say she was!" Jack exploded. "And how long are you guys going to go on comparing every young director with Logan and Kazan, when those two no longer work in the theater anyhow? You're like a baseball manager who sits in the dugout and refuses to field a team till he can get Babe Ruth. Mister, Babe Ruth is dead! And the ball game is waiting!"

"What do you do?" Klein asked suddenly.

Jack leaned forward, his face flushed in anger. "What the hell do you think I do? I'm a director!"

Klein smiled, looked to Jack's agent, said sadly, "In the theater it's a nice thing for a young man to have something else he does from which he earns his living. Till I had my first hit, I managed four apartment buildings in the Bronx for an uncle. I produced plays on the side. Some days I wish I was back managing buildings. What do *you* do?"

"I'm a process server," Jack finally admitted.

Klein started to laugh, "A process server . . . I should have known, with your *chutzpah*!"

Jack pressed forward in his chair, despite his agent's hand on his arm. "It's got a hell of a lot of advantages! I make my own hours. I can fit it in between classes and rehearsals and . . . and meetings with fat, self-satisfied bastards who call themselves producers!"

Klein stopped laughing. He stared at the agent, on whose face

190

was a motherly apologetic smile, "You asked for it, Kermit."

"Maybe we're going at this the wrong way," Klein said. "Maybe instead of asking can he get along with Julie West, we should be asking, can Julie West get along with him?"

He turned back to Jack, "Young man, I didn't mean to run down your livelihood. I was just surprised. Most young men, when I ask, say they work for their fathers, or at Macy's, or sell insurance."

"I tried insurance," Jack admitted. "Didn't like it. Who the hell is going to buy insurance from a kid?"

Klein spoke very soberly now, "This is a precarious business. Frankly, I don't like to encourage anybody or lure them away from a steady, stable job or profession. Because somehow if they fail in the theater they never go back and take up their lives again. You will not find any sane man or woman in this business. But by the time you discover that, it's too late. Because you're in it and you think the *rest* of the world is crazy. So I feel guilty about encouraging anybody."

"If I fail, I'll be back serving summonses the next morning," Jack said. "And I won't blame you."

"I have this fantasy," Klein mused. "The Bomb drops. The world is wiped out. Except for two people. And while one of them is scrounging around to find something to eat, the other one is saying, 'I have this great idea for a one-man show . . .'"

Klein turned to his phone, dialed, waited to be acknowledged. "This is Kermit Klein. I want to talk to Audrey. Audrey? Kermit. I have Jack Finestock here in my office. You know that young man, those two off-Broadway productions . . ."

Jack's agent threw in, "And the Paul Muni special on NBC!"

"And the Paul Muni special. Remember? Yes, yes, I think he could. I really do. Anyhow, let's set up a meeting. Tomorrow?" Klein consulted his desk pad. "Five o'clock! No, Audrey, no, I can't make it at three."

"I can!" Jack interrupted firmly, loudly enough for Audrey to hear.

Klein looked at him resentfully, then as if to teach him a lesson, Klein said into the phone. "Audrey, Mr. Finestock *can* make it at three. Your office? Good. He'll be there!"

191

Klein hung up, at the same time presenting his appointment pad to Jack. Puzzled, Jack looked at his agent.

"Go ahead. Look!" Klein ordered. "See if there is anything written in there for three o'clock tomorrow." Jack saw that from two thirty to six Klein's pad showed no appointments at all.

"Now, you might like to know why I said I was busy at three and free at five. Because, young man, I want to know if Audrey can keep her sober till five o'clock! But you are so goddamn anxious to have this chance, you'll do anything, say anything, be anywhere, any hour of day or night. I can understand that. I like to see a young man anxious for his chance. Frankly I am sick to death of old stars, old directors who have to be wooed and enticed and bribed back into the theater. I like enthusiasm. I like youth.

"Only remember one thing. In your enthusiasm, there is also great risk. She'll look better to you than she actually is. More sober. You'll compensate for her every failing, her loss of looks, her loss of youth. You'll cover all that up in your mind with your own fire for the chance. After all, for a young, unknown kid named Jack Finestock . . . you know that's not a very impressive name . . . you should change it . . . but, for a kid named Jack Finestock, it could turn out to be very important to be known as a man who directed Julie West. But you'll pay for that chance. Maybe for the rest of your life. So don't kid yourself, or me. Look at her with hard eyes. Assess the risk of failure as well as the chance of success. Now, you go there tomorrow, have that meeting, and you call me the minute you get out. And be honest with me. But more important, be honest with yourself!"

"Okay, Mr. Klein," Jack Finestock agreed, sincerely and respectfully.

The producer nodded, then turned to Jack's agent, "Sara! I want you to tell me honestly. Where else in this world, in what other business, would a mature, experienced man of fifty-six consider putting his future and reputation into the hands of a psychotic actress and a twenty-five-year-old kid?"

Julie West was standing when Jack first saw her. Her back was to the door and she was studying some portraits Audrey had hanging on her wall surrounding an old marble fireplace, autographed photographs from other stars, older stars, gone, dead, and buried stars, or just gone-to-Hollywood stars, which to Audrey was practically the same thing.

When Julie West turned to see Jack, it was not in response to the sound of the door, but as though she thought she was still alone, for she seemed greatly surprised. She smiled and put him at ease instantly when she held out her hand to him. He crossed to the old fireplace, took her hand. When he pressed it gently she pressed back. She seemed genuinely glad to see him.

Audrey let the moment establish itself, then she said, "Mr. Finestock, please?" She gestured him to a large chair near the desk. She offered, "Tea?" For the first time he became aware that they were having tea. Audrey's cup and saucer were on her desk. Julie's cup was on the mantel, where she stood, holding herself erect and still smiling. She had a good face, a good, mature figure.

Audrey spoke first, as agents always do. "Julie likes the script very much. Of course there are some changes she'd like to discuss with you. But basically she likes it . . ."

"I have some changes in mind too," Jack said.

Audrey continued, as agents will. "We don't think it should take long to get a rewrite. And if it does, that'll tell us something about the author that we might as well discover right away. Now, as to the young leading man, Julie thinks . . ."

Here Julie interrupted, softly, pleasantly, "Audrey, let the young man talk." It was said pleasantly enough, yet it put a greater gap between them than there actually was. For Julie West was no more than forty-one. And Jack was twenty-five. If he was a young man, she was definitely not an old woman.

He began talking, while sitting down, but soon he was on his feet, giving movement and force to his opinions, of which he had many. About the script. About changes. The proper young leading man. The structure of the play. The physical style of the production.

He began by addressing both of them, for he felt it was neces-

193

sary to win Audrey's approval too. But as he talked, and Julie stared, her eyes inviting his comments, he found he was talking to her and her alone. She never moved from her place at the mantel. Occasionally she would sip her tea. But never so that it interrupted his discussion. She picked up her cup and set it down without letting the porcelain make a sound when it touched marble.

At the end, Audrey looked up, soliciting her approval. Julie said softly, "I think we're going to get along very well."

With that single sentence Julie West had lifted him from that vast army of hopefuls, candidates, and students into the ranks of professional directors, Broadway directors. He shook hands with her before he left. He held her hand a long time while she reviewed some of the things he had said that had impressed her. He kept searching for signs of what Klein had feared. He smelled no whiskey on her breath. Saw nothing in her warm eyes, except possibly a slight astigmatic haze. She really should wear glasses, he told himself.

Once he reached the street, he made for the nearest drugstore, the first free phone. He almost dropped his dime, but finally succeeded in inserting it. He dialed.

"Well, Finestock?"

"She's terrific, Mr. Klein! She loves the script. And my ideas for the rewrite. In fact, we agreed on everything."

"Good, good," Klein said, as yet still guarded. "And how did she look?"

"Fantastic!"

"And ... and sober?"

"Oh, yes! Drank tea all through the meeting."

"Tea ..." Klein was reassured. "Well, that sounds great, Finestock ... Jesus, let's change that name now. Before I have the artwork done. Somehow, well to be honest, I don't think 'Jack Finestock' adds a hell of a lot of class to a production. Let's find another name."

"I like my name!" Jack protested.

194

"Look, kid, I have been sitting doodling, waiting for your call.
It doesn't doodle well. 'Jack Finestock.' That's all right for a pro-
cess server. What about . . . what would you say to Finley. Jack
Finley?"

"I like Finestock!" he repeated.

"All right, don't get sensitive. Think about it. Christ, if we don't
like the title of a play, we change it. What's so holy about a name?
Anyhow, I better call Audrey and start negotiating. Talk to you
tomorrow, kid."

Julie was warm, kind, pleasant, cooperative all through the
preparation period. And she drank a great deal of tea. Jack was
with her as much as he could be, during the meetings with the
author, with the designer, during the casting, when they sat in
dark orchestras of empty theaters and watched and listened to
an endless stream of handsome, sometimes talented young men as
eager as Jack for their chance.

The play concerned a love affair between an older woman and
one of her son's classmates, so no recognized leading man or star
would have been young enough. The challenge was to find a young
man, ready for stardom, with the youth and all the other qualities
the role demanded.

Through days of endless readings, Jack and Kermit Klein and
Julie West sat together. Occasionally, when a young actor seemed
to have outstanding quality Julie would reach out to touch Jack's
hand and press it. But always she was careful to be circumspect
about it. Always it was professional, never personal.

They had been forced, finally, to scout other shows in search
of the right young man. Together, Julie and Jack attended every
play in town. When they stood in lobbies between acts, because she
loved to smoke, he was constantly aware and flattered by people
recognizing her, being surprised for a moment, then pointing or
whispering, "That's Julie West over there."

The night they spotted Jimmy McDaniel was such a night. Later
they went back and saw McDaniel, who turned out to be a nice kid,
modest, frank, greatly flattered that a star like Julie West would

take the time to come back and see him. They took him to Downey's, a place where show people go who do not wish to contend with the tourists and starers at Sardi's

She was as warm and friendly with McDaniel as she had been with Jack during the first meeting. At the end of the night, when it was past three, she got up from the table and said, "You're a very talented young man. We'll be seeing more of each other."

That was Jack's cue to pay the check and take her home. He left her at her door, where he always left her.

"I think that's our boy," she said very pleasantly. Later Jack remembered having said to himself, I think she's attracted to him, personally as well. Which is great. Because it will make the whole relationship more credible onstage.

But most important of all, Jack had been watching her closely that evening. It was their first evening together when she had had any liquor. A single vodka, with a quarter of a lime squeezed into it. Just that, one drink. No more. In a way that was better than no drink. If Julie could take one and refuse a second, it meant she was past the danger point.

The first reading of the play went off without a hitch. Klein, the author, Audrey, Jack's agent, two important backers, the rest of the cast, and the stage manager were all there on the bare stage. His stopwatch before him on the long table, Jack conducted the reading. Some members of the cast gave simulated performances, others merely read their lines. The young man who played Julie's son seemed to have trouble with the dialogue, as though the language were foreign to him.

But Jack knew that first readings from actors meant little. If you knew your actor, you knew what he could do at the end of four weeks when it counted, not on the first day when it didn't.

Julie was extremely efficient and economical in her reading, only indicating the emotional moments, giving a sense of tempo to the scenes, and reaching, though vaguely, for the impact of her curtains, of which she had all three practically to herself.

When the reading was over, Jack and Klein got together in a

196

corner of the stage. They spoke quickly and quietly, without being overheard or taking too much time.

Klein said, "Good cast. Except for that one kid. What a mumbler! We're long but not too long. We're going to have trouble with Julie's scene building to Curtain Act Two. But we'll find it."

Jack Finestock said, "Don't worry about that kid. I've worked with him at the Studio. He's very good. And you're right about Act Two. I've been after Sid for weeks. But you know authors. And Julie, Julie will be just great!"

"Still no drinking?"

"Once. I saw her take one drink. Otherwise, it's tea," Jack assured him.

"Well, kid, keep her going that way and you'll make it. Because this is the best marriage of an actress and a part that I've seen in years," Klein said. "Now I want to show her the artwork on the ads. We're taking a full page in the Sunday *Times* week after next. Page two. That's a big break."

Klein gathered them all around the rehearsal table and laid out a proof of the full-page ad. Kermit Klein was announcing JULIE WEST in a New Play by Sidney Lamprecht. The names of the cast followed the title, and after that, in flattering type almost the size of the title but much smaller than Julie's name, was "Directed by Jack Finley."

Jack looked from the ad to his agent, and then to Klein. "What do you mean 'Finley'?"

"I thought we agreed . . ." Klein seemed betrayed.

"*You* suggested. I never agreed!" Jack shot back sharply.

"I guess we could change the ad . . ." Klein conceded grudgingly, indicating it would be a huge inconvenience.

But Julie West said, "Finley . . . Finley . . . I like that, Jack. And I've never had the chance to name a director before. 'Jack Finley.' 'Jack Finley.' I like it!"

She took his hand, placed her rehearsal pencil into it, pressed his fingers around it and made him write out, J a c k   F i n l e y.

"There, see how easy it is." She laughed. "Logan, Kazan, and Finley. It sounds like a law firm. So natural and easy. Please leave it?" Julie laughed in that way she had when she was warm and friendly and it made you want to do things for her. So he finally smiled at her and nodded. The crisis was past, and his name was changed. The rehearsal, which started so auspiciously, went on auspiciously.

The first time there was any hint of trouble was on the fourth day. They were blocking the dormitory scene. Julie's character, the mother, came to visit her son at college. Her son was out at lacrosse practice, but his roommate, McDaniel, was there. As the scene evolved, it led to a moment of physical contact between mother and roommate.

During the coffee break, Julie summoned Jack to her dressing room, shabby and plain as all dressing rooms are in theaters being used for rehearsals. The bulbs around the dressing table were unshielded and harsh. Julie sat before them doing her hair, which seemed a constant exercise with her. The light on her face made her seem not forty-one, but fifty-one. Her handsome face seemed ugly, her chin full and flabby. But she held herself proudly as she sipped tea from the small plastic cup which was part of the set of thermos bottles she brought to rehearsal each day in a leather case.

When she first said it, she spoke simply enough, but a chill seemed to run through her body.

"I can't stand for him to touch me," she enunciated each syllable quietly but meticulously.

"Who?" Jack asked, for he had not suspected anything.

"McDaniel. I can't stand him."

"We picked him together. You liked him."

"That was before I found out he was queer. Since then, I can't stand him to be near me. I don't want him to touch me in that scene."

"But that's what the scene is all about."

"I'm sorry," she said, taking a sip of tea from her plastic cup. "Find another way, rewrite the scene, do something!"

"In the first place, he isn't queer," Jack said. "If he were, I'd have spotted it from out front."

198

"I tell you he is!" she began to raise her voice somewhat.

"It doesn't matter what he is. If you don't like him, let's replace him," Jack offered, though he felt that McDaniel was precisely right for the part and promised great opportunities for inventive direction. "After all, if you don't feel right with him, you'll never play those love scenes in Acts Two and Three."

"I don't want to hurt him," she said almost sadly. "But we do have to think of the play. Above all, the play!"

"I'll tell Kermit. We'll start looking right away."

"Thanks, Jack, thanks." She reached out for his hand, held it tightly, "It's as much for your sake as mine, darling. I want your Broadway debut to be a hit. A big fat hit!"

Kermit Klein liked McDaniel very much, too. But like Jack, he felt it was far better to lose McDaniel than upset Julie. So they replaced him. Clinton, the replacement, was not as good, but if Julie liked him that made him better instantly.

Rehearsals went on. On the tenth day, when they were doing the first run-through of the final scene of the play without scripts in their hands, Julie seemed to take fire. She played the scene beautifully almost till the end, knowing every word of her dialogue perfectly and, for the first time, giving a true indication of the enormous power and subtle delicacy which made her a great actress. Jack and Kermit Klein sat side by side in seats in the eighth row.

Throughout the scene, from the middle onward, Kermit kept saying in a soft whisper, "My God . . . my God . . . she is great . . . great!" He reached over and pinched Jack's cheek. It reminded him of the way his rabbi did that same thing when Jack had finished his bar mitzvah *haftorah* without an error in the words or the singsong intonation. Kermit Klein was a nice, conventional Jewish man at heart, in addition to being a Broadway producer. But he was also unduly optimistic, for in a few moments, Julie began to go up in her lines. When the stage manager prompted her she turned to him, "You keep your fucking mouth shut till I ask for a prompt!"

It was the first outward display of temper or profanity Julie had betrayed during all the time Jack had worked with her. Now

199

she turned away, stepped out of the scene, pressed her fingers tensely into her face, and then down to her throat, leaving red pressure marks. Jack came running down the dark aisle, with Kermit Klein right behind him.

They leaped up the temporary steps to the stage. Jack went to Julie, Kermit lingering a few steps behind. Jack put his arms around her. "Julie?" She seemed to surrender herself to him, secure to have him there, to have his arms around her.

"I'm sorry," she whispered. "Sorry I flipped at the stage manager. Tell him."

"He understands. We're all under strain."

"No, tell him," she insisted in a whisper.

Jack turned to the young stage manager. "Bob, Julie is very sorry. She didn't mean anything."

The young man nodded, his face still tense and flushed. "My fault. I shouldn't have been so fast with the cue."

"Take me out," Julie said to Jack. He started to lead her toward her dressing room, but she said, "Home!"

"Julie, we've got four hours to go. We're on a tight schedule. Please?" Jack looked to Kermit, his eyes seeking help and reinforcement.

"Julie, honey," Kermit said. "Take a break. We'll work on another scene. Lie down and rest a while and we'll come back to this scene later."

She shook her head slightly, but quite definitely. Kermit moved around so that his face was close to hers. She hid herself in Jack's shoulder.

"Julie?" Kermit sought her.

Finally she answered. "Can I talk to you?"

Jack and Kermit exchanged glances, before Kermit asked, "Alone?"

"Both of you," she whispered.

Jack broke the cast for an hour, it was close to lunch anyhow. The three of them, Kermit, Julie, and Jack, went to her small, bare, dusty dressing room. She sat before her mirror, again fingering her hair in the pretense of doing it. She sipped tea again from her plastic cup. Her eyes followed them in the mirror, darting back and forth, from Kermit to Jack and back to Kermit,

200

depending on the moment, and who spoke, and to whom she spoke.

"I can't do it! I can't!" Jack's eyes met Kermit's in the mirror, over Julie's head.

"Look, honey," Jack began. "You're tired. You've been working too hard. We've all been working too hard . . ."

Because they misunderstood her, she said again, and more firmly, "I can't do it with him out there watching me all the time!"

"Who?" Jock asked.

"The author! The fucking author! That's who!"

"He sits in the last row. He's very quiet," Jack apologized. "If he has anything to say, he says it to me privately. He's been very good so far about cuts and changes."

"Of course," she agreed too quickly. "Why not? We are taking this shitty abortion of his, with his crappy dialogue, and making it sound like a play! Well, it won't work. It won't!"

"But it *is* working!" Kermit said, his face growing damp and fearful. "Julie, darling, we're sitting out there. We can see. It *is* working. It's the best role you've ever had. Certainly, the best part since your . . ."

She interrupted him by merely staring upward into the mirror, raising her eyes a minute fraction of an inch, sharply, angrily. Kermit had almost, not quite, but almost, said the one word she would not stand to hear.

She spoke almost wistfully. "Maybe . . . maybe I shouldn't be here . . . maybe for the sake of the play I ought to quit. After all, it's the play first. I've always said that. From my first days in the theater. You know that, Kermit."

"Yes, yes, Julie, I know," he lied.

"So maybe I ought to quit. And let you get someone who can do it. There's still time."

Through Kermit's mind shot a thousand details, the New Haven theater, the New York opening, the little money remaining in the bank, the Boston date, the loss of theater deposits, the advertising, the advance, the theater parties, all of which depended on his ability to produce Julie West. The Shubert Office hadn't been too sure of the script and only gave them the theater because of Julie. The pre-opening publicity was all Julie West. After all, the playwright and the director were both young, new, and not worth much space. His backers, what would they say if he had to resort to an overcall for more money, because his one big asset, Julie West, was no longer in the production?

Through Jack's mind went only one thing. If Julie West left the play it would make the whole venture unimportant to the critics. It would start rumors that could destroy his career before it got started. Jack Finley could not direct a star. Jack Finley could not bring a show in. Jack Finley had one chance, and it disintegrated before it got off the ground. His first play never even opened. Whatever else was dispensable to Jack in this production, this first chance, Julie West was not.

"Julie, you can't quit," he said. "I won't let you. I've sat out there, I've heard you. Remember the way we talked before rehearsals. Everything we ever said was in this play *is* in it! Now, if there's anything disturbing you, tell me! I'll fix it. But no more talk about quitting! Okay?"

She looked up at him in the mirror, reached for his hand and pressed it against her face as though it comforted her to have him there, so close. She said softly, "I can't do the final scene the way it is, Jack. That boy would never leave that woman at the end of the play."

Kermit's eyes and Jack's met in the mirror. Kermit's cued Jack: Talk to her, convince her!

"Darling, that's the strength of the play. The poignancy lies in the fact that such a romance could at best only be temporary. We have to leave the theater feeling sorry for you. And you do it so beautifully."

"Jack, I'm the one who has to play the scene so I can tell you. It's wrong! It won't work! I cannot play that third act if it ends with the boy leaving her!" she said. "I think you better get another actress!"

"Julie, please! I won't listen to that kind of talk!" Jack said.

Kermit interceded at that point, gently, concealing his panic. "Look, you two go on with rehearsal. I'll take the author out for a drink and discuss it with him. Okay, Julie?"

She seemed mollified. "And Kermit, darling, please explain to him that if he didn't come to the theater, everything would be easier. For everybody. Of course, don't hurt his feelings. I'd hate to get a reputation for being bitchy with authors."

Just before they broke for the day, the stage manager gave Jack a message to hurry over to Kermit's office right after rehearsal. The rehearsal itself had gone extremely well, except for the last minutes of the last scene. Again, Julie didn't seem to play that at all. But the rest of Act Three worked amazingly well for a play only ten days in rehearsal.

When Jack arrived, Kermit's secretary had already gone, so the door to his private office was open. Kermit called out, "Jack? Come right in!" When he entered he saw that the author was sitting at the far end of the couch. He was staring, hurt, angry.

Kermit said, "He's upset, naturally. He wants to know what you honestly think."

The author looked up at Jack. Tears glistened in his eyes.

"Sid, if it upsets her, lie low for a few days. Don't come to the theater. After all, we're past the point where there are going to be any big changes. A few cuts, possibly. And I won't make any until we meet and discuss every one in advance."

The author looked hopeful for the first time. "You must admit I haven't been difficult about cuts and changes till now, have I? Have I, Jack?"

"Of course not, Sid, that's why I'm so sure we can work together right through to opening. Only not in the theater, not around her."

"It would be a relief not to come to rehearsal," the author confessed. "The last few days she exudes hatred. Breathes it. I can feel it. All the way back to the last row. But she's great. You'll make her great, Jack, I know that. So who gives a damn about showing up at rehearsal every day!"

Jack was relieved, but only momentarily, for the author went on, "Now, there's one thing you have to do for me. You can't let her change the ending!"

Jack looked to Kermit. "Did I agree to change the ending?"

"He told her. I was there. I heard him. He told her the ending stays!"

"Thanks," the author said fervently. He crossed to Jack, shook his hand. "She's sick, that's what she is, sick! But you can control her. Whatever you say, she does. So you promise me that the ending stays, and I'll keep out of her way."

"Sid, your play wouldn't work with any other ending. That's the thing I loved most about it when I read it. So don't worry. I gave you my word. The ending stays."

Sid Lamprecht embraced Jack, turned to Kermit, with his hands still tightly gripping Jack's biceps. "With directors like him, there's hope for the theater yet! It's worth the struggle to write a play and get it on!"

Lamprecht left. Jack dropped onto the couch, exhausted. But Kermit was staring at him in such a way that Jack sat up expectantly.

"Kermit?"

"Tea," was all Kermit said. "Tea!"

"Kermit?"

"You know how much tea she drinks?"

"It's for her voice," Jack explained.

"That stuff is vodka! Pure vodka! One hundred proof! With a little coloring."

"How do you know?"

"When you were giving notes, I slipped into her dressing room. I tasted it. Vodka! She can drink it till the cows come home and you'd never suspect. It has no odor."

"She doesn't look drunk . . . I could swear . . ." Jack explained justified.

"Of course not! Her capacity is enormous. She never seems drunk. But she is! She is! That look in her eyes, that myopia, you said she needed glasses? All she needs is less "tea.'"

"I could swear . . ." Jack said, then he remembered. "That first day, Audrey's office, then too?"

"Then too. I know because I spoke to Audrey this afternoon. She admitted it. Said Julie needs it. But if we handle her right this can still work out."

Kermit rose from his desk chair, went to stare out at the dusk that was covering Broadway. From his window he could see the marquee of their theater. People going home from work were stopping in to buy advance tickets for Julie West's new play.

204

"Christ," he said. "If she would only . . ." but he interrupted himself. "Kid, she's got us by the balls. Without her, there's no production. With her, we're always one cup of 'tea' away from disaster. She can destroy us both. If I don't have a hit this time . . ."

"Don't worry, Kermit. I'll see her through it. I swear."

Sadly Kermit said, "Logan swore. Kazan swore. She almost destroyed them."

Jack got up, moved to the window, stood beside Kermit, and looked out at Broadway. The lights were on, though it was not yet fully dark. Huge electric spectaculars raced, ran, breathed steam, announced, proclaimed, sought, seduced, promised. And every so often almost hidden by the huge signs was the lit-up marquee of a theater.

Jack stared out, because to look at Kermit would have been too embarrassing, too revealing.

"I've never been able to say this out loud to anyone, Kermit. Because it doesn't make sense. I couldn't even explain it to my mother when she wanted to force me to go to dental school.

"Kermit, I have to be in the theater. Have to. It is not the lights. It is not the audience. It is not even the fame or the money that I know I'm going to have one day. It's just that I need to be here. I need to direct. I need to make plays look and sound right. To make them as near to perfect as is possible for something created by human beings. I have known that since I was twelve years old and my teacher took us to a special school matinee. It was my first time in a real Broadway theater! I sat there feeling, my God, I can reach out and touch this. This is real. It isn't TV. It isn't a big, flat, moving picture. It is real!

"But I felt something else, too. Even at the age of twelve. I felt, this is good but I can do it better. I even said that to one of my friends, on the subway going back to Brooklyn. The way he laughed at me, I knew I must never say that again to anyone till I could prove it. But I *can* do it better, Kermit! I can! And I will! And no actress, no star, drunk or sober, psychotic or sane, is going to rob me of the chance to prove it!

"Because if I don't do this, there is nothing else in this world I want to do. Nothing! I have to do this. I have to be the best in the world at it, or I have to die."

205

Kermit did not answer, only stared out the window trying to glimpse the reflection of Jack's face in the windowpane. Jack was utterly sincere.

"I'll bring her through, Kermit. I'll give you a hit!"

Kermit had heard that promise before, many times. Sometimes it worked. Most times it didn't. Yet each time, the director, whoever he was, was just as sincere as Jack Finestock. Sorry, Jack Finley.

Till the night before the New Haven opening it worked. The last run-through, on a bare stage, before they left New York, was most touching, most impressive. That last act still had a problem. Julie was not comfortable. But she was doing it, and it worked, not smoothly, not perfectly, but good enough for New Haven and a first public performance.

She kept drinking her "tea" and Jack kept watching. It seemed to him that she drank no more than before. But then he was not with her every moment of the day and night.

They arrived in New Haven in the rain. He dropped her at the Taft Hotel which adjoined the theater. He helped carry her bags to her suite. She carried her leather thermos kit herself. He set down her bags as she looked around the shabby living room.

"Christ, this suite again. They haven't redone this one for eleven years!" Then she laughed, "It's good to be here anyhow." She kissed him playfully. "And it's you, all you. They're all surprised, all of them. They must have been betting I'd never get this far this time. After my . . . my retirement."

"Darling, you rest," Jack said. "I want to go down and check the set. See how they're doing. Especially the lighting."

She nodded, releasing him. But just before he went, she reached out and pressed her face against his. "We'll do it. We'll make it. We'll have a hit! Now you run along," she whispered.

He slipped into the backstage door and found the stage almost dark, but the set was already hung. The designer was supervising the dressing of the set, some touch-ups and the placement of the furniture. Jack jumped from the stage into the aisle and backed up slowly, keeping the set in view all the way, checking the sight

206

lines. Ninety-five percent of the audience would be able to see all the action. The people in the fringe seats, well, that was just too bad.

He stood in the back of the house, in the dark, leaning forward, staring. Brooklyn to New Haven! Suddenly there was somebody beside him.

"It's always a thrill. Always. The first time. And the last time." It was Kermit. "How is she?"

"Okay. Fine."

"Ready to open?"

"She certainly is!" Jack said.

"Good. Good," Kermit said, not exuberant, not even sure, just hopeful.

They started to light the set. The differences between Jack and the designer were minor. Finally it was all worked out. He broke the crew for supper and gave everyone till nine o'clock and the first technical rehearsal.

When they had all gone, he couldn't resist going up onto the stage again and walking about the set. He felt the carpet under his feet, soft and luxurious. And each piece of furniture, costlier and more luxurious than any with which he had ever lived. Yet, in a way, all of this was his, for he selected it all, controlled it all. It was his. His set. His show. His success. Or his failure.

The technical rehearsal was the usual disconnected jumble of trying the entrances and exits to see if the doors worked and if there was sufficient clearance for the cast between doors and furniture. They tried all the major crosses to see if lines timed out right in conjunction with the number of steps it took. The lighting was being readjusted all the while, because with people onstage, lighting values changed.

Through it all Julie was fine, very serious, very industrious, very compliant, very helpful. When young Clinton had trouble with his cross to her, she volunteered to change her own previous cross so her new position would make it easier for him.

Kermit was growing surer, more relaxed. He even permitted himself to smile at Jack, who kept moving up and down the aisles

207

of the empty theater observing the stage, the various bits and pieces, calling out instructions and directions to the lighting crew, the actors, the stage manager.

It was past midnight. They were already into the cues for the last scene, which should go easily, since technically it was the simplest scene in the play. Kermit had already given the order to bring in the coffee and sandwiches for the late-night snack.

They were doing Julie's last scene, in which the boy leaves her. The scene with the last embrace, the last kiss, the farewell, and all the while her son was offstage, out in the hallway calling to his friend, with no consciousness of what had happened between his mother and his roommate. Now the friend, Julie's lover, had to say farewell and leave Julie onstage alone, the aging woman who has just lost her last romance.

For the first time that night Julie seemed to have trouble. That cross to the boy, and then away from the boy, it wouldn't work for her. She couldn't explain it. It just wouldn't work. Jack went up on the stage, walked it for her to show her how she had done it in rehearsal every day for weeks.

"I know, I know," she said. "And I told you it's never felt right. Never. Now that I'm here in the set I *know* it's not right!"

Kermit started forward in his seat, but restrained himself.

Jack moved to her, whispered to her, "Julie! It *is* right. I can see it. I can feel it. *It is right!*" She shook her head almost frantically. "Julie?"

"I can't do it this way!"

"We've run the whole play twice a day for a week now! You've done it every time!"

"The ending. They won't like it. They won't believe it. I can't open with that ending!" She was losing control of her whisper now, so that Jack had to think about the morale of the rest of the company.

"Julie, honey, just walk through it now," he whispered. "Then I'll break the others and we'll talk about it."

She nodded finally. She ran the remaining cues, including the boy's exit and her final moment onstage alone, but she was perfunctory, uninvolved.

With the sandwiches and coffee already in the wings, Jack

208

couldn't get rid of the company at once. So, while the rest were eating and drinking, Jack and Kermit moved back down the aisle till they were out of earshot of the stage.

Kermit said softly and unemotionally, "I would take the lighting down a couple of points."

"Why? The scene is daytime. It has to be bright. We're cheating as it is, for dramatic effect," Jack protested.

"I would still take it down," Kermit persisted.

"Why?"

"Why?" Kermit echoed. "Because if the critics get a good look at her puffy face, at her baggy eyes, they are going to forget the play. All night long they are going to sit there saying, She's drinking again, she's drinking again. And the play and you and me will go down the drain together, in a flood of vodka! Take down the lighting!"

"She doesn't look that bad. Besides she's supposed to be a mature woman, with a nineteen-year-old son."

"A woman forty can have a nineteen-year-old son. She looks like fifty-five. Older even. Take down the lighting."

"It'll kill the play. It'll kill the scene," Jack argued.

"Kill the play! Kill the scene! As long as you save her. If we all succeed and she fails, we all fail. They are coming to see Julie West in her first role since her breakdown. They will have one thing on their minds. One thing!" Kermit was pleading now.

"Okay, Kermit," Jack acceded grudgingly.

"Kid, the theater, all of show business, is compromises. The people who succeed are the ones who make the *right* compromises. Believe me, I'm doing this as much for you as for myself."

The designer, an experienced man, needed no long explanation. He had anticipated the request to take the lighting down as well as the reason for it.

The cast, having finished eating, drinking, and griping, began to drift back to the hotel. Soon only Jack and Kermit remained on-stage. They thought, they hoped, that Julie had gone back to her hotel suite. But when the rest had left, she came out of her dressing room. In her hand she clutched a few pages. When she reached them, they could see clearly that she had been drinking heavily.

209

She even seemed to have lost the ability to control her face, which appeared misshapen as well as sagging, puffy.

Her attempt at clear, precise diction only betrayed the fact that she knew she was drunk. Alongside him, Jack heard the faintest, whispered, "Good God" from Kermit.

"Jack, darling, I think I have something here. It's rough, of course, but I think it would work. Can I walk it, improvise it, just . . . just run it . . ."

"Darling, it's late, and you're tired."

"I know. But tomorrow we open. We can't be looking for an ending for the play the day we open. We have to find it now!"

Jack looked at Kermit, who nodded almost imperceptibly. But it was eloquent permission to do anything or say anything that would assuage her.

"Of course, darling, let's find it. Let's find it now."

"I have this idea . . ." she said, vaguely brandishing the pages on which something had been scrawled. She interrupted herself to take Jack's hand and sit him down on the couch in the set. Brusquely she motioned Kermit out of the way and he went.

She took center stage and, speaking half to Jack and half to the empty dark house, she said, "You see the play is the thing. We have to save the play. You know authors don't always know what's best for their own plays. I've had that happen before. Many times. You have to save the play from the author.

"This author doesn't know women. Doesn't know anything about love. If you want to know this author is queer! Else he couldn't write a final scene like this!

"This boy would never leave this woman! Never! He loves her too much. Age doesn't matter. It's this woman, this attractive, warm, graceful, mature woman who taught him how to love. He would never leave her."

"But, darling," Jack interrupted. "They can't be together at the end, we know that."

"Of course not! But . . . but *he* doesn't leave *her*. *She leaves him*. That's the only way. Despite his protests and his pleadings, she leaves him. For his own good.

"That's what *this* woman would do. Because she is fine and noble, and, above all, compassionate. She puts aside her own

210

desires for the good of this young boy who might be her own son. Yes. There is a strong sense of incest here. I know, darling. I have a son of sixteen. I know exactly how she feels. *She* would leave *him*. She would."

"Julie, darling, please," Jack interrupted. "We're eighteen hours away from opening. We can't rewrite the pivotal scene of the play and stage it and rehearse it in eighteen hours. We can't!"

"But I have it. I have it right here!" She raised her hand with the crumpled pages in it.

Jack looked out into the dark house, and Kermit's voice reached out to him, barely under control, "Jack, as long as Julie's taken the trouble to write it out, we should look at it."

But as Jack reached for it, she said, "It's just notes. No dialogue. Not much to read. Let me walk it for you. I can explain it better that way." She dropped the pages onto the couch and started to walk through the scene as it seemed best in her tortured, alcoholic mind. She indicated where the boy was, and how he played to her. Vaguely she suggested what he would say, and what she would say. Then how she would go off and leave the boy.

Through it all, both Jack and Kermit were pursuing the same desperate mental gymnastics, listening solely to find as many arguments as they could to talk her out of her idea. When she finished Jack was ready.

"Honey . . . honey . . . wait! Listen to me." He went to her, took both her hands in his. "Do you realize what you're doing?" She looked at him, her eyes barely able to focus on his. "In your desire to save the play, you're destroying yourself!"

"What do you mean . . . destroying . . . ." she gasped.

"Julie West is going to go offstage and give the curtain of the play to a young kid? I don't care how unselfish *you* are. *I* am selfish enough to say I want Julie West onstage at the curtain because the audience wants her there at the end. Not anybody else. Julie West. That's who they came to see. So you can't walk off at the end. For that reason, if no other, we have to leave the ending as it is!" He turned to seek support, "Right, Kermit?"

"Absolutely!" Kermit said.

"Julie, honey, let me take you back to the hotel and you get a good night's sleep. We'll do the play tomorrow night as it stands.

Then if it doesn't work, we'll change it before the Boston opening. Okay?"

She didn't answer his question but said softly, and it was terrifying to him, "I won't open. I won't open. I won't open." She started out of the set by herself.

Kermit seized Jack's arm, pressing it so tight it was painful. "Kid! I don't care what you do! How you do it! You have to have her onstage tomorrow night or we lose every penny of the advance, every theater party! She opens tomorrow night, in this play, as written. Or I close it here tomorrow for good! It's that simple."

"God, what do I do?" Jack pleaded.

"You want to know what directors get paid for? *This* is what they get paid for! To be smart and resourceful when a star presses the panic button. In the theater you can play your assets straight. But you have to be clever and shrewd and inventive with your liabilities. This is your time. You're either a director. Or a kid with nothing but ambition. And the world is full of those."

Jack started after her. He would have caught up to her in the lobby, except that he was intercepted at the stage door. By Sid Lamprecht, who was staring at him, desperate, frightened, angry.

"Sid, I didn't know you were here!"

"I've been hiding. Up in the balcony. That's why I worked all these years, sacrificed so much, so I could become a playwright and hide in balconies like a thief when my work is being performed. Do something with her, Jack! Do something! Because if this play doesn't work I'll . . . *I'll* do something desperate . . . desperate . . ."

"I ll . . . do . . . something," Jack promised, starting after her.

Sid went to the couch to pick up the yellow pages Julie had written and left behind. He stared at them, then looked up at Kermit.

"Nothing! No scene! Unintelligible scrawls! She was lying!" Sid said.

Kermit only responded sadly, "How much worse it is if she *isn't* lying. Did you ever think of that?"

When he knocked the first two times she did not answer. Finally

212

he heard a stirring, then her low hoarse whisper behind the door.

"Who is it?"

"Me. Jack."

"Go away! I don't want to talk to anybody!" she almost shouted; her voice and diction revealed that she was quite obviously drunk.

"Julie . . . please . . . I have to talk to you."

"You wouldn't listen . . . I told you what was wrong, how to fix it, you wouldn't listen . . ." she moaned almost pathetically.

"I couldn't. Kermit was there. I want to talk to you alone," Jack pleaded.

She was silent for a moment, then she said in a softer whisper, "Wait. Just wait." He could hear her moving away on bare feet. He waited. It seemed a long time. God knows what she was doing in there. More vodka? Or pills, even? He had heard all kinds of rumors and warnings from friends once she'd been announced in the play.

He resolved that if she didn't open in a matter of seconds he would call the manager. But there was no need. She was back. He could hear her unlocking the door. She opened it, not fully, but guardedly. She was smiling unsteadily and with great effort, but she was smiling. Her lips were freshly made up, the lipstick uneven and not covering her lips completely. She wore a wrapper of black crepe and lace, but it was old and frayed in places. Yet she held herself erect and proudly, as she had that first time in Audrey's office when she stood at the fireplace, poised, awaiting his entrance. Even now, she carried herself with the pride of a beautiful woman though she looked older than her years, drunk, bloated with excess fluids. Her shapeless chin and the fat which hung below it reminded him of his oldest aunt, a widow who ran a kosher butcher store in Borough Park.

His first and most urgent desire was to turn and run, even if it meant fleeing the theater for the rest of his life. For as she stood there at the door seeming to guard herself against his intrusion, she was being coy and seductive.

Oh, God, he said to himself, imagine my old Tante Susha being coy and seductive with one of her twenty-year-old delivery boys. Christ Almighty, run, run, run!

213

Instead he said, "Julie ... please?" But when he pushed the door she held firm.

"I don't want to talk about it!" she said. She was so close that he could smell her sour vodka breath even over her perfume, which was stronger than usual tonight.

"Neither do I, if you want to know the truth," he said, because he had to keep talking, had to keep her talking, had to get inside that room.

His answer must have surprised her, for she lost her coy, obscene smile. He capitalized on that, "I am sick to death of talking about it. If you want to know the truth, I'm sorry we had to meet this way. Why couldn't we have met at a reading of some other play? Or at the Studio? That night you did that scene from Chekhov. I was there. I saw you. You were magnificent!"

"Because the scene was right!" she said testily.

"I thought we didn't want to talk about that," Jack said, moving closer to her face as she peered out through the guarded, slightly open door. "You know, that night I was going to go back and see you. I wanted to, desperately."

"But you didn't," she flirted.

"What would I have said: 'Miss West, you are the greatest actress I have ever seen!' What was so revolutionary about that? Or: 'Miss West, you are a marvelous actress, but I don't care. I fell in love with you tonight. Your marvelously frank and lovely face. Your hair. Your breasts!' Because, Julie, you do have fantastic breasts. You know that, don't you?"

She smiled at him. For the first time he detected she was beginning to relent.

"Suppose I'd come back and said that, that night. What would you have said?"

She didn't answer, only laughed, a low, provocative laugh that proved to Jack that he had hooked her. So he said softly, pleading, "Julie ... forget all plays. Just let me in. Don't send me away. I'm not a kid any more. I'm a man, Julie. And I love you. I need you. To hell with plays."

She stared at him, no smile now, to see if he was lying. Evidently she believed him because she started away from the door, leaving him free to enter. He hesitated, then pushed the door open, closed

214

it, hesitated again, then threw the lock loud enough for her to hear and know. He had made his decision.

The living room was underlit. She had arranged that well. One floor lamp was on in the corner. The lamp on the table had only one of its four bulbs lit. She was standing again, this time at the window, and behind her in the vague and rainy New Haven night were the faraway headlights of cars on wet streets. He went to her, close, so close he could feel her breath as well as smell it. He could feel the warmth of her flabby, bloated body. From between her breasts the strong smell of her perfume seemed to rise upward like obscene incense.

He embraced her suddenly, pressing his face against hers, but not kissing her. He could feel the outlines of her body, her thighs too big, but her breasts still good, still strong and high. They were large. But he had always liked large breasts, he consoled himself. As a kid in high school he had only dated girls with overdeveloped breasts. He was trying to convince himself that he wanted her.

She moved her face to kiss him and though he wanted to avoid it, he didn't. She kissed him, her tongue finding its way into his mouth. It was swift and adept and could almost make him forget her breath which was bitter with too much vodka.

He hoped he could come erect, wanted to, strove to. But he did not. Not till, in order to avoid her mouth, he pulled back slightly and tore her wrapper apart and pressed his face hard against her breasts. The perfume helped. The largeness of her breasts, which were still shapely, the warmth of them, his own special desire for all breasts conspired finally to give him the erection he sought.

When she felt it pressing against her, she laughed, low, soft, warbling. Then she coquetted, "Do you usually work standing up? Or is it a hangover from Brooklyn hallways?"

He laughed, took her hand, turned her towards the bedroom. She started, he followed. Suddenly he embraced her from behind, cupping one of her breasts in each hand, he pressed them hard. She leaned back to feel his erection against her buttocks and she undulated there, teasing him, arousing him more. He spun her around and went at the nipples of her breasts, kissing them,

215

tonguing them. She pressed his head against her in such a way that he thought she was having an orgasm, for she breathed in small, delighted gasps. Then she laughed.

She said what sounded strange to him then, and always would, "Come, boy. Come."

She took his hand, led him to her bed which had been prepared for this moment as neatly as she could prepare anything. The smell of her perfume was strong around it. He noticed that in this room the shade was drawn. The only light was a small table lamp at the far side of the room, away from the bed.

At the side of the bed she turned to face him, and he kissed her again. Then she did not move, so he loosened her wrapper and let it drop, leaving her naked. The sight of her nakedness almost made him turn and run. For she was a fat woman, with good breasts, but still a fat woman. The alcohol had put pounds on her, on her thighs, her belly, her buttocks. This was no overdeveloped high school girl from Evander Childs, no budding fleshy young actress picked up after a night at a New Dramatists reading.

This was a woman, an old woman, his Tante Susha, even his mother. But the look on her face, with her eyes closed, told him that she fancied herself one of the most attractive women in the world. If he could close his eyes and forget everything else except her breasts and her cunt he might make it. He might. For the play. For Sid. For Kermit. But mostly and first- ly and lastly for himself, for Jack Finestock, for Jack Finley.

He went at her breasts again and when he felt her rising to his mouth and his tongue, he gently pressed her down onto the bed. He slipped out of his clothes and started toward the lamp to turn it off when she said, "I like the light!"

He would have wanted it otherwise, but he discovered that she liked to watch. She was a voyeur at her own intercourse, forcing him to ride above her so that she could see his face when she wanted to. Other times she closed her eyes and reached out and ran her fingers over his eyes and his cheeks. Then she would seize him with both her strong hands and press him close to her. All the while he worked away, thrusting, thrusting, thrusting. But he could not bring himself to come. The more she writhed and pressed him to her, the less he felt the need and the desire. Though she had

216

obviously had three orgasms during that same time, and had gasped and moved each time, breathing faster and more spasmodically with each succeeding one.

He decided finally to simulate an orgasm, because he knew it was not going to happen. He quickened his pace, and as nearly as he could, acted out what he thought he did in moments of such passion. Then he rolled off her, onto his side, and breathed more deeply and quickly then he had to.

She lay still. The first words she spoke were soft and contented. "We're going to have to work on our timing, darling. Now that we know we're good for each other."

He said, "New Haven always was a good tryout town." She laughed. Which was a good sign. At least she wasn't as negative and argumentative as she had been. "And Boston," he promised. "We'll fix everything in Boston."

"Uh-huh," she agreed. "Uh-huh." She groped for him, without looking towards him. She found him, her fingers playing up and down him till he came erect again. Since she had practically agreed to open tomorrow night, without changing the ending, he pressed his hand over hers as she gripped him.

In that moment, he remembered what Kermit had said, "You want to know what directors get paid for? This is what they get paid for!"

He turned on his side, towards her. Her eyes were closed, her face turned upward. She played with him and smiled. In a short while he was back on top of her and thrusting away.

She kept whispering in his ear, "Better... this time it's better..." She must have been right, for this time he had an orgasm too.

They slept a while after that. Then they went at it another time, and another. She did not drink at all. He made sure of that. Not vodka. Not "tea." Not even water.

She opened that night. Till the final scene she was at her best. Even in the final scene, though Jack noticed the letdown, the audience did not, nor did the New Haven critics. They loved it. Even *The Yale Daily News*, which made a practice of hating everything in the professional theater, loved it. Julie was a favorite of theirs, anyhow.

But problems that get solved in New Haven do not always stay solved. As though nothing had happened or been agreed to in New Haven, as though they did not get great notices there, on the train to Boston, Julie stayed in her compartment. Kermit was worried, kept urging: "Go in there. See her. A star shouldn't sulk after notices like that. Something's wrong."

"She's tired," Jack explained. "She's resting."

"Uh-uh," Kermit disagreed. "Psychotics don't rest. They have more energy than anybody. Go in there!"

So he went in. He found her lying on her bed. "I thought you'd never come," she said sadly, seeking comfort, reassurance. "I wanted to talk to you. About the ending."

"The ending is fine! It worked beautifully!"

But she could not be convinced by words. In a while he realized that. He was alongside her, kissing her breasts, letting her play with him.

There is a section of New Haven Railroad track just this side of Providence, Rhode Island, that is irregular and considerably bumpier than the rest of the ride. There are two things a young man should not try to do during that stretch: eat soup in the dining car, or try to be at his rhythmic best in a compartment. Neither works as it should.

When they got to Boston, Julie was not happy, not consoled, not convinced about the last scene of Act Three. There was more trouble, too. Kermit had found several messages waiting for him when they got to the Ritz. Calls from the Shubert office.

The Shuberts had had scouts up in New Haven. What was wrong with Julie West? Why did she look so terrible? Had she been drinking again? Was she heading for another breakdown? Could Kermit promise to deliver her for New York?

Finally, this kid Finley seemed to be pretty talented, but perhaps now Julie needed another director, an older, surer director? What if they found out that Josh was free for a few weeks, or that Gadge would take over to put on the finishing gloss for Broadway? How would Kermit feel about that? After all, being so close to a hit, why not do everything he could to protect it?

All Kermit would say was, "I am not replacing Finley. The show needs him. Julie needs him. He brought her this far, he'll bring her the rest of the way."

Kermit did not mention that part of his conversation to Jack. Only the part about how worried the Shuberts were about Julie's looks. Jack admitted that, despite everything, she was drinking, drinking more, drinking openly in his presence, which meant practically all the time. No wonder she looked so terrible.

"Then get her to stop!" Kermit ordered and pleaded.

"I can't," Jack admitted. "No one can."

"She'll look awful before she gets to New York!"

Jack Finley knew that, knew it better than anyone in the world. He was doing all he could, which guaranteed that she showed up each day for rehearsal and each evening for her performance. But no more than that. And that was not enough.

The Boston reviews, which were very fine, began to give hints of what New York might say about Julie. One of the critics, known for his straightforward, honest appraisal of what he saw, wrote: "It is good to have Julie West back under any conditions." That hinted at reservations about her looks. It was a grave warning, meant in the friendliest way, for this was a critic who loved the theater and loved Julie's work.

Jack used that review as his opening wedge in his determined drive to get her to stop drinking, at least till after the New York opening. But instead of convincing her, it angered her. When she exploded viciously, she was the one who hit him with it, straight out, "I turned down Josh for you! And Gadge, too! Audrey made a special trip up here to ask me. The Shuberts wanted me to give my consent to have you replaced. And I said no! No!"

She caught him unaware with that, taking him totally and completely by surprise. For he had done well in both sets of reviews, New Haven and Boston. The play was working. And Julie was showing up. Had they really, had they honestly been seeking to replace him? Or was it one of Julie's psychotic lies, invented to throw him off guard because of his attack on her drinking. He chose to believe it was a lie. He went to bed with her that afternoon

219

between the rehearsal and the performance that night. She would not let him go till it was too late for her to have any dinner. So she had to take two long, long drinks of straight vodka to be ready when the stage manager called "Places!"

During the first act and after Julie's entrance to great applause, Jack seized Kermit and dragged him out of the dark house and into the lobby. There he demanded, "Do you want to replace me?"

"For God's sake, kid, how can you say that? I've been fighting with the Shubert office for four days now, saying I *won't* replace you!"

Jack was immediately sorry that he had attacked Kermit. But he knew one thing. Julie was not lying. She had told him the truth. He felt sick. But there was no time, for Kermit was saying, "Instead of worrying about that, go in there and watch her. See what you can do about the way she looks. She's worse tonight than ever!"

Kermit had a special makeup man flown up to Boston at the end of the first week there. But Julie would not admit him to her dressing room. She had always done her own hair, and always would! And her own makeup! And always would!

She slammed her dressing-room door, locked it, and would not even admit her own personal dresser. The woman, who had attended Julie in each of her last four plays, sat outside the dressing room on the fire escape steps and wept. When Kermit tried to console her, she simpered and said, "It wasn't even like this the last time."

Kermit looked across her at Jack, for they both knew what she meant. Even during the play in which Julie had had her breakdown she hadn't been this difficult. Kermit gave a sudden jerky head cue to Jack, who left the weeping woman and went to Julie's dressing-room door.

He knocked. She would not answer. He knocked again and heard an object hurled against the door.

"Darling, it's Jack. Please? Let me in?"

"You did it," she screamed. "You brought him up here! I don't need a makeup man! I never have! I don't need one now!"

"Darling . . . please . . . open up? At least listen to me?" he

220

pleaded, when every instinct in him was crying, She's mad, let her stay in there forever, run, get out, leave this theater, leave all theaters for all time, before it's too late! "Julie . . . darling . . ." this time it was the intimate darling, not the good-morning-nice-to-see-you-at-rehearsal darling. "Darling . . . Julie?"

There was a long silence. Then she unbolted the door suddenly, angrily. He pushed it open. She was back at her dressing table staring into the mirror, fixing her hair, which was unkempt, stringy, all ends. She had been deliberately making herself even uglier than she was. A smear of orange lipstick sat crookedly on her mouth and the rouge was too thick and too high on her cheeks to seem natural even under stage lighting.

"I'm sorry," he lied. "But it wasn't our idea. The Shuberts insisted on the makeup man. I tried to talk them out of it. But when they get the smell of a hit they won't let any stone go unturned. You know that. You saved me from that. And I won't ever forget it, Julie . . . darling . . ."

He stood behind her, placing his hands on her shoulders. She kept working at her hair, staring up angrily at him in the mirror. His hands moved across her shoulders and down her throat to press passionately on her breasts. Only then did she press her head back against him, rolling it back and forth, face up so that he could smell her bitter breath.

"Send him away," she said, her voice softened somewhat by the yearnings that he had aroused in her.

"Of course, darling."

"And I'm tired, too tired." That made him glance sharply into the mirror to study her puffy face. With her eyes closed and the passionate look on her face, obscene as it was, she was telling him that she did not wish to appear tonight. That she wanted to be alone with him in her suite at the hotel. Or right here in the dressing room.

"Julie . . . we can't cancel a performance."

"Put on the understudy."

"When Julie West misses a Julie West performance there is no performance. You know that," Jack said.

"I can't help it . . . I can't." The imperious, impatient quality was coming back into her voice.

221

There was a knock on the door; Bob, the stage manager, was singing out his usual, "Half hour, Miss West, half hour!" But she did not move, she only rolled her head back and forth against him, kept her eyes closed, and smiled that little cat smile of hers.

"Julie..." he urged. "Julie, you have to make up, do your hair..."

"I'm not going on tonight. I... I don't feel well. I'm sick. Even Equity wouldn't make me go on if I don't feel well."

"Julie, you know what it'll mean if you miss a performance. The rumors. They'll say you couldn't go on, that you'll never go on. You can't risk that, Julie, I won't let you. For your own sake."

She did not seem to hear, or having heard, to care. Even when there was another knock and Kermit's voice reached out uncertainly, "Jack... how is Julie? Darling, how are you?"

"She's fine, Kermit, fine! She's just getting made up."

"Oh, good!" Kermit lied. "I'll hold the curtain ten minutes. But hurry!"

"Yes, yes, we'll hurry."

He stared at her in the mirror, then bent over and kissed her on the lips, upside down, and it struck her funny, so she laughed. But her arms went around him and drew him to her, while she rose up from her chair and pressed herself against him. She took his hands and drew them to her breasts, seeking to arouse him.

"Later," he whispered. "Now you have to make up, do your hair, and be ready for your entrance. Then later, Julie. Later."

He kissed her to guarantee his promise. She was assured. She assented. He tore some tissue out of the box and wiped the orange lipstick from her face. He sat her down, faced her toward the mirror, started to make her up, and she let him. Meanwhile she fingered wisps of her hair, pretending to arrange them. But finally he seized the hairbrush and worked on it himself.

There was another knock. Bob's voice again, this time inquiring rather than announcing, "Five minutes? Five minutes to places, Miss West?"

"I'm not going on ... I'm not going on ... I'm not ...," she said, letting Jack do her hair at the same time.

"Julie, you have to!"

She smiled and said, "Not Julie ... not tonight ...fuck 'em ...

222

fuck 'em all. They only come to stare at me as if I were an animal in the zoo!"

"Julie . . . tonight you have to. Because . . . " he started to improvise desperately, "because I finally have it! I have it! The idea for the new ending for the third act."

That made her drop her coy and languid pose. She sat upright in her chair, looked back and up at him, as he used the brush and the comb on her hair.

"You do? You finally understand what I've been talking about all these weeks?" she asked.

"Yes, Julie, yes, I understand, finally. The ending, it has to be changed. You were right all along. She should leave him. But I have to see the whole performance tonight before I can tell if my idea will work. So tonight, the hell with them, just do it for me. Just for me. Julie?"

She thought a moment, then reached for her plastic cup, her vodka. She sipped it as if it were ice water, slowly but in frequent swallows. Finally when the cup was empty she said, "All right, darling . . . for you."

Bob's voice, his knock, were at the door again. "Places! Places, Miss West."

Jack gave her his hand and she took it. He helped her to her feet, opened the door, led her out. But once she was clear of the door, she rejected his hand and went to stand in the wings ready for her entrance. If she felt unsteady, she did not betray it. She walked slowly, majestically, to the lighted area just inside the wings, ready to make her entrance into her son's dormitory room for Act One.

Kermit had been waiting outside her dressing room door. When he saw her safely in the wings, he whispered quickly to Jack, "Let's get the hell out front and see what she looks like!"

They went out the stage door, ran down the alley and into the lobby. Just before they entered the dark house, Kermit seized Jack's arm.

"Wipe that stuff off!" Kermit said helpfully.

Jack glanced in a mirror in the lobby. Her garish orange

lipstick was still on his lips. He wiped it off roughly, angrily. They went inside where Julie was already onstage and the applause had started. They stood behind the last row, Jack found himself alongside the makeup man who heard no words, saw no action, but focused only on Julie West's face with the clinical interest of a surgeon.

Midway in the first act, he signaled Jack and Kermit to step outside. They went with him, stood out in front of the theater, as the drizzling rain bathed the marquee, and they talked.

The makeup man spoke quickly, professionally, with no personal feeling at all about having been barred from her dressing room.

"Perfect she is not going to be. So I say, take down the lighting a few points."

"Even more than it is?" Jack asked.

"Even more. Because if you back-light her, or footlight her, you can't hide it all. Then I'll show you a couple of touches that I would do, around the mouth and under the chin. A different shade of makeup there would cut down on the puffiness and the shadows. But that's all. That's all anybody can do."

"Take down the lighting even further?" Jack considered bitterly. For he knew what the critics would say about a director who underlit a show.

"What's more," the makeup specialist went on, "I'd move her upstage more, too."

"Christ, they won't see her at all!" Jack complained.

"It would be better that way," the slim, small, bespectacled specialist said. Then for the first time he revealed any feeling, "What the hell does it do to them?... How can a woman have such great talent and be so...so...insane...that's the only word...insane!" He took off his glasses, revealing tired eyes. "I'll write out all the instructions, with samples of all the makeup, and leave it in your box at the hotel. I have to get the first plane out in the morning. Mary Martin is doing *Peter Pan*. At her age. She asked me to help her with her makeup. But at least she knows she needs help, she wants it. This one..." He shook his head sadly, then walked down the rainy street toward the Boston Common and the hotel.

224

Kermit kept his eyes on the makeup specialist as he said to Jack, "I know what you're going through, kid. And it's never any different. The details can vary, the cast can change, but it's always the same. Always. A kid your age shouldn't have to waste himself on a woman like that."

It was the only reference Kermit ever made to the fact that he knew exactly what had been going on for the last twelve days.

"Kermit . . ." Jack began, but he paused, not knowing how to continue. Kermit stared at him. Jack had to say it, "Kermit, the only way I could get her on tonight was to promise her . . . I promised her I'd change the ending, the last scene."

"You what?" Kermit demanded, outraged.

"If she hadn't appeared, if the word got back to New York, to the Shubert office, that she missed a performance, you know what that would do to all of us. Kermit?"

Kermit nodded. He knew. But in his mind, compromising the play was just as bad. Yet he realized that if he had been in the same situation, at the same moment, five minutes before curtain time, he would have made the same promise. He knew. Because he knew that every producer would have done exactly that to save his show.

So he said hopefully, "Maybe she'll forget about it. Or we can talk her out of it. I've seen actresses hate a scene till they play it right just once and the audience lets them know it. After that, they never have trouble with that scene again. I've seen it."

It was a forlorn hope, and he knew it. They stood in the back of the house, watched her perform till the last scene. In the last moments, she did it so badly that Jack realized she was letting him know that she would never change her mind about that scene.

When the curtain came down, Jack looked to Kermit and did not need to ask. For Kermit said, "I'll try to explain it to Sid. But I want you to know now, he can close the play. He has a legal right under his contract. If we make any changes without his approval. Especially after you gave him your word."

Desperate, and his mind working solely on what he had to do, Jack said, "I don't give a damn. Make me the heavy. But she is going to open in New York!"

The audience had applauded Julie longer and louder than usual this night. She took her bow with a modest smile, bringing the other members of the cast up front to stand with her and share in the appreciation. When she did things like that Jack found it hard to believe that she was vicious and destructive and psychotic.

But when he approached her dressing room he knew. For he could hear her voice, shrill, loud, rapacious, "Find Jack! I have to see Jack at once!"

Her dresser almost collided with him as she came racing out of Julie's dressing room.

"She wants you," was all the frightened woman could say. Jack calmed her with a gesture and sent her away with a pat on the shoulder. Then he hesitated and entered Julie's dressing room.

It was after midnight. They sat out in the empty house, Jack, Kermit, the designer, and two technicians who administered the lighting. They were waiting for Julie. She appeared finally, peeking coyly around the corner of the set. She was smiling, bright, not tired, not even drunk as far as Jack could make out. She was in the full flush of her psychotic energy. Suddenly it came to him, she was playing Julie West. The Julie West of the public image. The smiling, bright, gay, helpful, devoted star who spared no part of herself in her dedication to the play and the theater.

Kermit sent Jack up onstage with the same kind of shove that coaches use to send college boys out onto the football field. Jack went, with precision, haste. He went down the aisle, up the rehearsal steps, onto the stage to take Julie's hand and kiss her on the cheek, as though he had not kissed her half an hour ago and screwed her half an hour ago. It was like a new day starting.

He sat her down in the large chair of the set and turned to address Kermit and use him as a foil.

"Kermit, as I see it, and Julie was the first one to spot this, the last scene isn't of a piece with the rest of the play. That's why it won't work. And since we haven't been able to get Sid to rewrite it, I have been working on an idea of my own.

"But this idea has to be made part of the entire play organically. It will change some lines up front, in Acts One and Two, and it will

226

even change lighting cues in some places. We have to be more subtle, since the play isn't everything it should be.

"To begin with I'd like to take down the lighting key a few points. The whole lighting key of the production. And I would like to restage certain parts of the first and second acts."

Here, Jack interrupted himself intentionally, "Look, I can show it to you better than I can explain it." He turned to Julie, held out his hand invitingly, "Darling?" and brought her to her feet.

Then he began to walk through certain early scenes of the play, and soon Kermit began to realize and appreciate what Jack was actually doing. Every piece of restaging served to move Julie farther and farther upstage. Away from the harsh, revealing light. Jack was implementing, by subtle indirection, what the makeup specialist had urged so strongly.

He moved swiftly through her key scenes of the play, indicating here and there how he would begin the restaging first thing tomorrow afternoon. Kermit appreciated all that, and did his producer's mental arithmetic—restaging one act a day for three days would let them play three full performances in Boston with the new staging and the new ending, Friday night, Saturday matinee and evening. And then they would break the show and move to New York. With four previews in New York, it was possible to make it work and work smoothly and surely enough for the New York opening.

But that ending, Kermit reminded himself, Jack hadn't got to that new idea for the ending yet. But Kermit was patient, for this young kid of a director was demonstrating extreme poise, ingenuity, and guts in a desperate situation that would have made Josh or Gadge come screaming down the aisles.

Swiftly but carefully, Jack went through her scenes, tossing notes to Bob, the stage manager, so he would remind Jack at rehearsal tomorrow of intended changes in the blocking, cuts of lines, but mainly changes in Julie's position upstage of her present marks.

And now, now, the ending! Julie was waiting, leaning against the desk in the set and waiting. For her geniality, indulgence, and smiling patience were all dependent on one thing, that new ending. If it did not please her, Jack knew that she might explode, walk out, or do some other equally outrageous thing. So he went to her,

227

took her hand, and spoke softly and intimately to her and her alone.

"Darling, remember I told you once we could not leave that kid onstage at the curtain after you went off? No audience would stand for it? Well, I believe that more than ever! But I know the way around it. I know how *you* can leave *him* and still remain onstage right here in his own dorm! But to do that, to have the effect and the impact, we have to do it in an unusual way.

"So we will play the third act, as is, right up to that scene. But then when you and the boy are left alone onstage, instead of your son waiting for his friend and calling to him, your son is off waiting for you, calling to you.

"Now, instead of the boy sending you away, and breaking it off, you send him away, and break it off, as you've always suggested, Julie. And that way you are accomplishing two things. *You* are breaking off the affair with the young man. And you are subtly letting your son know what happened and that it is over. So the boy goes.

"Now, hear me, Julie, this is vital to the scene!" He gripped her hand hard now, "Once you hear him close that door, once you are alone, your young lover gone, you turn slowly downstage for the first time, to look at the door, then out front at the audience, alone, bereft. As though you'd performed an . . . an amputation . . . an emotional amputation on yourself without anesthetic. It must all be on your face, it must all come from you, but without a word of dialogue, without any weeping, perhaps even without a tear. A lesser woman would weep in a moment like this. Not you. Not Julie West!"

She seemed to have great doubt on her face as she asked, "I turn slowly . . . you mean . . . till then I play the whole scene facing upstage?"

"Exactly, darling!" he said with great fervor to cover his inner doubt that she would buy it.

Kermit Klein felt a red hot surge of anger. He almost leaped up from his seat. What an outrageous idea! What gall! This young kid of a director was looking to destroy them all! But Kermit held on. Patiently, against every impulse that was racing through him, he sat quietly.

228

Jack continued, "Of course, Julie, I don't want to overtax you. I don't know if you can play a whole scene with your back to the audience and still get the effect. I hope you can. But if you can't, say so. I don't want to force you. Julie?"

She stood there, leaning against the desk, fingering her hair, thinking. Then, without a word, she moved away from the desk, began to pace about the set, taking a position here, then a position there, coming to rest finally before the leaded-glass bay window that suggested the campus outside. She stopped there. Still silent, she began to feel the simulated paneled oak of the set, made to resemble typical traditional Ivy League dormitory décor. She touched it, played with it, running her forefinger over it, finding places in the design that intrigued her. All this she did with her hand at a spot just above her head, so that at all times her right hand was clear and visible to the entire audience.

Then she spoke for the first time, "Dialogue!" she ordered.

"There isn't any, yet. I have to write it," Jack said.

"Then improvise it, ad-lib it, fake it!" she ordered. "I need dialogue!"

Together, between what Julie felt was right and what Jack ad-libbed for the young man to say in the situation, they pieced together a rough scene. With the stage manager racing to write down as many of the lines as he could.

All the while Julie was facing directly upstage, away from the audience, looking through the bay window out at the painted flat that represented the campus. But her hand, her right hand, rested on the simulated carved oak paneling of the bay. Her fingers toyed with it, giving emphasis to her lines and allowing her to reveal very subtly to the audience what was going through her mind as she told this boy she loved that she would never see him again.

Then as she ordered him to leave her, to go out the door and join her son, suddenly her active, expressive, right hand stopped moving and gripped the woodwork of the bay, as though she had stopped breathing.

Without leaving the set, Jack simulated the boy's exit by opening and closing the door. Now he turned to watch her.

Julie's hand was perfectly still, motionless. She held that pose for a full ten seconds. Then slowly her hand slipped away from the

229

paneling, she turned to face the door, then to face downstage, her eyes wet, but the rest of her body straining to stay erect and not crumple.

Softly, in a gentle whisper, Jack said, "Slow, slow curtain."

Julie held the pose, long after the curtain would have descended in a real performance. Then she whispered, "Oh, God, how right that is! How right that feels!"

Jack went to her, kissed her in appreciation of her artistry. She pressed his face against her own cheek for a long time.

Kermit came down the aisle, applauding all the way, murmuring, "Brilliant! Brilliant!" Yet there was a reservation in his voice. And Jack knew it. He leaned back from Julie and said softly, "Go back to your dressing room. I'll pick you up later and we'll go out for a drink." They were past playing games about her drinking by this time. Julie released him, nodded, and started across the set with the poise and sureness of the great actress she sometimes was.

When she was gone, Kermit talked quietly but urgently. "It could work. Could be great. But we got problems, kid, problems!"

"Such as?" Jack challenged.

"Sid for one thing. He'll never approve the change!"

"He will when I get done talking to him," Jack said, sure, defiant.

"Will he?" a voice came at them from the wings. It was Sid Lamprecht. He stepped into the unshielded glare of the worklight. His face was fierce with anger, his disheveled hair indicating how he had tortured it while they were changing the ending of his play. "You bastard, you swore! You gave me your word! No matter what, 'We'll never change your ending. That's the thing I loved most about it when I read it.' Remember? And now to please a psychotic whore you destroy my play? You bastard!"

Sid leaped at him, and Kermit tried to intervene but failed. But Jack reached out with both hands and seized Sid by the coat, holding him so tightly he could have choked off his breath if he had wanted to.

In a hoarse whisper Jack threatened, "You keep your voice down, or I'll kill you! I don't want her to be disturbed! You hear me?"

230

His fury silenced Sid more than his words. Finally Jack released him. "And stay away from her and the theater till after we open!" Jack whispered. "I'll give you your first hit, but stay the hell away!"

Sid turned, glared at Kermit, and then slipped out of the theater and into the misty Boston night.

Once Sid was gone, Kermit asked quietly, so as not to enrage Jack again, "It's a cheat, but a brilliant cheat. And it could work. But what about her makeup? We can't make her look like something she's not. Jack? Jack?" He realized that Kermit was pleading. Kermit, the veteran, the man with the big hits behind him, the important name on Broadway, was pleading because he was at the end of his resources.

Jack never paused, never hesitated, because he had known for a whole hour how he would handle her.

"I'll keep the lighting in a low key all the way. I'll get her to use the new makeup. And then ... then ...." Jack paused wondering whether to reveal the rest of it.

"Jack?" Kermit pleaded, because he had had enough of surprises, strife, and shock for one night.

"Starting at the beginning of the last scene, I will have them sneak up the lights, very slowly, almost imperceptibly. So that by the time she finishes her scene and turns around, she'll be in full light."

"For God's sake, Jack!" Kermit protested. "You'll crucify her!"

"No, I won't! And you shut up about it! I'm not even going to try it till the last preview in New York."

"Jack, don't ruin everything!" Kermit pleaded.

"Don't worry. I won't!"

The new ending didn't work so well on Friday night mainly because the young man didn't know his new lines. But by Saturday matinee it did work. And by Saturday night, because Julie loved it and invested it with all her talent, it worked beautifully, and she evoked a thunder of applause, and, for the first time, bravos.

So it went the first three previews in New York. The men from the Shuberts who were there were only worried about one thing now, the lighting. One of them said, "That damned lighting is so low you need a Seeing Eye dog to find your way around the stage."

When Jack would not budge, they accused him of being too young, too opinionated, too aggressive. But he held his ground.

Wednesday night, the last preview, Kermit waited at the back of the house while Jack replotted the lighting cues for the last scene. Then they watched the whole play. Finally came the last scene. The lights sneaked up so imperceptibly that Kermit was not even aware of it till halfway through the scene. Then he became aware, too aware, and almost held his breath till the last moments, till the boy's exit, till the time Julie turned to face the audience.

The lights were up, Julie turned, and her face was revealed in all its bloated, puffy, sagging age. She seemed to have aged twenty years between the beginning of that scene and the end. Kermit gasped and said, "You can't do that to her!"

"I have already done it," Jack said very firmly. "And if you try to upset it, I will throw you out of the theater the way I did Sid! Understand, Kermit?"

There was no more discussion. Fortunately Julie had been concentrating so hard on playing the scene she had not been aware of the change in lighting.

The next night, opening night, Julie was tense and nervous and drunk but strong, because she was sure. For the first time since the first reading, she was sure, because she had the ending just the way she wanted it. And for her, at least, it worked.

It was a gala black-tie audience, because whenever Julie West was in a play it was an event. More so this time than any other because she had been ill and was making a comeback. The audience, even those professional Broadway-haters who came to vulture at openings, loved her and worked with her through the performance, laughing when she wanted them to, not daring to breathe when she held center stage for her scene leading up to the second act curtain.

For them there was no one else in the cast. No author, no director. Only Julie West.

In the last scene, which she played with her back to them, they

232

watched every move and nuance of her right hand, fixed there on the oak panel of the bay. When the boy exited, and Julie turned slowly, they gasped, but when the curtain came down there was the greatest applause Jack had ever heard in the theater. Bravos echoed through the theater. Julie was called back for eleven curtain calls.

As Jack went back to greet her, Audrey intercepted him and kissed him fervently, "You did it. She was great and you did it! And that ending, fantastic! She aged right before my eyes. Right before my eyes! Brilliant!"

Julie never went to opening-night parties. So Jack did not go. When he phoned Sardi's from her apartment, Kermit read him the few reviews that counted. *The Times*, *The News*, *The Post*, *The World-Telegram*, and *The Mirror*.

The Times started off, "Julie West came back to the New York theater last night. And that is always good news. But last night she performed the most brilliant change of character before the eyes of an entranced audience that I have ever seen. Literally aging without the aid of makeup, she transposed herself from a handsome, attractive woman in her early forties, to a defeated woman in her fifties, facing the rest of her life alone and unloved, by her own choice.

"Surmounting a play that has its faults, and a cast that was not up to her high standard, Miss West carried the entire production to a brilliant triumph on one of the more exciting opening nights of my time.

"The fact that she could carry off that final scene, wherein the author has let her and the play down so badly, gives true testimony to her greatness. For it is a sheer tour de force to play the entire scene with her back to the audience and then turn to reveal herself to be an old woman, as though she had aged a lifetime in the brief span of that one scene.

"Julie West has proved that all she ever needed, or needs, is a stage and an audience. She will supply the rest, as she always had."

Chapman in *The News* was equally laudatory, but not so verbose, and Watts was just as enthusiastic, but more moderate in his choice of words and comparisons.

When Jack arrived at the theater the next evening, there was a long line at the box office for tickets to future performances. The backstage doorman told him it had been that way since early morning. They were a hit! They were here to stay for two years at least! Or as long as Julie West cared to play.

Jack went back out front and looked at the cast photos and the cards. And at his name, JACK FINLEY. DIRECTED BY JACK FINLEY.

It felt good. It felt better than he had ever dreamed. It was worth it. Tired as he was, in body and soul and mind, it was worth it. The nights when he was terrified because he was sure that it wouldn't work. The days when he was driven to improvise and think and feel for the whole cast. The nights, and days, with Julie in bed. It was all worth it now, every strain, pain, and inner scar.

He went back to see if Julie had arrived. She was in her dressing room, working at her hair. Before her lay the review from *The Tribune*. To one side of it was the plastic top of her thermos. She did not smile when he entered.

"Did you see that?" she demanded.

"What?"

"*The Tribune! The Herald Tribune!* Kerr! That sonofabitch!"

"Julie, he loved you!" Jack protested.

"He said I was an old woman. An old woman! And you did it. You sneaked those fucking lights up on me! You made me look horrible, ugly, old! You did it on purpose! You did it to me! You bastard. You queer! You fucking queer! You did it to me!"

Her voice could be heard through all of backstage. Kermit came rushing in, crying, "Julie, Julie, what's wrong?"

As though she had never begged Jack to make love to her last night, she shouted, "Kermit! Get him out of here! I don't want him in this theater again for the run of this play! He goes! Or I go! That queer, that fucking queer tried to destroy me! Tried to destroy me!!"

Helpless, perspiring, Kermit looked to Jack, who resigned simply by stepping outside the door. He started across the stage

234

toward the street. He could still hear her, belaboring poor Kermit. "That queer! Did you know he was queer?" she was shouting at Kermit.

Jack Finley walked out of the theater, crossed the street and started through Shubert Alley. When he arrived at Sardi's, Vincent pointed out a short, bald, plump man dining alone, who had asked for him. Jack went over. The man rose, "Jock Finley?" he asked extending his soft, chubby hand.

"*Jack* Finley," Jack corrected.

"Not if you read Earl Wilson tonight. Hinted the only way you could get a performance out of that broad was to keep knocking her off. Said you had lots of jock-sock."

"Earl Wilson?"

"Yeah. Here I saved it for you." The man handed him *The Post.* At the same time he introduced himself, "Marty White." The name was familiar to Jack, for Marty was one of the few fabulous independent agents in Hollywood.

"If you don't have a date, have dinner with me," Marty invited. "I want to talk to you about representation on the Coast." Marty was seating Jack with one hand, while snapping his fingers with the other and calling, "Josef! Get Mr. Finley a drink!"

When they were both seated, Marty said, "I was there last night. What an opening! Any director who can get that kind of performance out of a drunken bitch like her is a real director. But you sign with me and you won't ever have to worry about opening nights, critics, reviews, or flops again. In fact, there is a package I'm putting together at Steiber Studios that I might fit you into right away, with those reviews you got today.

"Laddie, you're too good for Broadway, too brilliant to put up with the kind of horseshit that talent has to take on Broadway."

They shook hands on the deal before Jack left Sardi's. It was agreed that when Marty sent for him, after he had things lined up at Steiber Studios, Jack would come out to the Coast. Certainly within the month.

Marty's last words were: "And, laddie, use the name 'Jock.' It'll have conversation-value out there."

When he was out on the street alone again, Jack went through Shubert Alley and past the theater. There was her face, huge and lovely, far more lovely and much younger in these old photographs they were using than she had ever been during the time he worked with her and slept with her.

He said to himself, Screw you, Julie West! Screw all the Julie Wests of this world! I don't need you now. I never will again. I'm on my way. I'm on my way!

Yet here it was, seven years later. And he was out on location in the desert, with a huge, expensive company, shooting a picture, and he was in the same trouble all over again. As long as he was a director, he would never be immune from it.

If Daisy Donnell had none of Julie West's mad aggressions, her psychotic hatred, and her vicious accusations, the trouble was still the same.

The star! The girl! And she didn't look as good as she was supposed to.

What did a man do? What did a director do? If Kermit were still alive, he would have said: "Kid, this is where you earn your money. This is where you find out what a director gets paid for."

Jock Finley determined one thing. What Julie West had not been able to do to his career, Daisy Donnell would not be allowed to do. Somehow, somewhere, there had to be an answer, and he would find it.

They were knocking on his door now. Joe Goldenberg had done all the faking he could gracefully do. It was time to go on.

With his script in its magnificent Florentine leather snap binder, Jock started out of the trailer, down toward the lake edge, where the crew was waiting. And costing God-knows-how-many-hundreds-of-dollars every hour.

Jock was almost at the beach when the dazzling reflection of the strong sun off the water blinded him momentarily. He turned away instinctively. Then shielding his narrowed eyes, he stared out at the water, at the painful, shimmering reflection, and suddenly the idea seemed clear and almost too obvious.

Why did problems always seem so much more complicated than

236

they really were? What did it all come down to? The girl couldn't sleep. Her eyes showed it. The answer? Use the camera in such a way that her eyes didn't count in the scene. But how did you accomplish that effectively in a medium in which ninety percent of all acting was done with the eyes?

There was a way. Film is one medium where the audience can only look where the director permits it to look. Unlike the stage, where the audience is free to look anywhere, in film the director can point the audience and say, look there! And the audience will. The film director's art consists of accomplishing that subtly, so that the audience does not resent it, but welcomes it, is eager to do as told by the director. That is when a picture is successful and when a director is successful.

If you can't show them *her* eyes, Jock was saying, show them *his*. If you can't show them her *eyes*, show them *something* of her. Almost anything. Except the eyes. This called for a moment of inventive illusion. For sleight of hand. For cinematic creativity of the boldest, yet most skillful kind.

It could have been the sun coming at him off the water that inspired that. Or the sheer desperation of a man fighting for his creative life. But the idea came to him. Though it would mean a fight with Joe, and a long, long explanation to Daisy, and possibly even his first open break with Preston Carr, it was the only way, now. Jock was convinced of that.

First, he approached Joe. Could Joe give him the sun bouncing right off the water? An almost surrealistic shot, hazy, diffused, perhaps even a touch out of focus. So Daisy would seem to be a nymph, rising up out of the water. The way she might look to a man whose eyes had been too much affected by the strong desert sun. Then Jock would bring her out of the lake from about waist-deep in a slow walk, so that as she emerged in her thoroughly wet dress every detail of her body would be outlined, dripping hair, breasts with nipples standing out firm because of the cold water, curved belly with the navel clearly showing, right down to and including her pubic hair. All of that, enhanced, highlighted by the wet dress, yet all of it sensitively photographed so that it was almost an Impressionist painting, not a half-naked broad in a wet dress.

237

Joe considered the idea. Jock held his breath, reading the little man's eyes. If Joe said, can do, that would help with her and with Carr. Joe squinted out at the water, thought, then said, "You got to work fast though. We'll lose the angle of the sun."

Jock could have kissed the bearded little man who looked like a rabbi but thought like an artist. And work fast, Joe had said. So much the better! Jock sent his assistant to summon Preston Carr, then changed his mind, overtook the man before he got to the door of Carr's trailer.

Carr was reading yesterday's *Wall Street Journal*, which he put aside, asking, "Going to shoot around her?" knowing Jock couldn't shoot those eyes.

"No, Pres, no." He proceeded to explain the shot he intended to make and the help he wanted from Carr in convincing the girl. Carr listened, was intrigued. If Joe said it could be done, Carr agreed, it was worth trying. Because Joe, even when he didn't fully succeed with a camera, was better than most men when they did. Now, Jock suggested, would Pres go with him to sell the idea to the girl?

They found her in her dressing-room trailer, sitting before the mirror of her makeup table, staring at her incriminating eyes. Jock knew what she had been going through. He knew too that if she was to work at all today, he had to talk fast.

"God, honey, you haven't been doing anything to your eyes, have you?"

She didn't answer because she had and she couldn't admit it. The bottles of eye drops, four different prescriptions, were sitting on the table, opened. He reached for her hand, drew her away from the table, looked deep into her eyes.

"Whatever you do, leave them as they are! The way we're going to do this scene we *need* them this way!"

He fingered her lids as gently as though they were butterfly wings, to make sure they were untouched. "I don't want any makeup. Any eye makeup either. I want naturalism, realism. Let the illusion be in the eye of the beholder. Understand?"

She was so tense, so confused, she dared not even nod.

"We don't have much time, we're losing the morning sun. Joe says we can't shoot past eleven. We have to work fast. So just

238

listen. Remember, in the beginning I said to you our key word is *different*. Everything about you is going to be different than it's ever been in one of your pictures before. Well, that goes for the big love scenes, too.

"I do not want the perfect image, the perfect hairdo, perfect lips, perfect eyes. I do not want every woman in the audience saying to herself, sure, if I had a hairdresser two feet away, and a makeup man, and a dresser, and was planted on silk sheets, in a Dior night-gown, with a built-in bra, I'd look beautiful too.

"I want this love seen to be done the way real people really live love scenes the world over. Two imperfect people. You without a suggestion of makeup. Instead of the perfect dress or nightgown, the least perfect yet the most alluring dress in the world, a cheap cotton number. Instead of neatly ironed, it is thoroughly wet from your being dumped into the lake. Your hair is stringing down. I want everything going against you, every element conspiring to make you look less beautiful than you are, and then despite all that, your beauty emerges and triumphs over all and Linc realizes it!

"In Linc's eyes, hence in the audience's eyes, you, sopping wet, bedraggled, are the most beautiful woman he's ever seen!

"Now, we're going to do it exactly the way I said. As soon as Joe says the angle of the sun is right, I am personally going to carry you out into the water and drop you into it. Because I want you to experience the shock of the cold. I want to see your skin pucker with goosebumps. I want to see the nipples of your breasts turn hard, stand out dark and rigid. You get up, angry that Linc's horse dumped you into the water. You start walking back toward the shore. When you start back, you are angry enough to kill him because he's laughing at you. But as you come closer, when you see the look in his eyes change, the sheer love there, you begin to respond. It is a wooing, a seduction, done through his eyes. So that by the time you reach the shore and are out of the water and up on the sand, you welcome his putting his beat-up old sheepskin jacket around you to warm you. When he sits you down on the sand, you sit. When he kisses you, you let him. Your first kiss from this man. There have been other men, more than you can count. You have been a tramp till this man came along. But this kiss is like a

239

first kiss ever, for you. When he gently presses you back, you trust him, you lean back, you submit. And then . . ."

This was the tricky moment, because Jock had not mentioned this to Preston Carr before.

"And then . . . he will undress you. Yes. He will unbutton that wet dress, gently, pull it back so your breasts are completely bare, wet as they are, the drops of water glistening, the skin still puckering, the nipples still hard . . . he will expose them completely. Then he will kiss your naked breasts . . . and the audience will imagine the rest."

"I don't know . . . " she said. "I mean . . . I've never worked nude . . ."

"It will be a moment the world won't ever forget," Jock said in a whisper. He waited. She finally nodded.

She'd do it! She would do it! Without any of the reservations or fears he had anticipated. He kissed her on the cheek, "Good! I knew you'd see it our way," he said. "I'll send for you as soon as we're ready."

He and Carr left. As they crossed the stretch from the trailer to the shore, Carr said, "Man, I hope you never take it into your mind to sell me life insurance."

"They'll never even notice her eyes," Jock said softly. Pres Carr nodded.

Joe set up the scene. They walked through it, with Daisy's stand-in. Photographically, it would work. For Jock it would work. Pres Carr had a few minor suggestions to make, which helped. Now they were ready. Jock's assistant went to fetch Daisy. When she arrived, Jock ran through the action of the scene.

When it came time to shoot, Jock himself removed all makeup from her face, finger-combed her hair so that it would achieve the proper degree of disarrayed stringiness when wet. Then he kissed her on the cheek, pressed her hand for luck, lifted her into his arms.

He carried her out into the lake, careful to hold her above the water so that when he dropped her she would get the impact of the

240

cold water for full effect. Just before he dropped her he turned to look back and get the sign from Joe.

He whispered to her, "Stay under for a count of five. So I can clear, before you rise up. I want this in one take. I want it all, and I wish to God I could play the rest of the scene with you. Because I've got to have you! Do you hear?" This last he said with the urgency of a lover, though it was sheer performance on his part.

Then, before she could respond, he hurled her into the water, hard, as though trying to force her to go as far down as bottom. As swiftly as he could, he plodded hip-deep through the water, to the side, so that he was clear of the shot. From there, he turned to watch, slowly moving back, out of the water, never taking his eyes off the spot where he dropped her. Now, the count was five, six, then seven.

Finally she rose up from the water, panting, sputtering, hair stringy and clinging to her face, dress outlining her body. She started toward the shore, struggling at first, then slower. When she was in only a foot of water, she stopped, looked into the camera as Jock had directed her. Her figure was outlined in all detail by the sun's light as it reflected blazingly off the rippling water behind her. Her face, her eyes were never even seen. With the slight lens diffusion Joe had added, with blue water, brilliant golden sun, red mountains, and her body outlined in clinging wet cotton, this would emerge as the shot that would finally be chosen as the key of all advertising for *Mustang!*

Some critics would call it "Finley's Venus" because as Daisy reached up to brush back her hair with one hand, the other was crossed under her breast, so that in silhouette she seemed to have no arms, no hands.

With that as the master shot, the other takes moved swiftly. Preston Carr's reactions to seeing her come out of the water, his change from amusement at her being doused, to pity, to love, to arousal, all the Carr close-ups worked beautifully. Then the scene on the shore itself, the love scene, wherein he undressed her, that worked too. Though it required frequent dousing with cold water to keep her skin wet and glistening, to keep her nipples firm and tight.

241

But all this was easier since the lighting could be simulated and controlled with reflectors and arcs. And because Preston Carr was great in close scenes, having a deftness and delicacy that was sheer professional magic. His was so much magic that when he kissed her, she responded, actually, really, and he could feel it. Suddenly Jock knew it, too. The girl was in love with Preston Carr. That was why the scene worked so well. Jock knew that. And he resented it.

But he would forgive anyone anything by the end of that day. The desperate gamble had worked, or so it seemed. They really wouldn't know till the rushes came back from the lab tomorrow. But enough footage had been put in the can today to cut into one hell of a love scene.

Most important, it wouldn't matter about the girl's eyes. Thank God, they were over that. Perhaps now she would sleep better and her eyes wouldn't be a special problem anymore.

The next day, when the rushes were flown in, instead of waiting till after lunch as had been his practice, Jock interrupted shooting so they could be seen at once.

Preston Carr, Jock, Joe, Jock's assistant, Les Ansell, all crowded into the small projection trailer. Daisy Donnell never watched rushes of herself.

The film ran in the out-of-sequence bits and pieces in which rushes are printed. So the first, and only, master take of Daisy rising up from the water and walking toward the camera actually came last.

When it was done, there was silence. Till Joe said, "If I could do it again, I wouldn't. That kind of perfection is the sheer accident of genius. Or the sheer genius of accident."

It was the highest tribute a director could get. Especially from an old pro like Joe Goldenberg, who was not used to bestowing tributes, and who, on Academy Award nights, contented himself with a simple "Thanks. Thanks very much."

Critics, who lend pretentiousness to their own empty jobs by pretending that the films they review are important, would find all sorts of symbolism in that scene. They would write about it endlessly, comparing Finley to Antonioni, to Bergman. They would divine all sorts of Freudian and Reikian interpretations in it. And

242

not one of them would ever suspect that it came about as a desperate device to hide a terrified girl's weary, swollen, sleepless eyes.

One critic on a national magazine would write:

> Some film directors use naked breasts with the same finesse as butchers hang meat in shop windows.
> Not so Jock Finley, who can do as much with a few glistening drops of sea water on a naked breast as Dali can with unlimited paint, brush, canvas and technique.
> ... her breasts live ... their very pores seem to open to the camera's eye. Finley combines the utmost in intimacy with tenderness and respect.
> Finley has made a Madonna of a girl other famous directors have treated as a whore. Or worse, as a mere sex symbol.

And Jock would play his part. Knowing the patois and the game, he would give interviews in which he would enhance the Finley legend as one of the great *auteurs* of modern film by pretending that every scene and shot was carefully thought out and motivated by the director's deep psychological drives and each had murky symbolic overtones and intentions.

Now Jock wanted the rushes run again. But, strangely, the shot he watched most intently was not the Venus rising up out of the water, but the kiss, Carr's kiss on Daisy's naked breast. And her reaction. When it happened he glanced at Carr's face, in the dark trailer, with the reflection from the screen highlighting his handsome, brown features. Carr nodded his head as he watched.

It was approval of the shot. But for Jock it seemed to confirm what he suspected, the girl was in love with Carr. When the dailies were over, Carr said, "Good day's work. Great. Maybe now we're under way."

It was meant as a compliment. But Jock chose to take it as reproval. "We've got some great stuff in the can. We'll get more. And we'll finish on time, with a great picture

"Don't be nervous, kid," Carr smiled. "Six days behind schedule isn't much, after what we've been through."

243

"We'll make it up! Now that we've got her this far," Jock said, still a bit peevish.

"I think we will," Carr said thoughtfully. "I think we will."

Carr was confident but Jock was resentful. It was the director's prerogative to be hopeful, encouraging, expectant, especially as it related to the performance of an actress. And Jock would cede that right to no star. Not even Preston Carr.

CHAPTER

7

NOT since the court of Louis XIV has the simple natural act of fornication held such an important position in the financial life of a community as it does in Hollywood. So there was value, real, hard business value to having the word around, in restaurants, studios, commissaries, that Jock Finley was sleeping with Daisy Donnell. That they were making a great picture together because they were making great love together.

So from the moment that everyone on location watched that kissing scene and realized that Carr was only playing the scene but Daisy was living it, Jock knew what that could mean. He had confirmation of it within twenty-four hours.

With exposed film being flown out every day, with letters, phone calls, and other means of communication available, it did not take long for word to get around LA. Nor did it take long for the Owl to call. When he asked Jock to clear the communications trailer, Jock knew it was important, though Marty began in his usual placid way.

"Well, kid, so how's it going?"

"Okay. Fine. Terrific. Why?"

"Why? I'm your agent, I worry about you. I'm your executive producer, so I worry about the picture. I am looking for a block-buster."

Jock Finley knew that the Owl didn't ask him to clear the radio

trailer for such routine talk. There was a rusty fish hook here somewhere. The most direct way to find out was to say, "Look, Marty,
I'm in the middle of an important setup. They need me."

That brought Marty to the point, as Jock knew it would.

"Before you go, kid, how is everything? I mean, there's no
trouble, is there? I mean, with the girl."

"The girl?" Jock asked innocently. Though he knew. Better
than anyone, he knew.

"New York called me this morning. There is this item in *The
Reporter* about . . . let me read it to you . . . 'The big shoot-out on
the *Mustang!* location could be between a certain star and a certain
director over who is prime stallion of the herd.' Now, something
like that could worry a studio. Especially when they are already
talking a two-million-dollar advertising campaign to back the
picture. They are even talking a hard ticket roadshow. They have
the Music Hall panting to take a look. With all that, they wouldn't
want anything to go wrong now."

"Nothing will go wrong!" Jock Finley caught himself shouting.
He softened, "Look, Marty, the picture will get done. The picture
will be great. She will be great. Now, as long as I think it will help
the picture to screw her, I will. And when I think that depriving her
will help her performance, I will do that. Right now, I am doing
that. Now, that's between you and me. I don't want anyone else to
know about it! Understand?"

"Kid, you only have to tell me once," the Owl replied. He
knew, and Jock knew, that just as soon as he could hang up, Marty
would call the studio and *The Hollywood Reporter* and a few
columnists he favored.

The word would get around. By the end of the day, jokes would
be made about Jock-Sock Finley. How he got his name. That he
had more sex appeal than all his actors put together. That he used
it for those weird wonderful performances he got out of actresses.
That this was the greatest love affair since Bergman and Rosselini.
In La Scala tonight, people would say, "Big prick, big talent." And
would mean it, several different ways.

But correcting the gossip back in LA did not serve to change the
realities on location. Preston Carr, a sixty-two-year-old man, old
enough to be Jock's father, had taken this girl away from him, in

broad daylight. Right before the entire company. Nor was it just "this girl." It was Daisy Donnell. She might be notorious for her spasmodic, short-lived affairs with men she didn't marry, but that was no consolation to Jock Finley, who had a reputation of his own to prize, a pride of his own to cherish.

An actor needs great pride to deliver a performance. A director needs even more. He thought for hundreds of people in the company, led them like an army. He felt for an entire cast. Projected for the author. Protected a studio's millions. He was boss of everything, while seeming to be the solicitous servant of everyone. To walk that emotional tightrope every hour of every day a director needed confidence, pride, courage, hostility, gentleness but, most of all, a belief in himself.

So it did no good to be humbled a hundred times a day. As he was being humbled every time he needed Carr for a scene and Carr was found in Daisy's trailer. By the end of two days it became a location joke, if you want Pres Carr, he was "up in Daisy's trailer," a takeoff on the title of an old chestnut of a risqué stage farce.

Each time that Jock snapped, "Well, get him!" the entire company was suddenly very busy at jobs already done, because they didn't wish to embarrass Jock by staring at him when he had to say it. But it became worse, when on the second afternoon, Jock snapped, "Get him! I'm ready to go!"

Jock's assistant, Les Ansell, ran all the way to Daisy's trailer only to report back minutes later, "They... they wouldn't answer."

Christ Almighty! Three-fifteen in the afternoon! Not more than an hour's sunlight left to shoot by! And that sonofabitch was screwing that broad! What the hell kind of picture-making is that? From the great pro, the great King of Motion Pictures? Jock did not say it, but he didn't have to. Joe, who was suddenly examining and cleaning his lens, by the very act of being so damned busy, was saying it. Les Ansell, suddenly barking an order to some poor crewman to put something down or pick it up or do something equally unnecessary, was saying it. So was Joe's assistant, who said, "We better reload or we'll run out of film during the scene." That would eat up about ten minutes. Each one was saying it, in the most polite, sensitive, roundabout, but pointed way he could.

Jock Finley did not welcome pity. Pity was something he showed, not shared. It was what he graciously and self-righteously extended to actors.

Yet now he was the object of it. He would never forget that. Nor would he ever forgive the man who was responsible for it. There was an irony that Louise would have appreciated: Jock Finley, who never truly loved any woman, who used sex as an instrument, should be wounded this way. That Jock Finley who prided himself on being able to take sex or leave it alone, with any woman, should be so wounded by one woman. And one man.

There were only two courses to follow at the moment. To wait till Preston Carr arrived. Or to go to the trailer, knock on the door himself, and say, "Mr. Carr, I am making a film out there, if you don't mind. So if you have the time, between lays, and the inclination between urges, *we* are ready to shoot!"

That was a risk. Because with a man as sure of himself as Preston Carr, you had no way of knowing how he would react.

So Jock Finley sat down in his director's chair, saying to his assistant, with an outward show of indulgence, "Give everybody five. No, make it fifteen. Who knows how long it takes him to get it up these days?"

It was a cheap joke—no one knew that better than Jock—but it got the laugh. And he knew that it would be repeated in LA tonight, adding to the reputation of Jock Finley and no doubt reviving and recirculating the jock-sock legend, too.

Quickest to laugh, and loudest, was Tony Boyd, the young actor who was cast as the third principal in the love conflict in *Mustang!* In essence—stripped of symbolism and hidden meanings about the stifling conformity of our civilization, with the mustangs representing the last stronghold of individual freedom, etc., etc., etc., all of which the critics would discover—*Mustang!* was, for the audience, a love story with Western action.

It was now moving as a love story should: man had found girl, man was about to lose girl, to a younger man.

The younger man was Tony Boyd, recruited from a successful television series which had run its course. Boyd had turned out to be a fairly good actor. Several years ago, in New York, with no great parts to be had on the stage there, his agent had talked him into going to Hollywood just to do a television pilot for instant

248

money. But the series had sold and there had been a firm option on Boyd's services. So he had spent the last four years in the daily grind of the six-A.M.-to-eight-P.M. shooting essential to keep an hour series running.

Each year during the summer hiatus, young Boyd had gone back East to do a few weeks of stock, to try out a new play or revive an old one. Just so he could return to the Coast in late August and discourse on his great, stimulating, challenging, and enriching experience in legit, to which, he would have everyone believe, he was still devoted. Hollywood, TV, all the rest was just for the money.

Despite that forgivable sham, Boyd was a nice kid, vigorous, handsome, attractive, and ready to talk acting theory with Jock Finley, or oil, real estate, stocks and bonds with Preston Carr. Because he had sold his percentage of the TV series and come away with a capital gain of one million six net, Boyd was himself an investor, a speculator, a businessman of some standing.

So Carr didn't mind having young Boyd on the picture. Not until he worked a few scenes with Boyd who delivered his lines with that uncertain, unpredictable, unrealistic tempo of "realistic" actors. But with scene after scene, take after take, when Boyd hemmed, hawed, chewed his lips, or razored his thumbnail alongside his jaw before saying what should have been a straightforward, simple, uncomplicated line, Pres Carr was becoming more and more irritated. Yet when he complained to Jock, Carr did so privately, as a professional should.

"Look," he had said. "Half my performance is confidence. Knowing what the other actor will give me. I don't care that he's bad. Just let me know *how* bad and I'll do my end of the scene. They won't even know he's there. But I can't be left hanging. I need cues. I need them on time, with some semblance of sense. Then I'll give you a scene you can cut, tighten, and get by with. But I won't take his Method crap."

"I'm bringing him along," Jock had said. "Give him a few more days."

"I don't know if I can," Preston Carr had answered.

In other circumstances, at other times, Jock Finley would have called Boyd in, closed the door, flailed him with words, epithets,

249

and crushing, devastating critiques on his performance. This was a favorite technique of many directors, not only Jock, to totally destroy the confidence of a recalcitrant actor so that in the end the only thing the actor would have confidence in would be the director. And from that point on there would be no trouble. Jock would get everything almost the way he wanted it. But the actor would never quite recover from the experience.

Jock was not going to do that to Boyd. Not so much for Boyd's sake, but because it was a means of not letting Preston Carr have everything his own way.

When Preston Carr finally did arrive from Daisy's trailer, Jock was extremely businesslike, very director, very cool. There was a scene to do, and the light wouldn't last forever, he remarked in passing.

Neither the point nor the way it was made escaped Preston Carr. But all he asked was, "How do you see the scene?"

Jock explained. It was the first time in the picture that Linc, who had been having an affair with Rosie, the waif girl he picked up, realized that the young man, the Boyd character, might be just the right husband for her. If only the boy could shake off his hunger to take up the mantle of conformism, if he could really become his own man. In other words, what this girl needed was a man she could depend on, not a man who depended on others. That's why she fell in love with Linc. But now the time had come to give her gently over to another man more suited to her age. And this shot, this close shot, was the moment when Carr let the audience in on his decision for the first time.

The scene was simple enough, basic enough. But as Jock Finley, proud young man, stallion of the Hollywood Hills, explained it, each word took on two meanings, and three. The girl, the affair, the old man, the young man, the competition, every element in the scene was like ripping away dried gauze from Jock's crusty, sensitive, personal wounds and starting them bleeding again.

Carr kept listening, silently. If there were meanings beyond the scene itself for him, he did not betray it. He only nodded. So Jock kept talking. Around them there grew a circle of silence,

250

Joe, Lester, the camera operator, grips, makeup men, wardrobe, Carr's dresser, every one of them was hearing the painful explanation of the scene. Till finally Jock's explanation ran down and he ended by saying, "Let's try it, and we'll find it."

The close-up occurred in the scene where Linc was teaching the young Boyd character how to break a mustang stallion, fresh and wild and free and proud, just brought it from the arroyos.

As Linc watched the young man try it, the audience would see Linc first being critical of him, then gradually rooting for him, working with him, and finally being relieved that the young man had conquered—then suddenly struck by the important realization that this young man was the man for Rosie! It happened in a moment that changed from seriousness to Carr's famous subtle smile, then back to seriousness. So that, without a word, and by intercutting with the action of Boyd's scene with the mustang, the audience would get through Carr's eyes his entire thought process, all in honest motion-picture language, all without a word of dialogue.

"It would help if you'd play me back some of that horse track," Carr called to the sound man.

The sound man searched his recorded tape to locate the sequence Carr had requested. It was the clattering sound of the mustang's hooves on the hard-baked earth of the desert, sharp, sudden, spasmodic, desperate, frightened. With it came whinnies which were both pathetic and proud, terrified and angry. In that piece of magnetic sound tape was the story of the mustang's capture, fight, rebellion, and his breaking by Boyd.

With that sound in his ears, Carr started his take. His reactions were minute and precise. Jaw, eyes, lips, smile, his entire face played the scene. In his eyes one could see revealed not only his emotions, but the entire scene that he was witnessing.

When it was over, Jock said nothing to Carr, but only asked Joe, "Okay for you?" Joe signaled okay. With an obvious show of resignation Jock said, "Okay, then. Unless we can get a better one."

An experienced picture actor, especially a star like Preston Carr, knew when he had delivered a good scene. Sometimes you

251

had to do one over because of a shadow the cameraman didn't anticipate, or an intrusive, unwelcome sound on the track. But if all mechanical and electronic tests were met, you knew what you had done, and whether it was possible to do it better, or was worth trying to. In this take, especially because he wanted to avoid any conflict with Jock Finley, Carr had really delivered every nuance.

But he could not allow to go unanswered the challenge that was inherent in Jock's "Unless we can get a better one."

"If there's still enough light for Joe, I'll have another go at it," Carr said.

"Joe?" Jock asked.

"It was a hell of a take," Joe responded evasively.

"Is there enough light?" Jock demanded.

"We can add a few arcs. We can go, if that's what you want." This last was a caution, a fatherly plea to an arrogant, angry young man.

"Okay. Sound! Ready with that track again! Joe, I'll take my cue from you!"

Joe lined up everything again, moved Carr just a few inches for the opening of the shot. After he had checked everything, he said softly to Jock, "Ready to go."

"Okay. Let's make this a good one," Jock said, low, firm, in such a way as to anger Preston Carr. It showed in his performance. Halfway through, Jock had to say, "Cut! We're just not getting anything. Try it again. From the top!"

They reset and started again. Then again. And then a fourth time. At the end of the fourth abortive take, Joe Goldenberg said softly to Jock, "That first take is the one. You can't want better."

"*I can*," Jock said, by now not caring if Preston Carr heard it or not.

Word spread around location. People gathered. Even Daisy. Carr did a fifth take. And a sixth. Neither of which Carr was allowed to finish, for Jock cut in midway each time to say, "Christ, no! *That* won't do it!"

Joe Goldenberg suggested, "Look, Jock, we got to reload and the light's going on us, why don't we wrap for today and start again tomorrow?"

252

But Preston Carr was a man of pride too, great professional pride. He said, "One more!" Joe looked to Jock. Because it was Carr who had asked for one more, Jock was almost inclined to refuse, but he agreed, "One more."

The operator reloaded quickly. Joe made his lighting adjustments at the same time. So they were set to go in minutes. This time before he was ready, Preston Carr walked around outside the shooting area, breathing deeply and building up his inner dramatic energy, which had begun to flag from sheer physical exhaustion. He inhaled as deeply as he could and let go with exhalations that were sharp and aggressive. Then he was ready. He stepped into the circle of lights and faces.

Once he got his cue, he listened for the track, the hooves, the animal's terrified sounds, absorbed them, visualized the scene in his mind, saw the Boyd character and began to react. Whether it was being tired, or acting tired, Carr gave the scene the feeling of an older man, ready to let go to a younger man who had the vigor and the age this girl needed. It could have been the lighting, which had changed key somewhat due to the fading of the sun's intensity. Or it could have been Preston Carr's pride. He was going to be better than his best in order to prove something to this young bastard of a director.

Whatever it was, when the scene was over, everyone knew it was *the* take. Better than the first, which God knows, should have satisfied anyone.

When he walked out of the scene, Preston Carr was perspiring. When he turned, his shirt was wet through the back. How a man could perspire that much, doing a small, confined, intensely interior scene, was a matter of amazement to the younger men in the crew. But the old-timers knew that those small, close scenes, the ones in which you had to seem the most relaxed and thoughtful, were the very ones requiring the most projection, the most concentration, the most of everything you had.

Carr stopped at Jock's side as he was giving the order to wrap for the day. Jock looked sharply at Carr, ready, almost aggressive. But instead of the hostility Jock expected, Carr said, "You were right. There was a better take."

If Daisy hadn't come up at that moment to place Carr's expensive Italian knit jacket around his damp shoulders, the incident might have passed. But she did, and she kissed him on the cheek.

"I love it. Love it. That's acting."

"No, honey, that's directing," Carr corrected. "Any other director would have been satisfied with less."

At any other time, under any other conditions, those words said in just that way would have been taken as the compliment they had been intended to be. But Preston Carr had said them. To Daisy Donnell, who had worried about him, taken care of him, kissed him and, for all anyone knows, just had sex with him only two hours ago.

"Look, mister!" Jock exploded. "The first time I ever spoke to you I said, I am not like any other director. And I'm not! That first take was 'easy.' It might have been very good Preston Carr. But it was not good enough for me! I won't compromise! Not when I'm on the verge of making a great picture! If that offends you, or if it is inconvenient, or if it requires you to stretch your talent a little, that's just too goddamn bad!"

Jock turned and walked away. Someone said softly, "You don't have to be a prick to be a good director. But it helps."

That, too, would be repeated at La Scala, Mateo's, and Chasen's tonight. And in the studio commissary tomorrow morning. Though Preston Carr hadn't said it, Jock would always blame him for it.

Word did not take long to get back to LA. Before dinner, Marty White was on the radiophone again.

Marty's preamble was all praise, profuse praise. The word around the studio was great. "New York" felt great. The rushes were great. Everyone was just holding their breaths now, that Jock would be able to complete the picture without any flare-ups or walkouts, for which Daisy was famous.

"So, laddie, as a favor to me, but mostly to yourself, when you're this close, don't fuck it up. I got New York jumping out of their skins to make a gigantic deal. They'll finance our company. Six pictures. You'll be your own boss. There is nothing you can't have. Just play it cool down to the wire. Laddie?"

But Jock was not listening. His pride was a prisoner. And he meant to win it back. He would humble Carr, and he would

254

do it where Carr had humbled him, before the entire company.

"Laddie, the word is around town that the performance you are getting out of the girl and out of Preston Carr is fabulous. So I beg you, don't screw up! Please?"

Marty realized that Jock was not listening. "Kid? Laddie! God damn it, Jock, I am talking to you! I am trying to tell you something important!"

Jock smiled, said very sweetly into the radiophone, "Laddie, go get yourself blown."

And he broke off the contact.

Marty was right about one thing. Word was drifting back to LA and to New York. Word that exceeded in importance the gossip about who was going to bed with whom. There were repeated offers of feature coverage from *Life, Look, Time.* Two TV networks offered to do documentary coverage on how a great, or promisingly great, picture was really made.

Despite the studio's urging and Marty's insistence, Jock would allow no reporters or outside photographers on location. He turned aside all requests with the same line, "Moses and the Israelites spent forty years in the desert without *Life* and *Look.* We can spend four months here without them."

In the beginning, it had been because of Jock's uncertainty. Now it was because he felt he was sitting on a blockbuster, and he didn't want to dissipate any of the impact by letting it leak, bit by bit.

But New York had problems it could not ignore. The stockholders' rebellion, put down only months ago, was boiling up again. It would help to have *Life* or *Look* coverage and TV cooperation to promote the picture, if only as a sop to the stockholders, to persuade them to withhold or soften their judgment on management for another few months.

It was on this pretext, to plead with Jock for a change in publicity policy, that Marty made his own personal safari to the location. In a private, rented helicopter, which, to Jock's annoyance, descended right in the middle of, and ruined, a perfectly acceptable take, the Owl arrived. He had timed it so that he knew he was

255

close to the lunch break. But not so close that he couldn't watch Jock Finley at work.

The scene involved Carr and Boyd, with Daisy in the background, reacting. While it was in essence a dialogue scene and was written that way, Jock was unhappy with it. Carr and Boyd did well enough with the dialogue. Boyd knew his lines; better still, he said them as if he knew them. And there was a minimum of shit-kicking with his dusty-toed boot, and nail-shaving on his jaw, and lip-sucking in the middle of sentences. Preston Carr had cured him of that by pacing his own lines faster and cautioning Boyd, "If you go too slow, kid, they'll cut the hell out of you on the Moviola."

That had been enough to scare young Mr. Boyd out of his eccentric New York acting tricks and into a decent pace.

So that, all things considered, the scene was working fairly well. Marty, watching it, thought It's a nice scene and you need a few nice moments in a picture with so much action, so much naked sex. After all, if a picture hoped to play the Music Hall, nice was necessary.

Preston Carr felt it was a routine scene. Not great, but then not every scene in every picture could be great. If it advanced the story, didn't hold up the pace, helped enrich the characters, that was enough for any scene to be worth its time on the screen.

But Jock Finley was not satisfied. Joe accepted it. Sound okayed it. The assistant was giving the order: "Okay. Next setup!" when Jock turned away from the scene and said crisply, "Wait! Hold it!"

It could have been Marty's presence. Every director has a tendency to showboat a bit when there are outsiders on the set. Directors have little opportunity to let the world know what it is they really do, or how brilliant they really are, or what they invented as distinguished from what the author, long forgotten, had put down on the page to begin with. So almost every director does a fancy bit of inventing on the set when there are visitors present.

It was pardonable that Jock did some now. For with the Owl here, it was not mere vanity that motivated Jock, but hard knowledge of the fact that what the Owl saw would be used by him for years in selling Jock Finley. Time and time again he would be able to say, and would say, "Why I saw that boy take *dreck*, and turn it into gold! Right before my eyes!"

So that Jock Finley had a practical reason for what he did now. "Let's break for lunch! And we'll come back to this!"

Joe Goldenberg, his assistant, Preston Carr, Tony Boyd, all of them were caught in the middle of that moment of relaxation that follows a scene done satisfactorily, professionally, acceptably.

Joe asked, "Something wrong?"

"No," Jock said, "but if I was looking to make a picture in which nothing is wrong we'd have been done two weeks ago. Not wrong is one thing. Right is something else. We'll come back after lunch and do it right!"

Cryptically, with no further explanation, he turned to Marty and said, "I'll be in my trailer." He walked off, with the clear intention that the Owl pursue him. But Marty White, a man used to power of his own kind, did not pursue. Instead, he took the moment to speak to old friends. He exchanged cordial hellos with Preston Carr, kissed Daisy Donnell, which everyone did, every day, instead of saying hello, or how are you. Then he approached Joe, who was just dismissing his own assistant after orders concerning the requirements for the afternoon's shooting.

Veterans of each war have their own special vocabulary, meanings, unspoken understandings. So, too, the veterans of early Hollywood wars. To them the Jock Finleys would always be upstarts, to be observed, tolerated, accepted somewhat, but never fully.

"Well?" the Owl asked.

"Lot of good stuff," Joe said.

"Will it cut?"

"Sure!"

"The girl?"

"Never better."

"Carr?"

"He's the King."

"So?"

"I'll be glad to have my name on it," Joe said, which was the ultimate in praise from Joe Goldenberg.

"Finley?"

"If only he didn't turn it into a vendetta."

"Him and Carr?" Marty asked. Joe nodded. "Carr and the girl . . . they're screwing around, huh?"

"Not in front of the camera," was all Joe would say and all that was pertinent, as far as he was concerned.

Marty nodded. Joe had said it all. Everything was fine. As long as Jock didn't try to revenge himself on Preston Carr.

Marty arrived at Jock's trailer to find the young director deeply involved in his script. When the Owl started to talk, Jock quieted him with a sudden, harsh, "Christ, Marty!"

Marty sat quietly through the ensuing minutes as Jock studied his script. A waiter brought lunch for two from the commissary, set it up, served it. All without a word. Jock kept poring over that scene and over his notes, which were on the back of each preceding page, and on colored pages interspersed between script pages. Then he looked off, past the Owl's gleaming bald head, toward the window, toward that fragment of the mountain range visible through the small opening.

Something had just happened in Jock's mind. The problem had been solved, because suddenly he said, "Yeah?" catching Marty speechless, which did not happen very often. "What's the pitch, Marty? You don't rent a helicopter, fly out here just to have a lousy lamb stew for lunch. What's up?"

"Well, kid," Marty began. "I got a call from New York. They feel we are missing some big chances at publicity. If *Life* wants to give us a spread, possibly the cover, it would be foolish to say no. After all, with an eight-million-dollar picture, twelve million by the time you count prints and advertising, a little pre-selling can't hurt."

"*Life* gave *The Greatest Story Ever Told* a big spread, with the cover. And it turned out to be the biggest bomb ever told," Jock said, passing up the lamb stew for his iced black coffee.

"You know what they say about George Stevens, it takes a big director to make such a big flop. An ordinary *shmuck* couldn't have done it," the Owl cracked. Then he pushed a piece of gray lamb around in the gravy, studying it as he said, "New York would also like to talk a deal. But I'm stalling them. The more they press the more I stall. I figure if the picture is as big as everyone thinks, no deal made now is good enough. If the picture bombs for any reason, they'll find a way out of any deal we make. So I say, we don't risk anything by waiting, and we have everything to gain. That's why it's nice to deal from strength. Of course . . ."

"Of course" was a key phrase in the Owl's vocabulary. It was a signpost, a clue, a signal that it was time for Jock to stop paying attention to his iced coffee and to listen.

"Of course, the main thing is that New York is so close to a great picture they can taste it. But the closer they get, the more nervous they get. After all, they have stockholders to worry about. So they are keeping their fingers crossed that nothing goes wrong at the last minute."

"Such as?" Jock asked coldly.

"Such as . . . well . . . the girl . . . she is prone to breakdowns and if anything happened to her . . ."

"The girl is fine! She feels great!" Jock said, but he did not add, except that she will not get into bed with me again.

"Good. Good," the Owl said. "And they are worried, this Boyd kid, can he cut it in a feature? Does he have balls on screen? Will he be worth anything to the picture?"

"He will be good. Fine. Adequate to the demands of the part. The kids will love him. That's important."

"It certainly is," the Owl hastened to agree. These days everyone worried about what "the kids" would like.

Suddenly time was short. Jock's assistant was already knocking on the trailer door to announce lunch was over and the crew was back. So the Owl had to talk fast and Jock knew that now the real business of the meeting would come up for discussion finally.

"There is one other thing that New York is worried about. That is, well, friction. For example, I would like to be able to go back to LA, call New York and tell them that you and Pres Carr are getting along just fine . . ." the Owl let it hang.

Jock let it hang too. He finished his coffee, picked up his script binder, started to the door. The Owl was still waiting for an answer. At the door, Jock turned, and said softly. "Marty baby, tell you what. You get in your nice rented helicopter, fly back to LA, call New York and tell New York that no matter what they hear, everything is going along just fine. *For example*, you can tell them for me when I think that, for the benefit of the picture, it is good for Preston Carr and Daisy Donnell to shack up together because it helps their character relationship, I encourage that. New York is not to worry about who is getting into bed with whom. They are only to worry about what they see on film. Nobody, hear me, sweetie, nobody fucks any girl of Jock Finley's without his permission! Got it?"

Till that moment Marty White never realized how deeply hurt Jock Finley was by what Preston Carr had done. Knowing that, he could appreciate fully for the first time what Joe Goldenberg had been trying to tell him.

"As for anything else," Jock continued, "you come out there right now. And you'll see with your own eyes what I am going to do with that scene. Then you can go back, call New York and tell them that I am paid to make pictures! Not to fuck movie stars!"

Jock didn't merely leave that trailer. He exploded out of it, launched like a missile. He headed for the setup, where the crew was awaiting orders. With no word to anyone, Jock began to walk through the scene by himself, first being Carr, then being Boyd, then Daisy. Everyone else stood around and watched, silent. Carr came to join them. Then Daisy. Then young Boyd. Glances were exchanged, looks of concern, but no one said a word until Jock spoke suddenly, "Okay! This is the way the scene is going to work!" He snapped his fingers at the propman. "Lariat!" The man nodded, moved, said, "Yes, sir!" all in the same single instant.

Jock took up a position in the center of the area, with cameras, chairs, reflectors, unlit arcs, crew, Joe, Carr, Boyd, Daisy, all around him. The Owl stood behind the camera, hidden from sight but peering past the viewfinder at his frenetic client.

"We are dealing here with a scene in which age is getting ready to give way to youth. Dealing with a scene in which the older man can see the handwriting on the wall. It's a matter of time, brief time, when this young girl who thinks she is in love with the older man, but who is really only in love with the image of her father, will form a more natural relationship with a man closer to her own age."

260

Now Marty began to look, not at his own client who was doing all the talking and acting, but at Preston Carr. To see how he was reacting to a description, which while precisely applicable to the picture, was also precisely applicable to his sexual involvement with Daisy Donnell. The way Jock was using words like "older man," "man closer to her own age," "more natural relationship" made it clear that he was working off his hatred in full view of everyone.

If Joe Goldenberg had been wrong before, it was only in understating the danger. But there was nothing the Owl could do now, except listen. And hope for some opportunity to be able to talk to Jock before he started back to LA.

Right now, it was all Jock. He had center stage and he was not yielding to anyone.

"Now, how do we make the point, without hammering it home with words? How do we see the realization of the older man? The way he surrenders dominion over this girl whom he loves, but whom he knows he is going to lose? How does he hand over the mantle of successor to this younger man, this stronger, tougher, more virile man? In other words, how does age, which must inevitably lose, give way gracefully to youth and retain the audience's sympathy, affection, and loyalty?"

By now the propman had returned with the lariat and was standing by. Jock snapped his fingers. The man came forward to offer the coiled rope. Jock took it. He let out coil after coil till there were about ten feet on the ground, and he was able to manipulate it like a long, thin snake. He played it as he talked.

"This! This is the symbol! Of skill, of long experience. The older man uses it while he plays the scene. When he instructs the younger man in the lariat, he is really talking to him about the girl, about life. He will loop it over that fence post at the corral gate, free it, then loop it again, time after time, easily, gracefully. Loop, disengage, reel in, loop, disengage, reel in. All through the scene. And *you* . . ."

He turned suddenly to Boyd, "You will watch him, admire him. Listen to him. But only toward the end of the scene will you get the idea, when he actually hands you the rope. At that moment you, and the audience, will realize that he is giving the girl to

261

you. Entrusting her to you. Handing her over to you with his hope that you will use the same skill with her. Because she is a sensitive girl, and he knows it. He loves her, but he also knows he is too old for her. The next day he will ride off and be gone. Before he does he'd like to know she's going to be in dependable, loving hands."

Boyd nodded. Preston Carr stared. There was neither dissent nor acceptance on his face. Only a serious, thoughtful attitude. If he was furious, Marty could not detect it.

Now Jock beckoned Boyd out to join him in the scene. Ad-libbing the dialogue, Jock played the rope lazily, then let it fly through the air. It did not make the post, but Jock played the scene as if it had. He jerked it, in a simulated effort to free it, reeled it in, let out the loop again, threw it, disengaged it, reeled it in.

He ad-libbed the entire scene that way, following the sense of the dialogue but not the precise words, only some of the key phrases. As he did it, the scene began to come alive, to take on greater meaning. When he had talked his way to the end of it, he turned, handed over the coiled rope to young Boyd who took it. Then Jock walked out of the scene, as if making a proper exit.

In all of this, he had never once asked Preston Carr whether he could do the scene that way. Or if he wanted to. It was a simple courtesy you extended to any star, even if he was not the King, even if he was not paid a million dollars up front, with tax benefits. Because the degree of skill required to do that kind of roping, which Jock had only been faking, was considerable. And to do it while playing a scene, with the cameras on you, to do it timed to the key words, might turn out to be impossible. So that Carr might have to end up doing it in little bits and takes to be edited together later.

So the least a director did, if he was a thoughtful, sensitive man, was to ask the star. And in private. Not before the entire company. However, all that Jock Finley said was, "Let's walk through it a time or two and see how it works. Boyd! Pres! You ready, Joe?"

Joe nodded, came forward with his viewfinder so that he could move freely to follow the action, looking for his most advantageous angles. Boyd was standing in the middle of the set, rope in hand. Preston Carr left Daisy's side, came forward, took the rope. Jock squatted low, just forward of the camera. So Marty had to move to keep the scene in sight.

"Whenever you're ready, Pres," Jock said, cool, sure.

Preston Carr hefted the rope, let out a few coils, snaked it on the ground, reeled it in, threw a lazy loop, reeled it in again. He made a pass at the corral post. He missed. He reeled in. He hefted the rope again, made another pass. He missed again. Then Carr used a few lines of dialogue to go with the throwing action but the rope missed again. He was feeling his way, searching for something. But he had not yet dropped that loop over that fence post, which was the key to the whole attitude, purpose, and meaning of the scene, the skill of the older man. Through it all, Carr was very, very thoughtful, concerned, uneasy. Or, Marty asked himself, was he unwilling? Marty and Joe Goldenberg exchanged glances. Joe's glance said, This is what it's been like; Marty's said, Any other star would walk out.

Carr tried the scene again, still looping out the rope, still missing the fence post, reeling in, using the dialogue, still concerned, troubled. The crew stood by at a respectful distance, watching, listening, wondering when the King would blow up and stalk out. But he didn't.

Not even when Jock said, "Obviously, it's too complicated. Tell you what. Joe! Give me an angle that cuts out the fence post. Later we'll bring in one of the wranglers and just get close-ups of one loop after another ringing that post and then intercut them. Carr throw, cut to close-up, Carr throw, cut to close-up. It won't be as good but it'll do."

A director, a good director, especially a brilliant director, did not do that. Not to Preston Carr, not to any star. If a star was inadequate to a challenge, the director found a polite, diplomatic, face-saving way around the awkward moment. He did not expose the star's limitations in front of the whole company. That is, if a man was a brilliant director and not Jock Finley, if he was a brilliant director and not a man who has been eased out of a lady's bed by a star almost twice his age.

There is a special silence that descends on picture sets at certain moments. It has weight, substance. It hangs there, responsive to every sound, every breath. And unless someone does something, or says something to dispel it, it seems like D-Day minus ten seconds, forever.

It was Preston Carr who spoke first. "Smitty," he called to a propman. "Get me two ropes. One brand-new. One used. Age it if you have to."

"Yes, sir, Mr. Carr," and Smitty, older than Mr. Carr, was hustling on his way like an errand boy to carry out the King's orders.

"Corinne!" Carr called to the script girl. She was up from her chair, came forward with her inevitable stopwatch hanging from her neck, her script book open to the scene.

"Yes, sir?"

"I want you to follow me, every word of the way. Before, when we were depending on words alone we needed them all. But now, with this idea, where we *do* it, as well as say, we don't have to say nearly so much . . ." Carr turned to Jock. "Jock baby, you don't mind if I walk through it and make a few cuts, do you?"

"Not at all. Whatever feels comfortable for you, sweetie."

"Look, do you mind if I make a suggestion or two to Boyd?" Carr asked.

"Of course not," Jock said. "As long as it doesn't go against the scene."

Carr came to the center of the corral set, motioned to Boyd to take up his position. Carr looked around, found Daisy just out of camera range, called to her softly, "Darling, I want you to be there . . . right over there."

He went to her, took her hand, and walked her gracefully to the far end of the fence. He set her where he wanted her, and then because he couldn't seem to resist it, he kissed her on the cheek and playfully tapped her nose, then started back to Boyd.

"Now, kid, this will help me in the scene. You see, if I am turning this girl over to you, and trying to get across to you that she needs a younger man, but one with sensitivity, skill, understanding, *I* can't let the audience know that. That means I'm showing off, saying to the audience, 'Oh, what a nice guy am I.' *You* are the one who has to let them know it. So when I am making my last loop, just before I reel in for the last time, hand you

264

the rope, and thus the girl, you look from me, to her, then back to me. I want to see it dawn in *your* eyes, that you realize suddenly what I'm doing. Got it?"

Only now did Carr look to Jock, to say, "That should be a close-up, that look on Boyd's face, shouldn't it?"

"Exactly!" Jock agreed, though he was quite angry that he hadn't said it first himself.

By this time, Smitty was back with two ropes. One fresh and new, with the label still around the looped end, the other, used, not so light in color.

"This one used enough?" Smitty asked.

Carr took both ropes, hefted them. Looped each out a time or two. He turned to Jock.

"What do you think? A new rope, so that when I hand it over, it's fresh and clean, symbolizing the relationship between the girl and the young man as being fresh and clean? Or the used rope, so that I am handing over to him a girl who is no longer fresh and clean, but if used with care and skill will do a man for his lifetime? Which is going to go better with the critics back there in New York, Paris, and London?"

Marty would never know how much sarcasm was intended by Carr's question. Or if the mention of London was deliberate, to scrape Jock's wounded pride a little. But no matter what Carr intended, there was only one way Jock took it. Retaining his control, smiling, Jock moved into the center of the area, looked at both ropes, then said, "I think the new one is better. The idea that the relationship will start fresh, clean, new with a younger man . . . that point is made better with the new one." He took the used rope from Carr and tossed it off into the group of waiting crewmen.

"Ready?" Jock asked.

"Let's try it," Carr agreed.

Jock looked to his assistant, to Joe. "Everybody ready! Stand by!"

Each man moved to his job. In the arena of the scene, Carr was merely indicating his action without really doing it, was making small hand gestures that simulated the rope-throwing without letting go the lariat, and was saying to himself, without uttering a sound, all the lines, so that he was sure he had the new, cut version of the scene in mind.

Jock did not interfere. When Carr was done, he turned to seek out Jock among the faces that crowded round the camera, "Ready!"

Jock signaled his assistant, who went through the usual commands to assure that everyone else was ready, then he turned it all back to Jock for the final "Action!"

Preston Carr snaked out the rope, said his lines slowly, carefully, alternating his gaze from the rope to Boyd to see if the young man was getting the import of what he was saying. Then Carr reeled in the rope, so when it came time to hit a key line he could let it go again. It dropped neatly, cleanly over the fence post. Then as he took a pause to see the effect on Boyd, he jerked the rope free, reeled it in, saying his lines about how careful one must be, how sometimes with a woman a delicate touch can achieve much more than strength or force. With that, and exhibiting a delicate touch, Carr let go of the rope. It landed gracefully over the fence post.

With the cut dialogue, with the graceful, easy way Carr handled the rope, looping it over the fence post, jerking it free to reel it in again, the scene took on a poetry of motion and words that truly entranced young Boyd. So that when the time came for him to look over at Daisy and make the connection, Boyd did it so naturally that even Jock didn't know for sure if the boy was acting or not.

At the end of the scene, Carr reeled in the rope slowly, coiling it as he did, so that it was ready to hand over. Then he held it out. Young Boyd took it, his actor's admiration so clear on his young face that it could rightly have been called awe. But since it fit the climax of the scene so well, no one would fault him for it. Now Carr walked out of the scene. And there was no mistaking what it all meant. Audiences that would not understand a word he had said, would know it, feel it, and not miss the words at all. And that was when picture-making was really an art.

"Cut!" Jock said in a low, whispered command. As soon as he did, Boyd walked over to Carr, held out his hand to him.

266

"Jesus! Man! That is acting! I just hope I didn't do anything to spoil the scene, Mr. Carr."

"You were swell, kid. You gave me exactly what I needed."

"Boy, and they talk about acting in New York!" Boyd went on. By that time Jock Finley had reached Carr's side.

"Terrific, Pres! Just terrific!" but he could have meant it more, and used more original and less clichéd words.

"Soon as you walked through it with the lariat I could see what it would do for the scene," Carr said graciously.

So, while in full hearing of the company, Carr was giving Jock all the credit, there was not a man or woman there who did not realize that Carr had taken Jock's idea and made it into a scene by the way he cut the dialogue. He had given it life, grace, depth, and meaning by his use of the rope for accents. He had been at complete ease doing what Jock had intended to be a great and humiliating challenge.

Marty joined them at that point. He could only shake his head in awe and reverence, hold out his hand to Carr. "They don't do it like that any more. Kids! They talk theory. They know all about acting, except one thing. How to act! What a lesson! Every young actor in America should have to go to school and watch that scene."

"It was your client's idea," Carr said modestly. "That's the way pictures are made. A good idea becomes a better idea. Everyone helps." He walked away, as though oblivious to friction, resentment, conflict.

Marty turned to Jock waying, "Brilliant! Kid, that is a terrific scene! They'll talk about that one for a long time. I never knew Carr could handle a rope like that. Terrific! Keep it going that way. Don't let anything upset it." Though Marty was talking in impersonal pronouns, he knew, and Jock knew, exactly what he meant.

"You have to drive him. If you want his best," Jock said, almost grimly, as though he had suffered a defeat.

"Just take it easy, kid, What have you got left? Another week, ten days?"

"I'm saving the big scene for the end. It might take a week. Or a month. But I won't quit till I get it my way."

"The big scene?" Marty asked, searching his memory. "The stampede of the mustangs? You already got that in the can."

"The breaking scene," Jock said.

The breaking scene, the Owl was asking himself, what the hell scene is that? But he didn't press it. "Oh, yes," he said. "The breaking scene. Well, how long can one sequence take?"

"This one could take a long, long time," Jock said, thoughtfully.

"Whatever you do, do it carefully. You have a classic here," Marty said. He would have said more, much more, but Jock's assistant had some questions that needed to be answered at once. The Owl started for his helicopter. His elation over the scene diminished, replaced now by his fear of what Jock Finley might be planning. If only young men with talent had less mischief in them. Less pride. Yet without pride where would their talent be?

CHAPTER

8

IT had been accepted for some days now that Preston Carr and Daisy Donnell no longer appeared in the commissary for dinner. They were always served in Carr's trailer. And usually certain choice foods which Carr had flown in from LA or New York.

But this evening was different, perhaps because of the events of the day, the roping scene that had gone so extremely well. Whatever the reason, this night Carr had arranged a table for just the two of them. When they made their way through the large room, some of the old-timers in the crew rose up, reached out, and shook Carr's hand and congratulated him. There was a camaraderie among the old-timers of the picture business which no longer existed in these days of foreign locations and hit-or-miss independents. Then each person in the industry, from lowliest grip to the biggest star, belonged to a studio. Now each picture was a separate deal, so no place was really home. One hardly ever worked with the same people twice.

Jock had just begun his own dinner of rare roast beef when Carr and Daisy entered. He kept a fixed smile on his face as he ate. But he could not avoid hearing some of the old-timers who commented on how today was almost like the old days, and, "Remember when we were shooting *Red River*?" and that today was "almost as good as the scene Pres did with Lionel Barrymore in *Surrender*," which went back to a time when Carr had been about the same age young Boyd was now.

Though very rare roast beef was Jock's favorite food, tonight it was bloody sawdust in his mouth. Mumbling something about "damned Western beef!" he shoved back his plate and asked for coffee. The waiter suggested another, possibly rarer, cut. Jock refused. Just coffee. That seemed a little too long appearing. He got up, strode out of the commissary. Careful, of course, to smile his greetings to Daisy and Carr.

Alone, in the cool desert night, he started away from the camp. Till he was far enough to stand in almost complete darkness and stare at the distant, arid hills.

He had to tell himself that the appearance of Daisy and Carr in the commissary had nothing to do with his sudden exit. It had been the food. But more, it was the demand pressing on him to create or invent a way to finish the picture. Some way which would exceed all the fine things he had achieved in the earlier scenes. It would be a defeat of enormous consequence if he were to be accused by the critics of letting his film sag at the end. With greatness so close, now it was Jock himself who was demanding of Jock Finley, the director, some way to "guarantee" the picture.

It all depended on Preston Carr's important final scene. Which was fortunate. For in some way Carr had been able to rise to every challenge and demand that Jock had devised, to exceed them, in fact. More, Carr did it with a sureness, ease, and professionalism on which today's crop of young actors and directors prided themselves, but which, in their youthful arrogance, they tried to deny to the old-timers.

Yes, this man Carr had it, had it all. And knew how to use it. If Jock had been testing him, and he could grudgingly admit by himself, to himself, that he had been, then it was the tests that had failed, not Pres Carr.

Of course, Jock hastened to justify himself to himself by protesting that what he had done had always been in the best interests of the picture. For example, that roping scene today was one of the great ones. Who gave a damn how it came to be! That was the creative process, that a man, a director, invested his own emotions, his loves, hates, and hostilities for the benefit of the film. Which, in the end, was the only thing that mattered.

Whatever anyone might have said, about Jock, about Carr,

about the girl, or about who was sleeping with whom, Jock's final recourse, and the world's final demand, would be, what was on film? If it was there and great, then no one in this world would remember for very long what had happened in whose bed. In the folklore of Hollywood, Jock Finley would merely take his place in the line, that long line, of men Daisy Donnell had slept with and never married. The men she had allowed to use her, because actually she had been using them.

The only important thing to Jock was that the film which emerged would have greatness stamped on it. That in those places where it counted to a director, people would talk about the greatest performance of Preston Carr's life in a meaningful role in a meaningful picture. That they would talk about the time that Daisy Donnell gave the one "real" performance of her entire career.

He was justifying himself, consoling himself, yet somehow he did not feel consoled. The Jock Finleys were not born to lose. When they finally did, it was to death, and death alone. And they were not born to die young. He had proved that when he went out, in a mortally reckless way, with that hand-held camera. That was something he could do only because he had such utter belief that there was a fate in store for Jock Finley which exceeded that of ordinary men. Other young men might die untimely deaths but not he. Other young men might lose girls but not Jock Finley. He had to believe he gave her up, and he manipulated it in the best interests of the film.

Now his problem was Preston Carr. And that last scene.

He stared toward the motor pool where all vehicles, personal and company, were parked for the night. He found his own red Ferrari, leaped into it without opening the door, perhaps because it had been Preston Carr who pointed out to him that young smart-ass directors tried to impress everyone by leaping into and out of their Ferraris without opening the door.

Jock started up the car. The powerful roar sounded even louder in the quiet of the desert night. He pulled away, headed out across the wide, flat wasteland, raising a trail of dust that hung in the air, refracting the moonlight and giving it substance.

He could have ridden straight out to the makeshift corral

where all the equipment stood, silent, shrouded shadows. But he cut a wide path around it, circling and approaching from the far end. He pulled up at the corral, leaped out, walked around among covered cameras, booms, monster cranes, platforms. He climbed the corral fence, sat there a while, then leaped down, crossed the corral, slipped through the far fence, and walked out into the desert, feeling the gritty, hard-baked earth under his boots, stopping every so often to kick his heel into it, to get the feel of it, the sound of it.

He stopped, looked up toward the mountains which rose out of the flatland. In the moonlight, huge grotesque shadows hid there, patches of light, large oceans of darkness. Suddenly, a sound made him turn, the sound of another living thing moving close by. There were animals out here at night, but not particularly dangerous ones. Desert jackrabbits, coyotes too, they said, but he had never seen one. Jock turned swiftly, somewhat tense, then suddenly completely at his ease again when he saw that it was Joe Goldenberg coming toward him.

"Something wrong?" the older man asked. He was filling his caked-up pipe as he approached. That was an after-hours luxury for Joe. Between takes and setups there was no time to fill a pipe and really savor it. But in the evening, after dinner when he was planning his camera angles for the next day, he loved a fragrant, easy smoke.

Jock did not answer. The older man drew close, started to light up. Using the jet flame of his pipe lighter to its fullest, he was also able to glance at Jock's young, strong, pensive face, at the blue eyes, now narrowed, hard, calculating.

"Anything wrong?" Joe asked again.

Jock smiled. "Wrong? Hell, Joe, I'm going to make you famous!"

Amused and concerned, Joe said, "It's about time."

This was Joe Goldenberg who by his own artistic creativity had made famous half a score of young directors.

Jock Finley began to move about, looked across at the mountains, up at the night sky, which was lavishly silver with stars, and was lighter blue than it should have been at this hour.

272

"What's it about, Joe?" Joe puffed and wondered if Jock meant life, or the picture, or the relationship between himself and Preston Carr.

"This picture," Jock said. "What's it really about? A man in the declining years of his life realizes that he has to pass something on. And that 'something' is a plea for individual freedom. The world is getting too complex, too big, too involved for mere human beings. There is no place any more, no frontier, nothing left for the individual to conquer. The world is all technology, equipment, machinery. Man is being plowed under, made to serve the machine that man himself invented."

Joe had heard some of the greatest in the business talk that way, expounding long, involved meanings that no audience in the world would ever appreciate, no matter what you put on film. But if from all that mass of turgid thinking and raw, unrefined feeling there emerged one thought that an audience did grasp, then it didn't matter how right or wrong, how explicit or confused was the director's thought process.

"Joe, how are we going to let the audience know that, feel that, be part of it? Because I don't want spectators. I want participants. I want them to be *with* Carr! To *be* Carr! At the most crucial moments of this picture! I don't want this picture seen! I want it experienced!"

Joe puffed away, silent. There was no good director he knew who hadn't at some time said this same thing and in somewhat the same words. Joe knew that what they were really trying to say was that they were so immersed in the film they were making that they wished the whole world could feel as intensely about it as they did.

But that was good. Because Joe had a creed about pictures, if you couldn't believe in them fervently you shouldn't be making them. In these days when pictures were being made in such profusion because even if they were no good and satisfied no one, they could still recover their cost on TV, it was good to hear someone who did care so deeply.

A good part of Joe's art was in listening. Because by listening to what directors said, in their vague, esoteric, confused way, he could become infected with their feeling, help it germinate, give birth to some new technique, angle, trick of lighting that would capture and further the director's intention.

Joe himself had said once in an interview, "To directors, especially young ones, I am like a psychoanalyst. If I listen to them long enough something good comes out of it."

"I want the audience," Jock was saying, "to be overwhelmed. As simple human beings are being overwhelmed by the world around them. I want the desperate anger of a wild beast fighting what it knows must be its last free fight. And I want the determination, sweat, muscle, drive, of Carr, the man who has to corner and cage that animal. I want it continuous! I want it simultaneous! I do not want to have to break it up into shot, shot, shot. Man, beast, man, beast, man, beast. Wide, medium, close, wide, medium, close. I do not want conventional treatment in this segment of the film. I want an overpowering experience that will leave the audience wet, limp, terribly sympathetic on behalf of that animal, and almost hating Carr, even while they admire his skill, his strength, his determination. And then . . . then if, while they're feeling that way, Carr suddenly says to himself, I can't do this to such a noble beast, and turns, raises that tailgate, takes off the halter, slaps the animal on its flank, and sends it leaping off that truck and back to the hills, free again, they'll want to come up out of their chairs and kiss Preston Carr. So that if he never makes another picture, or makes a hundred of them, they'll remember this moment of this picture as his greatest."

Jock paused a moment. When he started again, it was in a more intimate voice, soft, solicitous, apologetic.

"Joe . . . I don't know if you'll even be interested in the effect I have in mind . . . and if you're not, say so and I'll call in another man just for this one sequence . . ."

Along with the apology there was an undercurrent of challenge in Jock's tone. Exactly as he had intended.

"What I have in mind is new, daring, maybe risky. So maybe a younger man with far less skill and experience might go at it with fewer inhibitions. I would like this sequence, which is to me the major sequence in the picture, I would like it to be done in multiple screen."

274

"Multiple screen? You'd have to re-equip every theater and drive-in in the country for one sequence in one picture!" Joe protested.

"Not if we do it all in the lab. With opticals. Not if we put the whole effect of half a dozen screens on every frame of film so it can be shown on one screen. Multiple images, instead of multiple screens."

"Interesting," Joe conceded. "Of course, there's the matter of cost..."

"I'll go to the studio. Or to New York if I have to. I'll get the money!" Jock said, determined, almost angry. "But if I get it, can you do it, Joe? It's no disgrace to say you can't. It's a new technique. Different from anything you've ever done..." Jock's eyes seemed to be searching the vast, dark horizon. Actually they were fixed, poised, awaiting Joe's answer.

"Anything that can be done with a camera, I can do," Joe said softly. "And if you feel it's what you want... and you can get the budget for it, okay by me! I'd love to try something like that."

Jock's eyes were smiling now, almost dancing. Because part of his strategy in getting the added budget depended on his being able to say, "Look, Joe Goldenberg would love to do it! So it can't be such a wild idea."

"Of course..." Now Joe qualified his commitment.

Jock felt his elation might be premature. "Of course what, Joe? What?" Jock could, on cue, display a young-boy air of intense interest in what the other person had to say, when all the while he was only concentrating on how he would refute it.

"Cameras are cameras, film is film, cutting is cutting. All that can be handled if there is enough time, enough money. But ... but, footage, my boy. You need footage. You can't cut, splice, edit, frame by frame, unless you have enough footage of that horse and that man to begin with.

"If you want that man's eyes, and the ridges of muscle in his arms, and his face, grim and taut, all at the same time so that we know it is life and death, you can't just take those few frames. You have to shoot and shoot long, long sequences to get the precise effects you want, in order to have just the frames you

275

need so when you put it all in multiple image it makes that over-whelming experience you're talking about. Footage! Lots of it, that's what you'll need."

"But with enough footage, you could give me what I want?"

"*I* could!" Joe said, saying at the same time that what Jock wanted did not depend on him alone. Jock turned to Joe, looking puzzled, almost hurt.

"If I get you enough time, enough budget, we can get all the footage we need, can't we?" Jock asked.

"The total effect," Joe began, "depends on how close we can come with the camera. On what lenses we use. But if we are close, very close, it will become apparent, sometime during all that foot-age, that we're using a double for Pres. Now, true, with six images going at once, or eight, you might figure you won't get the audience discrimination you get in single-image projection. But if you get the total immersion you're after, you'll have them concentrating to such a degree that they won't miss a detail. So you can't have any giveaway frames that even let them suspect it's a stunt man."

Jock absorbed that, seemed to think about it.

"Joe . . . Joe, what if we didn't use a double . . . would we have the problem then?" Jock asked almost casually.

"Christ, you can't ask Pres to do all the footage for a sequence like that out in the hot sun. It would mean days on end! Do you realize what that would take? The energy, the strength?"

"Strength? Those arms of his. I wish I had power like that."

"At his age, five or six days of that kind of horse-wrestling in the desert sun . . ." Joe shook his head. "He won't do it. And you can't make him. No contract in the world can make him."

"I can't make him do anything, Joe. We both know that. He does what he wants, the way he wants. Fortunately he's great, his instincts are great, so we're way ahead of the game as a result."

Now Jock began to play his own scene in high gear, using a device he had always found most effective. You gave someone a part of your innermost self, as security, as a bribe, in order to disarm them and make them believe what you wanted them to believe.

"Joe, I can't fool you. I wouldn't even try. Sure, I hate the

276

idea that he took that girl away from me. Because I . . . I have
a feeling about . . . I can't say I love her . . . maybe I don't know
what love is . . . But she is an unusual experience in my life, in the
life of any man. And I would have wanted it to go on and on and
on. But she fell in love with him. My fault! She didn't find what
she wanted in me. Or maybe I staged that first love scene between
them too well, too real, and she believed it. Who knows, maybe
deep down in my unconscious mind I was making that match
months ago when I decided that I would cast her opposite him.

"Whatever it was, however it happened, I blame myself for
it. Not him. I don't resent that man. I respect him. I feel that
he is better for her than I am. I couldn't admit that to anyone
else. But I feel I can tell you.

"What I'm trying to say, Joe, even though I hate what he did
to me over that girl, I respect him too much to *order* him to do
anything. I can only ask, hope. But command? Never. Not Preston
Carr!"

Joe, who was not fooled often, believed that.

"Joe, if you think it's possible, I'll talk to the studio. And
if they go for the extra budget, only then will I ask Pres."

"Good. Let's not get involved in this kind of shooting unless
he wants to do it," Joe warned.

"I give you my word!" Jock said, his baby-blues on overtime
now.

Early next morning Jock called Marty White to request a meeting with the studio. Within two hours Marty called back. The
meeting had been arranged. Both the studio head and the president
would be there. The place would be LA, since the president was
due to be at the studio for one of his periodic trips to discuss stories
and production.

The meeting was held over lunch in the small private conference
room that adjoined the studio head's office: the president, the
studio head, Jock, and the Owl—just the four of them.

Because the president had no idea of what bombshell this young
maverick director might come up with, he had passed up his usual
double martinis before lunch, to be alert, ready for any onslaught.

The lunch was orchestrated with pleasantries. How pleased they
were with the footage. That love scene on the lake shore, they

277

were sure such poetic nudity would even be welcomed at the Music Hall. Of course, let's never forget that hand-held footage of the stampede. The president said whenever he began to lose faith in the picture business he went into his projection room in New York and ran that sequence and his faith was restored.

By now the studio head and the president were vying with each other to say whatever they thought might please, flatter, soften this young monster of a genius in whom they had invested more than seven million dollars.

Finally, over coffee, the president declaimed, "So that's why I can say to you, my boy, anything within our power to grant, you have only to ask. And if the stockholders won't kick, the answer is yes."

Jock started slowly, softly, about the "new" film, the "new" audience, the "new" critics, and how demanding they were. But once satisfied, there was no limit to their loyalty, expressed in terms of dollars at the box office. Take *The Graduate*, for example. Not the greatest film ever made. Not anywhere near the greatest. But it had that thing, that "in" thing the kids loved, so it was doing fantastic business.

They needed such a new attack in *Mustang!* The stampede, the love scene, the use of nudity, all that was part of it. But it needed one thing more. Jock exposed his plan for the use of the multiple-image technique for the climactic horse-wrestling scene.

Sure, multiple image had been used. But only as a stunt. Never this way before in any big feature. Never for total immersion. It was the kind of novelty worth millions in publicity, in added revenue, in critical acclaim. Of course, with the kids it was just the sort of thing, the new kind of thing, they went for.

Relieved on the one hand that Jock had no unreasonable demands to make, but concerned on the other, about getting into any added expense, especially one that might create an open-ended drain, the president was cautious. So naturally the studio head was cautious. And what did Joe Goldenberg say, the studio head wished to know.

"We've had extensive discussions about it. Joe is so enthusiastic, I'd hate to go back and tell him we've been turned down."

278

So Joe Goldenberg said it was possible, the president mused, greatly impressed.

"Possible? Joe thinks this sequence would be the crowning achievement of his career! It will be his third Academy Award!"

Well, the president considered, if a man as stable and experienced as Joe Goldenberg said that ... suddenly the president asked, "Preston Carr? What does he say? Is he willing to do it?"

Jock shifted into his most sincere mood now, his baby-blues glistening with tears which verged on being shed.

"I haven't asked him. Because I know what his answer is going to be. Then if you turn him down over a lousy half million dollars, he'll be brokenhearted. He'll never forgive any of us. I won't ask him unless I have your approval in my back pocket. Unless we're willing to go through with it."

They understood, naturally, the president, the studio head. The president turned to the studio head, "We can do it on the lot? Technically, I mean?"

"I'll get hold of Walter. I'll find out."

They got Walter. They found out. It would take some new equipment. Not much. Most of it could be hand-built right on the lot. But it was feasible to proceed with the shooting. Only, Walter warned, get enough footage of Carr in the can so you don't get caught short. But Jock was quick to tell them that he and Joe had gone all over that and were prepared with a shooting plan. Finally, the president said, "Kid, go ahead! Make the picture your way! We have the utmost!"

They shook hands all around. Jock started for the door, with Marty right behind him. The studio head whispered something to the president who then called out, "Oh, by the way, kid ..."

Jock turned, Marty turned. "Yeah, boss?" Jock asked.

"Publicity is after us all the time. They got a lot of pressure from *Life* to shoot the picture on location. They think it's a cover story. What do you say?"

Jock considered it a moment, smiled, shook his head. Then he borrowed a bit from Marty, "Boss, a picture is like a girl. As long as she's considered a virgin, people are respectful. As soon as talk gets around, she's old-hat, used. We still got our virginity.

We're going to hold onto it. It'll only make *Life* more anxious for it when we finally do give them something."

"If we hold them off too long they might sour on the project," the president warned.

"Blame me! Tell them you got this crazy boy director who sits around naked, smoking pot while he works, so he doesn't want to be photographed by *Life* or anyone else." Jock laughed and closed the door.

The president and the studio head smiled, too. Till the door closed. Then the president said in an anxious whisper, "Get me a martini! Double!"

In the parking lot, where Marty was depositing Jock in his own Rolls so the chauffeur could drive him back to the airport, the smallish agent was asking gingerly, "What have you got to lose, letting *Life* come in and cover the last sequence? From the way you describe it, it could be fantastic."

"It will be fantastic!" Jock declared.

"Then all the more reason for *Life*!" Marty urged.

"Marty! That decision is made! Forget it!"

There comes a time in the relationship between agent and client on the western shores of this continent when the client starts to give the orders. That time is when the client has just achieved, or everyone feels he is about to achieve, a huge success. From that time on, the client is really boss.

Till then, politely or otherwise, by suasion or force, by the manipulation of truth or falsehood, the agent makes all the decisions and gives all the orders.

Right now, in the career of Jock Finley, he had just crossed that invisible meridian. He had just become boss. And he would be, from now on.

So the question of *Life* coverage was closed.

CHAPTER

9

On location, the day had not been lost. Joe had been shooting backgrounds, usually second-unit stuff, to use for intercutting when Jock would need a shot or two to bridge time lapses, or when two sequences wouldn't cut or lend themselves to a natural dissolve without some intervening footage.

When Jock's red Ferrari pulled up at the shooting location, Joe was intensely involved in lining up a long pan shot of the mountains. It wasn't till he came away from the camera that he saw Jock.

"Well?" Joe asked.

Jock made an okay sign, giving it his big, white-toothed smile. "All the way! Half a million! More if we need it. They're crazy about the idea."

"Good. Good," Joe said, smiling, but not too warmly. Not warmly enough for Jock.

"What's wrong, Joe? Change your mind?" Jock's expression turned from boyish happy to cooler, mannish concern.

"We'll . . . we'll talk about it later," Joe said, conscious of the fact that his crew was standing around, awaiting his go-ahead, and listening. "I'll be back in about an hour. Drop into my place? We'll have a drink," Joe invited, trying to seem casual.

"Drop into my place!" Jock corrected. "I'll be waiting." He leaped into the red Ferrari, revved it up, backed out with a speed that required a sharp stop. Then he took off with a sudden rasping of tires on desert earth.

Almost two hours later, Joe was back from location, showered, dressed in brown flannel slacks, an open shirt, and an old corduroy jacket, the leather elbow patches of which were also worn through. But it was Joe's way of relaxing, nostalgically. For the jacket had been given to him years ago by Katharine Hepburn after a picture they did together.

Jock was naked, just toweling himself after a cold, stinging shower. He took his time about getting dry, as if he were exhibiting his strong, young, muscular body. Joe, who had a sculptor's eye, thought to himself, Oh, to be that young again. It was no wonder the girls went for this outrageously impertinent, aggressive, vulgar young man. There was a kind of beauty about him.

Jock took his time to dry his feet, poising first the one, then the other on the arm of the chair, so that his young, vital genitalia hung loose, free. If he was self-conscious it was only to be proud.

"Scotch or brandy?" Jock invited, for Joe was known to drink brandy before dinner, ever since his illness about six years before.

Joe poured a short brandy, with just a splash of soda, as he asked, "Have you thought about it any more?"

"That's all I've been thinking about! What do you think I went to LA for?" Jock asked.

"I mean about Pres," Joe said, and he started to sip his drink.

"What about Pres?" Jock asked, pulling on a pair of salmon-colored silk boxer shorts, made for him in Paris.

"Ever since you mentioned this the other night, I've been observing him." Joe knew he must proceed cautiously.

Jock added to Joe's uncertainty by suddenly turning away to the bar to mix himself a Scotch and soda. There on Jock's back was a multicolored bruise, now more yellow than blue, the last trace of the injuries sustained during the stampede episode. Whether his back was turned in resentment of Joe, or to remind the older man that Jock bore the physical wounds of this picture, Joe could not know. But he was well aware of Jock's back, of the healing bruise, of the fact that he was being rudely upstaged by a thirty-one-year-old savage. Joe's every impulse was to get up, put aside his

282

brandy glass, get out. If he were on a mission of his own, he would have done just that. But more was involved here.

"I have been watching Preston Carr," Joe said.

"When?" Jock asked sharply, turning to Joe to get his answer.

"Today," Joe said.

"Today? You mean at lunch, don't you? He doesn't come out for breakfast. You haven't shot him today. So it must have been at lunch."

"Yes, at lunch," Joe admitted. "What difference? I had a chance to really observe him. To talk to him." Joe took another sip of brandy. "He's tired, Finley. Tired."

"He should be," Jock smiled. "Up screwing half the night!"

"It doesn't matter to me, why. The fact is, he is tired." Joe paused before he added, "And I don't think he is up to it."

"Up to what?" Jock asked, not smiling now.

"The horse-wrestling sequence," Joe said. "Not the way we discussed it."

"Did you say anything to him about it?"

"No," Joe said softly, in face of the rage evident in Jock Finley's face.

"Good! Let him make up his own mind! About whether he is up to it!"

"Don't you think a doctor might be a better judge?" Joe suggested.

"Doctors always say no!" Jock declared dogmatically.

"Not always," Joe disagreed, as sure in his soft way as Jock was in his loudness. Jock glared at him. But, Joe decided, better to have a crisis now than a catastrophe later.

"When I had my second attack," and this was the first time Joe had admitted to anyone in the industry that he had had two, "I wanted to go back to work. My wife kept saying, go to the doctor, let him decide. Because she felt the same way you do, doctors always say no. So I went, had a series of tests, had a long talk with my doctor, and he said, 'Of course, sure, go ahead, go back to work. More of my patients drop dead golfing at Hillcrest than working in studios.'"

"What's the point?" Jock demanded impatiently.

"The point is . . . " Joe started to say, "the point is . . . several points. First, we don't know ... and with a man like Preston Carr you usually don't find out till after ... but he might have had a heart attack and kept it absolutely quiet. The first time he retired, eight years ago, how do we know it wasn't because of a heart attack? A doctor would know. And if Pres ever did have an attack, he can't do this sequence."

"Well, if that's the way you feel, then by all means we'll call in a doctor."

Joe felt reassured, till Jock continued, "Or would you rather do the EKGs yourself? After all, you seem to be the expert in this field. You meet the patient in the dining room. You observe him. You make a diagnosis. He is too tired to do the sequence.

"It so happens, and you know it, that a tired man is what we *need* in that sequence! It has to be Linc's last effort! That's the last horse he's ever going to wrestle and defeat! The first one he's ever going to turn free! And for that whole sense of last and too old, tired is exactly the quality I want! That I need!"

Now Jock started to pace up and back, imprisoned suddenly by the narrow confines of the trailer. In his silk shorts, snug against his flat abdomen, hugging his flat, narrow back, he seemed to have all the nervous energy of a boxer ready to go up into the arena at Madison Square Garden.

"I *want* him tired! I want that camera showing every line, every crease, every pucker around his lips, every wrinkle around his eyes! I want it all! This man is too old for this girl! What the hell do you think that roping sequence is all about? We are not making a drawing-room comedy with Melvyn Douglas and Irene Dunne, or Rock Hudson and Doris Day!" Jock said, wiping out two generations of stars in one sentence.

"We are making a picture that is real, honest! That has wrinkles, warts, and breasts that are starting to sag! We are making a film that is going to be a classic! And for a classic, I do not cheat angles, take fake shots, or use stunt men! You know that! You knew it from the start!" Jock turned away to make a fresh drink.

One thing Joe did know, you did not argue with arrogant young men. Especially, arrogant, hurt young men.

"Look, Finley, you're making a realistic picture? Okay, let us be realistic, too. What will happen to your film if the big sequence, the main confrontation of the man with himself, which is what is going on in that horse-wrestling scene, what if that sequence is never shot at all?"

Jock turned back demanding, "Never shot?"

"Suppose we are halfway into it . . . and something happens?" Joe asked. "Where are you going to be with a half-shot sequence that you can't cut, can't finish? A sequence without which the picture cannot live? What do you do then?"

"He'll make it!" Jock said firmly.

"What if he doesn't?" Joe kept asking, not belligerently, not loudly, but persistently. "Where are we?"

"We'll face that if we get to it!" Jock said.

"If we get to it, it's too late. Forget about anyone else. Think of yourself. To come this close and boot it will leave a scar. On your career. This is a picture you almost gave your life for."

Joe pointed out the yellowing, fading bruise on Jock's tan back, the white stripes where adhesive strapping had held dislocated ribs in place. "Are you going to risk it all now, just because . . . " Joe didn't finish that. He was about to say, "Just because you hate that man?" But he didn't have to say it. If Joe knew what he meant to say, Jock Finley knew it better.

"I want this picture authentic! Real! Right down to the last foot. But as I promised, I'll let Pres decide," Jock finally said.

Joe was relieved, so relieved that he finished his brandy in one, long sip. Jock used that moment to ask, "If he decides to do it, give me your word you won't try to talk him out of it, won't say a thing."

Sure that Preston Carr would not agree, Joe found it easy to promise, "I give you my word." He held out his hand to seal the agreement.

As their hands clasped, Jock said thoughtfully, "Plan your shots both ways. With Carr. And with the stunt man."

"Of course," Joe agreed quickly, relieved.

"Good!"

Most pictures are being edited even as they are shot. The editor, working with bits and pieces, cuts them into a rough semblance of the scene as it appeared in the script. Though it lacks music and sound, and dissolves and fades, and is jerky and jumpy, because sometimes some of the interstitial bits are not even shot yet, an experienced eye can get a feeling of how the picture is going by viewing a rough cut of most of the sequences.

Jock's editor, a girl named Mary Horne, a plain girl with thick glasses, had been working by herself at the studio, taking each week's film, cutting it roughly into the form it would assume when Jock came back to the studio to go to work on it himself.

If an editor doesn't cut exactly as the director would, some editors, when left alone in the early stages, still come up with touches that can delight a director. Mary Horne was such a girl. She was of the New Wave too, and had an eye for things that Jock liked. So on Jock's last three pictures, as soon as she was available, Mary went on his payroll and had charge of the rough, rough cut, working on her own.

Mary was a lonely girl, with no attachments, no regular sex life. So she had hours to spend, day and night, in the editing room, alone with the Moviola. Everyone knew she was Jock's editor, and loyal; that she never talked, never betrayed enthusiasm or disappointment, only quiet confidence in Jock Finley. There was talk that, at one time, when he first arrived in Hollywood, Jock had had a brief affair with Mary. If one studied her body, and forgot that plain face, one could see that it might have been true. But no one knew for sure, except Mary and Jock Finley.

Mary found nothing unusual in Jock's call from location, to fly down with all the cut film. Late in the shooting of a picture, yet while there was still time to reshoot and add scenes without prohibitive cost, it was a good idea to review what was already rough-cut. Although it seemed to her to be easier, and it would make more sense, for Jock to fly back to LA and see it there, rather than haul all those cans down to location, if that's what Jock wanted, that's what Mary would do, without question or discussion.

She arrived, turned over the cans of film to the projectionist, with precise instructions as to the order of screening. At the end of the day's shooting, Jock invited Preston Carr and Daisy to see the rough cut. Jock did not expect that Daisy would avail herself of the invitation, but she did. So all four of them crowded into the projection trailer, Pres, Daisy, Jock, and Mary.

To nonprofessionals a rough cut is jumpy, spasmodic, just bits and pieces with some scenes too long, others cut too short, with gaps for film yet to be edited, with an occasional bit of black and white footage suddenly appearing amid the color. To the unpracticed eye it might seem quite senseless and unimpressive, but to Preston Carr, who had lived his life with daily rushes, rough cuts, trackless scenes, missing dialogue, the bits and pieces that eventually grow into a completed film, this rough cut was very, very impressive.

The sequences in which Daisy appeared nude from the waist up, which showed her breasts to be sagging ever so slightly, made her dig her nails into Pres's hand. But he pressed back reassuringly and whispered, "Great! That is truly real. Great!" The love scene on the shore was almost perfectly edited. Even Daisy liked that, she, who usually could not bear to watch herself on the screen. Pres Carr patted her arm, gently, reassuringly, lovingly, during that sequence.

The lariat sequence worked well, though Jock knew as he viewed it that it would have to be edited again. He whispered to Carr, "You know we're going to recut that, Pres."

"Sure," Carr said. But it was obvious that he was delighted with what he was seeing.

The rough cut was over as abruptly as some of the scene changes were abrupt. Suddenly the film was gone and there was only the white-hot light reflecting off the screen, assailing their sensitive, wide-pupiled eyes. The lights came on and Jock said, "Pres, let's go back to my place for a drink."

The invitation was so exclusive that both Daisy and Mary left, going to Daisy's trailer at her invitation. Pres and Jock went to Jock's place.

"Okay, kid, what's the trouble?" Pres asked as Jock handed him his Scotch over ice.

"Trouble?" Jock smiled. "After what you just saw? Trouble?" He laughed.

"You didn't show me all that film just to let me know how the picture stands. It's no secret. We're in good shape. The story works. The characters work. I don't mind telling you, I like it better than anything I've ever done. Thanks to you, you bastard." Carr smiled. Now that the picture was practically done, he could afford to joke and be generous about their disagreements, their competition.

Jock grinned, disarmingly, as though he, too, could be relaxed and generous now.

"Okay," Preston Carr said. "Now what's up?"

"They have seen the rough cut at the studio. They figure this picture is worth its weight in gold. If we can finish it with the same feeling of total and complete realism that makes what you saw so great."

"Yes . . ." Carr said, feeling his way cautiously.

"We've got only one more important sequence to shoot."

"The horse-wrestling sequence."

"The studio wants me to do it in a style that's never really been properly used before in a feature. Multiple image."

"Could be sensational," Carr agreed, for the idea was fresh, and so it appealed to him.

"There's only one trouble. To get the kind of footage that can make it work, we need about six to eight times as much footage as normal shooting would require. And we have to work with lenses that give the audience the same feel we have in the stampede sequences. But we have to be much, much better. Because if we can't top the stampede sequence we're heading for an awful let-down at the end of the picture."

"So?" Carr asked, beginning to grow somewhat wary now, alert.

"So to get all that footage, to get it right, to do it without making it an obvious cheat, we would prefer not to use a stunt man," Jock said, in his low, slow manner, with his baby-blues at about a hundred and ten percent sincere.

Carr did not answer at once. Then, "That day at the ranch. You said we would use a double."

"Of course! And it was always my intention!" Then Jock added hastily, "You understand I'm not saying you have to. Or that it's an order. I'm only saying, I was asked to ask you. By New York. So I'm asking, Pres."

288

Carr thought a moment, a very long moment, during which Jock refilled his glass with that special aged Scotch whiskey Carr drank.

"When my doctor considered this script, his first question was, 'They'll use a double in the horse sequence, won't they?'" Carr said. Then he was silent and sipped his icy drink. "I'll think about it overnight."

He put down his glass, started out, stopped at the door, turned back. "I didn't work hard all my life to throw it away for one sequence in one film. No matter how great it can be. Especially now. That girl. I love her."

Jock couldn't resist saying it. When he did, it sounded not malicious, but helpful, almost respectful, as though submitting it for Carr's serious consideration, "Pres, she never marries men she goes to bed with."

"Maybe that's been her trouble up to now," Carr said simply. And he left.

They did not show up in the commissary for supper, Carr and Daisy. Jock sat at the head of his long table, alone. When Joe came in, he ate with his substitute assistant and two other men, but he moved over to have his coffee with Jock.

"Did you ask him?"

Jock nodded.

"Well?" Joe continued.

"He's thinking about it."

"He's a fool if he does it!" Joe said heatedly, because he had expected Carr would reject the idea completely.

"It'll be one of the greatest action sequences anyone's ever seen!" Jock exclaimed.

"I called LA," Joe said soberly. He started to load his pipe so as to avoid Jock's steel-hard stare. "Sam Hosfeldt was his dresser on *Fool's Gold*, the time he 'took a rest' just before the shooting was over. It *was* a heart attack."

"So?" Jock asked.

Joe was lighting up his pipe, using the jet-flame, eighteen-carat-gold lighter, as he puffed and talked. "If he *were* to agree to do

289

it ... and anything *happened* ... *everybody* could be up the creek. The insurance company, I mean, they don't know about this heart thing. They could claim fraud. And if your picture never got finished the studio is left with one of the most expensive ... disasters ... in history." Aromatic blue smoke filled the air around them.

"What did you do, call your lawyer too?" Jock asked angrily.

"I didn't have to call any lawyers," Joe said, sniffing at the fragrant bowl of his pipe, all of this to avoid looking directly into those blue, blue eyes. "Remember one thing, kid, they'll forgive you for making a bad picture. But they won't forgive you hanging a rap like this on a studio. No lawyer in any studio will approve any contract with you, ever again, not without all kinds of warranties and bonds. It could ruin you."

"He won't do it, anyhow," Jock said. "That business of thinking it over is just a stall. He won't do it, so don't worry." Joe seemed relieved, free to talk about other matters.

"How did it look, the rough cut?"

"Great! Sorry I didn't have you in to see it, but you know her, she's so damn sensitive about seeing herself I didn't want to make it any more difficult for her."

"I understand," Joe said, rising. Then as an afterthought, "I have it all figured out, the shooting angles. If I use a telephoto lens I don't think they'll be able to tell it's a stunt man. You'll get all the excitement you could want. And when you add the sound to it, hooves, whinnies, you'll have it all. All!"

"Good! Good!" was all that Jock said, rising and starting out. He was halfway across the compound to his own trailer when the communications man came running after him. There was a radiophone from LA. Urgent. Jock went back with him, got on the phone.

"Hello! Yes?"

"Kid, it's me. You alone?" Marty's voice asked.

Jock dismissed the radio man with a gesture.

"Yeah, Marty? What's up?" It was Jock's alert, cool, impatient voice, the one ready to find fault with anything.

Diplomatically, the Owl started, "I hear the rough cut looks great. I understand Carr loved it. Even the girl liked it."

290

If the CIA were as swift and as accurate in securing information as the Hollywood underground, we would be in much better shape in the Cold War, Jock was thinking. Who could it have been? Not Mary. She never talked. Not the projectionist, surely. Carr? The girl? Why would they have been calling the Owl? But he knew Marty. And he knew that if he waited, the third subject Marty mentioned would reveal the real reason for his call.

"Kid, they have decided on a hard ticket roadshow. For openers, twelve top cities across the country! The talk is great! Would you believe they've even got two offers for the album, and the music not even written yet!"

Marty is really laying it on, Jock was thinking. What's coming must be pretty bad.

"Oh, by the way . . . "

Here it is, Jock said to himself. Marty killed you with his "By the ways" and his "Oh, before I forgets."

"Yeah, Marty?" Jock fed him, very cool, but ready to be very angry.

"That whole thing about the multiple image and Carr . . ."

"Yeah, Marty, what about that whole thing?"

"Do you think Carr can do it? I mean, it's one hell of a concept! Great! Absolutely great! But you think he can do it? Physically, I mean?"

"Why shouldn't he be able to do it, Marty?" Jock led him on.

"Well, I . . . seems to me . . . didn't he have some trouble about eight years back on another picture? They had to lay off shooting for four weeks . . ."

As many agents do, Marty White had a way of leaving sentences hanging in order to find out how much his client really knew or what he really thought about any given situation. But Jock was in no mood to help him out. He just let Marty hang. In midsentence.

Then he asked, most sincerely, "You still there, Marty?"

"Yeah, yeah, I'm here."

"Good. I thought we got cut off. You were saying, about some picture where they had to lay off shooting for four weeks because of Carr. What's the point, Marty?"

"Well . . . well, the point is, do you think Carr can do those horse-wrestling scenes? Give you all the footage you need, and

291

still finish the picture?" Marty finally asked. "For example, where are you if you got a whole picture, a marvelous picture, exciting, good, real, with lots of sex and action, but the last sequence never gets on film? You know?"

"Have I got everything on film so far, Marty?"

"Sure, kid! That's the point! You got something great going. Protect it!"

"Marty baby, who's been talking to you?"

"Nobody! Why would anybody ... look, kid, I'm only thinking about you. I want you to finish this picture! I want it to be great! For your sake!"

"For *my* sake," Jock reiterated acidly.

"Okay! I'm your agent! And executive producer. Sure! I stand to make a buck. I don't deny it. But don't forget, because I am your executive producer I am saying to you, take it easy! Don't drive him too much! Don't take chances! Don't screw it up now!" Marty's voice was stronger.

"Any other orders, Mr. Executive Producer?"

"Look, kid ..."

"Marty, I have looked for the last time. I have listened for the last time. Now you look, and you listen. This picture got to where it is thanks to my effort, my guts! Not yours! You guys are the wheelers, the dealers, the salesmen, the moneymen. But people do not go to theaters, do not flock to drive-ins, to see your contracts or your figures.

"You could get up in person on a stage and show them exactly how you connive and maneuver, how you got to be an executive producer on my back, but no one ... no one, Marty ... would pay a nickel to see you do your act! Pictures! That's what they come to see! *My* feelings, *my* imagination, *my* brainchild, that's what they come to see! So don't tell me how to do what I do!

"And now, if you want to fire me, Mr. Executive Producer, go right ahead! And then who the hell do you think is going to finish the goddamn picture?"

"Kid ... kid! Laddie ... you got this all wrong. I didn't call up to fight, or give orders. Only to caution, to advise, to ask. Take it easy, please. That's all."

"Who called you?"

292

"Nobody! You know how rumors are in this town. You hear them in your sleep."

"Well, go back to sleep, Marty. Or better still, while I return to worrying about tomorrow's shooting, you take yourself off to Chasen's. Have some nice cracked crab on ice. And a tender Steak Diane. Because I have put it up to Carr. If he doesn't want to do the scene, I'll use the stunt man. So, no sweat. It's that simple."

Relieved, Marty said, "Good. I'm glad."

"I'm glad you're glad. Now, Mr. Executive Producer, go out and get yourself laid, for a change, and leave me alone!" Jock slammed down the phone.

Furious, Jock was crossing the compound toward the trailer, no longer wondering who it could have been. Joe Goldenberg, obviously. The key piece of information, about the four-week layoff on Carr's picture eight years ago, Joe had discovered it, now the Owl knew it. Obvious. Logical. Irrefutable. Halfway across the crusty compound, Jock stopped, pivoted in a sharp right angle, headed straight for Joe Goldenberg's trailer. He did not knock. He turned the knob briskly, opened the door with such force it slammed against the wall, causing the whole aluminum structure to tremble.

Joe, who was puffing away at his pipe, poring over his script under the glare of a small, powerful tensor light, looked up, startled.

"You keep your fucking mouth shut!" Jock exploded, harshly, hoarsely. "You stay where you belong! Behind that camera! And get me everything I put in front of it! But stay off the phone! You hear! Getting people to call me, to beg, plead, warn!"

When Joe answered it was indulgent, fatherly, yet with great, great contempt. "Young man, I do not like anyone coming in here and rudely interrupting me when I am working. I do not like being shouted at. I do not like your vulgarity. I do not like your orders. Most of all, I do not like your accusations, which are both false and ridiculous."

"You called Marty White!" Jock accused. "How else would he know about Carr's condition?"

Joe did not raise his voice. But somehow there was more contempt in him the quieter he became.

293

"Because I know a fact and Marty White knows the same fact, does that mean we have a conspiracy? Isn't it just possible that he is worried, as I am worried? That he made some inquiries? As I did. And that since we *are* dealing with a fact, he was able to discover it, just as I was? No, I did not call him. Now, do me a great favor, get out of here! Please?"

Jock paused, poised to answer. Then he changed his mind, turned and started for the trailer door. As his hand gripped the knob, he was arrested by Joe Goldenberg's words.

"Do me one other favor."

Jock turned to him.

"Don't kill him?"

Anger rose into Jock's face, flushing his tan cheeks, knotting the muscles in his jaws. But Joe continued.

"He is a man of great pride. In his way, a great man. And because the world has made him a hero, he owes it a debt which he feels very strongly. Don't make him do it."

"If he does it, it's because he wants to! And it won't kill him!"

The instant Jock opened the door of his own trailer, he knew she was there. The fragrance she used in the evening hours was strong and familiar. He had tasted it on her breasts many times. He closed the door, turned, and did his best to seem surprised to find her sitting curled up in the one comfortable chair in the small place.

The lamp over his work table was the only light in the room. It caught her white gamin's face, painting it pathetically soft, except for the two pronounced planes of her cheeks which photographed so well. She wore a light, sheer black dressing gown, and the intentionally casual way it was gathered around her made her breasts not only obvious but unavoidably attractive.

She was smiling. But she was tense. She had had a few drinks. He could tell that from afar. When he drew close to her, the pupils of her eyes betrayed the use of considerable medication, too.

Her smile was spasmodic, flickering nervously on her tense face. "I . . . I wanted to see you . . . I . . . I had to see you . . . about

294

that scene in the rough cut ... you know where I'm alone and I first begin to realize that I might be in love with him ... "

"Oh, yes ... " Jock said. To himself, he said that this was what they all said about her. She was never satisfied with her own performance. She must never be allowed to see rushes or a rough cut. He had been wise to follow the rule till now, when all she had left to shoot were reaction shots to Carr's big, final scene.

But she was obviously so tense, he had to humor her. For Carr's sake. For his own sake, too. Anyone who lived in Hollywood long enough grew expert in the signs of incipient breakdowns. One learned to identify that mix of alcohol and sedative pills that led to the final "miscalculation" in which too many pills were taken, always "by accident." The patient wound up deadwhite on a stretcher, being carried into an ambulance, and there was a flurry in the newspapers for a few days.

Jock had been through several of those, two with girls with whom he had had affairs. It was always a calculable possibility in this business, and almost always it was pretty young girls who were involved. Though not so young any more. Nor as pretty as they used to be.

Looking at Daisy now, he saw it clearly. So he knew he had better humor her.

"Yes, the realization scene. Where you're alone and getting dressed. You think about it and realize you want to attract this man, have him make love to you, so you get undressed and start to dress all over again. But this time, no dress, no undies, just that sleazy dressing gown, which is the most elegant you have. It worked perfectly in the rough cut. When I put the right kind of music behind it, you'll love it!"

"It ... it could be better," she ventured.

With tense actresses, Jock had a rule: Encourage them to talk. Once they talk it all out, they generally convince themselves. So he fed her, "How? What would you suggest?"

"Well ... well, what I would like ... the way I see it ... " She rose, a touch unsteady. She started to play the scene in pantomime. As he watched he was saying to himself, Good God, if only she could do this in front of a camera. It was there, it was all there, even in her terrified befuddled mind, the intuitive talent was there.

295

But fear robbed her of most of it when she got in front of a camera. That's why she had had to depend on that face, that body, those breasts, the special dresses that tucked under that lovely behind to make it the most photographed ass in the world.

She went through the whole scene, including playing the reflection angle before the little wall mirror that hung on Jock's closet door. While she was doing that, Jock caught the look in her eyes. She was not so frightened, not so confused or detached that she was not glancing into the mirror from time to time to seek his reaction. She intended to seduce him. She was working at it. She was being her prettiest, her most provocative, her most alluring. There was the heavy scent, her black dressing gown, under which it was now apparent she wore nothing. She was employing it all deliberately, and on him.

When she turned away from the mirror, as part of the scene she pretended to be playing, she let slip the gown so that it parted and there was that stunning white flesh against the black, her body outlined by the gown. He moved to her, took her in his arms, kissed her. It was a brutal kiss. Hungry and angry. But she let him. She welcomed him. She helped him.

Whatever tricks she was supposed to know and perform because she was the world's love symbol, she used. There were moments now when Jock felt that she was so desperate for him that she had resented every moment she had had with Carr, that she had been hungry for Jock all the while.

Passion saved up for weeks poured out of him. They made love not once but four times. And still she seemed not to have had enough. Her arms and legs locked around him hurt where his bruises were still healing, but it was an exciting hurt. It was the kind of pain that added to his ecstasy, the tighter she embraced him the more the pain. The more the pain, the greater his enjoyment of her. She seemed to know it, for she enjoyed it all the more, too.

There was no part of her immune from him. And no part of him she did not touch, feel, embrace, kiss. He had been to bed with her scores of times in recent months, but it had never been like this. Never.

Even while he was in the throes of his sexual aggression, so that she was his partner as well as his enemy, a part of him, way back

296

in his brain, the part that remained ever aloof, critical, observing him, judging him, doing the thinking, while the rest of him only felt, or acted and reacted, that part of him kept saying, "She came here to seduce me. She came here wanting this. *He* doesn't satisfy her. She needs me. *She needs me!*" It added exultation to his desire, triumph to his satisfaction.

It had never been like this before, he kept telling himself. His was the final victory. If they could all know it now. She had come back to him of her own accord. Her story about the rough cut, the scene that could be done better, was only her excuse. And transparent at that. So that she could find a reason to play the scene and let him seem to take the initiative in an act of love that she desperately needed.

Two hours later, three, it made no difference to Jock, he lay on his back, naked, calm, smoking a cigarette, watching the smoke curl upward in the dark room. He reached out to approximate the ashtray. But he was confined by her soft blond head just under his shoulder, pressed against his chest. She was breathing lightly, regularly. She might have been asleep. But she nipped at the tight tanned skin of his chest, her little teeth tantalizingly painful. It was a playful thing, perhaps meant to start the act all over again. But he was saying to himself, Christ, baby, what do you think I am? How many men could have come this far with you? Is there no such thing as enough?

He was smiling in the darkness, priding himself on his performance, his animal ability to gratify in a way that only more gratification was desired. Jock Finley, the kid with jock-sock, who could do more with sex on the screen, and off, than any young director alive!

This was one of the great moments of his life, and he would remember it for as long as he lived. Daisy Donnell and he. Together. The great lovers. And she had come here practically right out of Preston Carr's bed! Man! If there were some way of letting the whole world know!

Gently, so as not to disturb her too much, he reached out to find the ashtray, drop his cigarette into it. She nipped at him again. She knew somehow that pain was good for him. Aroused him. He was turning back to her when it struck him. Instead of

297

embracing her, he hovered over her, looking down at her white face, the closed eyes. The passion he expected was not there. The face was poised upward toward him, the lips open, awaiting his kiss, his tongue. But this was not the passionate face of a girl, as he knew girls.

Once he was aware of that, he became aware, back there where the thinking went on, where the calculating, the observing went on, that in all the times before, when they had been together, working on the script, discussing the part, arriving at her decision to do the part, during those times when *he* carried on the love affair, she had never been so voracious. Once, twice was the most it ever happened in any one encounter. And always he had been the aggressor. As though in order to win her for the picture he had had to give her something of himself. It had been a payment in earnest, a kind of barter.

Did it mean she had not been in love with him before? And was she now? Or was it something else? Now as he mounted her, entered her, he thought more about that than he did about the very act of making love in which he was engaged. This time the intercourse was routine, without anger or passion. When he was finally at the last of his thrusting and had rolled over on his side, he felt suddenly not satisfied, only free, no longer required to perform. No, he realized, no satisfaction. Just relief, freedom. And the chance for a fresh cigarette.

She lay there, head against his chest, eyes stealing upward to glance at his lean, angular face. Her fingers traced a design on his chest, her long nails causing his skin to react and to pucker till he pulled away finally, laughing. "Don't!" he said in the coy, almost coquettish way that girls, not men, use when they don't wish you to stop. But he really had no more desire. He was as empty as he could ever remember being, except for that time with the nympho airline stewardess in Copenhagen.

"I should have met you a long time ago," she said suddenly. "First."

To himself, Jock said, Christ, not that one again! Every girl says that, with damn near every man, damn near every time. As though if she had met him first, he would have been the only one, instead of the tenth, twentieth, or fiftieth.

298

But when she said, "It would have been wonderful. To love to-gether and work together, like this," Jock glanced down at her by just flicking his eyes.

"Don't worry about that scene. It's great the way it is. But if you insist on doing it over, I'll go back to it when we're finished." It was a delaying tactic. He did not intend to do the scene over, ever. But if he could keep her stable, alert, interested, till he had finished with her reaction shots in Carr's big scene, that was all he wanted.

"I think it's important for my character. The most important scene I have in the whole film," she said, with the schoolgirl intensity she assumed whenever she talked about acting as though it were a holy undertaking. "It's where I make my big inner change. Where I go from being a tramp on the loose to a girl who is really, truly in love for the first time."

She was disgorging to him almost word for word what he had fed her in that long siege when he was wooing her to do the picture. Was she so confused that she did not remember? Or was she just beginning to understand?

"You see," she continued in the little-girl voice he had heard her use in more than one film, "unless I get that scene right, my whole character falls apart. I mean, like, the last big scene, where he's wrestling with that horse, and I'm supposed to be reacting, what am I feeling? That I want to see him conquer that magnificent animal or that I don't? Do I want him to win because I love him? Or do I want him to lose because I love him too much to see him deprive that animal of its freedom? You know what I mean?

"Of course, the whole thing, that scene with the horse, I think it's cruel. I mean, I think that there are animal-lovers the country over, the world over, who are going to hate that scene."

For the first time, he began to really listen to her, to be truly involved in what she was saying. Because for the first time he felt not fear, not concern, but anger. He did not change the pace or depth of his breathing. His chest continued to rise and fall in the same steady rhythm so that her head which was pressed against it could not detect what went on inside him. Nor did he puff at his cigarette any faster than before.

299

Cool, laddie, cool is the word, as he asked, "Why would they hate it?"

"Well, nobody likes to see an animal that wants freedom be tied down, whinnying, rearing, trying to bolt and break loose. No audience is going to want to see Pres Carr, of all men, hit that beast across the muzzle with his hat. And then pull in on that rope to bring that animal practically to its knees. That's painful, brutal, cruel. It's . . . it's terrible . . . so unfair."

"Unfair?" Jock asked softly, inviting her to continue. "That mustang is ten times as heavy, ten times as powerful. The man can win out only because he is sharper, wiser, craftier. It is civilization against wild brute power, that's what the scene is all about."

"I wouldn't want to see it!" she said in sudden, passionate revulsion. "When it comes on the screen, I'll turn away! So will most people! You'll see! I think it's a mistake!"

"I'm sorry you feel that way," Jock was seemingly thoughtful.

"You ought to think about it," she said, encouraged to feel she had made some impression. "And especially in a multiple-image sequence, that would only make it more brutal."

"That's what people want these days. Brutality. Violence," Jock said.

"I'll bet you that women won't like it!"

"Women are more sadistic than men," Jock invented. "It's a scientifically known fact."

"I don't think that the women of this world who've loved him for thirty years are going to want to see Preston Carr do anything as cruel as that! And I told him so!"

So, finally, it was out. They had talked about it. How else could she know exactly how Pres intended to do the scene. That touch about whipping the animal with his hat, only Carr could have told her that. They had obviously discussed it, and in great detail.

There was only one thing more he had to find out. "What did *he* say?"

"He said it was a good scene. It belongs in the picture."

"I mean, did he say if he was going to do it. Or was he going to ask me to use a stunt man?"

"He . . . he doesn't want to do it," she said in a soft voice. It was

300

her own tiny little-girl voice, without any pretense at acting or trying to achieve any effect except simple honesty. She was terribly frightened about what might happen to Carr. She could not hide it, nor did she attempt to.

To Jock it was all very clear now. Everything that was different about her tonight was because of it. Coming here, seducing him, her seemingly insatiable hunger for him, all so that he could prove himself time and time again. Because like all women, no matter how stupid they were, they knew instinctively that sexual pride was man's worst enemy, and woman's best friend.

She had come here tonight for only one reason, to make him promise not to force Preston Carr to do that scene. And she had done it with all the cold, calculating intention of a professional whore turning another trick with another John. She was the one who had called Marty White, who was, after all, her agent, too.

He got up, reached out, lifted her to a sitting position on the side of the bed. She was naked, her eyes cast down. He raised her face. "Tell me one thing. Are you going to marry him?"

She tried to turn her face away. His grip on her chin was so tight it hurt. "Tell me!" She started to weep. He released her. She was going to marry him. And that meant one other thing. She had not slept with him.

If he weren't so sorry for her, he would have laughed. These past weeks, she had been deprived. No wonder she seemed to enjoy him tonight, even though that was not what she had come here for.

One other thing, he knew now how it felt to be used. Louise would have gotten some satisfaction out of that. To know he had been led on by a woman who didn't love him, for a purpose not having anything to do with love at all. He could only salvage his own pride by demeaning and pitying Daisy, saying to himself, Poor, poor kid, so warped and twisted that the only way she can show her love for Carr is to come here and act like a whore to get me to screw her. Man, how wacked up can you get?

But to her he said, "I won't make him do any scene he doesn't want to do."

"Cut the whole scene out!" she pleaded.

"I can't do that," he said. "But I can fake it. It would be the

301

only thing in the whole picture that isn't real or true. But for you, I'll do it."

She kissed him. This time, at least, the feeling was genuine, even if it was only appreciation. And she was ready to give herself to him again. She was pressing against him, her fingers playing with his ear and the hair on the back of his neck. When he felt himself swell, he eased back from her.

"You don't have to do that," he said. Not harsh, not loud, softly, with pity. But within himself the anger was great.

Tired as he was from his sexual exertion, he did not sleep much. At six-fifteen the next morning, when it was nine-fifteen in New York, Jock Finley was up and on his way to the communications trailer to put through a call to the president.

Presidents of major film companies, when they receive long-distance calls from the Coast, at nine-fifteen New York time, know instinctively it is bad. Nobody in California gets up at six-fifteen to call New York unless there is trouble, big trouble that can't wait.

So, while he was motioning his secretary to prepare him a double Alka Seltzer, the president lifted the phone, summoned all the sweetness he could to ask, "Well, kid, how is everything?"

He was surprised and worried when Jock's reply was serious, sober, uncomplaining.

"Boss, I've been considering it ever since you asked. Maybe I have been unreasonable. I think it might be a good thing to have *Life* come down and do a story on us shooting the last big sequence."

"You do?" the president interrupted, gulping his Alka Seltzer; then he continued, "I'll tell Publicity right away and they'll check with you about when and how, all the details!"

"Just one thing," Jock warned. "It'll be your idea. I want to be as surprised as everyone else. Okay?"

The president, who in his mind was already playing the scene at the stockholder's meeting and taking credit for a *Life* cover, was quick to agree. "Okay!"

Jock hung up, leaving the president free to drink the rest of

302

his Alka Seltzer, which he now discovered he no longer really needed. He drank it anyhow in anticipation of the next call. From the Coast. Or London, Paris, Rome, Madrid. Time was when the sun never set on the British Empire. Now it never set on picture companies whose interests were as extensive as the Empire, and from which it was never impossible to receive phone calls.

Some days the president yearned for the old days of a quiet law practice when the most exciting thing he had had to do was give a subtle routine bribe to a Federal Communications Commissioner or a New York State Supreme Court judge. But for him those days were gone never to come again.

CHAPTER

10

THE day to begin shooting the final sequences of *Mustang!* came up clear and golden bright.

At dawn the camp was already alive with activity. A long caravan of jeeps and trucks was shaping up. The generator trucks, location dressing rooms, commissary truck, equipment trucks, which carry cables, reflectors, cameras and track, a huge monster crane, sound booms, and recording equipment were lining up under the alert, tense command of Jock's assistant.

Every need of every member of the company must be anticipated, considered, provided for. There could be no last-minute lacks, failures, or delays. For the actual shooting locale, which Jock had named the battleground, was some miles away from the camp. There, desert, mountains, landscape were virginally free of roads, houses, power lines, poles, or markers of any kind which bespeak civilization. Jock wanted it as primitive as it had been a hundred years ago, a thousand years ago. So if by unlucky chance some transcontinental jet drew vapor trails across the sky they would have to stop and wait and shoot that take again. Because if you had some footage with vapor trails and some without you couldn't edit, intercut, or match shots without eye-disturbing contradictions. So no take with trails would be acceptable here.

Jock and Joe Goldenberg were in makeup with the stunt man,

Art Ryan, who was stripped to the waist, and turning this way and that under Joe's expert gaze.

Finally Joe decided, "We'll start with some Max Factor's Seven N body makeup. I think that'll match Pres's tan. If it doesn't we'll switch to Pancro twenty-six."

"What about size, musculature?" Jock asked.

Joe took another long look. "It'll work. With my telephoto I can be close enough and still keep the details vague enough."

"Impact!" Jock reminded. "Don't forget, I want total immersion!"

"You'll get it," Joe said in his methodical way, turning to Art again, looking at his face. Joe was businesslike, intense, completely devoid of the feeling he had displayed the day before.

"You want to see Art alongside Pres?" Jock asked.

"In a while," Joe said. "In a while." Then he nodded his head. Suddenly he had reached a decision. He started out of makeup. With a small head motion he invited Jock to follow. They were outside, in the midst of a moving, noisy wagon train of the nineteen-sixties.

"I want to thank you. For not forcing Pres to do it. And to show my appreciation, I would like to make a suggestion. About the editing."

Jock played it straight, cool, his baby-blues at modest appreciation, eighty percent. "Joe, no matter what our differences, I admire an artist. You know that. So anything you have to suggest..."

"Let me tell you how I would like to do it," Joe began. "First the big master shot. The animal far off to that side, the man off there. The last two creatures alive on this desert. Then the man begins to approach the mustang, who eyes him but cannot flee because he is staked by that lariat around his magnificent neck. As the man moves in toward the animal we move in slowly, changing focus, going all the way from wide panorama to a wide two shot, finally man and animal. The move in should be slow, building suspense. Maybe we even intercut a reaction of the girl, and of Boyd. Their faces tell us of the danger waiting here for Carr.

"Now, man and beast are closer together. The animal pulling,

306

twisting, rearing, trying to free himself of that rope. Carr, a close-up, as we see his conflict on his face. His admiration for the animal which symbolizes freedom, against his need to tame that animal so he can convert it into a material asset which means security to him. It has become a choice, his way of life against that animal's freedom. We need that from him. Then he decides, moves in, seizes that rope. When he does, the animal will naturally rear up, menacing him with its hooves.

"At that point *explode* into your first multiple image! Don't dissolve into it, explode! Two shots simultaneous, rearing animal and man, plus sudden close-up on Carr. Play both images till the next moment of impact when the animal, after rearing up again, comes down almost on top of the man, again explode! Into a three-image shot! With each pivotal change in the battle, explode into another image. We keep adding images, with enormous impact, the animal close, the man close, man and animal, the flailing hooves dangerous as knives, the man's hat a weapon against the animal, the girl's fear, Boyd's admiration and concern. So that we achieve the staccato effect of exploding into each new phase of the battle instead of merely adding to it. It will be like percussion in a symphony!

"Impact? When it is at its full peak and you have six images going at once, on each single frame of film, you'll have impact! The fight from the aspect of every important character, simultaneous, instead of the routine, usual method of intercutting. When you add the sound, hooves, terrified whinnying, Carr's voice, the girl's gasping fear, you'll have an experience on film that will have been worth it."

"That's what I was always aiming for," Jock said. "And your idea about exploding the added images onto the screen so that it gooses at each moment of danger is just great. Great!"

"I'm glad you like it," Joe said, feeling free now to confess. "Because . . . because otherwise I don't think it could work."

Jock's look was a question which demanded answering. "Unless I can shoot Ryan from the rear all the way, we can't get in close enough. We can't maintain the illusion. If I can shoot Ryan from the back and then get facial actions and reactions from Pres, I can get away with it, and still not overwork him. Just give me time to

307

get the right opening shot of Pres and the mustang. Then I can work around him.

"After that, exploding each added image will keep the eye and the mind so bombarded with effects that I don't think anyone will ever notice it's Ryan."

"Great!" Jock said, as if he meant it. "Terrific! I can't wait to get started!"

Jock turned away and hadn't gone five paces when both of them became aware of a copter that was flailing its way into sight from a westerly direction.

"Yesterday's rushes?" Joe asked. "So early?"

"Could be," Jock said.

They watched the copter set down to one side of the staging area. But even so, the force of its mechanical gale and its sound combined to terrify the captive mustangs which reared up and threatened to bolt their ropes. Finally, the wranglers managed to hold them. It was tricky business, rounding up matched animals that could be used interchangeably, keeping them under control, yet not robbing them of their natural savagery and wildness, which would be necessary for the scenes. For days the wranglers had combed the foothills seeking, singling out, pursuing, capturing additional mustang stallions, all roughly the same size and color. Jock had specified stallions, so that when the animals reared up he could get a good, full shot of their genitals and also because stallions would be prouder, more combative, more menacing. He was sure the audience would sense that and it would add to their sadistic and sexual excitement.

The copter had landed, whipping the desert dust into millions of tiny projectiles. Now its blades came to a slow wisping stop. The bubble opened. A young man leaped to the ground.

He was tall, frail, with beach-boy-blond hair and he was dressed in extremely well-tailored chinos. His air of casualness was so studied and precise that Jock instantly recognized he was a homosexual. Not blatant, not overly obvious, but quite distinctly homosexual. The young man turned back to the bubble. The pilot handed down a Valpak and several bags of photographic equipment, cameras of differing shapes, sizes, and makes, and many cartons of film.

308

Jock turned to Joe, "What the hell is that?" he demanded, with a look of unlimited surprise and indignation. Disturbed, angry, Jock started toward the tall photographer.

Before Jock could say a word the visitor introduced himself, "Manning. *Life!*" He held out his hand. Jock shook it, inwardly congratulating himself. Manning was excellent, one of *Life's* best. In fact he had done the best series on the Vietnam war that had ever been done. And the Nixons had wanted him for the wedding. Manning on the assignment meant great pictures and practically a guarantee that the story would not only be used, but would also get enormous space and, in all probability, the cover.

"Oh, Manning! Yes, I know your work. But what are you doing here?" By this time Joe had joined them.

"Haven't you been notified? New York cleared this. I'm here to photograph Carr's big horse-wrestling sequence," Manning said.

Jock's eyes flicked from Manning to Joe and back to Manning. "They never told me ... I gave orders ... look, there's a union rule, only a union still photographer is allowed on a picture set! Right, Joe? And I assume that covers locations too."

"We cleared that. We always do. Now, if I can get settled ... and have a look around ..." Manning said with bristly impatience, as though from now on this entire huge production existed only for the purpose of being photographed for *Life*.

Jock turned to Joe, playing a man speechless at an accomplished, irreversible, and stunning fact. Joe started away, beckoning with his eyes for Jock to follow him. Jock started after Joe, but Manning called to him, "What's this?"

"Caravan, staging for the move out to location."

"Good place to start!" Manning said, reaching down to select the right camera for the caravan shots.

When Joe had escorted Jock out of earshot, he asked in a frightened whisper, "God Almighty! Do you realize what this means?"

"We'll have to change our shooting plan. And the editing," Jock said. He wouldn't say the rest of it. He wanted that to come from Joe.

"Change the shooting plan?" Joe demanded, angry and tense, because he was terribly fearful. "We can't do it at all!"

309

"Can't change?" Jock pretended to misunderstand.

"Can't shoot," Joe said. "We can't use Ryan, not with him around. It won't be a cover story. It'll be an exposé! Of how this real, real picture is actually a big, big fake! A cheat! If he gets wind of that, if he gets his camera on that, then Art Ryan, the stunt man, becomes the hero and Preston Carr, the King, turns out to be a phony. You can't do that to him! Not after what he's done for this picture!"

"You're right!" Then suddenly, Jock said, "I'll call the studio! New York! I'll tell them to get that bastard off our backs."

Joe shook his head, "All you have to do is tell *Life* they *can't* shoot something then they're *sure* there's something to hide. You'll never get rid of him!"

"Christ, Joe, what do we do?" Jock seemed to plead.

"I wish I knew," Joe said, pulling at his short white beard.

Manning joined them now. "I'd like a jeep. So I can get some shots of the caravan as it moves to the location. First I want it moving against those mountains. Then as it goes over that rise. And if no one is using the copter I'd like to get a few from the air. The serpentlike effect as it makes its way, single file, across the empty desert. By the way, where's Mr. Carr? I'd like to follow him from Wardrobe to Makeup to location. People like to know what a star goes through before he actually does those shots they see on the screen."

"He's not out yet," Jock said. "Joe, would you go see if he's ready," Jock used it as a signal to Joe to prepare Carr for the news. Joe nodded, started away toward Carr's trailer.

"Oh, by the way," Manning said. "Exactly what did New York mean about a new multiple-image technique?"

Jock explained the multiple-image idea, adopting Joe's explosion concept as his own. "You have to shoot ten times normal or more, to get enough footage," Manning said.

"I figure it'll take two or three weeks. Though when it's edited, the whole thing may only run four or five minutes. Probably the most exacting four minutes of film in history," Jock predicted, feeding Manning's interest.

"It's a great idea! Extremely exciting! Simultaneous montage instead of sequential montage."

310

"Precisely!" Jock said. "And with much more impact. Audiences these days, especially kids, need to be surprised, jolted, lifted, assailed, assaulted, by impressions, feelings, sounds, sights. The human mind is too surfeited with single-dimension things like TV to care any longer, even to pay attention. We are going to stun the audience, rock it, beat against it, totally bombard eye, ear, and mind!"

It could do no harm, Jock realized, to drop a line or two here which could be quoted later. For he knew that Manning usually wrote the text that appeared with his photo stories.

Later, from the quotes that Manning might pick up from Jock and use in his article, the picture company's advertising department could select quotes and attribute them to *Life*. So that actually Jock Finley in the name of *Life* would be extolling the virtues of Jock Finley, director, and of Jock Finley's super film, *Mustang!*

"I am not only going to give them their first experience with honest story-integrated multi-image, I am going to explode them into it, frame by frame! Yes, I said explode!"

Thus Jock enlarged on his views of the "new" film. In so doing he gave Manning some intimate insights into his theory of motion picture-making, all with the pretense of making him a confidant and a colleague.

"Not many people can appreciate what we do. Not even most critics. Sure, they like our films. But as to knowing, caring how they're really made, appreciating the fine points, I guess it takes another artist."

How successful Jock had been in establishing a rapport, a camaraderie with Manning, he realized only when he turned to catch Manning staring at him, attracted to him with a look Jock had seen before in the eyes of girls, and in the eyes of other homosexuals over whom he seemed to exert enormous attraction. It worried him sometimes, when he wondered if he did it intentionally. Or did they misinterpret? Or was it that there was about him a sexual magnetism that knew no bounds, and to which neither sex was immune? He hoped this wouldn't lead to a pass. It had happened to him before, more than once. Most recently in England. He had never been able to handle those moments comfortably or easily.

311

And if there was one thing he did not want to do, it was to offend Manning.

Joe returned. He said only, "Jock . . . Pres would like to talk to you."

"Excuse me," Jock said to Manning.

Left alone with Joe, Manning watched Jock walk away. "Fascinating director. Bold. Must be very strong with his people. A tyrant, I'll bet. And what energy! Even when he just *talks* about making pictures."

"Yes," is all that Joe said.

"I'd better get going on those caravan shots. Later I'd like to talk photography with you, if you don't mind."

"I'd like to," Joe answered. He started after Jock.

As Joe opened the door of Carr's trailer he could hear Jock saying, "We don't change a thing! We go right ahead and shoot as we planned . . ." and he turned to include Joe, "Just as we discussed it this morning, understand! Pres opens the master shot, then we go into the wrestling, Ryan and the stallion, with Ryan's back to the camera all the way. When we get that, we'll figure out your close-up reactions, Daisy's, Boyd's. It'll take time but it'll work. So screw him. And *Life!*"

All the while, Carr was sitting before his dressing table mirror, letting the makeup man work on him. He had not said a word. Only after there had been a lull of some seconds, did he ask thoughtfully, "You can't get rid of him?"

Jock deliberately looked to Joe, so that he was reflected in Carr's mirror and Carr could see him. Joe shook his head.

"Not this *faygelleh*," Joe said. "I know the type. He'll cling like a leech. The harder you try to shake him the worse he'll get. No one is as nasty as an offended fag."

"Anything we can do, Joe?" Preston Carr asked.

Joe shrugged. Then he made a sudden desperate suggestion, "Shut down shooting for a while. Say there's been a new script idea. The scene has to be rewritten . . ." but it was so obviously implausible that Joe didn't even finish.

"We'll do it as we planned!" Jock kept inisting. "After all, I gave you my word!"

"Sure," Carr said. "Your word. But my career. My reputation."

312

Joe glanced at Jock, Jock looked back, his baby-blues projecting one hundred percent sincere. *"I'm* not going to let you do it."

Preston Carr turned to Joe, "How long would it take, Joe? To get all the footage we need?"

"Look, Pres, it's ridiculous . . ."

"How long?"

"You know how it is with animals. You get lucky it could take ten days. You get unlucky it could take ten weeks. With a sequence like this, all that sudden movement, all that violence. It may take longer. Lot longer."

"Joe, I want to ask you something."

"Sure, Pres, anything."

"Will it work . . . if we do it . . . If *I* do it . . . will it work as we expect? Will it be worth it? Will it be better than with a stunt man?" Carr asked.

Joe fumbled, looked into the mirror at Jock, whose blue eyes looked back, waiting, expectant. There were times in his life when Joe Goldenberg would have liked to be able to lie. To lie well, convincingly. But he never had. And certainly not to a man he respected as much as he revered Preston Carr.

"Real is always better, Pres. I don't have to tell you that. I'll be able to come in closer, use different lenses, get you from better angles. With a stunt man, it's all back, all horse, no man."

Carr sat staring into the mirror. When the makeup man wanted to add another touch, Carr waved him away. Jock signaled the makeup man to get out. He did. Jock gestured Joe to leave. Joe left, but reluctantly, lingering at the door, to hear what, if anything, Jock would say. But Jock said little. He only patted Carr on the bare, tanned, muscular shoulder and said, "You're the boss, Pres!"

They were riding out to the location in a specially built command car, equipped with radiophone and portable refrigerator. In front, alongside the driver, sat Joe. In the rear seat, Preston Carr, Daisy, and Jock. Carr had not told them his decision. Joe was afraid to ask. Jock didn't dare ask, lest he seem too anxious.

Carr spoke suddenly, "How many shooting hours you figure we have a day?" It was directed to Joe.

313

"This time of year, the light we need, four, maybe five."

"Could we break it up? Two hours action, two hours reaction shots. Is that possible?" This was directed at Jock.

"We'll do it any way you say, Pres, including sticking to the original plan." Jock could afford to be gracious now, for it was obvious that if it were humanly possible, Carr would do the scene himself.

"Two hours a day," Carr considered. "In that sun . . ."

"You don't have to do it," Daisy interrupted, in a way that betrayed that she had said those same words to him a dozen times before they ever got into the car.

Suddenly Joe suggested, "I can decide I don't like the light. I call off shooting for today. That'll give us time to think, at least."

No one in the car had to say it, since everyone knew it. Joe most of all. He could not plead bad light to one of *Life*'s best action photographers and get away with it. And even if he could, Preston Carr's pride wouldn't let him.

No more was said. The car pulled up at the location where the trucks, vans, and jeeps had already assumed their battle array. Every vehicle in its proper place for its function in the day's combat. The crew was at work. The wranglers walked tethered mustangs about. It was remarkable how alike the animals looked. Place any two side by side and one could have picked out some singular small difference. But when all eight of them were paraded by, they looked alike, almost identical, in size, color, musculature, markings.

Just before Jock opened the door, Carr said, "We'll do it. We'll go as far as we can. All the way, I think. But we'll do it."

We. The plural, the collective pronoun. Agents, when they used it meant "You'll do it." But other people used it when they knew instinctively that what they were about to do might be beyond them. They needed the help, the confidence one got from not being in it all alone.

When they got out of the car, Jock slapped Carr on the shoulder, a gesture of respect between men. A silent tribute to one who understood and would do his best. Jock was cool, silent, sober but not quite grim. His baby-blues were at an underplayed seventy-percent-silent-sincere tribute to courage and dedication.

But inwardly there was an excitement unequaled for Jock since

314

the day of the stampede. It was going to happen! The first time he had read the script he had known this was the big scene, that it demanded highly unusual treatment if *Mustang!* was to become the classic Western. But at that time even he had not dared to dream it would be done this way, without stunt men, with multi-image and with the camera practically staring into Preston Carr's face, showing every tense line and wrinkle, every drop of sweat. Close and tight on Preston Carr's chest, biceps, and arms, showing every straining, bulging muscle. The anatomy of a man fighting for his life, with every muscle, tendon and nerve exposed, tense, working together. We would be looking right into his eyes, the camera an opthalmoscope to read his thoughts and his emotions. The real thing, life-and-death combat, man against animal, one fighting for his freedom, one fighting for his life.

The rest of the picture, two hours of exciting sex, character conflict, stampedes, all of it was to Jock only introduction, preparation, the launching platform for this great climactic scene. Now he was going to have it his way, no cheats, no fakes, no doubles, no stunt men. Preston Carr all the way!

That was what films were supposed to be. And great motion-picture direction, too. Finding life, re-creating it for the camera and making it look real by making it be real. No more illusion. No more trickery. Bombard the senses, overwhelm them, with truth, truth, truth! He would have liked to shout it to the world now. But cool, laddie, cool was the word.

While Jock and Joe Goldenberg lined up the master shot, Carr was being subjected to the final touches of the makeup man. In the shaded area created by an open tent, he sat before a mirror, bare to the waist, lending himself to the careful professional scrutiny, the dabs and touches of a man who worked silently and seriously. Daisy sat to one side, watching. Carr was aware of her, her white face, so carefully shielded from the sun, for her features did not lend themselves to tanning, losing character somehow when they did. She tended to freckle, which was not good for her sex image. For in the idiom of film, freckles meant virginity and were only good for Doris Day.

So Daisy's face was pale, sad. As Carr turned from time to time to allow the makeup man easier access to a particular angle of his jaw or his cheek, he glanced at her, his eyes bright, merry, trying to reassure her. She smiled back, the stiff, uneasy smile, which was more nearly herself than any other facial gesture she knew and which she only used unconsciously.

Manning found them this way. He had circled the location in the copter, taken all the airborne shots of the encampment and the battleground. Now, hearing that Carr had arrived and was in Makeup, Manning entered to take some shots. He worked with a proficiency and speed that made Carr respect him at once. Had it not been for the slight mechanical sounds of his camera one would not have known he was at work. He did not pose, set, or take a shot. He shot simply, easily, from angles that caused one to wonder how he knew what he had in focus. But his gallery of prize-winning photographs, of which there were some in every volume on the art of photography, were proof that he knew his craft as well as any man in the world.

Once when Carr glanced up to see him in the mirror, Manning shot and smiled. It was the only time he smiled. For he had caught an expression of Carr through the mirror that pleased him.

But that was the only sign of approval or personal involvement Manning exhibited in all the shooting he did that day.

On the battleground, Jock and Joe Goldenberg were walking off the distance that would separate man from animal in the wide master shot. They were learning the feel and texture of the terrain underfoot to see if there were hazards to warn Pres about, to see if shadows would help or hurt, to see how long it would take for a man to make that slow, determined walk from one side of the frame to the other. For this was one shot that Jock did not intend to cut or edit, he wanted it all in one take. He wanted it to be slow, almost unbearably slow, for suspense, to start the scene at its slowest to serve as contrast for the build of the scene, the explosions into other aspects as the screen split into two, then three, four, five, and six images. For a climax so powerful, the best contrast

316

and preparation was slow, quiet, solitary action, as though this man and this beast were the last two things left alive on earth and they were about to fight for dominion over it.

So Jock walked it off, silently, playing the mood, feeling the moment for himself. Joe watched, following the entire move in his portable viewfinder, which had the proper aspect ratio for seventy-millimeter film. On a screen and with the lens Joe would use to shoot it, this scene should give an audience that feeling of seeing the entire world.

Jock finished his walk to the stake where the animal would be tethered. He turned and started back to Joe. When they were face to face, Joe could see the perspiration starting down the side of Jock's jaw. If it was that hot for Jock, what would it be for Carr, an hour from now, Joe was thinking. He did not say it. But Jock could read it in his eyes and he resented it. Joe said only, "Ready when you are."

"Okay, let's try it," Jock decided. He turned vaguely in the direction in which he last saw his assistant and called out, "See if Mr. Carr is ready!"

The assistant, far to the other side of the battleground, was giving orders to one of the wranglers, who was trying to keep a rearing beast in submission. But he left at once to run all the way to the makeup tent. In a few minutes he returned with Carr and Daisy. Manning followed a few feet behind, till Carr and Jock were face to face. Then Manning moved nimbly, quietly, taking a succession of shots with such rapidity that the clicking sounds seemed to blend and be continuous.

Jock and Carr walked out to the position Carr would assume at the opening of the shot. Then together they walked through it. Jock talked, Carr nodded. Brief, curt nods, businesslike, thoughtful. When they had walked it, Jock turned to call out, "Okay, Joe, we're ready to walk it for you!"

Everyone on the location jumped to his working post, for this was a technically difficult, as well as an important, shot. To give visual impact to the feeling that man and beast were alone in this place, Jock had decided on a long, slow dolly shot that seemingly traveled across virgin desert.

As man approached beast, the camera would move in as well.

317

Lens focus would have to be carefully changed, but Joe's temporary assistant, a good man, should have no special trouble with that.

The part that might go wrong, and often did, was laying the track just ahead of the camera dolly so that the move could be continuous and smooth without any track ever appearing in the shot. It was almost as if a railroad track were being laid down immediately ahead of a slow-moving locomotive.

Two crews of four grips each would have to slip in from each side and lay the two-by-eight track, plank by plank, before the wheels of the moving dolly, ever so careful never to get so far ahead as to appear in the shot. In that way Jock's vision of a desert untracked, unpopulated, virgin of footsteps, equipment, or habitation, would be realized, yet the camera would always move on solid track and the shot would be stable, smooth, free of any eye-jarring jerks or jolts.

For two hours before Jock and Preston Carr arrived, Joe's assistant had been rehearsing the grips, so by now they could put down the two-by-eights swiftly and smoothly. They were ready for their real test as Carr walked the scene for the first time.

Joe rode the camera, to watch the entire slow move through the lens finder, except when he was leaning in over his assistant's shoulder to watch him change focus as the move progressed, as man approached beast and camera approached both, till finally the frame was one huge two-shot, man and beast.

When they finished, Joe gave some notes to his assistant. The grips were told to slow it down just a trifle, for the danger of track showing up in the shot was too great as it went this time.

Now they were ready to walk it all again so that Jock, too, could ride the dolly and see the shot before they went for a take. Once more, Carr took the long slow walk in the hot sun, his shadow, small, moving like a terrier at his feet, just ahead of him on the red, crusty, desert earth.

When Jock had viewed the walk, he turned to Joe, nodded his head. Joe nodded back. They were ready. Jock signaled his assistant who called out, "Quiet! We're going for a take! Quiet!"

Preston Carr moved back to his starting position, to await his cue. The makeup man, as usual, rushed out to take one last look,

318

make one last correction, dab away one last gleam of perspiration. But Jock called out, "Damn it, don't touch him!"

The makeup man turned to Jock, explaining, "But the sweat . . . "

"I want that sweat!" Jock shouted. "I want real, honest-to-Christ sweat. I don't want it sprayed on or painted. I want it to come from within! Naturally! Damn it, let's walk it again! Sorry, Pres, we're working for an enormous effect here!"

Carr started again, from where he was, across the hot desert earth, in the sun, his shadow moving before him. He reached the point at which he was about to pick up the tether and Jock called out, "Okay! Fine! Let's do it! Just that way! And everybody stay the hell away and in your places!" Jock looked to his assistant, who took over.

"Places! Mr. Carr, please?" As Preston Carr was walking back to his starting position, the assistant made sure everyone was at his post. For this shot, Jock rode the camera, too, just behind Joe, straining to see past his head and through the finder. The assistant gave the action cue on a sign from Jock. Carr started walking. The long walk, slow, just as it had been discussed and rehearsed. The operator changed focus flawlessly. The crew moved the camera dolly in on the track laid so carefully and with such precision by the grips. Joe watched. Jock watched. At the point where Carr and the animal were close, Carr bent down to yank the tether from the stake. But Jock called out, "Cut!"

From the way he said it, Joe knew he was dissatisfied. He turned to Jock, who exclaimed, "Christ Almighty!"

"But it was good!" Joe protested. "A damn good take!"

Without another word, Jock called out, "Christ, Pres, wouldn't you know? Screwed it up. Track in the shot. Sorry, old buddy. But we have to do it again."

"There was no track," Joe Goldenberg protested in an angry whisper.

"I saw track!" Jock said in an equally angry whisper, and he pretended to be too much in a hurry to discuss it. He only turned to his assistant and called, "Get 'em cracking! I don't want to impose on Pres!"

The assistant gave the orders curtly. Everyone resumed his

starting place. The whole shot was done over. Joe followed it meticulously in the finder, with Jock just behind him, close, peering over his shoulder. This time when the shot was over, Joe said softly and without looking back, "This one is perfect!"

Jock did not answer, but only said to his assistant who was waiting, "Give everybody ten. I want to talk to Mr. Carr." While the assistant was calling, "Everyone is on ten! Everyone take ten," Jock walked over to Preston Carr, who had come back to the protective shade of the open tent. Daisy was dabbing his neck, where it wouldn't interfere with his makeup. Manning was shooting that tender moment. Jock strode in, slipping between Daisy and Carr, put his arm around Carr, moved him a few paces away. Manning followed, close enough to shoot tight, intimate, candid shots as the King and the brilliant young director talked over the scene.

"I am not going for cinematography in this shot, Pres. Sure, it has to be a startling shot, stunning in its sparse grandeur. But that's only background. It's character I want. It starts your big scene! Bigger than any scene with the girl or even the stampede! This is the picture! This scene and what it says about your character, about freedom, civilization. I am looking for things far beyond mere camera excellence. So if I seem finicky or overly demanding, it's your performance I'm thinking about. It's honesty I'm thinking about. And it may take time to get it. I'll go slow. We'll have long breaks, as often as you want, just ask for them. But I won't quit till we get it right. And I'm sure you wouldn't want me to."

Carr did not answer, just nodded his head, as if to indicate he understood, he would cooperate. Then he turned, walked into the shade of the tent. Manning had covered it all, heard it all.

As Jock turned to go back out to the camera post, he caught a look in Manning's eye. It was admiration. Possibly more. Damn it, he hoped that fag wasn't getting any ideas.

They did the scene again, twice more before the long lunch break. It worked well both times, and on the three times after the break. But the fourth take of the afternoon, which was no different from the last three takes, was the best one, the right one, for in this one the shadow preceding Carr as he moved across the earth was longer, more foreboding.

320

For some reason known only to Jock, and for which he had only his own demanding, precise, untutored instinct to go on, that shadow was exactly the proper length. That shadow was what made this last take exactly the right one, and all the others, good as they were, not good enough.

He would never be able to explain it—not to the critics who would rave over it, and say it was "Jock Finley's signature" on the scene, or to anyone else. But there was something inside him that told him it was right. And that was the mysterious element of his craft, which he possessed and most other men in this world did not. That take, that shadow, would be more eloquent than all the dialogue in the world.

Carr was resting in his air-conditioned trailer, naked except for a blue-and-gold sculptured towel thrown across his middle. Daisy was giving him a glass of iced Scotch when Joe Goldenberg came to call. It was something Carr had asked him to do and which Joe would do for the rest of the shooting schedule.

"Well, Joe?"

"I wish I could fault him," Joe said, taking pouch and pipe out of his pocket and starting to load. "But he has instinct. That last take was the one. Though any of the others would have been acceptable to damn near any director I know."

"But it was good?" Carr persisted.

"It was great!" Joe reassured.

But as Joe took those first deep puffs a man needs to get his pipe going, he was wondering to himself. Preston Carr had never needed such reassurance before. Why now? But Joe did not say anything.

"As long as it was good," Carr said, taking his icy glass, sipping his Scotch.

CHAPTER

11

THE next morning when they drove out to the battleground, Carr and Daisy rode in one jeep, Jock and Manning preceded them in the command car.

The presence of the driver inhibited conversation, but Manning did ask, "How much do you plan? How much just happens?"

Jock smiled, a grim smile, and not looking at Manning, said, "I could ask you the same thing."

"But I shoot life," Manning said.

"So do I. Except in my work, we choose the story we tell. We put the elements together. We wait for the chemistry. That chemistry becomes life, reality, actuality. Take yesterday; I knew there was a great take lurking there, waiting. I knew it the first time I read the script. I knew what the elements were. But how to use them best, what was exactly the correct, the most striking, most truthful use of them, that only emerged when the shadow was at the right angle and the right length. When it happened, I knew it. You did too. It's what makes you the artist you are."

Manning nodded soberly. He made a mental note, that statement would be something for his text. He had already considered, very favorably, a still of Carr, with that long shadow, as the shot for the cover. But he would consider favorably, and discard, a hundred shots for the cover before this was over.

"Is it difficult getting a star like Carr to do the same bit over and over?" Manning asked.

"He didn't get to be King by being stubborn or rebellious. He's very cooperative, very constructive. In his field, there is none better. No one gives more of himself to a character or a picture."

They reached the battleground, leaped from the car. Jock started away quickly, deliberately. Manning, fearing that Jock wished to escape, followed as fast. Suddenly Jock stopped, turned to Manning, "Look, never ask me questions about Carr in the presence of anyone, even a driver. Now, if you want to know the truth, Carr has to be babied, coaxed, driven, seduced, used. He's a star like any other star. He has something. A personality. But not a hell of a lot of creative brains. You have to take him through it time after time. You saw that yourself. You want him to sweat, you work him till he sweats. You want him to walk tired, you work him till he's tired. My job is no different from yours. Except that you only shoot reality. I have to take make-believe and make it look like reality. And most times with actors who, deep down, probably don't give a damn! Except about what's left after taxes."

Jock had a technique with interviewers, a conscious, deliberate way of making them feel they were the only ones in the world who really understood him, or the art of the motion picture. Of the dozen or so young men in the world who were considered brilliant young directors, Jock Finley knew best how to use an interview to his own advantage. Confronted by another person who deemed himself creative, inventive, an artist, as Manning did and had a right to, Jock was working to his best possible audience.

"Look, off the record, he's giving the performance of his life, because I have pushed him, pulled him, badgered him, bullied, and ridden him like no other director he's ever had. He must hate me. When this is over I doubt that he'll ever talk to me again. Oh, maybe when he wins the Academy Award. But not before, believe me. But I don't mind. In fact, I'll know I'm getting the best he's got, if he winds up hating me.

"I am not in this business to make friends but to influence people. People who see pictures. So I am going to be just as tough and mean a sonofabitch as it takes to make a great picture."

When he was sure that Manning had ingested all that sufficiently to remember most of it for future reference, he added, "Watch. The next week or ten days. You'll think I'm brutal. But I like that

324

man. I respect him. Still, he's an actor. Which includes certain shortcomings. So when I drive him, it's for his own good, and for the picture! Remember all this, when you see the picture open in New York."

Having said that, Jock started away, toward the camera.

The key to the day's shooting was the moment when Carr seized the end of the tether from the stake and snapped the rope against the earth, causing it to make a sound as sharp as a pistol shot.

It was both a punctuation and an overture. It was the prelude to the beginning of the battle between man and beast. As Jock expected, the sharp sound itself was enough to make the beast rear up, its hooves flailing, menacing, high above Carr's head. But there was enough distance to give Carr safe clearance. Then the beast came down, sharp hooves landing and cutting into the desert crust.

They did a first take, a second, a third. None satisfied Jock.

"All the excitement of a travelogue," he muttered to himself, but just loud enough for Manning to hear.

During the fourth take, by accident, Carr miscalculated and came closer to the beast than he had planned. The beast reared up, poised in mid-air, hooves scything. Then it came down so close that the hooves barely missed Carr's head. Everyone froze, waited, then started to breathe again.

That's it, Jock said to himself, it's that element of danger, if we can re-create that and the camera can catch it, that will make the shot!

Jock conferred with Joe about the angle, the best lens to give them a close-up effect yet keep the camera far enough away so as not to menace or be menaced by the frightened beast. Technically, it was feasible, but Joe raised the question of Carr's safety. After all, Art Ryan, the stunt man, was waiting around. But Jock insisted on Carr's face. If they could come close, he wanted the element of danger written there, in Carr's eyes, his tense jaws, his tight muscles.

Finally, Joe said softly, "*We* can do it, if you can get *Pres* to do it."

Jock called a lunch break, a little early in the day, but he needed time, talking time.

325

While Pres relaxed in his air-conditioned trailer, eating very little of the lunch sent in by the commissary, Jock talked quickly, fervently, about the need to have the audience appreciate the danger Linc was facing. It couldn't be said in dialogue. Daisy's reaction shots would help, of course, but only to reinforce. The audience must see it, feel it for themselves. For that reason, Jock had decided that he wanted a shot in which the camera would be in close and Linc would wind up practically between the mustang's hooves when the animal came crashing down after rearing.

To achieve this proximity, this impact, Jock said, he had decided to use Ryan in this angle. Carr ate slowly, carefully, listened, nodded. Across the trailer, Daisy was sipping hot tea, which was all the lunch she ever dared tax her nervous stomach with. Pres didn't look toward her. He knew what she was thinking, feeling. He stared past Jock, he chewed thoughtfully. "The point is," Carr said finally, and with irritation, "you'd like me to do it. But you don't want to ask. You're running this like some kind of boy scout troop. You want volunteers, without even asking for them. Well, ask!"

Jock hesitated, then softly, "Okay, Pres, it would be better if you did it. I want *your* face, *your* shoulder muscles, *your* biceps. I can get a more honest shot if it's really Preston Carr, not Ryan. But I'll understand if you say no."

"I'll let you know after I finish my lunch," Carr said, turning away from Jock, dismissing him. As Jock opened the trailer door, Carr called to him, "Look, kid, with me, play it straight! I'm in this all the way. You know that. So don't try to con me. That only makes it tougher."

Jock turned, his baby-blues at about one hundred and ten percent hurt innocence, "Jesus, Pres . . ."

Carr interrupted, "I'll see you out there after the break."

Jock stood in the doorway, long enough to register a pained, hurt, misunderstood moment, then exited, as he used to when he had been a young actor with a flashy but shallow talent. The hurt look lasted only as long as it took to come down the three steps. He crossed the temporary compound, briskly, eagerly.

Inside himself, he was saying to Carr, Oh, you bastard, hate me, resent me, insult me, accuse me, dismiss me, do any fucking thing

326

you want, only do the scene my way. It's my picture! Make it my way!

When the lunch break was over, Carr and Daisy were in the makeup tent precisely on time. The sun overhead had already started its arc of descent, so that photographically it was at its best. Though combined with the heat of the baked earth, this was the most punishing time of day.

Jock and Joe were out in it, conferring about it, looking up at the sky, looking back at the camera, looking up again, talking, deciding finally. Joe went back to make some camera adjustments, to change his lens, to add a filter. Jock moved into the shade of the open makeup tent.

The makeup man was applying some Factor's body makeup to Carr, who lent himself easily to the operation. Jock drew close, saying to the makeup man, "I want real muscles, real sweat. So don't overdo that gook." The makeup man nodded, put on another dab, then a final touch, and he was gone.

"About before, Pres, I'm sorry. I don't try to con you. It's that I know how much I'm asking and I feel guilty. Maybe I get so wrapped up in any picture I make that I forget the people. I warned you that first time. I have a tendency to drive, to overdrive, myself and everyone else. With you I'm trying to guard against that. So I try to be diplomatic. I guess it comes out phony. I'm sorry. Straight out, that's what I should be. And you too. If there's anything I ask that you can't do, just say so. Straight out."

Carr nodded, not indicating if he had been placated. But Jock knew quite well, it would be a hot hot day here in this desert hell before Preston Carr, the King, admitted that there was anything he couldn't do.

Give me a nation of actors, Jock had always said to himself, and I could be elected President!

"We're going to cover this three ways. The mustang in foreground, you facing camera. You in foreground, the animal facing camera. Profile, man and beast. Whichever take gives us the optimum in danger, hooves, your muscular arms, your eyes, is what we'll use. Though I may decide later to intercut all three. That's why the proximity has to appear practically the same in each take, so that we can cut without compromising the perspective."

327

Carr nodded. A straightforward nod of understanding. No enthusiasm. But no protest either. The director had spoken. The King had agreed.

They were set up. Jock sent for Carr. He could see instantly that Carr was too dry for the take he wanted. So he found a pretext, walked Carr out to stand in the sun ostensibly to fully review the place and purpose of this sequence in the course of the entire battle scene. Carr listened, kicking at the earth, staring at the far mountains, glancing up at the hot sun. Finally, a rivulet of sweat made its way down the slight depression in the middle of his bare chest. It was Jock's cue. Now he was ready. He went back to the camera. Action was called. Carr, as Linc, moved into scene, bent down, seized the tether from the stake and snapped it fiercely, loudly.

The animal, a different mustang from the one used before lunch, reared up, prancing on its hind legs, terrified. Its forelegs scissored in mid-air. Carr's grip on the tether was tight, strong, so that the animal, high up, seemed to dance at the end of it. Then after a moment, hooves, animal, all came down so close to Carr that Jock gripped Joe's shoulder as the little man peered through his viewfinder. But Joe did not move, nor did anyone in his crew. With cold proficiency they stood by their equipment till Jock released them all with "Cut!"

At the command, Carr did not release the tether. He held it tightly till a wrangler could run out and take over. Then Carr turned away, his face grim, almost ashen under his tan. He was angered, his lips tight, his jaws locked in a hard, muscular fury. Jock came running up to him.

"Sensational," Jock began to say.

But Carr interrupted him. "You pull that on me again, I'll beat the hell out of you!" He reached out suddenly to seize Jock's shirt and hold the young man close to him.

"Christ, Pres, what are you talking about?" For once, at least, Jock was truly innocent, truly puzzled.

"Don't switch animals without telling me! If I get to know them, I can figure them. And how close to get to them. I thought this was

328

the one we were working with before lunch. Suddenly when he's up there, rearing over me, I look up and see his muzzle with a little white marking on it, I realize, Christ, this isn't the one! I don't know how he's going to land. And there I am, close enough to him to smell his breath! Don't ever do that to me again!"

Jock held still till Carr finished and released him. To struggle would only have called attention to Carr's grip, and his anger. There was also a touch, just a touch, but it was real, a touch of fear in Jock Finley, that young and strong as he was, this sixty-two-year-old man could really beat the hell out of him. He had the strength for it. And if he were ever to become angry enough, he could do it.

Not since Jock was a small, blond kid in a poor section of Williamsburg, taken over by Negroes, had he felt such fear of imminent physical punishment.

As Carr started away, Jock called out to Tex, the chief wrangler. The man came running. While Carr was still in sound of hearing, Jock berated Tex severely. Under no condition, never again, no matter the reason, was any animal to be substituted on Mr. Carr without his being told! It was a rule never to be broken! By anyone! And Jock said it loudly enough, viciously enough, so that everyone would hear it.

Then, he called to Preston Carr who was halfway back to the welcome shade of the tent, "I'm sorry, Pres! I guess it was my fault for assuming they wouldn't do that."

Manning caught it all. The shot of Carr gripping Jock's shirt. The close intense words from Carr to Jock. From Jock to Tex. Jock making his apology.

What Manning did not capture was Jock's feeling as he walked back toward camera. For he was thinking, Sonofabitch! So that's what made that take so good. Surprise! He didn't know the animal.

Jock crossed to where the crew was setting up for the new angle, head-on of Carr, across the mustang's body. Joe was busy supervising the setup. So busy that Jock felt he was being deliberately ignored. When Joe turned, unable to avoid him, Jock looked into the smaller man's face to say, "You think I planned that!"

Joe shook his head, negative, but not very convincing about it.

329

"I had no idea they switched animals! What the hell have I got a chief wrangler for? To keep things like that from happening!"

"We're ready for the next angle," was all Joe said. "And we'll be losing the sun soon."

This time, this angle, because of the perspective, it would not be necessary for Carr to work quite so close to the animal. Depth and the right lens would give the impression of their being closer. Jock had Joe explain this in detail to Pres. Then he let Carr determine the proper proximity. They were ready to walk it. The assistant enforced quiet. Just before Carr made his move to pick up the staked tether, Jock called out: "Take a good look at that animal, Pres! Make sure this time!"

Carr glanced in Jock's direction, a look of guarded appreciation or it might have been resentment or even controlled anger. But Carr did stop, did take a good look at the animal, recognized what was the now familiar small white marking. Then Carr walked through it, giving the tether less snap, evoking less rearing, less danger, till Joe knew he could get it all with the lens he was using.

Once set, Jock signaled. The assistant called out the orders. Jock called, "Action!" Carr started the scene. But the animal did not react as expected. He reared too much to one side and not above Carr. So it would not cut with the previous angle. Jock knew it even before Joe said it. They started again. The same grinding routine of detailed preparation and orders, which can sometimes make motion-picture-making the dullest work in the world. Another take, another problem. They had to go through it all again.

By now, Joe Goldenberg was saying, almost to himself, "We're losing the light, we're losing the light . . ."

So Jock called out to the crew, "We have time for only one more take. Get the lead out, guys! We have to make this a good one! Come on, damnit!"

Every man hustled, every man was ready. Carr was ready. Joe was ready. Jock stood just behind Joe, peering through the viewfinder, as he called out, "Action!"

Carr moved toward the mustang; glancing at it, then at the tether, he reached down, jerked it up, snapped it with the crack

330

of a pistol shot, raising a cloud of dust along the earth and giving added interest to the composition of the scene. At the same instant the frightened animal reared up on its hind legs, its quarter muscles magnificent, a Bernini statue in a Roman square. And just beyond, framed by the mustang's hooves, was Preston Carr's brown, tense face, his eyes glaring up at the animal, defiant for combat, for conquest. The look on Carr's face said it better than anything else could. It was man against beast and the man was not giving way. At the last moment, as the beast came down, his hoof brushed Carr's shoulder! It did not strike it fully, but came close enough to inflict a long, abrasive scrape which brought blood to the surface instantly so that it was in the shot.

Everyone gasped, except Carr. To Jock, Joe, Daisy, Manning, to every man and woman on the battleground, that moment was the moment when the entire picture could have been destroyed. Only Carr played it out to what he felt was the proper instant to end the scene, then he tossed aside the rope. From all sides they ran out to surround him. Jock and Manning were the first. Jock talked, Manning shot. This was blood, real blood, this was a man deliberately close to disaster. This was Life.

"Pres? Pres!" Jock kept asking.

"Get me some Scotch," Carr said in a low, hoarse voice. Jock gave the order to the man closest to him. Now the young company doctor arrived to take a look. He handed his kit to Jock to hold. The doctor took out alcohol and sponges, wiped away the blood, which was not spurting but oozing in a wide irregular patch of many small droplets. He held Carr's wrist as he worked on the biceps, dabbing it with stinging alcohol, wiping away the blood, assuring himself that it was only a scrape, no serious bruise, no break.

The whiskey arrived. Carr seized the glass with his free hand, took a long drink, then a shorter sip. He handed the glass back, saying only, "Ice." The doctor suggested Carr go back to the shade of the tent and lie down. Jock called a sharp command for a jeep. But Carr ignored that, started back on his own, with Daisy at his side.

When Jock asked about the prognosis, the doctor said, "Keep

331

the wound clean, it will dry up in a few days and be gone. You realize a change of skin color will be noticeable for some days."

But Jock had already decided to have that biceps made up to show blood in all future takes. Since the entire elapsed action of the finished sequence would be only minutes, all continuous, a wound sustained in this early shot must seem to continue to bleed through the entire sequence. But more, that touch of blood against all that tan skin, those powerful muscles, would make excellent color and composition. He was glad now that he decided to have Carr do the sequence without his shirt.

As Jock was handing back the medical bag, the doctor, instead of taking it, said, "I have to talk to you."

They started away, doctor and director, away from the crew, who were wrapping up production for the day.

A little way out into the desert, the doctor said, "I wouldn't worry about that scrape. Be careful with your makeup, keep it clean, it'll heal in three or four days. But . . ." he said, turning back in the direction of the battleground to make sure he was not being overheard. "But I would worry about something else if I were you. When I was treating him, I could have done this . . ." and he put his hand on Jock's biceps and pressed it. "Instead I . . ." and he took Jock's hand by the wrist to hold out the arm and dab at his biceps as he had done with Carr. "Because I wanted to feel his pulse. Don't push that man too far."

"After a shock like this, his pulse would be bound to race," Jock said.

"Just don't push him. And don't make me say any more than I have. I don't want to compromise the company. After all, they pay me." The doctor took his kit from Jock, started back toward the camp.

Jock kicked at the desert dust, thinking a moment, then crossed the battleground, where men were raking and smoothing the earth to obliterate footsteps, hoofmarks, and tire tracks in preparation for tomorrow's shooting. Jock found his assistant waiting for orders for tomorrow. But Jock said only, "Find Joe Goldenberg."

Almost an hour later, Joe opened the door of Jock's trailer. He was already puffing on his pipe.

"Drink?"

"No thanks," which meant Joe had had his quota of two pre-dinner drinks with Preston Carr.

"How is he?"

"Okay." But it was the kind of answer a man made when he was awaiting information, not giving it.

"He say anything?"

"Only that he got too close."

"He wasn't in pain? Or ... or resentful?" Joe shook his head. "Good!" Jock rose, started to move back and forth. He talked to Joe, yet for the most part avoided his eyes, except when he intended to make a special point or sought to determine Joe's reaction.

"He worries me, that man," Jock said. "I hoped he'd be more cautious. He knows perspective, he knows animals. He had no right to get that close. I know he's doing it for the picture, for the performance. Unless ..." here he glanced at Joe, "unless he's doing it to prove something. To himself. Or to her. Or to the world.

"If that's what it is, we have to protect him against himself. Subtly, of course. We have to arrange our schedule so as to keep him from overdoing. I'll need your help. Tomorrow, for example, are we better off going to reactions of Daisy and Boyd, or finishing Pres's sequence from the third angle?"

"The best way," Joe suggested, "is finish off the third angle tomorrow. Then take your time with the reactions, Daisy and Boyd. Especially now that you have the accident and the blood to work with to enhance their reactions."

Jock turned on Joe suddenly, "I know how we can do it!" He started to the bar to make himself a fresh drink, "Sure you won't have one?" Joe shook his head. "We'll tell him we need all their reactions in several grades of lighting so we don't have matching problems when we edit. That way we can spend a whole day with Daisy, a whole day with Boyd and give Pres two full days off. Okay?"

Joe nodded. But it was a slow, considered, almost grudging nod. Then he asked, "Finley, are you scared?"

"Damn right! And why not? The man simply will not protect himself! He takes risks I wouldn't take at my age!"

"I didn't mean that. I thought you knew something that I didn't."

"I saw what you saw! So I'm concerned! And I think I have good reason to be! Now, let's work together and get him through this in good shape. Right?"

"Right," Joe said in his quiet, understated way.

The next day was devoted to the third angle of the scene. It was set up, Carr walked through it several times. They tried one take which was aborted by an equipment failure. The cable feeding power to the camera cut out. They tried a second take, and a third. The fourth one was good, acceptable at least. Then they broke for lunch.

During lunch, Jock and Joe discussed the advisability of going for another take, or settling for what they had. Jock decided on another take. So after lunch they started up again. Instead of one take, they worked as long as the afternoon light would allow. For on the first two takes, it was Carr who aborted before they were complete. He seemed to suffer a memory failure, the kind that will overtake an actor in a dialogue scene sometimes, when he goes dry in his lines and has to say, "Sorry. Let's do it again."

It was strange for Carr, so it troubled Jock. Carr was forgetting the progress of the scene, or else was fighting it. Or perhaps it was the memory of that moment when the hooves came axing down close enough to injure him. By the time the light became critical, in mid-afternoon, they finally got that one take which everyone felt was the right one.

Whatever was troubling Carr, Jock knew it had resulted in the best take of the day. Carr was on his way back to his trailer when Jock intercepted him at the edge of the battleground, "That last one was great, just great!"

"Thanks," was all Carr said. At the moment a wrangler was leading the animal by. Carr took the opportunity to slap the animal on its shiny flank, a gesture of affection and respect. The wrangler led the spirited animal away, forced to use all the strength in his tough hands to control him.

Jock chose the moment to say, "You can take it easy tomorrow, Pres. Joe thinks we're better off getting the reaction shots as we go, less matching problems later."

"Oh?" Carr responded in a way that indicated he had expected to do the entire battle from start to finish in continuity, no

334

matter how many days it might take. But he only nodded, continued toward his own trailer.

Jock watched, measuring the man as he went. Wondering did he look different, walk different than he had before? Of course, at the end of a day's work in the hot sun a man should look different, appear tired, slump a bit. Or would Carr never look the same again to Jock, after the doctor had said what he did?

The next two days were given over to reaction shots. The first day Daisy. And she was better than Jock had anticipated. The fear the audience should feel later, she felt and exhibited. It looked true, real, because it was true, real. She did not know what the doctor had said. She didn't have to. Her own instinct about the man she loved told her the same thing the doctor's expertise had told him.

Boyd's reaction shots, on the day after, were simple, straightforward, craftsmanlike. He had a contempt for reaction shots. To him they were the phoniest part of a screen actor's performance. To exhibit love, fear, hatred, anger, amusement, concern, in little snatches, removed by hours, sometimes by days or even weeks, from the event or person to which or to whom you were supposed to be reacting was, to him, the worst kind of fakery. It was file-cabinet acting. But he did it, neat, cool, economical, controlled. Because if you were too big in your reactions you looked hammy.

So Boyd's reactions were always done with a consciousness of his friends in the East, who never hesitated to write him and tell him how awful he looked, when he was being paid six thousand dollars a week and they were working for Equity scale and getting $167.50.

In his own mind, Jock had long passed the point where he expected greatness from Boyd. If the boy was adequate in the role, that would serve the picture well. It would give Preston Carr and Daisy Donnell the complete attention of the critics, which was as it should be.

There would, of course, be several younger homosexual critics who would stamp Boyd's acceptable performance as "great," because it was so "self-effacing and modest, subordinating himself to the picture as an artist should." As if it were intentional on his part to be less than he might have been, and not that he was doing all he could do within the limits of his own small talent. For those critics, his limited reactions would conjure up the days of the lamented Jimmy Dean, and even Brando's first pictures.

But Jock would know the truth. And though he would recommend Boyd to other directors, he had already made a big mental note, stay away from that mediocre television bastard in casting any future pictures!

336

CHAPTER

12

Dawn of the first day of Carr's big battle sequence was one of those desert mornings when high, thin clouds spread milkily across the blue sky, presenting an insurmountable matching problem. Clear, pure blue desert sky was what they had been having. To work with anything less would severely limit, or make impossible, intercutting any good footage of today with that of previous days

They could work low, Jock thought, almost excluding the sky, keeping the action against the background of the mountain range. Such a low angle might be damned interesting. Though it would be different from what he had planned. Still, he decided they would try it that way. If nothing else, it would be a rehearsal, on film, of the entire battle sequence. It would tell him what the potentials were. He could study the rushes, perhaps come up with additional highlights, action and moments of conflict and danger beyond those he had been able to visualize from applying his own creative imagination to the script.

Over coffee, at the breakfast table, Jock revealed his plan to Joe.

"With that sky, I didn't figure you'd want to shoot at all today," Joe said.

"Suppose we come up dry, what have we lost, a few thousand feet of film? But if lightning strikes . . ." Jock left it hanging.

337

"If lightning strikes, you'll spend days, weeks maybe, trying to recapture it, because that sky won't cut."

"Even if it won't, we'll learn something. Pres'll learn something about the fight. It'll be a run-through."

"You don't use a star like Preston Carr for rehearsal," Joe said, picking up his notes and his script, which was now down to the few pages of the big scene, folded in the middle, frayed and dirtied by endless handling. He started away from the table.

"Joe!" Jock called in a low voice so as not to attract the attention of the others. Goldenberg turned back, waited. "Has he said anything? About how he feels? About any pains?"

"A proud man is not likely to talk about pain."

"Is it something you've seen? Detected?" Joe shook his head. "What, then?"

Joe made a small beckoning gesture of his head. He started for the exit. Jock followed. When they were outside, they walked along one side of the compound, so that while the convoy was shaping up all around them, the noise kept Jock and Joe from being overheard.

"When I had mine," Joe began, "the doctor said after eight weeks I could do anything I wanted. In moderation. Except one thing. Drive a car that didn't have power-steering. He forbade any continuous strain on the muscles of the arms, shoulders, chest, and back."

"How can Pres possibly do that wrestling scene without involving those muscles?" Jock asked.

"If I were you, I would think seriously about going back to the idea of Ryan. *Now.*"

"He's been talking to you!"

"He hasn't said a word!" Joe protested.

"At the end of every day, when you go into his trailer, he doesn't talk about it?'

"No."

"What does he talk about?"

"He only wants to know how it went. If we got everything. If I'm satisfied with what I've done."

"If you liked his performance . . ." Jock suggested, unable to conceal his resentment that the star would use a cinematographer as a sounding board when Jock Finley was his director.

338

"We're old-timers together," Joe explained. "I think it makes him feel better."

"No wonder he was never as great as he could have been! He can't put himself completely in the hands of his director! Has no confidence. Can't let himself go!"

"He was never this way before," Joe said. He realized an instant too late that what he had intended to be a placating comment would be interpreted as a slur by Jock Finley.

"With other directors, you mean!"

"I didn't say that," Joe began to protest. But Jock never let him finish.

"Sonofabitch! After the way I worked with him, built this character and this picture around him, got him to do things that he himself admitted he's never been able to do before. And now he doesn't come to *me* for reassurance! When he saw the rough cut he couldn't find enough nice things to say. Now he won't talk to me. Won't ask me, am *I* satisfied, do *I* like it, do *I* think he's doing fine, no!"

"Don't hate him!" Joe pleaded.

"Hate an actor? No, I do not hate actors. Any more than I hate a bad set. Or crappy dialogue. Or flat lighting. They offend me. But I do not waste my time hating them. Even the biggest of them. Even your King!"

If they were not so close to finishing, if Joe Goldenberg did not feel a sense of obligation to Preston Carr, if he did not know that they were making a great picture, he would have quit. Right there.

Instead, for Carr's protection, he decided to appease Finley, for he felt the young man's anger could be dangerous.

"Finley, you're coming to the end of a great picture. No one can take that away from you. No critic, no audience, no one who ever sees that picture will walk out without remembering your name. No matter what Pres does, or the girl does, the picture is you. So you have nothing to lose. Unless ... unless you don't finish.

"Now, when I said the man has never been like this before, I didn't mean he's never been like this with any other *director* before. I meant I have never seen him uncertain about *himself*. I've never seen him ask for or need reassurance.

"So it isn't you. He thinks the world of you. As a director. He doesn't want to upset you, doesn't want to limit your imagination by making you think you have to carry him, baby him. He doesn't want to make his problems your problems. He wants this picture to be as good as you do! That's all it is."

"There's another reason . . ." Jock suggested. "Guilt!"

"Guilt?" Joe asked, incredulous.

"Yes, guilt! What the hell are we talking about? Right now! Let's face it! You're saying to me, 'Take it easy, he's an old man who's had a heart attack and if we ask him to do justice to this scene it might kill him.' Right?"

"All right, suppose it is?"

"Let me remind you, Mr. Goldenberg, that we are in this situation because of Preston Carr's failure to be honest with me! Before he signed to do the picture, he might have said to me, 'Finley, I want you to know that I've had a heart attack. Unless we can work within the limits of that, I can't do your picture.' Or was honesty asking too much? From the King! Who gets paid one million bucks a picture, up front! Instead, he lets me come right down to the wire, with the big scene in the picture staring me in the face! Then he sends you to plead with me to go easy with him. I do not call that honest, decent, or even professional!"

By now Jock's voice was coming up strong. Joe was growing nervous, self-conscious lest they be overheard. So when he defended Carr, it was in a whisper, but a strong, resentful whisper.

"He did *not* ask me to talk to you! *I* did not ask to talk to you. If you will recall, *you* wanted to talk to *me*!"

"Only because by your actions, your attitude, you led me to believe you had something to say to me. Something of importance!" Jock answered, also in a whisper, but no less furious than before.

"Yes, I did have something to say to you! If you do it right, and with regard for the man's physical limitations, he'll give you everything you need. Maybe not everything you want, but enough to make you a great picture. Work *with* him, not against him. Encourage him, don't challenge him. He is a proud man. He will try to outdo himself. And if he does, it can be . . . it can be bad, for all of us. That's what I had to say."

"What about today?" Jock asked, ignoring Joe's plea.

340

"I don't like that sky." Joe looked away from Jock and out toward the battleground and the sky above it.

"Even if we angle low, keep off the sky, use the mountains?"

"That's a possibility. But the odds don't favor it," Joe said, staring across the wasteland at the mountain.

"Suppose I use Ryan for a rehearsal, on film?"

"Okay with me," Joe said, still waiting for some response to his desperate plea.

"I'll check the weather. Talk to you later." Jock walked away, giving Joe no promise about Carr, about going easy, about not challenging him. Joe watched him, the fear he had felt before much stronger now.

Half an hour later, Jock sent word to Joe by his assistant. The weather for tomorrow indicated the possibility of rain. That could mean the loss of two days, not one. So that today would be a rehearsal, on film, of the entire battle sequence. With Ryan. Jock sent word to Carr that he would not be needed for the day.

Since the only shooting left involved him, Carr was puzzled by the brief message. He made it his business to attend the shooting, out of costume, wearing a steel-gray cashmere jacket and a crimson cashmere turtleneck shirt. Aside from the fatigue obvious in his face despite the fresh sunburn from days of recent shooting, Preston Carr looked almost as Jock had first seen him at his ranch.

Jock and Ryan went off by themselves, to the middle of the battleground. Jock was talking the scene. With great sweeping gestures of his hands and his body, he moved like a prizefighter enacting a past fight. When Jock Finley was intense, he was total energy, movement, physical power. To explain a scene, and to enact it, was as satisfying an exercise to him as having sexual intercourse. And generally he did it with even more gusto.

Now he was explaining to Ryan precisely what he would like to get, and at the same time, admitting that a great factor in the scene, the beast itself, would to some degree determine the course of it. But within the limits of those unexpected elements, Jock was explaining what he hoped to have on film at the end of shooting.

Ryan listened, nodded; his eyes were keen, narrow, active, flicking from Jock to the stake where the animal's tether would be tied. He was correlating Jock's words and movements with the

341

actualities of the situation. But mostly Ryan was nodding, thinking. Jock went through the whole scene, the attack on the animal,
the use of the rope, moving in, whipping the mustang with the
hat, holding the beast close in at the muzzle, cowing it, almost
bringing it to its knees, finally exercising complete domination
over it, leading it to the ramp and up into the waiting truck and
captivity. The later moment, when Linc paused, reacted, and freed
the animal, would be a separate, close take and of course not
involved in this rehearsal. When Jock was done, Ryan nodded
thoughtfully.

"Pick the animal you want to work with. Because once we start,
the camera is going to roll continuously. I want this all in one
take." Then Jock added, "A take we can use, if we have to."

At that phrase, Ryan looked up sharply at Jock.

"This is your chance, Art. You're in this picture or you're not,
depending on what you do today." Jock turned and walked away.
Ryan stood looking after Jock for a long beat before he started
toward where the wranglers had the mustangs in tow.

When Jock got back to camera position, Joe Goldenberg had
just come away from the finder. As though nothing had passed
between them an hour ago, Jock said to Joe, "I want to be able to
keep going so we can get the whole take in one continuous flow. At
least we'll go as far as we can. How much have you got in there?"

"Almost four hundred feet."

"Reload! Take no chances!" Jock ordered.

Joe did not argue, only passed the order to his assistant. All
the while, Preston Carr and Daisy were sitting close by, in the
shade of the open tent, watching. The import of what Jock had
said was not lost on Carr. Now Jock seemed to spot him suddenly.
He came over to greet him, to inquire about his shoulder scrape.
Then, as though it were an afterthought, Jock explained, "We're
doing a rehearsal on film. I want to find out if we can take it all
without having to edit. So I'm making Ryan run through it. Then
you and I can study the rushes and see where he went wrong. And
what we'd like to aim for when you do it."

"Good idea," Carr agreed.

"Love that jacket," Jock said. "You got to tell me the name
of your tailor when we get back to LA."

342

"Had it made in London," Carr said, but he was looking past Jock at Ryan who had begun to walk one of the selected stallions across the battleground.

The animal was reluctant, bridling, but not fierce, not rebellious. So Ryan led him back to the wrangler and walked another, and another. The fourth mustang seemed to have the proper degree of fight. And Ryan approved him. The chief wrangler took over the rope, led the animal away to give it a shot of mild sedative. The mustang would become somewhat more manageable then. He brought it back, fixed its tether to the stake.

Ryan looked the beast over again, then turned to call out to Jock, "Whenever you say!"

"Walk it for Joe," Jock shouted back.

Ryan made a signal of approval and moved back to his starting position. He paused there a moment, thoughtful, then when he was ready, he gave a curt wave of his hand to Jock, who checked with Joe, and then called out, "Go!"

Ryan walked the scene, indicating, but not actually doing the business. He bent down, pretending to loose the tether, to pick it up. He moved forward and back as he would once the animal was in the scene. He swung around, his back to camera, then around again, facing it, and moved forward as he would to back down the mustang, and he retreated when it would be proper to give ground to the animal. Finally he used his hat as a weapon, replaced it on his head to free both his hands again, and then working with what would be the rope, he feigned bringing the animal up close, dominating it and walking it up the ramp of the open-backed truck.

Jock looked at Joe, "Okay?"

"Okay."

Jock called out to Ryan, "Okay, Art! That's the way we'll do it." Then, to make it appear an inspiration of the moment, Jock added, "Tell you what! Let's try it with your shirt off." Jock looked about, calling, "Makeup! See if he needs body makeup! Now, Joe, what about you?"

Joe Goldenberg stared at Jock, at Ryan, then looked through his viewfinder, and finally back to Jock, "Okay for me." But he could not completely conceal his anger. If this was only a rehearsal on film, why the need for Ryan to remove his shirt? And if it wasn't a rehearsal, why hadn't he been told? And Joe was conscious of Preston Carr sitting there, staring, furious.

Jock Finley had not planned it, but at that precise moment Manning took a sly shot of Carr. Carr was too angry not to be alert to every sound, every move. He turned, glared at Manning, who used it as the moment to take yet another shot, star in anger. Then Manning moved away, turning his camera on Ryan and the makeup man. With a flip, Manning changed lenses, got a shot of the makeup man adding some tan to Ryan's already tanned, strong body.

When the makeup man was done, he turned to call, "Okay, Jock!"

Without looking to Joe, Jock asked him, "Ready?"

"Ready," Joe answered, biting back his anger.

"Let's go!" Jock called on his assistant. The assistant shouted all the orders necessary to dispatch each man to his job and to eliminate all unnecessary movement and sound. Now Jock took over. He glanced first at Carr who was staring grimly out at Ryan. Then Jock called, "Action!"

Out there alone, his shirt off, his chest deep, his muscles clearly outlined, Ryan started to the rope, picked it up, snapped it to excite the animal, all of which was already on film, but he needed it as a lead-in to his own scene. Then he snapped the rope again, jerking the animal's head, causing it to resist, rear and pull back, all in an attempt to free itself from the rope. Even though the animal had the usual dose of sedative, it took all the strength of Ryan's arms and legs to hold fast, all the power of his shoulders to keep from being turned. The effect of man on beast and beast on man, their wills, their muscularity, came through clearly. Ryan's strength and his speed afoot, which allowed him to make effective countermoves to the mustang's resistance, were graceful and impressive.

One thing more was impressive. Ryan was thirty years younger than Preston Carr. And Preston Carr, watching this duel of man and beast, realized that, realized it more than any man there. Carr was living every move, every twist, every turn, every lurch, every surge of strength, every exertion of Ryan's magnificent body. All

344

of it kept reminding him that this was a man thirty years younger.

The battle continued through the phases outlined by Jock. But each phase took longer than he had anticipated, because the animal was fiercer than Ryan had expected. But for Jock's purposes the more fight, the better the scene. It must never be easy or allowed to appear easy. It must tax the man to the utmost. So the longer the struggle, the more intense, the more the outcome was in doubt, the better.

When he called, "Cut!" at the moment when Ryan dropped the truck gate imprisoning the beast, Jock felt an enormous surge of satisfaction. The scene worked! It did precisely what it should for the climactic scene of the picture! He turned to Joe to ask if he had gotten it. But he discovered that during the action Preston Carr had left his chair and moved toward the camera and had been peering over Joe's shoulder to see how it looked.

"Joe?"

Joe Goldenberg, with Preston Carr standing alongside him, said, "Got it."

Carr said nothing. He started away. Jock called to his assistant, "Take half an hour. Clean up the battleground. I want to try it again!"

At that, Preston Carr who had almost reached the shade of the tent, looked back, stared at Jock Finley, then continued past the tent toward the jeep which would take him back to his air-conditioned trailer. Daisy hurried after him, barely catching up with him as he climbed into the jeep.

They did the scene with Ryan one more time before lunch. And twice after. Of these three takes, one was a complete washout, the animal being too sedated or too timid, too free of fight. The second was good but not particularly notable, because Ryan had had trouble getting his hat back on after he had used it.

The final take of the afternoon, just before the right light deserted them, was the best of the day. Ryan had caught the feeling, gained sufficient confidence to work the spirited mustang in such a way as to achieve maximum fight, hence the maximum exultation of conquest for the audience.

345

Jock ordered all four takes flown to LA, rushed through the lab, to be back the next morning at the latest.

If Jock needed justification for his decision to work with Ryan, he had it the next day. Though it did not rain, it was one of those gray, windy days which can afflict the desert suddenly. The sky was thick with layers of clouds in threatening, glowering shades from light gray to dark. The wind whipped the clouds, driving them like dirty sheep. The whole sky seemed to be racing in one direction. An occasional gust of wind sucked up the dust, drove it across the compound like pellets of steel.

Jock welcomed the weather. Not only because it fulfilled his prediction to Joe, but because it would be a welcome day off in which there would be time to view Ryan's rushes, to consider, discuss, decide on future plans. The first call from LA reported that the rushes were out of the lab, but that the copter would probably not be able to make it due to strong adverse winds. But Jock got on the radiophone. He spoke to the manager of studio and finally to the studio head. And when the cost of a day's delay was thoroughly considered, the pilot was ordered to take off.

It was a rough flight. At the moment of landing, a sudden strong gust almost carried the copter into a generator truck off to the side of the landing pad. But the landing was effected. The cans of film were handed down and rushed to the projection truck. When Jock got word that he could run the film he did not invite Joe. This first running he wanted all to himself.

Standing in the truck, crouching somewhat, Jock viewed all four takes. The first and the fourth were very good. He had them run again. The fourth was the one. He ran that again, and yet again. That was it. The scene, the struggle, the impact, the color, the excitement he had been hoping for. If there were moments when it was too obviously not Carr but Ryan, another take or two could fix that. But the fact was clear. If Jock had to, he could finish with Art Ryan. The only question now was, would Preston Carr realize that? And if he did, what would he do about it? For deep in Jock's mind was a director's absolute conviction that he must have Carr in this scene to give the picture the honesty he demanded. And to give himself the satisfaction of having executed it exactly as he had conceived it, so that weeks from now he would not have to leave a projection room, or months from now leave a preview theater, rebuking himself for not having been strong enough, despot enough, to have insisted on what he knew to be right.

He had to have Carr! In fact, the better Ryan looked in the rushes, the more sure Jock was that he had to have Carr! Having determined that, he sent for Joe Goldenberg, ran the first and the fourth takes for him. Joe watched, expressionless. Jock commanded the projectionist to run them again.

Then Jock asked, "Well?"

"There's no question it will work," Joe said.

"I know the scene works! I want to know what you think about Carr!"

"When I said there's no question, I meant there is no question in my mind that Ryan can get away with it," Joe explained. "A little different angle and I'll give you a take that I defy anyone to say is not Carr."

"And if I don't just want to get away with it, then what?" Jock demanded.

"I don't understand." But Joe did understand, very well, too well.

"I want that scene! But I want it honest! I want Carr!"

"Finley, please!"

"And I want to know what you'll tell him, if he asks you. And he will ask you," Jock challenged.

"I'll level with him," Joe said simply.

"Meaning?" Jock pursued him.

"I'll tell him what I saw. That I think Ryan can do it, that very few people, aside from real pros, would spot him as a double. That's what I'll tell him," Joe declared, quite firmly.

"Okay," Jock said. "Thanks for being honest with me."

"Can I go now, *boss*?" Joe asked.

"Sure, Mr. Goldenberg, sure."

Joe left the trailer. The projectionist had seen it all, heard it all. Though he had tried to busy himself in order to appear not to be aware, he called attention to himself when he couldn't resist lighting up a cigarette.

Without looking at him, Jock said, "Go make pictures! Knock yourself out, plan, write, dream, shoot! Then at the last minute something like this happens."

347

"Yeah," the projectionist commiserated.

"Would *you* know?" Jock asked suddenly. The startled projectionist could not answer a question he did not even understand. "Seeing those takes, would *you* know it was Ryan instead of Carr?"

His professional skill challenged now, the projectionist put on his thoughtful grimace. "Well...I...I could tell. After all, there's only one Preston Carr," the projectionist said.

"Exactly! You just said it! There's only one Preston Carr! And they'll know it. Everyone who ever sees this picture will know it! We can't fake it. We're not *allowed* to fake it! It has to be Carr. You're absolutely right!"

Jock left the projection trailer, started across the windy compound, his eyes almost completely shut by the tiny particles being driven against his face. Above, the sky was growing blacker. Clouds, striations of many shades of threatening gray, moved with the pace and purpose of attacking armies. Off in the distance, he could see where rain had already begun to fall.

His opening line, what to say, how to say it, was what Jock was considering. The projectionist's words could be a place to start. Or perhaps best with a man like Preston Carr was to say, "Pres baby, relax! Nothing to worry about. We'll work with Ryan. With a few different angles in his big scene, and a few close cuts to you, they'll buy it all. They'll never know."

But Jock's debate in tactics became academic suddenly. For across the compound, coming at him, was Preston Carr, hatless, his hair windswept. He was on his way to find Jock Finley. There was no doubt about that as he headed for Jock, confronted him in the middle of the compound. The wind was sharp and shrill, as it will grow sometimes in the desert, so Carr almost had to shout, "I heard you got the rushes back!"

"Yeah, Pres."

"Did you see them?"

"Yeah. They were ..."

But Carr interrupted, "I want to see them for myself!"

"Sure, Pres. Sure. Any time."

"Right now!"

"Okay!"

348

Jock started to escort Preston Carr back to the projection trailer but Carr halted him.

"Alone!"

"Sure. Sure, Pres. Anything you say."

Jock stopped, Carr did not miss a step or a beat but continued on toward the projection trailer. Jock stood with the wind behind him, driving his chino pants against his legs, driving his tweed sports jacket against his back. He put up his collar, buttoned the flap, all absentmindedly as he wondered what his next move must be. Joe. He decided it must be Joe. He started for Goldenberg's trailer.

The projectionist was just finishing rewinding the rushes when Preston Carr entered. He was immediately alert, attentive, respectful, for he was of the old school, when stars were revered, idolized, looked upon as the mainstays of entire studios, providers of thousands of jobs. A star was royalty. And Preston Carr was, of course, the King.

"Yes, sir, Mr. Carr!"

"Finley said you have the rushes. Run them!"

"Yes, sir!"

Carr pulled up a camp chair, sat down. Resting his elbows on the narrow wooden arms, pressing his fingers together, steepling them against his lips, his thumbs supporting his chin, he settled in to watch. The rushes started. Carr's eyes were framed by tight, tanned, wrinkled skin. They were fixed and demanding as he evaluated the action that moved before him.

The color of the scene was clear and bold, red earth, sky, dun-colored mountains. The beast was a remarkably strong, graceful animal. But Preston Carr saw one thing and one thing only. Ryan, a good thirty years younger than he was, moved with the strength and ease which an older man must either admire or hate.

In a little while, Carr became aware of another thing: certain betrayals, subtle and gross, of the fact that this was not Preston Carr on the screen. It could never be Preston Carr. There were moments when he could pick out Ryan's face unmistakably. There

349

were mannerisms that were not Carr's. And ways Ryan moved
that Preston Carr did not. And even from the rear, one could
see that Ryan's shoulders sloped like a certain great prizefighter's,
while Carr's did not, his coming straight out, firm, broad, which
made him such a delight to expert London tailors. And Ryan had a
way of toeing out, while Preston Carr toed in somewhat, just
enough to give him that famous, distinctive walk.

Suddenly the film was over. The white light reflecting off the
screen hurt Carr's eyes, causing him to turn away slightly.

"Once more!" he said. Now he leaned forward in his chair, one
elbow on his thigh, resting his chin in that hand.

The film started again.

Jock Finley had crossed to Joe Goldenberg's trailer. He found
Joe reading one of four new scripts sent down by his agent in hopes
of attracting his interest, his enthusiasm, his signature on a contract. In his own way, Joe Goldenberg was a star too.

At Jock's intrusion, Joe looked up, removing the cold pipe from
his mouth. Dog-earing the page, he put aside the script.

"He's in there, watching the rushes."

Joe did not answer, just knocked his pipe against the side of the
deep ashtray to empty it. He started to fill it again.

"He's going to discover it for himself. Shoot it any way we like,
we can't get the man and the beast on that screen at the same time
and still keep secret that it's Ryan. We have to do something!"

"What are you going to do?" Joe asked, transposing from the
collective to the singular with one pronoun. He started to light up
his pipe.

"I don't know," Jock said, waiting for some suggestion. But Joe
busied himself, relighting his pipe. So Jock said, "You must have
been in a situation like this some time, somewhere, before. What
did they do?"

Joe thought a moment, sucked on his pipe, let the smoke escape
slowly from the side of his lips. "Once. Once we were in South
America. At a place on the Amazon. Where the current is very
strong. And the river takes a sharp turn, so you're suddenly in

350

the rapids without any warning. We looked that over, figured it seven different ways to the ace. Till finally the director decided that we'd use a stunt man. But even the stunt man was reluctant. Reluctant? Hell, he was frightened. But the director insisted. 'We need that shot!'

"So we set up. I was on the high shore, just at the curve. That way I could pick him up as he came around the bend, hold him into the rapids, follow him on through. He was using a small native canoe, about like a kayak. We figured, if we're lucky, we get it in one take. If not, we have to go for two. So we're set up. We get the word on the walkie-talkie. We start grinding. Round the bend in the river comes that little boat, in all that angry white water. This stunt man, in his makeup he looks like the star, and we've got him all the way. Coming toward us, into the rapids below us, till the current suddenly sweeps him sideways, then catches him broadside, whips him over, swamps him completely. And he disappears from view. Lost!

"It took four days to locate his body. It was found by a small tribe of Indians downriver about twenty miles."

Joe stopped as if to relight his pipe. Instead, he said slowly but quite pointedly, "We never did try that take again. And when it came to cutting the picture, because we were too long, they cut out the entire river sequence. All of it. And the picture was a good picture, got good reviews, made money.

"Sometime in the future, if you can ever use eight hundred feet of gorgeous South American color, in seventy millimeter, of a man getting killed before your eyes, I have it. In a vault. At Paramount."

Joe looked down at the flame of his lighter, but stole a glance across the flame at the grim, angry face of Jock Finley.

Without a sound or a knock, the door of Joe's trailer opened suddenly. It was Preston Carr. He was obviously startled to find Jock here. But it did not change what he had come to say.

"Joe, I want you to come with me! I want you to look at that film!"

"Sure, Pres." Joe took his old corduroy jacket from the back of a chair. They left, Pres and Joe, with no invitation to Jock. The two of them started across the compound. Jock watched them from the top step of Joe's trailer. Two figures, leaning against the

351

wind, crossing the open space, dust whipping around them. They disappeared into the projection trailer.

An hour later, Preston Carr came to find Jock Finley in his trailer. Joe Goldenberg was not with him.

"We just saw them, studied them, discussed them. It can't be faked. Even if you wanted to, and you don't." Then he accused, "That's why you had Ryan do it. To prove that."

Carr paused. "And to show me up. With a man thirty years younger than I am. Okay! You proved both things. And I am going to do it. But on my own terms. Only two takes a day. One in the morning, one in the afternoon. Two takes! That's all! And if it extends the shooting schedule a week, two weeks, or three, I don't give a damn! First, I want my doctor flown down here. And Axel Steenstrup, my trainer and masseur. I want him here from tomorrow till we're finished shooting. I'll be ready for the first take in five days."

Having said that, and Jock having nodded to each of his demands, Carr turned and left. Whatever Carr had said, and meant— I'll do it but on my own terms, I'll do it but only after I've had a chance to get in trim, I want to be treated like a champion, rubbed, scrubbed, and tubbed—it all added up to, I'll do it! To Jock Finley that was the one, the only fact of any importance.

Carr's pride had committed him to seeing it through, all the way. If there's one thing I know, it's actors! Jock Finley congratulated himself.

What took place in Preston Carr's trailer with his physician on those five afternoons, no one else knew, not even Daisy Donnell. Nor was Joe Goldenberg present or privy to the examinations, discussions, advice. But what happened between Carr and Axel Steenstrup, his masseur and trainer, was public business. Twice each day, Preston Carr and Axel ran several miles on a track they roughed out, circling the compound. In sweat pants and sneakers they ran steadily, each time for more than an hour, each time stepping up the pace, putting more and more pressure on Carr's legs, on his heart, only stopping when Axel felt that the King was fighting for breath a little too hard.

For a man already in very fine condition, the regimen was not too taxing. It was a matter of accustoming his well-tuned body, mainly his legs, for the long, sustained takes. The pivot of his struggle with the animal, the ability to withstand the animal's power, would rest finally in Carr's legs.

There were other exercises too. Calisthenics for those stomach muscles which would be put under great strain in rope-holding, pulling, forcing. Exercises for arms, chest, back, which Axel improvised to fit the special demands of the scene. He rigged up a chinning apparatus which employed the crane on the back of one of the trucks. He affixed a lariat to a high stake, at the head height of a rearing horse, so that Preston Carr's muscles could become used to the precise angle at which the greatest strain would occur. Manning was delighted. He was getting exclusive shots of a star in intensive training for one single sequence. So he worked almost as continuously as Carr. There seemed no end to Manning's interest or his raw film. For a time, Jock entertained the distinct suspicion that Manning was falling in love with Carr, with his strong, mature physique, which grew stronger from his workouts and more bronzed from constant exposure to the sun.

At the end of each workout, morning and afternoon, Daisy was ready with Carr's sweatshirt and towel. Axel shepherded him to his trailer, which was kept warmed or cooled to an even, constant seventy degrees. There Axel worked on him with alcohol, and alboline. His big, strong hands kneaded out the knots, firmed up the muscles, caressing them and beating them alternately, digging sharp, strong fingers into areas which were tight or tired. Across back and chest, up into shoulders and into biceps, Axel's hands worked. All the while he was urging, "Breathe deep, Pres, real deep!" while Axel himself seemed to fight hard for breath.

Each afternoon Carr and his doctor closeted themselves in Carr's trailer for about fifteen minutes. When the doctor came out he spoke to no one, but seemed to maintain a confident air. When Daisy asked Carr, his reassurance was constant and smiling,

"Don't worry, honey. He says it's fine, just fine." Occasionally he added, "I'll beat that sonofabitch. I'll beat him!"

During the days of conditioning, Jock Finley went about his own business. Overseeing the bits and pieces Joe was shooting. Talking with Manning. Consulting by radiophone with Marty White, with New York, on schedules, release dates, advertising, promotion. Through it all there was building within him a storm of anticipation about the big scene, the scene yet to come. Ryan's success with it had only made him hungrier to do it all with Carr. Carr's determination, his dogged, driven desire to be better at it than Ryan, was working out even beyond Jock's hopes.

On the fifth day of training, when Carr was on the table following his afternoon workout and Axel was kneading his back, Jock knocked on the door of the trailer. Daisy opened the door, called back to Carr to announce Jock. After a pause that seemed too long, Carr finally invited him in.

Jock stared down at Carr's huge, brown back, with the muscles standing out clean and firm. He smiled, "You could go ten rounds with Cassius Clay right now."

"With Joe Louis," Carr corrected, making a joke. And a comment.

"I wondered how it's going," Jock said, his baby-blues at about ninety percent respectful humility. Carr did not answer at once. "I ... I'd like to be able to plan. When do you figure you'll be ready, Pres?"

Now that Jock had asked the question straight out, Carr answered, "Axel figures another two days. Right?"

Without interrupting his deep, digging, rubbing motion Axel nodded.

"Friday?" Jock evaluated. "Why don't you take till Monday, maybe even get a day or two of rest over the weekend?"

"Monday?" Carr asked Axel.

"Oh, sure," Axel said.

Jock nodded, smiled. "Doctor say anything?" he asked.

"Everything's fine," Carr said.

"Good!" Jock enthused. Then, "You know I miss those end-of-

354

day drinks we used to have. I've got a trailer full of your brand that I'm going to be stuck with, unless you start drinking again soon."

Carr did not answer, just smiled, turned his head away, as Axel started to work on his neck muscles. It was all cool, polite, antiseptic. Jock knew now that he had lost something of this man. Be it friendship or respect, he had lost it.

He left, still smiling, a fixed smile, expressionless. As he stepped down from the trailer he found Daisy waiting to enter, carrying a bottle of alcohol she had gone to fetch from Axel's supplies. His smile suddenly felt uncomfortable on him. She said nothing. But her eyes were accusing.

"Hi," he said with great warmth.

"Hi," she answered simply, without any feeling.

"Some day when this is all over . . . " he said, "I want to talk to you."

"Why? What are you going to say?" She was capable of a naïve directness which was usually surprising. Used to hearing her speak dialogue which was written, and cute, in what was supposed to be her style, one never quite got used to simplicity or directness from her.

"You really want to know? Okay! A man doesn't get over you. Ever. Do you know that?" he asked. "You must. Other men must have told it to you."

She shrugged, avoided answering by asking, "Did Pres say when he'd be ready?"

"Monday. We're going Monday."

She nodded thoughtfully. There was a moment of silence between them. It seemed she might ask him something, and he was waiting to hear it. But she became conscious of the bottle and her errand, so she continued up the steps into the trailer.

Jock lingered, watching. Damn, he said to himself, imagine having had that girl in your room, in your bed, for weeks and never laying her. And for a man as strongly sexed as Preston Carr.

Jock Finley was halfway across the compound when he stopped suddenly, looked back at Carr's trailer. In one single moment of regret and loneliness, he realized that whatever he thought of her, her strangeness, her sickness, her promiscuity with a hundred directors, actors, agents, psychoanalysts, and God-knows-who,

355

maybe even gas station attendants, in his own way, he loved her. He missed her. And if he had the chance . . . and maybe he would one day . . . who could know how long this thing between her and Carr would go on . . . he'd go back there. He'd find out. For he secretly harbored the ambition that if she were not under the obligation of having to look so perfect, learn her lines, act and react on cue, carry on her shoulders the burden of multimillion-dollar-investments, if perhaps she were freed from all pressures, all tensions, she could yet be a woman for one man alone.

Yes, he had to find out. One day.

Some women marry alcoholics to reform them. Some men marry beautiful but sick women to cure them. It is always a noble delusion with a pathology all its own.

Monday morning the weather was almost perfect: the air clear, the sky blue, the layer of clouds, thin and stretched across the mountain top, disappeared early under the strong sun. It was the desert at its clearest, driest, brightest. Joe Goldenberg would start working with F-10 filters this morning.

Anticipation, excitement, was evident in every area of the camp. From the way breakfast was served at six, to loading the trucks, shaping up the convoy, moving out and setting up on the battleground, everything moved with precision and zest.

Jock made a half a dozen helicopter trips from compound to battleground and back. If the others were excited, in Jock there was a fever. A creative man can sense, with almost unerring premonition, when he is on the verge of a great moment. The writer can feel it in his fingertips. The artist too. The actor. The director. All of them.

They talk, sometimes, about creative accidents, about creative people resigned within themselves to making a flop and then suddenly waking the next morning to discover they had a hit. But the really great ones know. They know in advance. They anticipate and welcome the challenge.

That was the way Jock Finley felt today. It was the same feeling he had when he had pursued a girl for whom he had had an ungovernable hunger. When he would be on his way to meet her, with already enough clues to know that he would have her that afternoon or that night. Jock Finley had that same sexual hunger and anticipation for big scenes when they were about to happen.

And this one would be the biggest.

Manning had it, too. Whether he had generated it on his own, or whether he had simply grown so close to Jock, he, too, felt the excitement building. He felt it now as he hovered over Preston Carr in the makeup tent: shooting Carr's strong physique in the mirror, head on, then from angles that highlighted the depth of his chest, the profile of his distinguished face, then from over his shoulder, catching a glimpse of Carr's serious face in the mirror. All the while, the makeup man was bringing Carr's chest and back to the same dark brown as his face. In the background, holding Carr's robe, was Daisy. And to one side stood, Axel Steenstrup, Carr's trainer, silent, watching.

Manning got them all. In a swift, silent succession of shots, unobtrusive, highly proficient. He worked with a still camera with the same confidence that Joe Goldenberg exhibited with a Mitchell. And if one were to put Manning's shots side by side in sequence, they would have had the flow and movement of a motion picture. It was more than skill with Manning. It was instinct. There was never enough time for mere skill in the once-in-a-lifetime, get-it-the-first-time-because-it-will-never-happen-again world in which Manning lived.

When makeup was finished, Carr stood up. Daisy placed the silk robe about his shoulders. And Manning remembered shots he once took of El Cordobés, the great matador, when he was being prepared for an important engagement in Madrid. This moment with Carr had the same feeling. Manning slipped out of the tent, almost colliding with Jock who was coming to see if Carr was ready.

Manning looked Jock in the eye, direct, naked, and whispered, "I hope it works for you! It'll be just fantastic! Good luck!" He pressed Jock's arm, a strong caress.

"Thanks," Jock said. But inside himself he said, You fucking fag, next you'll kiss me. In front of all these people.

Before Jock could reach the shady area of the tent, Carr was coming out, followed by Daisy and Axel. Carr's doctor was nowhere around. This by prearrangement. But the three, Carr, Daisy, and Axel, constituted an entourage. Now Jock joined them

357

as they started from the tent area toward the camera position and the battleground beyond.

On the way, Jock talked, straight, professional, routine talk. Carr was to select any animal he wanted. When he was ready they would walk it. When he was satisfied, and Joe agreed, they would go for a take. That would be the only take of the morning. So there was plenty of time, no need to rush. Carr was to do it as he felt it. If he started with one animal and didn't like it, he was to abort the take and start over again.

Manning was getting it all, from a distance but still intimately, with a telephoto. Jock. Carr. Daisy. A two-shot of Carr and Jock. When the shots showed up finally, they would favor Jock. And Manning would realize that he had betrayed something about himself. But it wouldn't matter. The pictures would be excellent portraits of two of the best men in their profession in serious discussion about their work. There was a genuineness about these portraits which would later cause the one of Carr to be placed on exhibit at the Modern Museum in New York.

The entourage thinned out as they reached the camera position. Daisy and Axel dropped out there. Jock and Carr, preceded and shadowed by Manning, moved on to where the wranglers held several mustangs in readiness.

The animals were skittish, lively, nervous, almost as if they, too, sensed the importance of the scene. These were all mustangs captured and brought in during the past forty-eight hours, under Jock's orders, so they were fresh, strong, neither hindered nor inhibited by lengthy exposure to ropes, men, corrals. Jock wanted this uncivilized wildness in the animals so they would challenge Carr and demand all the strength and fight he had to give.

With the practiced eye of a skilled rancher and a horseman, Carr moved from animal to animal, touching, feeling, slapping a flank, looking into a muzzle. There was admiration in his eyes. If Appaloosas were by now highly bred and had the regal quality of champions, these wild animals were bigger, stronger, with a nobility that reflected the freedom, the untrammeled spirit which was theirs, and which would make one of them the proper antagonist for Carr. For he, no less than Jock, was seeking that animal which would give him the toughest fight, the best scene.

358

He selected one by taking the rope from the hand of the wrangler. He led it out, away from the herd, and it took strong hands and arms to make the animal follow, then to force it to walk around. But Carr, his legs strong and firm, took up a position and by the strength he applied to the rope caused the animal to move around him, describing almost a circle. The mustang pulled, reared its head, scampered suddenly, but always Carr held him in, forced him to move, move, move, approximating an irregular rough circle. Finally Carr had satisfied himself as to the way the animal moved, its tendency to favor one side or the other. Suddenly he let out the rope. The animal, sensing the promise of freedom, started away with a single powerful move of both his head and his body, but Carr checked him at the last instant, bringing him up sharply.

All this was done without a word to Jock or the chief wrangler. Finally, when he was ready, Carr turned to the chief wrangler, "I'll go with this one, Tex. Dope him up." Which meant, give him a mild sedative to keep him manageable during the scene.

Jock took his cue, turned away to find his assistant, gave his orders quietly. The assistant called out commands to the various crewmen involved. When they were all in place, Jock moved out into the center of the battlefield. Using a bull horn, he addressed the entire company.

"Okay, now we are about to do the most important sequence in this entire picture! This is Mr. Carr's scene, all the way. I want him to have everything he needs. And I want him to have the utmost cooperation from every man in this company! I don't want him to do a great scene and then find it's been ruined by some careless bastard! I want every man, every piece of equipment exactly where it should be. And absolute quiet! I don't want a single, hear me, not a single unnecessary sound or movement! I don't even want a single unnecessary breath! A great man is at work here! On a great scene! Maybe the greatest of his career! I want cooperation! Respect! I want the best you men can give him!"

Jock crossed to Carr. With his baby-blues giving out one-hundred-and-ten-percent sincere, he said, "Once I say 'Action,' it's all yours, Pres! Be great! As only you can be great! Show 'em who's King!"

Carr didn't answer, only looked hard at Jock, till it was Jock who turned and started back to the camera. He was wondering, had he laid it on too thick? That last bit could have been a high school coach doing an imitation of Pat O'Brien doing an imitation of Knute Rockne. He should stop pressing. Maybe he should have followed his own admonition—give the scene to Carr and get the hell out of his way.

Carr moved across the hard, gritty, desert floor toward the mustang. He looked it over, felt the taut stake rope, then moved back to the point from which he would make his approach to the scene. He stopped, looked out across the desert at the mountains in the background, and then squinted toward the mustang, and suddenly called out, "Okay, Joe?"

Joe called back, "Okay, Pres!"

Jock threw in, "Action!"

The camera started. Preston Carr moved to the stake, felt the rope, then snapped it loose. He cracked it against the earth. The animal responded, trying to rear up. Carr began to circle, away from the animal and to his left, which was also away from the camera. At first the animal drew back, reared till the rope became too painful around his proud, strong neck. Then suddenly he changed tactics and charged toward Carr, who sidestepped with the ease and grace of a matador, always moving around and away from the animal, always tightening and shortening the lariat.

Several moves, and man and animal had come closer together, Pres Carr trying to stay to the side of the mustang, away from the rear hooves, at the same time not too close to its mouth and those vicious teeth.

As Pres worked, Joe's assistant was gradually changing focus, the camera was slowly stealing in, smoothly, as the crew kept carefully laying track, so that it came closer and closer to the proud, angry, terrified face of the animal and the taut, grim, brown face of the man. The camera panned slightly as man and animal edged nearer and nearer to the ramp and the truck.

Jock watched, saying to himself, Good, good, good. Carr's face was all there, as sharp, wily, quick, penetrating as the wild mustang's. Carr's eyes, which could communicate to an audience what he was thinking without a word being said, an ability that

360

made Carr so great in close-ups, were working at their best now. The way it was going, Jock felt he might not need any close-ups. He would take them, but he might never really need them. As Jock stood behind Joe, peering over his shoulder to see what the camera saw, he was sweating as much as Carr, straining with every move of Carr's, every exertion, till he became aware that he was no longer breathing, and that there was a pain of tension deep in his chest. When he did breathe it was in small gasps, and it sounded so strange that Joe turned to catch a glimpse of him. Then Joe turned swiftly back to his work.

Carr, his brown chest, back, shoulders, and biceps straining and showing every muscle, was gradually moving in so close to the mustang that he could now whip off his hat and use it as a weapon. A few more twists of the rope and man and animal would be less than three feet apart. From there, given enough physical strength, Carr would be able to control him, walk him to the ramp and start him up. Then a sharp blow on the hindquarters and the animal would be inside, a captive!

Slowly, with the animal pulling, trying vainly to rear up so he could use his front legs as weapons, Carr maneuvered him toward the ramp, using great effort, great skill. As they reached it, the animal reared slightly, lifted both forelegs off the ground, not more than a dozen inches, but it was enough to cause the beast to come down with one hoof on the ramp, one off, and to throw Carr off balance, wrenching the rope free of his hand.

The animal reacted instantly to its sudden freedom. It reared up and Carr had no defense but to duck away, ruining the shot. Yet he recaptured the rope with his left hand, so that the animal could not break entirely free and trample him, or anyone else, as it well might have in its wild, fierce victory.

"Wranglers!" Jock called out.

Tex and four men rushed out to assist Carr. Tex moved swiftly, cautiously to Carr's side, seized the rope and started his own struggle to shorten it and move in on the animal. One of the other wranglers threw a second lasso and missed. But a third wrangler looped the beast as it was turning swiftly to one side and away from Tex. Now with two lassos on the mustang, controlling him was safer, simpler. They herded him away to the corral.

361

Carr leaned against the truck, breathing hard, painfully. His mouth was open, sucking in great gasps of air. And he worked as hard to expel each breath as he did to suck it in. By the time Jock, Daisy, and Axel reached him, he was breathing with some semblance of regularity.

"Oxygen!" Jock called out. A crew of three men, under the supervision of the assistant, wheeled out an oxygen tank. But Carr refused the mask when it was offered to him. A few moments against the truck, surrounded by Daisy, Jock, the oxygen crew, and with Axel's strong hands assisting his breathing, and Carr was able to walk toward the tent on his own.

When Carr was somewhat relaxed, sitting in his camp chair, sipping warm tea with a shot of Scotch in it, Jock came to see him.

"Just talked with Joe. He says it is one of the greatest takes he's ever seen! Till that goddamned animal stumbled. Tough break or we might have had it all in one first take."

Carr nodded, sipped his tea, said nothing.

"Well," Jock said. "Maybe we'll get it this afternoon. Take it easy. Have your lunch sent over here, relax."

"Two things, you can do."

"Sure Pres, anything that'll help!"

"First, have the carpenters take a look at the ramp. Maybe they could sink it into the ground an inch or two."

"Good idea!" Jock agreed. Right now he would agree to anything. "Eddie!" he called out to the chief carpenter.

"And another thing, have Tex give the next one a twenty-five percent bigger dose," Carr suggested thoughtfully.

"Sure thing!" Jock said, rising from Carr's side and starting to look for the chief wrangler.

As Jock moved swiftly away from Carr's side, he almost collided with Carr's doctor. Jock left. The doctor silently prepared two injections, one of vitamin B-12 and one of calcium, to fight off muscle cramps. He said nothing while he was administering the shots. But when he was going over Carr with his stethoscope, he said softly, "I watched that scene. Why can't you just pick up where the animal tripped at the ramp? It looks simple to me."

"It won't cut," Carr said.

362

"Don't talk when I'm listening to your chest," the doctor said. "I would think it could work so it would cut."

"A different animal, a different angle, it would be like we missed some frames."

"I said don't talk!"

"Okay."

The doctor motioned Carr to sit up. He did. To turn. He did. The doctor listened long, attentively, to his back. "In any event I wouldn't do it more than another time. Maybe two. But that's the most.'

"Well, I'll try . . ."

Daisy returned and so that was the end of all conversation. Except that just before the doctor left, he said, "It can't do any harm to take a couple of whiffs of oxygen. Before the take and after."

"Okay," Carr agreed, never intending to.

In the second take everything went more smoothly. The animal was prepared well enough in advance, with a larger dose of sedative. Carr needed less time to get ready for the scene, to walk it. Joe needed less time to get set. It was almost with a sense of relief that Jock called, "Action." This would be the one, the blessed one, in which everything worked right, he said to himself.

But now, as the scene progressed, as Carr reined in the beast, twist by twist of his strong capable hands, as he moved in closer, finally close alongside the animal, leading it carefully to the ramp and up, Jock became uneasy. There was Carr's sharp slap on the animal's hindquarters, the yank at the rope that freed the tailgate so it could drop into place, and the beast was caged. The take was done. Jock called out, "Cut!"

Axel and Daisy rushed out to Carr's side, the oxygen cart reached him before he was five feet from the truck. But he refused all help. He moved, on his own, more easily than this morning, to the shade of the tent. Jock watched. The man was perspiring freely, as they all were in this hot sun. He was breathing deeply, but there was not the terribly tired, painfully panting exhaustion of this morning.

363

Before he went to the tent, Jock waited till Joe was free of anyone in his crew. Only then did Jock ask, "Well, Joe, what did you think?"

"Fine! We got it all. All in focus. No problems."

"I mean," Jock asked, "what did you think of that take?"

"It worked fine."

"Better than this morning?"

"Well, the way he got that beast up the ramp was beautiful. Only a man with long experience handling animals could have done that. A real professional job!"

"Better than this morning?" Jock repeated.

"Well . . ." Joe began to say slowly, thoughtfully. "There might have been more fight in this morning's take. That's possible."

"That's what I thought," Jock said. He walked away from Joe, toward Carr who was sitting in the shade, sipping some tea, still breathing heavily but this time with no need of assistance from Axel. Only Daisy hovered over him, wiping his face with a makeup towel. He was smiling up at her, at the way she worried about him so unnecessarily.

Jock exchanged a few pleasantries with Pres, congratulated him on the scene, but discovered that he had to reassure him. For Carr was troubled, something in the scene, clean as it was, seemed lacking to him. Jock assured him, "We have one good clean take in the can. That's something!"

As he was saying that, Joe joined them. Carr turned to him, "What did *you* think, Joe?" Joe nodded. Between Joe Goldenberg and Preston Carr, two old-timers, that nod meant no flaws, no technical difficulties, a perfectly acceptable scene.

"Then we're halfway home," Carr said, beginning to smile more freely now, with more energy and enthusiasm, mainly to reassure Daisy. She kissed him on the side of the cheek, leaving traces of lipstick. But he turned his head to catch her lips, to kiss her full. And now it seemed she wouldn't let go.

"We'll see what the rushes look like," Jock said, keeping his tone as happy and disarming as he could. "Then maybe we'll take one for insurance tomorrow and we'll be all set. Except for close-ups, mainly to give us accents and room for editing. If we should ever decide to use the first part of that first take, we'll have some options if we can cut to a close-up or two."

"Right!" Carr agreed.

Jock slapped him playfully on the shoulder, walked away, starting across the desert toward his red Ferrari. With a roar of the high-powered engine, Jock was on his way back to the compound.

When he arrived at communications he put in a call to the studio, got the cutting rooms, found that Mary was, as she usually was, hard at work. Pretending he had forgotten his script and needed it to give instructions to his cutter, Jock dispatched the radio operator to find his script or his assistant. Once the man was gone, Jock spoke low and swiftly.

"Mary, listen to me! I can only say this once! Soon as today's rushes come out of the lab, get a look at them. And if that second take looks too placid, too easy, alongside of the first take, I want you to lose them both. I don't care how! But get hold of that negative! Burn it! Drop it into acid! Cut it to ribbons! But get rid of it! Understand?"

CHAPTER

13

NEXT morning, Jock was up early. He was the first man into the commissary, first fed, first out. He jumped into his red Ferrari, drove out to the battleground. There he worked with intense and painfully obvious concentration. Script and notes in hand, he walked the battleground, testing, considering, pacing off, figuring his close-ups.

So that when the radio call came in from LA, his assistant had to dispatch a driver to fetch him. But Jock would not forsake his planning. So that a second call from LA was necessary. This call was quite frantic. The head of the studio was calling.

Finally, harried, worn down by interruptions, Jock surrendered himself to be driven back to take the call. When he reached communications, his assistant was with him. The communications man handed him the phone as Jock demanded angrily, "How the hell am I going to get this picture made if I keep getting interrupted? I'm out there figuring out my close-ups and . . ."

On the radiophone, the studio head interrupted, "Jock baby . . . will you shut up a minute and listen? Please? Listen to me?"

"Okay! What is it this time? *Look* magazine? Or *The Wall Street Journal*? We've got enough trouble with *Life!*"

"Jock . . . baby . . . listen to me! Sit down! Relax, you hear! You relaxed?"

"I am so goddamn relaxed I am going to blow right through the top of this damn trailer. I have told you time and again, no calls, except at lunch break or after shooting!"

"Jock . . . Jock . . . baby . . . this is an emergency! Please?"

"Emergency? Yeah? What?" Jock's baby-blues turned from one-hundred-and-ten-percent-indignant to about ninety-five-per-cent-grim-silence-before-the-end-of-the-world.

"Jock . ... yesterday's footage . . ."

"Yeah?" As though he dared not ask.

"Kid . . . we don't know how it happened . . . but it . . . it got ruined . . ."

"What the hell do you mean ruined?" Jock demanded in his-anger-on-the-surface-but-mortally-hurt-deep-down tone that any other director would have criticized as being too obvious. Then he stared at his assistant and at the communications man, venting his anger, while asking their solicitude.

"Something in the mix, they think. They don't seem to know. But it doesn't matter. The stuff is ruined!"

"Good God! All of it?"

"Every damn foot!" the studio head said.

"Oh, my God!" Jock exclaimed. "And he was so great! So great! I don't know how to tell him. I don't know . . . look, do me a favor, hold on, I'll get him. I want you to tell him."

"Me? What can I . . . I'll have Robbie speak to him . . . he's in charge of the lab . . ."

"Robbie? You're going to make Preston Carr talk to an under-ling?" Jock asked, almost quivering with hurt and indignation on Carr's behalf.

"Okay. You're right. I'll hold on. Get him!"

Without a word from Jock, the assistant turned and started out. But Jock overtook him, "I'll do it!"

They were back in minutes, Jock grim, his lips tight, his eyes barely holding back tears. Carr was wearing an expensive, flowered silk robe made by Charvet in Paris. His hair was tousled. His eyes betrayed the fact that he had been wakened just for this. The odor he brought with him carried a touch of a woman's perfume, fading, but distinct. If he was angry at the intrusion, it did not show. He took the radiophone.

"Yes?"

"Good morning, Pres! Sorry to bother you so early. But we got a problem! We got a big problem. Huge! And we are hoping you'll understand and cooperate."

"Yeah? What?" Carr asked, warily. He had heard that opening line many times before in his career as a top star. It could mean anything. That the leading lady needed a week off from shooting for an abortion, or that the wife of the president of the company was coming out to the set with a group of relatives and would like to have lunch with Preston Carr in person. So he was annoyed, but not particularly concerned.

"Pres. We're in a jam. Something went wrong. In the lab."

"Yeah?" Carr repeated, noncommittal.

"Yesterday's footage. Ruined!"

"Both takes?"

"Every foot!"

"Christ! And some of it was damn good. I thought sure that second take would do it!" Carr said, betraying not only his expectations but his hopes. And, in a way, his fears.

"Believe me, if there was anything I could do . . . anyone could do . . ."

"I see," Carr said softly. He handed the phone back vaguely to anyone who would take it, left the trailer, not angry, but troubled, greatly troubled.

Meanwhile, on the phone the studio head was calling, "Pres? Pres? You there?"

Jock took the phone, "He's gone."

"What do you mean gone? I was just talking to him!"

"He just walked out."

"Just. Just walked out . . . he was that angry?"

"Not angry! Hurt! Something you wouldn't understand. A man puts his guts, his life on a piece of film! Then some stupid, sloppy, careless bastard treats it like shit! A man doesn't get angry at something like that. He only wants to break down and cry! But you wouldn't understand!"

Jock, indignant for both of them, handed the phone back to the radio man. And the studio head's voice could be heard, "Jock . . . sweetie . . . listen to me . . ."

Without taking up the phone, but loud enough for the studio

head to hear, and strong enough to impress both the radio man and his own assistant, Jock called back toward the radiophone, in righteous wrath, "Fuck you!" And he walked out.

He raced across the compound area, caught up with Carr at the steps to his trailer, "Pres? Please?" Carr stopped, turned to him. "I can't tell you how sorry I am. And there's nothing I can do to make up for it. But I'll tell you what. The rest of the way, we'll go at any pace you want. One take a day instead of two, okay? One take every other day and intersperse the close-ups in between, okay? Anything you say."

Carr nodded, said nothing, went up the steps, into the trailer. Jock caught a glimpse of Daisy as the door opened and closed. Knowing her as he did, it took only a glimpse to recall totally her morning look, untouched by any cosmetics, hair unmade, the little-girl look which made her far sexier than her clichéd picture image. Those were the times, in the early mornings, when he made love to her because he wanted to. He would want to now. Partly because of the way she looked. Partly because his urges always came up strong and sharp when there was impending conflict as there might be with Carr. Once Louise had said to him, "In an emergency other men generate adrenaline, you generate sex. Why is that?"

He had never tried to explain it. To her. Or to himself. But he knew it was so.

He would feel that desire all day long. He would wonder if anyone else was conscious of it. That on this day when Preston Carr might, for good cause, blow higher than a kite, might even walk off the picture for a few days, or a week, he, Jock Finley, good old Jock-Sock Finley, would go around with a perpetual erection for Daisy Donnell. Many times during the day, he would be tempted to say to her slyly, or aloud in front of the whole company, "I want to fuck you! Right now!" It was one of the ways he anticipated combat.

An hour later, the Carr entourage reached the battleground. Instead of sending for Jock, Carr left Daisy and Axel at the tent and went to seek him out. Jock was talking to Tex, the chief wrangler. But at the sight of Carr, Jock turned abruptly, went to meet him, as nearly as possible out of earshot of anyone else. Carr spoke first, quickly, quietly, right at Jock.

370

"We'll stay on schedule. Two takes a day. Another day. Two. Three at the utmost. But I want to wrap this week! I want to get the hell out of here!"

"Anything you say, Pres," Jock answered. But all the while, inside, Jock was saying, Anything you say, you bastard, just so long as you keep working, doing that goddamn take over and over, till I get what I want!

Joe Goldenberg was sorry to hear about the burned-out footage. Not frantic, hardly even surprised. Just sorry. He said nothing, did nothing, except to concentrate on his Mitchells, his lenses, his filters, worry about the light, and search the sky for menacing clouds and vapor trails. So that when Preston Carr was ready for the morning take, Joe Goldenberg was ready.

The morning take was routine. Tex had tranquilized the animal, the stronger dose, according to Carr's instructions. The animal behaved quite well, resisting, fighting back, eventually succumbing, being led up the ramp into the truck. When Carr pulled the cord, the gate dropped into place. At the impact of gate against truck body, Jock called out, "Cut!"

Carr was met by Daisy. She threw his cashmere polo coat around him, and, with Axel's help, she shepherded him back to the tent, to his chair, his warm tea. Axel's strong hands worked on his back, shoulders, arms, legs. Carr breathed with difficulty but without pain.

That impressed Jock most when he reached Carr's side. The man was breathing hard, but not painfully. Quite different from that first take, where that damned animal tripped on the ramp at a crucial moment. That would have been the take. Did it mean that it was getting easier for Carr, that he was gaining in skill and strength with each exposure? Not likely. He had always had the skill, the strong hands of the horseman. It must be that damned tranquilizer.

All these suspicions assailed Jock's mind as he exchanged a few post-scene comments with Carr.

"How did it feel, Pres?"

"How did it look?"

"Good!" Jock let that settle. Because a director should never

never tell a star he didn't do well, or that it looked too easy. But neither could he let the star's confidence prevail too long, "Good enough to let me know you're getting ready for the great one! The right one! Feel that way to you?"

"I thought it went damn well," Carr said.

"Right! But between damn well and great, there's a difference, one hell of a difference. I'd hate to wrap Friday and then have you say two weeks from now, 'Christ, I'd like to do that scene over.' I'd rather wait, right here, no matter how much it costs, till you're satisfied it's *the* take. But relax, we'll have a go at it this afternoon."

As Jock turned away, he almost collided with Joe Goldenberg, and wondered how much Joe had heard. So he lingered as Pres asked, "How was it, Joe?"

Joe was shoving his pipe into the fine English leather tobacco pouch Vivian Leigh had given him after a picture in which she felt she had been photographed at her very best; "I thought it was very good," he said.

In the picture business, words have vastly different meanings and values, depending on who says them, how they're said, and under what circumstances. A perfectly simple, declarative sentence such as Joe's could have meant many things. Depending on inflection, on emphasis.

It could be reassuring, if read, "I thought it was very *good*!" That could have been sincere, honest, straightforward.

But if read, "I thought it was *very* good," it became equivocal, since it took on a tone of belligerence, thus casting the shadow of doubt.

Of course, if it had been read slowly, each word with equal value, and with an almost perceptible, thoughtful pause between words, it could have betrayed underlying, deep-seated doubt—the threat that, on second thought, the opinion might well be different.

But the most painful and disturbing reading of all was the one in which the accent fell on the first word, "*I* thought it was very good." For that meant, I don't give a damn, I thought it was good! Even if I'm the only one in the world who thought so, and I probably am!

Unfortunately, that was the reading Joe Goldenberg had given it. Not because he felt that way, but because he harbored such resentment and distrust of Jock Finley that he had automatically assumed that Jock did not like the take.

That night, in his calmer moments, when Joe was alone, after dinner, he would sit in his trailer, yearn for his wife and his big comfortable home in Beverly Hills, and ask himself what the hell he was doing here anyhow. And then he would admit to himself that the take actually had not been very good. It had been, at best, routine, possibly even acceptable. And whatever else an ambitious bastard like Jock Finley was, did, or thought, he knew a scene when he saw it, and he was right about this morning's take. It was not very good.

But that would come later, when Joe could retire from the conflict and be by himself. For the moment, he was ready to defend his opinion and the take and Preston Carr. But there was no need. Jock was satisfied with Joe's answer. For he knew there was no comfort in it for Preston Carr. Precisely because it was intended to comfort him.

While he was having his lunch of cottage cheese, fruit, and tea with a shot of Scotch, Preston Carr was saying over and over to himself, while smiling at Daisy whenever she caught his eye, "*I* thought it was very good. *I* thought it was very good." Exactly as Joe had said it. The more Pres replayed it in his mind, the less sure he became that it was good, the more certain he became that it had been intended to let him down easy. It made Joe Goldenberg a sweet man, but a minority of one, nevertheless.

As for Jock, he simply waited. He knew. Oh, that Joe, if he had been rehearsed for a week he couldn't have given a better reading. It was no surprise to Jock when, after lunch, the request came to join Preston Carr in his tent, where the King was lying on the rubbing table while Axel worked him over, slowly, comfortingly.

"How do you feel, Pres?"

"Fine. Fine. Sit down."

Jock sat so that his face and Carr's were at the same level. Now it was possible for Carr to speak softly, thoughtfully, the only inflections being those induced at odd moments by the pressure of

Axel's hands on his back or his shoulders or under his stomach.

"I think I know what the trouble is . . ." Carr started, "I almost felt it. But I wasn't sure. Till Joe said what he said. It was good. Technically, as Joe sees a take, it was fine. But I think we had that animal toned down too much."

"He had exactly the dose you asked for, Pres."

"I know. I asked for too much. Maybe the answer is half that dose."

"You're the boss, Pres. Say the word," Jock replied quickly. Not too quickly, he hoped.

"This afternoon, let's try it with half that dose," Carr said. Axel pressed down extra hard at that moment, so much so that Pres turned his head and looked up at him. "Take it easy, will you, Ax?" Axel resumed his routine, usual pressure.

"Half dose," Jock repeated, before Pres could change his mind. "I'll tell Tex."

The animal for the afternoon take was being readied. From where Tex straddled the rail of the corral, he dropped the lasso around its neck easily. The animal reared, bringing its hooves up high, sending out a challenging whinny that was both angry and fearful, opening wide its strong jaws, which could be a devastating, bloody, bone-breaking trap for a man's arm, shoulder, or head. But Tex's strong tug on the rope, tightening the noose around the graceful throat, brought the animal down finally, held it at bay, angry and fierce though it was.

By the time they were ready for the take, the sedative appeared to have taken effect. The beast was easier to lead to the stake than seemed possible only a short time before.

When every man of the crew was in place, and Jock had the word from Joe, he cried out, "Action!" Preston Carr paused, took a deep breath, then exhaled slowly and started forward into the scene.

He lifted the rope from the stake, snapped it on the dusty ground. The mustang reacted, rearing, whinnying, turning, and twisting its head to get free. The battle had begun.

Jock, peering over Joe's shoulder, watched, scarcely breathing.

374

This was more like it. This was a far better scene. Not perfect. But more like that first one, the one that fouled up at the ramp. If only Carr could keep it going this way!

And Carr was so good! Big, strong, expert with his hands, using that rope as well as any tough, experienced young cowhand. He moved agilely, quick on his feet, balanced, exerting leverage in the right spots at the precise moments, so that he was always in control. Yet his face betrayed the effort, the great strain, letting any watcher know, intentionally or not, the demands such exertion made on a man his age, despite his splendid condition. All this was perfect for the story, for the character.

Jock became aware now that his own fingers were digging with painful force into his thighs, as he bent to peer over Joe's shoulder. He was so much in the scene himself that he was sweating, straining, feeling in his chest the pains that Carr must feel, and which one day an audience must feel.

This scene was close. If it was not *the* take, it was close enough to make most people in this world believe that it was.

Now Carr had the rope shortened to about five feet, the coil in his left hand, the short rope in his strong, powerful right hand. He was moving in alongside the mustang, whose fierce, frightened eyes and powerful arched head indicated his hatred of his oppressor. Carr was not more than three feet away from the powerful jaws now. Suddenly the desperate, terrified animal lashed out with its head, turning on its oppressor, its large white teeth snapping in a single vicious blow to end its torture, its imprisonment.

The sudden move evoked an instinctive countermove from Carr. He was swift enough. If anything, he was too swift. He escaped the surgically sharp teeth, but his swift, sudden move resulted in a severe muscle cramp in his right calf, drawing the leg up sharply in violent pain so that for the instant he was a man with only one leg, pivoting on it, trying to hold the rope, with no base, no fulcrum from which to exert pressure.

It took no order from Jock to catapult the wranglers into action. Tex and two others rushed into the area of combat. Two ropes looped out, but unfortunately intercepted each other. Now Carr was yanked off balance. Still holding the rope, he went down onto the crusty earth. The animal jerked once more, suddenly raising

375

its head high and hard, as though it smelled victory over its enemy.

Though Carr never let go, the rope, bitten into by the animal's powerful teeth, snapped. The animal was suddenly free to rear up, to trample its enemy with hooves which had been toughened and sharpened for a thousand days on desert earth and mountain stone.

At the same time the whinnying of the wild, free animal set up a response from those mustangs still imprisoned in the corral. The air was filled with frightening noises.

The animal reared up over Carr, who lay with his bad leg under him, unable to move, except to roll from his left side to his right. As the mustang was poised in mid-air, a rifle shot rang out. Hit or not, the animal was deflected just enough to crash down not on Carr, but straddling him. The sound of the shot so terrified the beast that it bolted across the desert, away from battleground, vehicles, equipment, humanity.

From the way it galloped, hobbling somewhat, it must have been wounded. Not fatally, probably in the flank.

No one noticed, for everyone rushed to surround Preston Carr, who lay, exhausted, gasping for breath, clutching at his right calf, trying to diminish the unbearable pain of the cramp. Axel, the doctor, and Jock were closest to him. Jock gave his assistant, Les, an order by a simple hand gesture. Les Ansell shoved and commanded the others away, permitting only Daisy and the four men.

In the background, the cries of the terrified, rebellious mustangs in the corral still shattered the air, sounding loud and shrill. The wranglers stood guard on the rails of the corral, ropes in hand, to lasso them one by one and quiet them down.

The sound was so penetrating and enveloping that the doctor had to speak in a half-shout to be heard, "Pres! Pres! Let go! Let go, do you hear?"

But it took the physical effort of both Axel and Jock to pry Carr's grip from the painful leg. The doctor indicated that they had better hold him for the next few moments. He tried to straighten the leg from its cramped, grotesque attitude to one more normal. But it was so painful that Carr gasped, making a sound that resembled a sob. He was breathing in short gasps now, barely

376

sucking in air, as though to breathe more deeply would have meant too much effort, too much pain.

The doctor opened his kit, filled a hypo with a muscle-relaxing solution, was able to inject it into the rigid calf only after forcing the needle in. In a few minutes Carr seemed able to breathe more easily. The pain was receding somewhat. Now the doctor gently forced the leg down, as if opening a sprung steel hunting trap, so rigid was the tortured muscle.

Carr was on his back, sweat pouring from his face, his hair damp, glistening. He stared up at the blue desert sky to avoid their eyes, especially Daisy's. He knew she was crying. He knew if he saw that, it might shatter him completely because the pain was so great. The fear was so great.

Each man wonders, in time, when it will happen to him. Or how. And who will be there. Those last times for the experiences he values most in life. With whom will it be and where, when he makes love for the last time? What will be his last satisfying piece of work? His last journey? His last meal? His last cigarette? His last breath?

When will it happen? Where? And will he know it at the time?

Preston Carr, a man of sixty-two, had thought about that. Many times. Especially in the last eight years, since his first heart attack. It had shadowed and diminished his lovemaking, every time. It had been in his mind every time he had read a picture script. It had been most insistent on those three days when he had begun his last three pictures.

Now, as he lay on the desert, giving way slowly to the sedative effect of the injection, he was wondering, God, does it happen here? Is this the last take of my last scene of my last picture? Is this the way it ends? For the King? Lying on my back, in the dust, in pain, helpless?

Jock had said nothing. He hovered there, useless, lost, wondering. Instinctively, he put his arm around Daisy to comfort her. He watched as Axel started gently to manipulate the leg, which was growing less and less resistant. The doctor, assured that his patient was at least free of the worst of the pain, turned away to ask the assistant for a stretcher.

During all this, Jock was asking himself, What now? Was there enough footage to manufacture the one last great scene? Propped up, with aids hidden from the camera, Carr could give him reaction shots, simulated-action close-ups, in which his face, aided by makeup, could seem to be his face in those tense moments in the struggle. Or if Jock could use the first take, or part of his last take, intercut the close-ups, then go to the one take when he successfully herded the beast into the truck, that might work. It might just.

He had better get hold of Mary at once. Now, God damn it, now, he was sorry that he had destroyed those two takes, one of which, if not what he really wanted, might have been passable. Would have been passable. Or would have seemed as if it might have been passable.

Those are the successive delusions movie minds pursue when things get hairy on a picture. A shot a director would not have accepted two days before, suddenly looms larger and better as his troubles grow worse and worse.

Finally he assuages his taste, his artistic demands, by telling himself that no one else has the same high standards he does. That the audience and the critics, not knowing what he set out to do, or might have done, will think that what he has is not only acceptable, but good. Not only good but fine. Not only fine, but great!

To be a movie-maker you must console yourself on your failures and end up convincing yourself they are triumphs. Except that the rest of your life you relive moments from pictures, when it might have gone better, when you might have been more inventive, more brilliant, and with precisely the same elements. Except possibly for luck. Or a moment of inspiration.

It was not inspiration that was lacking now, not for Jock Finley. It was luck. Luck in the form of a sixty-two-year-old man trying to be forty. And a wild beast who by now was back in his desert hills, free, if hobbled and bleeding somewhat. But free. Now, by some strange irony, it was Jock Finley, with his neck in the noose, trying to twist, turn, and break free of the big fact that his only salvation was Preston Carr, his health, his aging muscles, his tired, rebellious leg.

This was underscored and made doubly apparent to him as he

378

tried to help lift Carr to the stretcher. But there were enough hands, so Jock was not needed. He rose and as he did, he saw Manning shooting away, quietly, efficiently, unobtrusively. If Manning saw him in any way except as a fit subject for a photograph Jock could not tell it from the look in the homosexual's eyes. Right now, those eyes, which had been unusually kind, attentive, and searching toward Jock in recent days, saw nothing except what the lens would reveal. With a camera pressed against his face, Manning was as impersonal as a surgeon.

Preston Carr was back in his trailer, leg loose again. The muscle relaxant was affecting his entire body now. The doctor made sure Axel was administering the hot packs properly, then he left. Daisy, of course, would not leave.

Jock's assistant, posted at an unobvious vantage point for the purpose of observing the doctor's exit, reported to Jock at once. Jock started from his trailer, hurried to overtake the doctor, to walk alongside him across the compound.

"Anything we can get? Anything you need flown in from LA?"

"No," the doctor said.

"He's all right, isn't he? I mean, a muscle cramp like that won't leave any permanent damage? I'd hate to think it could cost him."

"He'll be okay," the doctor said, adding, "He'll be able to continue after a few days." As Jock was about to nod, relieved, the doctor continued, "I don't want him to. But he'll be able to continue. Which is all you care about anyhow."

"Just a minute, Doc..."

"*Doctor*, if you don't mind. And that *is* all you care about. So don't bother to deny it. Now if you are going to do it, listen to a few words of advice. Limit him to one take a day, not two. And try to get this over with as soon as possible. He is showing signs of fatigue, heart fatigue. I don't like it. If there were any way of stopping now...rewriting the script...doing the ending with some other character..."

"There isn't. And even if there were, he wouldn't allow it." The doctor nodded sadly. "I'll take it as easy as I can," Jock promised.

379

The doctor settled for that and continued walking. Knowing what he most wanted to know, Jock had no need to accompany him any farther.

Now he was aware that Manning was at his side.

"Well?" Manning asked.

"He'll be okay."

"The picture?"

"We'll shoot on. But carefully."

"Good."

Manning said it with the same sense of proprietary interest Jock expected from a studio head, or a president, someone having a piece of the venture.

"I discovered something a little while ago," Manning said. "I know now what makes him the King. He has two dominant attributes. He is strong, tough, and attractive. And he suffers well. You feel sorry for him. He is more attractive and sympathetic in pain than in his full strength and vigor. I think that's the thing that evokes such loyalty from women. He lets them love him, mother him, and desire him all at the same time. I've got some shots of him in agony that are fantastic. He has a face like Greek sculpture when he's in pain. Especially when he tries not to show it but it's too intense to conceal. That's when he was King, as far as I'm concerned."

Manning did not expect a reply or wait for one. Jock watched the blond homosexual walk away, and it seemed that he had been trying to tell Jock something. But either Manning had expected that his cryptic comment was very clear, or he dared not make it more explicit.

Jock started toward his own trailer. On the way he passed Joe, coming from Carr's place.

"How is he now?" Jock asked.

"He's sleeping, so I assume he's okay," Joe said, waiting.

"I wish we could stop with what we have," was all that Jock would say. He continued on to his trailer.

Within the hour, Jock called Mary at the studio. When he reached her, he emptied the communications trailer.

"Mary, honey, I want you to answer this question. But only after you've thought about it carefully. If we didn't have another foot of film, of Preston Carr I mean, would it cut?"

380

"Good God, what happened to Pres . . ."

"Nothing happened! Nothing! Now, review in your mind all the footage we have, then tell me."

There was a silence of almost twenty full seconds, which is a long time when eight and a half million dollars and your own lifetime reputation are hanging in the balance. Jock was sucking on his underlip, his eyes reflecting naked concern, fear, desperation.

"Jock . . . if you want to get away with it . . . yes. But if you want a big finish to a big picture, I don't think so. Mind you . . ."

"Forget the mind you's and the postscripts! I like first impressions, instinctive answers! The explanations only diffuse, confuse, and mislead. We haven't got what we need! Right?"

"Right . . ." she granted, though now it was somewhat reluctant. "Look, Jock . . ."

"I don't want to look. I only want to know what the situation is. And you told me that."

"I don't want to take the blame for . . .!"

"Blame? What blame?" Jock demanded. "What's there to take blame for?"

"Sorry, Jock."

Jock Finley had that rare ability to make everyone else assume his guilt. "See you when we get back. Be about six days, seven, maybe more. Depends."

He cut off the conversation with a flick of the switch.

It would take two full days for Carr's leg muscle to recover sufficiently for him to stand. Since the second of the two days was Friday, it was no great strain on the budget to let Saturday and Sunday go by without working. At the end of four days, Carr's muscle should be so well rested that he could move without revealing that it still hurt, though the pain would be a low-grade constant ache, of which only he was aware.

With no shooting for four days, most of the company was free to leave for the weekend. Carr and Daisy, the doctor and Axel flew to Carr's ranch for a few days of rest and relaxation. Carr invited Manning to go along, and he did. He also invited Jock, who declined gracefully, suspecting the offer was only a gesture, a courtesy.

381

The copter pilot and the wranglers worked Saturday and Sunday, driving, rounding up, selecting nine new mustangs which in color and size fit the standards Jock had established.

By late Saturday Jock grew restive. Actually he missed a woman. This was the first time in three weeks that he had actively, consciously missed any woman. Except Daisy.

At such times as this, when the intensity of his work was suddenly interrupted by accident, weather, rewrites, or long delays of any kind, with Jock it did become a case of any woman. There need be no strong individual attraction. They had only to be girls who were amenable, good-looking, and who could serve to release his tensions and his hostilities.

He could have flown back to LA. Louise was there. And she missed him, too. He was sure of it. If she didn't love him, she wouldn't have left the way she did. And Louise was someone he could talk to as well. She understood what his ambitions, his frustrations were. She listened without interrupting. And then, every once in a while, when the spirit moved him, she was not only willing and cooperative but hungry to make love with him.

He decided to call. Fortunately he found her at home. But her first words were no comfort.

"What's the matter? Is it raining?"

"Why don't you fly out and see for yourself?" he invited. But she had a date. For the entire weekend? The entire weekend. And this time she did not offer to break it.

Immediately, Jock consoled himself with the fact that the jerk was right there and she couldn't talk freely. But, no, he discovered, the man was expected soon. Louise was getting dressed, and that's why she had no time to talk. She only had time to say that she had heard the picture was going well, a little behind schedule, but well. In Hollywood, everyone knew everything about every picture. Sometimes even more than the man who was making it.

When he hung up, Jock had the distinct feeling that he had been brushed. And by Louise. Lulu. She had never done that to him before. That other jerk, it must be serious with him. Well, screw him. Screw her! He'd take care of her when he got back to LA. He'd have a long, long weekend with her, lay her twenty times, and then turn her free for the jerk, whoever he was!

But it was still Saturday. Darkness was closing in. And there was nothing to do. Corinne, his script girl, was no Louise for looks but she wasn't bad-looking. If her legs were stocky, the rest of her body was not bad. And those tits. Classic.

But he discovered Corinne, too, had taken advantage of the weekend and gone off. With one of the wranglers, it turned out.

Jock walked across the deserted compound feeling alone in the one way he hated to feel alone. Being alone was great when people besieged him and he had to fight for his privacy. Great when, after a weekend down at the Springs with some young starlet, he was able to drop her off and feel alone and free and used up. But to walk around with this big feeling in his crotch and have no place to take it, that kind of alone Jock Finley did not like.

He could have gone back to LA. But he knew that would have been as bad. There's only one thing worse than being alone in LA—being alone in LA and having a venereal disease.

He hated that town, and its environs. All his frustrations and defeats he blamed on LA. The Coast. It was a syndrome common to all indigenous New Yorkers when anything went wrong out there. It was never themselves. It was always the Coast that was to blame, LA.

But by the time he had had his second solitary drink in his beautifully designed and appointed trailer, Jock Finley was ready to admit to himself that there was one reason and one reason only why he didn't dare show up in LA alone. They knew. They all knew. About him and Daisy Donnell. About Daisy and Preston Carr. So LA was the one place he could not go.

He was pouring his third drink when he stopped suddenly. There was a place he could go. And perhaps he should have thought of it sooner. Dave Graham. He was still in the hospital in Vegas. While he was off the critical list now, he had a long way to go to overcome some of the more lasting damage he had sustained. Sure, Jock could drive down to Vegas, see Dave in the morning, give the poor scared bastard a much-needed lift, then drive back and still get a good night's sleep before Monday's shooting.

The more he thought about it, the more he sympathized with Dave. Those studio bastards, after the initial outpouring of defensive sympathy and money, they had deliberately forgotten

383

Dave. Studios did not like to have disaster of any kind attach itself to a picture. Especially a big picture. It was not superstition. It was cold business practice. It was bad for the image, and a constant source of questions during promotional interviews later on radio and TV. Sometimes the disaster got to be more important and newsworthy than the picture itself. So pay the bills, but expunge the memory.

By the time Jock had decided to drive down to Vegas, he was indignant on Dave Graham's behalf. Somebody had to remember that brave little guy!

It was less than an hour's flight into Vegas by copter. But no more than a two-hour drive the way Jock drove. The desert night, the open Ferrari, the empty roads, bright under that clear white moon, all made driving desirable.

He had been underway only a matter of twenty minutes when he found himself saying, Jock Finley driving almost two hundred miles to make a hospital call, and with an erection that could satisfy any woman in the world. Christ, he was like a hard-up nun with no place to go but a charity ward. He joked bitterly, good thing Manning had gone down to Carr's ranch.

Carr. In the last few days every mention of that man's name set Jock to cutting and recutting that last scene in his mind, with all the takes and bits of takes that they had in the can. The crucial moments in the battle. A part of this take, a part of that one, and the interstitial bits that might make it cut smoothly.

Of course, you were never sure till you were leaning over that damned Moviola, examining the footage frame by frame. Because sometimes you swore you had a distinct recollection of a particular piece of film only to discover after hours at the Moviola that that piece had either never been shot or never been printed. Yet you could remember it so clearly that it had more reality for you than film that was actually passing before your eyes.

Now, as he drove along in the cold desert night, the wind rushing by him to keep him cold, alert, keenly awake, he felt he could cut the scene with what he already had if he were forced to. And it would cut. Well. Damn well!

Suddenly, in his elated state, he found himself doing a hundred and twenty-five miles an hour and he grew afraid that he might destroy everything, as he had before in moments of impending triumph.

He knew that much about himself. He had that impulse to over-do, stretch his luck, see how far and how fine he could draw it. He had almost done that while shooting *Black, Man, Black*—when he had deliberately seduced the star's white girl friend, knowing full well that being blond and beautiful she meant more to the star than she ever could to any white man. That had almost led to a walkout, to the star's quitting, with the picture not yet two thirds finished shooting.

And England, that had been his fault, too. There had been no pass from the fag star, though the star was a notorious homo, with two convictions for accosting on his record, in the days when it was still illegal there. What had really happened was that the star had been amenable, perhaps too amenable to Jock's new, vigorous direction. He had actually welcomed Jock's vivid, intense, un-subtle attack on a scene, in contrast to what he had been used to doing under the guidance of British directors.

Till it had become a game with Jock. To see how far he could go toward remaking a great star's performance so that the critics would sit up and pay attention not to the star, but to Jock Finley's direction. Only then had the star rebelled and threatened to quit if Jock were not replaced.

Don't overdo when triumph is so close, must not overdo, Jock kept saying to himself. Going over a hundred and twenty-five miles an hour was one way of overdoing. He knew damn well that Ferraris and Mercedes 300 SL's had been known to flip over at high speeds, even though they were supposedly designed for just such driving.

He took his foot off the accelerator in a gradual continuous move so that the car braked itself and slowed down to eighty. He proceeded at that speed till he could see the distant glow in the desert sky. Vegas. Its perpetual neon night sky was no more than fifty miles away. If, from some other planet, some species really was studying us, then by night Vegas was what they were seeing.

He reached the outskirts, rode on into town along the Strip and thought, as long as he was here, why not take in a couple of the late shows. So he started marquee-shopping for the best night-

385

club shows, or one where a friend might be appearing. He knew
Buddy Hackett from when Buddy had done that not-so-good musi-
cal on Broadway. And Berle from TV. He had met Dean Martin
twice at parties. And Lena Horne.

Now, a huge sign, so bright you could read *The New York Times*
by it from a block away at midnight, proclaimed that "TONY is
back". That's all. Just TONY! No last name needed.

Since one of Tony's kids had had a small part in *Black, Man,
Black*, Jock had gotten to know him. When shooting was over,
Tony had sent him a fifteen-hundred-dollar gold wristwatch, "For
being so nice to the kid," the card had said. Tony had even asked
Jock to direct him in a picture, but Jock was already committed
to go to England. For though Tony's original and basic profession
was singing, something he still did with more impact than any
other man, he was also a picture star and a producer as well.

Jock decided to drop in and catch Tony's midnight show. For
one thing he was sure of a table there. He turned back, approached
the casino from the opposite direction, and drove in. Surrendering the Ferrari to the parking boys, he entered the lobby where
the perpetual gambling tables were going full tilt. The same faces,
it seemed, were always here in Vegas. At least the same types.
The ones too white. The ones too red, too suddenly burned by the
desert sun. The dead faces. The expressionless ones. The ones
staring in awed surprise at this unnatural way of life.

When Jock reached the door of the huge nightclub room, Tony
was already on. The place was jammed, but quiet. No drinks were
served when Tony was on. Jock asked the captain for a table, but
he was hushed at once, and then rejected in a sibilant whisper,
"Sorry, sir, not even standing room tonight." He gave his name
to the captain, who was completely unimpressed. So he wrote
out a note, signed it merely "Jock," gave it to the captain with
a ten-dollar bill, "See that Tony gets this as soon as he comes off."

Jock was at the blackjack table, not playing, just watching,
when Tony moved in alongside him.

"Hi, kid."

"Hi, Tony."

386

"Hear you're making a hell of a picture. Wish you'd do one with me sometime. How's it coming?"

"Great."

"Need anything? Got a bed? Got a bird?"

"Just drove in. To see one of my crew. Guy had a lousy accident."

"Oh, yeah, I read."

"Only be here overnight. Start driving back right after visiting hours tomorrow. We begin shooting again Monday morning."

Tony nodded his head, almost imperceptibly. Without looking around he raised his left hand, snapped his fingers. Instantly, there was a captain in dinner jacket at his side. Still watching the action on the table, Tony said, "Friend of mine, Mr. Finley. Give him the Sheik suite for the weekend."

"Senator Wardle's in the Sheik this week."

"Move the prick! Mr. Finley is a friend of mine."

"Sure, Tony, sure." The captain was gone.

Tony turned to Jock, "In about an hour go up to your suite. My next show isn't till three ayem. But if you're tired, skip it. No offense."

It seemed Tony had said all that Tony wanted to say, then he lingered a moment to add, "That's a nice thing. Taking time out to visit that poor bastard. Ought to be more like you in our fucking business."

He patted Jock warmly on the back and moved away through a mass of people who revered him. Complete strangers called him "Tony." He smiled at some, frowned at others. No one ever knew why he did either.

Jock watched a while longer. Gambling, whether he was watching or playing, had never been able to hold his attention for very long. If all that was involved was money, a game lost interest for him very fast.

He stopped at the desk. The key to the Sheik suite was waiting for him. He stepped into the elevator, pressed the "Penthouse" button, was sent upward with a surge that he felt in his scrotum. In a desert that stretched almost endlessly, men built structures twenty and thirty stories tall, and then had to design high-speed elevators to whip you up without a second's loss of time.

387

When he opened the door of the Sheik suite, all the lights were on. He looked around the living room. True to its name, the suite was designed as a version of a Sheik's tent, as such a tent had been dreamed up by a Chicago gangster and a Jewish fag decorator. From the ceiling, which was completely draped in striped fabric to resemble the top of a tent, to the bar which was made of blond wood with chrome inlays, the whole room was an affront to Jock's taste. He had never been a dévoté of traditional décor in his pictures, but he had never been guilty of taste such as this. Right now he felt that he might vomit.

On the bar, stood five full bottles, Scotch, bourbon, vodka, gin, Napoleon brandy. The tax stamps were still intact. The bucket was full of fresh ice. The glasses shone. Jock went to the bar, opened the bottle of twelve-year-old Scotch, fixed himself a drink. He had taken only the first sip when there was a knock at the door.

Tony, he thought, dropping by for a breather or maybe to talk about a picture. Jock called, "Come in!" and the door opened. It was not Tony. It was a tall girl, blond, about twenty-one or twenty-two. She was as tall as Jock, dressed in a mini-version of an evening gown which let you know instantly that she was gifted with a magnificent pair of breasts. She was pretty, too. Though Jock could see that she was the kind of blonde who at thirty would be overweight, brassy, with hair greening from too many dye jobs.

But she was a long way from thirty now. And she lisped, "Tony sent me up. He said you were alone."

Tony thinks of everything, Jock said to himself. Especially Tony thinks that everybody thinks the same way Tony thinks. Tony can never stand to be alone, so he thinks no one else can. So the nice thing to do, the Tony thing to do, is send up a little gift. If you were a friend of Tony's, it meant free booze, free birds.

For a moment Jock hesitated. She misinterpreted his reaction. "Don't worry. It's on Tony," she said. "He wants you to have fun. Said you're a right guy. He also said you're a movie director. That true?" Jock nodded. "He says you're very good."

Jock smiled, nodded. To himself, he said, Here it comes.

"You know," she said, "I could have been in movies. I still could be. I'm only twenty-two. Honest. And some directors I know say I'm very photogenic."

388

"I can see that," he said, smiling.

She smiled back. "I started out for Hollywood. I'm from Gary, you know. I started out for California but I landed here. But some day . . ."

"Let's talk about it."

"You will?"

"Sure. Sit down."

"Can I have a drink?"

"Sure."

"Scotch, rocks. Triple. Saves time."

He made the drink, handed it to her, sat down at the far end of the couch. He watched her, smiling somewhat. She looked at him over the top of her glass.

"Gee, you got terrific blue eyes. And you're younger than most of Tony's friends. Usually they're old men. Forties. Fifties. And fat. Or else too skinny. Ya ever notice, comes a time when a man either gets too fat or too skinny. Y'ever noticed that?"

"Uh-huh," Jock said, sipping his drink.

"Their skin hangs loose on them. Or else they got big bellies. Most men are pretty ugly, you know. Except when they're young. I can talk that way to you, because you're still young. And I bet you're well built, hard. Even Tony . . ." but she stopped at that. No one said anything personal or critical about Tony. Not in Vegas.

"So you think you ought to be in pictures . . ." Jock said, putting down his Scotch.

"You mind if I finish my drink first?" she asked, almost a bit pathetically.

"Take your time, honey, take your time."

It took about ten minutes. She finished with some reluctance, sucking at the melting ice till all taste of Scotch was gone. Rising suddenly, she asked, "How do you like it?"

Jock looked her over, "Fine! You look great!"

"I didn't mean that," she said. "Most of Tony's friends like it different ways. Any way but straight. What about you?"

"Straight. For openers."

"Here? Or you want to go in there?" she asked, vaguely indicating the master bedroom of the suite.

"How many rooms are there?" Jock asked.

389

"This suite? Four. Why?"

"We'll try 'em all," he said smiling.

She smiled too, thinking he was joking. But he wasn't. They did try them all. Till it got to be a game. Dealer's choice, she called it, when she started suggesting sexual tricks from her repertoire, which made him wonder how long she had been at this, to be only twenty-two and know so many ways to arouse a man, and satisfy him.

There was no part of her own body she did not use, no part of his she did not kiss, fondle, or embrace. Several times he fell asleep between rounds. Each time he was awakened by her, each time in a different way.

Dawn was just breaking. He had fallen off to sleep, his last conscious thought being that for once in a long time he was truly, finally empty and could not respond. Then, in his deep, exhausted sleep he began to be vaguely awake and conscious of a warm, moist feeling in his groin. That part of him which had been exhausted began to come to life, to grow, to become erect once again, in response to the tiny, darting stabs of her warm, wet tongue. When he moved as though to avoid her, she reached out to him, her hand offering him a glass of Napoleon brandy over ice.

She interrupted herself long enough to say, "You work on this."

She went back at him, her nails digging into his thighs, her tongue, pointed and making longer bolder moves now, moving the full length of him, till finally he felt so full and erect that it seemed he might burst out of himself.

Then she took him into her mouth fully and worked at him with an increasing fury that made him realize that she was building to an orgasm herself and he gave himself to it completely. Only the sound of her, the sucking sound seemed offensive to him. Damn it, he said to himself, why did she have to make that sound. He tried to push her away at the last moment but she persisted and could not be put off till finally he exploded in a burst of pain and ecstasy, the seminal fluid erupting out of him like hot lava.

They were both breathing hard, in short, spasmodic gasps. She had had an orgasm too. He wondered why, or how. In his loins the pain was beginning to subside now. He became aware of the brandy glass, still in his hand, untouched through the entire experience, so he sipped at the cold, burning liquor a time or two. She reached for the glass and he surrendered it to her. She sipped at it, then let it accidently rest against his warm thigh. The icy burn made him jump.

"Sorry, honey," she said, warming his thigh with her cheek and handing back the glass. He took it, but he did not drink from it again. Then he fell asleep and she let him.

She stayed with him through breakfast, and till early afternoon, when he had to dress and start the long drive back. Even then, she seemed reluctant to go. He showered, his third in the past twelve hours. She watched him dress, through the mirror, from where she lay on the bed.

"You're great," she said. "You're terrific. I wish Tony had more friends like you." He interrupted buttoning his shirt to turn toward her and smile. "You'll tell Tony you had a good time, won't you?" she asked.

"Sure!"

"And you won't forget. I mean, if you ever have a Kim Novak part. Or a Daisy Donnell part. You won't forget, will you?"

"I'll find you, wherever you are."

"I'll be here," she said. "I'll be here." And he had no doubt of it.

When he had dressed, he reached into his pocket, pulled out the engraved gold money clip the Negro star had given him after *Black, Man, Black* had finished shooting. He slipped out three new hundred dollar bills, folded them twice, and flipped them playfully to her.

"Oh, no!" she protested. "It's on Tony. If he ever found out I took anything from you he'd be hurt. He's very sensitive, you know. And he's got a terrible temper. Terrible."

"*I* won't tell if you don't," Jock said. She thought a moment, looked at the three new bills, and then said softly, "I could use it. My little boy needs his tonsils out. And everything's so damned expensive these days."

"I know," Jock said, picking up the money and slipping it between her very good breasts.

He was twenty-seven miles out of Vegas when suddenly it struck him. Christ, Dave Graham! He had never remembered to go to the hospital. And it was too late to turn back. He drove on. About ten minutes later he pulled into a small town, drove up to the gas station, and leaped out. He went to the phone booth, dialed information, got the hospital number, and placed a call to Dave Graham. But he was put through to the floor desk.

He learned that Mr. Graham was asleep and not allowed to take calls right now. And how was Mr. Graham? He was coming along fine. And how was his eye? Sight had been restored about forty percent in his damaged eye and was near perfect in his good one. What about the head injury? That was coming along, so all in all, considering his original injuries, Mr. Graham was coming along very nicely.

"Well, I'm certainly glad to hear that," Jock said. Then suddenly he found himself asking, "Would it be possible to come up now?"

"I'm sorry. Visiting hours are ten to noon, three to five," the nurse's voice said firmly, adding, "There are no exceptions, only in cases that are on the critical list."

"Don't I know! I'm down in the lobby now," Jock said, sounding as hurt and frustrated as he dared. "Look, do me a favor?"

"If I can," she said.

"When Mr. Graham wakes up give him a message for me? Tell him I drove down from location to see him but got here too late. And I had to start back, because we start shooting early tomorrow. But I'm glad he's feeling better. Tell him that?"

"I certainly will," she promised.

"Thanks," he said, about to hang up.

"Wait a minute! You never told me your name."

"Oh. Finley. Tell Dave, Jock Finley drove down to see him."

He jumped back into the Ferrari and headed west on the two-lane blacktop, going about ninety miles an hour.

When he returned to the encampment, he found a long list of phone messages waiting for him, four from Marty White. All four

392

frantic. Jock went to the radio trailer at once, located Marty through his service, reached him at Hillcrest.

When Marty was plugged in, he exclaimed, "Christ, kid, where you been? I hear the whole company knocked off for the weekend. So I call your home. I call the location. Where were you?"

"Drove down to Vegas," Jock said.

"For a little action, huh? Well, you deserve it, kid."

"I drove down to see Dave Graham," Jock said simply, almost reverently.

"Oh?" Marty reacted, respectfully. "And how is he?"

"Fine. He feels fine. He's going to be okay. That one eye may be a little less than perfect. But I think he'll be able to work again. But better than that, *he* thinks so. And that's the biggest part of the battle."

"Right, right," Marty agreed. "Ready for tomorrow, kid?"

"Ready!" Jock said.

"Think you'll wrap this week?"

"Possible."

"Good, good," Marty encouraged.

"Okay, Marty, got to get some sleep. I'm beat."

"Of course. Driving down to Vegas and back. And the way you drive. But it was damn nice. Not many guys in this business would be so thoughtful, believe me."

"Thanks, Marty. Good night." Jock hung up, his baby-blues smiling impishly, as he was saying to himself, Oh, Marty baby, have I got a girl for you.

Two days later in *Daily Variety*, a brief item would appear in Army Archard's column:

> On the horn with Tony from Vegas the other ayem, discovered one of those unreported goodies that make no business like show business. Jock Finley interrupted shooting his wide-screen, multi-mill Carr-Donnell road-show epic *Mustang!* to drive down to Vegas and visit Dave Graham, mending after serious location mishap. No people like you know who.

CHAPTER

14

Iт was dusk by the time Jock Finley came out of the radio trailer. His assistant was ready with a long checklist of those things set for tomorrow, and of those yet to be set. A fresh herd of wild mustangs was in the corral. Jock went to inspect them at once, before it grew too dark. His assistant hurried alongside, referring frequently to his clipboard, from which he controlled the entire production.

Among phone calls still to be answered was one from the studio head, who was in London, where they had another big picture in production and in trouble. The assistant had checked with the Carr ranch, and with the doctor, twice, once yesterday, once today. Carr seemed okay, the leg was being rested, the pain was almost gone. The rushes from Thursday were in. Mary called, urgent. She wanted to talk to Jock at once. Joe Goldenberg had gone home for the weekend, would be back early tomorrow.

Jock stood at the corral, one leg up on the rail, looking over the sand-colored mustangs, all of whom fit the standards he established to make them interchangeable. There was one, however, which seemed taller than the rest. If Jock had been given to creating or believing fables about the animal world, the kind that appeared regularly in *The Reader's Digest*, he would have said to himself that that one was king of the herd. Taller, somewhat stronger, better muscled in the flanks. That one was a beauty. If that one could be gotten into the scene, and if it worked as it might, that would be something, he thought.

But there was Carr to think about, too, to keep whole and well, till they got this final take over with. So Jock would settle for any of these animals in the right scene.

By now Jock's assistant came racing back. He had Mary on the phone. He had found her at home. Jock went to take the call. What Mary wanted to tell Jock was simple enough. She had cut the battle footage four different ways. It wouldn't work. It just wouldn't cut. She wanted Jock to know that, before he decided to wrap the final shooting. She suggested that, even if it were a cheat, an obvious cheat, he might consider going back to doing the entire sequence with Ryan. Or at least get the master scene with Ryan from the right angle, with the right cuts and cover shots so that they had it all in the can, in case they never did get it with Preston Carr.

What about the multi-image cutting, Jock asked. With enough close-ups, that would work fine. Except that to make it most effective, Jock should have the one basic master scene in a piece. So that the mounting introduction of additional images would add to, would build, instead of becoming distracting cuts that diminished the effect, which might be the case if all the bits were not in total conformity with the master scene.

There was no way around one fact. The big scene could not be a cheat without revealing that the multi-image concept was nothing more than a technical trick. If the critics started suspecting that, it could spell disaster for the film and for Jock as far as the important critics were concerned.

Jock listened, said little, tried to calm Mary. But within himself, he knew, and very painfully, that if Mary got excited, if Mary thought the whole picture was in jeopardy from the critics, that was bad. For Mary was one of those expressionless picture people. Most times, you could look straight into her full, plain face, look right into her spectacled eyes, and not read a clue there as to whether she liked a scene or not. With Jock, and even before Jock, she had learned not to intrude her opinion, even by reflection or indirection, unless and until she was asked. So if Mary was volunteering, calling twice, there was something to worry about.

About Ryan, Jock had never intended to release him till the

396

scene was finished and truly good. But he knew, too, that he must never let Ryan try that scene again as long as Preston Carr was still on location. If, finally, after another week, Carr couldn't make it, for whatever reason, then Carr would be finished. Thereafter Ryan would do the scene, as many times as Jock wanted, or needed. But not till then.

Carr had been at this one scene more than two weeks now. Not more than five hundred seconds of film, in two whole weeks, and now Mary said nothing would cut. The past two weeks had been wasted.

If Mary knew that, if Jock knew it, there was a damn good chance that the head of the studio might know it too. That must have been the reason for that call from London. And if the studio head got excited, if the phone calls started going back and forth from London to location, from LA to location, if the secretaries in the studio head's office got wind of it, it would be around the commissary by tomorrow morning, around the studio by noon, at Chasen's, La Scala, and Mateo's by dinner time.

Mustang! could get a bad reputation. Next thing you knew there would be items in *The Hollywood Reporter*, in *Variety*, in syndicated columns, all of which could have repercussions, worldwide repercussions.

Jock knew he couldn't settle for less than he started out to get. And he must move fast. When Carr showed up, he would put it to him. One take, one great try, succeed or fail, they'd go with that.

No, Jock decided, that sounds too corny. That one big take, that give-it-your-all, wouldn't help. Not with Carr. Not, actually, with any star. For if that one big take didn't work, you had ruined your actor psychologically for any further takes. Good or bad, if an actor felt he had given it everything he had, any star would be dry and useless for further takes of that same scene as long as he lived.

You must never let a star know that any take was *the* take till it was over, till it was good, till it need never be done again.

Carr, Daisy, Axel, Manning flew back to the location just after dusk in Carr's private jet. When they disembarked, they seemed to be one happy family. Carr was rested, fresh, smiling. Daisy had lost that just-about-to-cry look which had shadowed her face the past two weeks. Axel was confident, a trainer bringing a champion into town for a title fight. Manning was relaxed. He seemed almost pleased.

They all had dinner together in the commissary. It started with Carr's own imported gray caviar. And there was a good white wine sent to Carr by a business associate, from his own vineyard in France. They were tasting the wine, exchanging expert opinions about it, when Jock, hearing they had returned, came into the commissary. All four greeted him as though they were truly happy to see him.

He responded in kind, his eyes twinkling with that shy warmth he usually reserved for TV interviews on the publicity circuit when he opened a new picture or a new play—the kind of interviews when he was introduced as America's young genius in film, as America's answer to Bergman and Antonioni.

At first he used to be embarrassed by such introductions. Then he developed that shy, warm smile that said, it would be foolish of me to deny that I'm a genius, but don't embarrass me by saying it out loud.

That was the look he gave them, disarming, unaffected. But in one glance he took them all in. None of the scars of the accident, the leg cramps, the fear, was visible in their eyes. It must have been a hell of a weekend. And the King looked great. At least as good as he had looked in the last three weeks. They exchanged small talk, the flight, weather at the ranch, weather for tomorrow. The scene was never mentioned by anyone. But later, when dinner was over, when Carr and Daisy had retired for the night, Jock sought out Manning.

The photographer was not in his quarters. Jock walked across the dark compound in the crisp night air, searching for him. Jock's weatherproof jacket was too thin for the cold desert night. He should have zipped in the fleece lining. He decided to go back to do that, and he would have, except that he noticed a figure dressed in well-tailored chinos coming away from the corral.

He didn't recognize the face. But the cut of those chinos, the very slim figure could only have been Manning. Then he saw the beach-boy-blond hair in the moonlight. Manning. Boyish and even more so by moonlight. Handsome, too. Now Manning saw Jock and stopped. Resentful or guilty, he stared at Jock as though he were an intruder, a spy.

"Hi," Jock said, casual, friendly. Manning did not respond at once, except with a defensive, hostile stare. But once the photographer was past the point of surprise, he relaxed and answered in a guarded tone which tried to equal Jock's casualness.

"Oh. Hi, Jock!"

"Good weekend?"

"Great! Lot of fun."

"Quite a place!"

"Takes me back to my covered-wagon days," Manning said, smiling. "If you have to rough it, that's the way. Ever see his wine cellar? Fantastic!"

"How was he?" Jock asked, trying to toss it off. But even in the moonlight Manning's handsome face, the sudden arrested quality of his eyes, indicated clearly there was nothing casual about the question to him.

"I think," Manning said, "I think he's okay. He's certainly not edgy. He let me shoot him, and her, all weekend long. He seemed to like it. I've got a great series, 'The King and the Queen,' which we can break the week they get married. He promised me an exclusive on the wedding."

"So they're really getting married?" Jock asked.

"Yes, they are!" Manning said, smiling, genuinely happy about the whole thing.

"Say anything about the scene? His leg . . . anything at all?"

Manning hesitated for an instant, considering whether to reveal a confidence. His thin, boyish face caught the light of the desert moon as Manning said quite soberly, "He likes you. Did you know that? He thinks you're one of the best directors he's ever worked with."

"He does?" Jock Finley asked, baby-blues at ninety-five percent modest.

"He thinks you got things out of him no other director has, since he became a star."

"He said that?"

"Late at night. Daisy'd gone off to bed. Ax, too. But Pres didn't

399

want to sleep. Neither did I. So we just stayed on, drinking, talking. That's when he talked about you."

"Did he say anything about her and me?" Jock asked.

"He never discusses her. He's in love with her, worries about her, protects her. But he never never said a word. About her acting, or her fears, or her ... anything." Manning finished, not finding the right word.

"I always had the feeling," Jock said, getting to the real point, "that he resents me because of her. That it stands between him and the scene as it ought to go."

"I don't think so. I get the feeling he's trying, trying very hard. It troubles him that he can't do it as well as he might have ten years ago. I get the feeling he thinks he's letting you down. And he doesn't want to, no matter what he thinks about ...."

Manning didn't finish. He had said too much. Jock smiled. Manning was embarrassed and felt compelled to say it finally: "He admires you as a director. But as a human being he thinks you're a prick."

Coming from the elegant, blond homosexual, in his cool, precise speech, the word sounded almost as elegant as he was. But it didn't diminish by a single degree Jock's anger, his resentment. Any man insulted thus to his face would smile. Only a boor would exhibit anger. Jock Finley was never a boor except when he deliberately chose to be.

He smiled, his baby-blues ingenuous, soft. "Thanks. I was afraid he was really beginning to like me. A star will do more for you if he hates you than if he loves you. That way he's trying to prove something. That's when he's at his best. Thanks."

Jock's reaction had suddenly shifted the initiative. Now it was Manning wanting to know what would happen tomorrow.

"Are you going to keep pushing him?" he asked.

"I'm going after the take. The way it ought to be. I won't press him or push him. I'm willing to sit here and wait for the right one, all week, all month if I have to."

Manning heard it, nodded thoughtfully. He did not seem disturbed, even though Jock's dictum had overruled any plans Manning might have had for his own next assignment. Having come this far, he couldn't quit now. He had to stay through to the finish.

400

Especially to collect on Carr's promise about an exclusive on the wedding. Still, he did not seem disturbed.

Jock was about to turn away when he spied a second figure coming from the direction of the corral. It was Axel. Automatically, Jock's mind went back to Manning's having called him "Ax." Before Jock could control them, his eyes flicked from Axel to Manning, revealing his surprised conclusion more clearly than words could have.

Manning was neither embarrassed nor shy. He smiled. "Among those who know, it's as American as apple pie, dear boy." Manning started away. Axel saw Jock, changed his direction somewhat so they would not cross paths. Jock stood and watched. Sonofabitch! Axel, too? Yes, "Ax," too, it seemed.

Jock started back to his own trailer, feeling alone, really alone. Suddenly he was thinking about that young pathetic blond girl in Vegas. Tony's favor. With the skillful, educated body, hands, tongue. And the kid with the bad tonsils.

Next day was a good day. The sky was blue, virtually cloudless. Joe Goldenberg was back, having arrived before breakfast. Jock was ready. Once he talked to Carr, Carr would be ready.

Having decided against the strategy of "this is the one big take, win, lose, or draw," Jock spoke to Carr in a terse, understated, undramatic way. First, he inquired about the leg. The leg was fine, Carr said, submitting himself to Jock's hands for examination. Carefully, professionally, Jock manipulated the King's calf and thigh, seeking any knotted places, any tense, sore areas where there would be an instinctive betraying reaction. Calf felt fine, thigh felt fine. When Jock asked, Carr said there was no pain at all on walking.

Did Carr want to rehearse the scene once, with a heavily sedated animal to refresh his memory, to get back into the movement and rhythm of it? Carr reacted, curious, his brown face suddenly surprised, his eyes suspicious. Why would Jock think he needed rehearsing, in a scene he had done a dozen times? A fight which he had fought in his mind a thousand times?

Jock explained. There was one thing, one unique thing, which,

401

if they could capture it, would be worth all the struggles, the pain, the risk. There was one animal out there, one princely, no, one kingly animal which could not be described. In fact, if Carr agreed, Jock would like to show him the beast.

Gingerly, suspiciously, Carr accompanied Jock to the corral. The wranglers were at work, roping each animal, getting each ready for the day's selection parade, inoculation, and shooting. Each animal was being staked down in a different part of the corral, each with a wrangler close by, all waiting for Carr to appear and select.

The stallion Jock referred to was off to the far right side of the corral. But by virtue of his size, he was easily the most identifiable. Carr, a horseman by trade and inclination, spotted the animal at once. Leaving Jock's side, moving ahead faster, at his own pace, Carr approached the fence where the beast stood tethered. The animal pawed the ground, then suddenly tried to rear up, only to be arrested by the rope and brought down. He turned to one side, then the other, to avoid the tether, elude it. Finally he pulled back sharply, to back out of it. But each move only served to choke him more, causing him to gasp, to make a strange sound that almost had overtones of human protest.

Carr watched. Jock moved alongside. Staring at Carr, then at the beast, he said, "That's beauty! Power! Royalty in animal form."

Carr didn't answer, just stared. His eyes said it all. He admired the animal with a connoisseur's eye.

Jock sensed it. Without revealing his own purpose, he said softly, "Course he's bigger than the others. There'd be no matching up. If we use him, we'd have to get it all. One take."

Carr nodded. Softly, he said, "You can only fight that one once. If he loses it might kill him. If he wins, he'll be uncontrollable, free. You'd never catch him again."

"Never!" Jock agreed admiringly. But now he had shifted his look, from the stallion back to Carr. The man was truly taken. So Jock dared to risk it. "Would you go all out, Pres? For a take with him?"

Carr never took his eyes off the animal. "Yes, I would!" There was no doubt in his mind that he could take this animal. Then he

402

added, "But I want him when it's over. I'd like to own that animal."

"He's yours!" Jock said. Then since Carr was so deeply involved, Jock asked, "You want to run it once with another animal?"

"Uh-uh," Carr shook his head, putting aside all need for rehearsals, refreshers, preambles. "I'll take him right after lunch. See that he's fixed up."

"Okay, Pres! You've got it!"

Word got around, as it will on location or in a studio, that this was the shot! This was *the* take! This was the time when everything was on the line! Once Pres had singled out that beast, once Jock had given the orders to his assistant that there would be no take in the morning, but only one after lunch, everyone seemed to know that this was something special.

At the battleground, Joe made meticulous preparations. Instead of one Mitchell, two were loaded, ready to go. This was the kind of take when you didn't want to risk even that one-in-a-million chance that something might go wrong in the camera.

Carr had his lunch in his trailer, chopped steak tartare, lettuce without dressing, hot tea. Enough for the energy he would need. Not enough to tax his stomach or his heart, or to give rise to loginess or heartburn.

While lunch was being fed to the company, Jock went out to the corral. Tex was getting his instruments ready, syringe, sedative, alcohol. Jock climbed up onto the rail, watching every movement. Tex was sizing up the animal, doing his mental mathematics, poundage of beast in relation to dosage, a rough estimate. He was just drawing the solution out of the inverted, rubber-capped bottle, when Jock called softly, "Tex . . ."

The chief wrangler, who was from Arizona and had spent most of his adult life in Hollywood, but was nevertheless called "Tex," turned, seeing Jock for the first time. "Hi, Jock." He walked over, hypodermic in hand, held it up, "That ought to do it."

"Is that too much?" Jock asked.

"The dose we been using. Adjusted to a bigger animal. Figure

403

he's more than a hundred pounds heavier than what we've been handling. Maybe two. He's a brute," Tex said.

"Sure is. Magnificent!" Jock admired. "I wonder what would... no ..."

Tex looked up at him, "What?"

"Pres has never been happy with any animal even with the reduced dose. Leave it to him, he'd rather have them raw, tough, with all the fight they have to give."

"That's dangerous."

"Pres doesn't count danger. He's only interested in the scene, how well it goes. He's not King for nothing."

"That's true," Tex agreed. "I could cut it further."

"What would happen if you ... if you didn't give him anything?" Jock asked, his eyes fixed on the animal, turned away from Tex, so that when the wrangler looked at Jock, he saw only the side of his head.

"Brute like that? Full power? That'd be something! I'd like to try my hand at that myself," Tex said.

"Keep a secret?"

"Sure," Tex promised.

"We have to go through the motions of sedating the animal. Because of the insurance company. But Pres doesn't like it any more than I do, or you do. He'd like to have a go at this one in the raw. Only no one else can know about it, except him, me, and you."

It was a statement. But it sounded like a question, needing an answer, demanding one.

Tex looked at the beast, then slowly pressed down on the syringe till all the sedative squirted out onto the dry earth.

"Not a word. To anyone. You hear? We could all get into trouble." Jock made him a co-conspirator with those words.

"Just the three of us," Tex assured him.

Jock looked at his wristwatch, the one Tony had sent him as a gift. Almost two-fifteen. Ready to go. He slapped Tex on the back, started across the battleground in the direction of the camera.

Joe was just checking out both Mitchells, which were rigged in tandem. So Joe was ready, too.

Now, if Preston Carr was ready, this one was the one. Or could

404

be. Jock could feel it in his stomach, in the tingling in his finger-tips, the subtle, aching, trembling tension in his legs. In the old days, Jock's days of legit theater, he used to call it the opening-night feeling, the once-and-for-all feeling. With pictures, he hadn't had that feeling often. During one picture, he had it not at all. Usually nothing was risked, except shooting time, which was only money. If you didn't get it the first time, or the tenth, you could do it the second time or the twentieth.

In pictures there was rarely that one-roll-of-the-dice-and-make-your-point-or-crap-out excitement. Rarely, if ever, was there the threat that if you didn't get it now, you could never get it. Chances were bought for dollars in the picture business. Grief was in de-fending how you spent the money or if you took too long.

What the hell kind of picture-making was that? Where was the involvement, the excitement? If a man couldn't get a hard-on about a scene, why make the damn picture to begin with?

This feeling he had now about Pres Carr's big scene was the same feeling he had had about the most talked about scene in *Black, Man, Black*. In that picture the story called for the white girl to be in love with the Negro star. And he loved her because it tortured him, angered him, and it allowed him to revenge himself on the entire white race by beating her, attacking her. So that their every sexual encounter was a battle, an act of aggression, sexual sadism, a physical battle, from which she came away bleeding at the lips.

If the relationship was clear, Jock felt, then you could afford to be subtle with your camera, as he had been in that scene. Shot in silhouette, with both people naked, the black star and the white girl. Jock had actually shot it that way. Both naked, and their shadows on the carefully lit wall: from the black man's first approach, through the pursuit, to the way he cornered her on the old brass bed, so that the bars cast prisonlike shadows on the wall. Then the two bodies in a furious assault one upon the other. The whole act of intercourse, black man on white woman, with the bars on the wall behind them, signified the prison in which the black man had lived all his life, and from which he was now escaping by his invasion of this white girl, who symbolized forbidden white society.

405

Then Jock's touch at the end, after taking the entire scene from start to finish, in one long take of mounting excitement, all of it in silhouette, both bodies, with her breasts as clear but more provocative in silhouette than they would be head-on, after even a suggestion of the star's erection—which critics argued over, some saying they could see it and it had artistic value, others saying it was an accident in point of view—after the whole take in silhouette, at the very end of the scene when the fury was over, she moved slightly so that her head, unshadowed and in the clear, hung down over the side of the bed. And you saw the littlest trickle of blood on her lips. That was the only head-on, actual, non-silhouetted moment in the entire scene, and it had been great.

Afterward, the critics argued. Was the blood on her lips a symbol of her loss of virginity to the black man? Or was it evidence of their sadomasochistic relationship? No matter. To Jock, the fact was they all talked about it, wrote about it, and people went to art theaters all over the world to see it.

That was his kind of picture-making. The two whole days before he shot that scene, he went around with this same excitement in his stomach, his legs, his groin. Not even daring to get laid, for fear that, with his sperm, the whole idea would come gushing out of him and be wasted. He had needed a hard-on to shoot that scene the way it should have been shot. The fact was, though he never told anyone, during the shooting of that one long continuous take, he did come in his pants.

A man could not explain that to anyone. Either you felt that way about making pictures or you didn't.

Jock felt that way. He felt it now. And if God was good, this take was going to pay off. He would know soon enough. He would know it before anyone else did. Not exactly. He would know it a few seconds after Preston Carr knew it. That was where it would all hang. On Preston Carr's reaction when he discovered the truth about that untreated mustang.

The doctor was just finishing with Carr's blood pressure, one-thirty over ninety. For a man his age, damn good. His heartbeat, rhythmic and strong, a good seventy-two. The leg muscles all smooth, free of knots. General tone, a slight hint of tension. But he had seen actors have that degree of tension even before a love scene. It was a natural state for good actors. Without tension they transmitted nothing.

If he were examining Carr for an insurance company, he would have passed him for up to a million. He nodded. Carr knew what it meant. He smiled, his tan flat cheeks dimpling in the way that had excited hundreds of millions of women the world over for many years. Daisy, who had watched the whole procedure, smiled, free of worry for the first time in some days.

They drove out to the battleground: Carr, the doctor, Daisy, Axel, and Manning. Manning went along ostensibly to shoot Carr in every moment, aspect, and attitude preceding, surrounding, and following his big scene. Actually, and Jock spotted this instantly, Manning went along to be near Axel. In his cool, controlled way, Manning was a schoolboy with a crush. Only not so obvious. He was a high school freshman who allowed himself to admire the school athlete, because in our culture, the only man another man is allowed to admire freely is an athlete. But Jock could read it, clear and bold; Manning loved Axel because Axel was the physical thing that Manning was not. But he was so subtle about it that no one else detected it.

Jock wondered if Preston Carr knew about Axel. If he did, how could he stand to have the masseur touch him? It gave Jock a chill merely to contemplate it. Closet queens, hidden fags were the worst kind. Unless even worse were the overt writer-type fags, who were always making a merit badge out of their sickness.

Now Manning was shooting Carr as he unbuttoned and removed his elegant silk-lined cashmere shirt. He stood, naked to the waist, in his work-type dungarees, boots, and battered old hat, all the costume he needed for the scene. Jock waited just outside the shade of the tent as Manning finished shooting. Playfully, Carr tapped Daisy on her nose, a sign of good luck between them. Then Carr started into the sunlight, toward Jock.

"Okay, boss," Carr said, as though surrendering himself to higher authority.

"How do you feel, Pres?"

"Doctor checked me out. Great!"

407

"Good!"

"Going to use the big one?"

"Just as you said," Jock answered, smiling.

"Good!"

Carr walked out toward his starting position on the battle-ground. Though it had been abused, pawed, battled over for two weeks, it had been kept in good condition with constant scraping and raking, so that it looked as virginal as it had in the first take. Jock let Carr move ahead of him, wanting to size up the way he walked. Had that severe cramp really disappeared without leaving any traces? There it was, the famous Preston Carr walk. With perhaps a hint of a hitch. Or was it that Jock, who saw him writhing on the ground, knew where the weakness was, so he imagined the hitch was there. How strong Carr was, whether he was free of pain and strain, would become apparent very soon.

The assistant arranged, supervised, ordered, and prepared every detail that preceded the making of the shot. So that when he turned the action over to Jock, every man, every piece of equipment, was in precisely the place it ought to be.

There was a long, an almost unendurably long, silence, perfect, complete. Jock looked out at Carr, who was brown, naked to the waist, muscular, ready to spring into action. Jock looked at the beast, nimble, tall, strong, alert, more so than anyone suspected, except Jock and Tex.

Jock took a deep breath, then commanded in a bristling, hoarse voice, "Action!"

Carr absorbed the cue. In one long instant, one deep breath, he transformed himself from Preston Carr into Linc, the character. One could see it, one could feel it happening to him. Then with determination and a remorselessly slow pace he started across the battleground, reached the stake. He issued the challenge to the beast by jerking the rope free, cracking it on the ground, creating a sound so sharp and true the sound technicians would not have to simulate it later.

The sound, the sudden tug of the rope on the mustang's neck, caused the animal to pull back and rear up. But Carr's control of the rope aborted the move when the beast's hooves were no more than four feet off the ground. Suddenly the animal turned

408

its head, and whether it was the greater strength of this animal, or the lack of sedation, the move caught Carr by surprise, almost ripping the rope free from his strong grasp. Carr's swift, instinctive movement, his viselike hold, his sudden twist of the rope around his right hand, kept it from being torn free.

But the mustang's powerful move, his sudden threat, had done something to Preston Carr. He knew now. And for the first time. This beast had far more fight to offer than the others. Far more danger, too. Too much, perhaps.

This was the instant, never part of the original scene, when he must decide whether to go on with it or quit. That bastard Finley had done the one thing he had commanded never be done! He had surprised him in full view of the camera!

Jock knew it, too, knew it well. He crouched just behind Joe Goldenberg, peered over Joe, past the camera, at Preston Carr and he waited, breathless. For this was the moment he feared. The moment when Carr would discover what had been left undone and what the risk was. The moment when Carr might quit.

Manning, alongside Jock, caught that moment on film, too. Carr in hesitation. Instinctively and almost at the same instant, he turned to catch Jock's grim face. Not on film. But with equal veracity, in an expression Manning would not forget.

All the rest, Daisy, Axel, the doctor, the entire crew, knew nothing except that for some reason this scene was different. It promised to be more exciting, more a battle between Carr and beast than any of the others.

But Carr had to decide. His fury over his suspicion of Jock's deception and his pride kept urging him. Go on! Do the scene! Beat this magnificent animal! Break it! Subdue it! Force it to your will! Let them know who was King! And is still King! You can do it! You've got the arms for it! The legs! And the heart! Do it! Do it! Do it! Do it to that bastard Finley!

His hand tightly on the rope, his legs spread far enough apart to give him a solid base, Carr did not yield. Instead, he used his free hand to snatch his big, broad, sweat-stained hat and scale it away. When seen in the film, it would be interpreted to be the moment when Linc decided on his final confrontation with the mustang. But Jock Finley knew better.

409

"Son-of-a-bitch!" Jock said, in a low whisper.

Joe Goldenberg turned, angry. Manning close, edged even closer. Both photographers were alert to some possible ruinous technical detail Jock might have discovered that they had not.

"His goddamn hat! Now the scene won't cut with the other footage!" Jock explained in an angry whisper. But he dared not interrupt the scene now.

Softly, Joe Goldenberg said, "Not with any footage of Ryan, it won't cut."

Joe turned back to his camera and his field of action. Jock, aware that Manning was staring, forced himself to watch the scene. Now it had to be good. Now this scene had to work. And on Preston Carr's terms. With that one gesture of his hat he had made sure that this scene would be Preston Carr. All of it. All the way. Or it would never really be.

Now, both hands free, and with an overpowering desire and need to avenge himself on Jock Finley, Preston Carr addressed the animal, which tried to rear up. He jerked the rope suddenly. The mustang resisted, pulling back, its neck arching low toward the ground because of the rope which grew tighter and tighter. Then, suddenly, the act of backing away had become only the springboard for attack. The animal sprang forward, rose up and sought to trample Carr with its sharp hooves, coming down so close to him that Carr had to roll to one side, his leg going out from under him.

In that instant, Jock felt a cold hand on his groin. Damn it, not again! Not the leg cramp! This time it could be fatal! But Carr was on the ground, scrambling to one side, not hobbling, but rolling, eluding, getting up all in one move like an expert wrestler, all without losing his grip on the rope. He was on his feet again, circling, confronting the beast. By design or not, he moved swiftly, so that his body did not block the shot. As Carr pivoted before them, Jock could see that his back was scraped, bloody from his bruising roll on the rough desert earth. When Carr's face was turned toward them again, at last Jock could see there anger, determination, the fear of a man who had been close to death and knew it.

With the rope as his lever, and his source of control, Carr forced

410

the animal to one side, then to the other, making it respect, respond. He set up a rhythm, side to side, side to side, treating the animal like a circus horse, not giving it any leeway, not giving it an inch of freedom beyond what he intended to give it. Every time the animal tried to rear up, he cut it down, shorter and shorter. Each time it backed off, he jerked it up sharply. Always circling, moving, away, away, away, so that he would never be caught by surprise again, if the beast sprang forward.

The mustang, unhampered by any drugs, was proud, strong, with great power in its neck. Its legs were hard as marble statuary. In its wild brain was the memory of that moment of promise when it had almost vanquished its tormentor. It would not give up. Not easily. Not quickly. Each moment when it seemed to flag and acquiesce was followed by another sudden, desperate lunge, backward or forward, or by an attempt to rise up in order to crash both sharp hooves down onto Carr.

Carr could feel each surge, forward and back, could evaluate it. As a prizefighter taking punches from an opponent can tell if his strength is waning. This beast was not growing weaker. Carr knew he would never outlast him. He would have to conquer him. And he would have to do it soon.

Had the scene gone on longer than he had expected, he asked himself, or was it only tougher, more taxing? Did he feel it more in his back and shoulders, or did his chest hurt more because of that sudden unexpected shock of being hurled to the ground? All Carr knew was that it could not be allowed to go on, for the beast grew stronger as he grew weaker.

He would have to head for home soon. Now. One great, powerful effort to move in on the beast, to shorten the rope, to come up alongside, to turn him suddenly and run him, not lead him, but run him onto that ramp up into that truck!

Else the whole scene would distintegrate. If he knew nothing else, Preston Carr knew deep in his guts, in his balls, that this take had everything this scene had ever promised, more than he had ever realized. He had to see this one through, he had to save it, even though that bastard Jock Finley had lied to him, trapped him, almost killed him.

Whether it was anger, pride, or a desire to overcome Jock

411

Finley, he did not know. But Carr started now on the final thrusts of his battle.

With deliberate deft strokes, with skillful movements of his body, he shortened the rope, foot by foot, moving in closer on the animal, from the left side. As the animal pivoted, tried to turn, Carr held him in check with his strong arms. His back muscles felt as if they were going to burst. He used his shoulders as levers. When he was only three feet from the animal's proud, fierce, frothing muzzle, Carr made one sudden last move, pulling the animal in close, closer than he had been to any of the others before him. Holding the rope tight, Carr turned the animal about with a sudden surge that called on his entire body. Then with tight rein, Carr ran him toward the ramp, to it, halfway up it. Releasing the rope, he slapped the animal hard on the hindquarters with a sound that cracked across the desert. He pulled the loop, slipped the noose on the tailgate. The slats dropped down into place.

As though it had been rehearsed, the mustang let go a cry that transcended any whinny Jock had ever heard. It was the pain of a free thing being imprisoned. There could not have been a more perfect ending to the scene if it had been written for the effect. Carr, whose action was to turn away from the truck at that moment, did not turn, but stood there looking at the beast with a sense of vindication, victory, and pride on his face, as well as of admiration for the beast.

At the sound of Jock's "Cut!" Carr slumped forward, gasping and breathing hard, no longer the character, Linc, but Preston Carr, sixty-two years old, his tanned face and chest almost yellowing before their eyes, his chest and back spasmodically sucking for air, the muscles of his arms tight, so his arms hung limply out from his body. He leaned against the truck, slipping gradually to the ground before anyone could reach him.

They surrounded him, Daisy, Axel, the doctor, Manning, Jock, Joe. From the ground, he looked up at them. He could read their faces as if they were electrocardiograms. Gasping, while trying to smile, he said, "No, I . . . I did not have a heart attack. I'm fine. Okay. Okay!"

Before Axel would touch him, the doctor had to pass on him.

412

Pulse. Stethoscope. Nod. Axel got astride Carr, helping him breathe with powerful pressure from his strong hands. Carr worked at breathing deep, exaggerating each intake and outpouring of air, deeper and deeper each time. Slowly his healthy brown color came back full, the sickish yellow disappeared. Daisy knelt beside him, wiped the sweat from his face with a towel. Manning stood tallest of them all so he could get a clear, clean downward angle of Carr's face and Axel's hands and Daisy with the towel.

Jock knelt alongside Carr, saying, "Great! Great! The greatest take I've ever seen anywhere, any time!"

At first it seemed Carr was not aware of him. But then he was. He looked at Jock, who was smiling. Carr said nothing. But the look on his face, the accusation there, made Jock's smile go dead. His eyes, bright and sparkling with success one moment, became suddenly sober, defensive.

"It was a great scene! One of the greatest ever!" Jock said in justification.

Without a word, Carr extended a hand to Axel, who gripped it, lifted him to his feet. Daisy threw the cashmere shirt over Carr's shoulders. Carr started away, stopped, turned back to Jock, "Sorry about the hat bit. But I just seemed to *feel* it that way. You know how it is," making little secret of his reflection on New York acting. Carr continued into the shade of the tent. He lay down on the massage table, letting the shirt slip from his shoulders, exposing his broad back to Axel for a massage.

Jock could catch a glimpse of him from where he stood, could see the strong brown back, still working spasmodically to breathe. Then Carr was obscured by Daisy and the doctor, who surrounded him with great concern.

Joe Goldenberg, glasses up on his forehead, pipe and pouch in hand, digging for tobacco, came up to Jock.

"We got it. Both cameras. Great scene. Great!"

"Thanks," Jock said, with little enthusiasm, little conviction.

"There was one moment there, one second of hesitation, when I thought he was going to blow the whole thing. When it seemed it might be too much for him. But he was great. Just great!"

"I want some close shots, reactions, big close-ups of his face

413

in tension, agony, combat, pain. So I can explode them into multi-image for added effect to get his inner struggle and his outer struggle at the same time."

"We can get all those starting tomorrow," Joe assured him. "A few long days and we'll have them. We'll use arcs and reflectors if we have to."

"Yeah. I'd like to finish up this week if we can," Jock said.

"We can do it," Joe said softly.

That evening Carr did not come into the commissary. Nor did Daisy. Axel did. The doctor did. Manning. But not Carr. Nor did any of them approach Jock's table. An occasional grip or electrician or propman came by to congratulate him.

Jock accepted it with seeming modesty. But it was not modesty. It was elation kept in check. It was anger at Carr. It was expectation of the inevitable confrontation with him.

The sonofabitch hates me, Jock was saying to himself. The greatest scene he's ever done, the one they'll remember long after they've forgotten his whole thirty years of picture-making, and he hates me for it. He should thank me. He will, one day, when he gets that Academy Award. But right now, he hates me.

Well, Jock argued within himself, don't go at it tonight. Get those reactions, those close angles, that shot where he frees the beast, all the shots we need for the multi-image effect, get every last foot we're ever going to want in the can and on the way to LA before any confrontations.

Joe was just leaving the commissary, tossing a greeting at Jock with his pipe-holding hand. Manning left. Axel followed a few moments later. Suddenly Jock realized that except for a half dozen of the crew, he was alone in the place. He downed the rest of his coffee from the thick white mug, got up, started out.

Outside, the dark sky was lit by a moon which was only half risen over the mountain. It diminished the brightness of the stars somewhat. Still, they were plentiful, endless to the far horizon, where the glow of a small town could be seen in the distance.

No place to go but back to his trailer. Nothing to do but figure tomorrow's angles and setups. But the big scene, the big challenge

414

of the picture was over. It was like having pursued a reluctant girl till you've finally had her for the whole weekend, then here it was Sunday night. The fun was gone, but she was still here, and she talked too damned much.

CHAPTER

15

THEY started early the next morning. Carr was up, ready, eager to begin his last close shots. He took direction beautifully, giving Jock everything he asked for, more than he asked for, every nuance, every bit of subtlety he had accumulated over the years.

Though the feelings and emotions Carr was called upon to simulate were extreme, since the scene was a man in a life-and-death struggle, his reactions were precise, almost delicate. He used his strong face, his piercing eyes, his chin, his lips.

Every part of his face had meaning and purpose in the scene. But especially those black eyes. The way they darted, the way they fixed, the way they stared, considered, gauged, decided, the way they moved ever so slightly, yet conveyed moments of enormous calculation, fear, anger, admiration for the beast. By simply following Carr's eyes an audience could follow the workings of his mind in determining the next move he must make to overcome the animal. To watch Carr's eyes project thought and feeling was like looking into a pulsating human brain at work.

Through it all, Carr listened, waited, took cues, did his bits, was ready to accommodate himself to the next setup. During the breaks between, when the crew had to change angles of lights, reposition the camera, move reflectors in or back, Carr was quiet, waiting. He had no word to say to Jock. If he made any remarks they were to the crew, or to Daisy, if she was close by, or to

417

Manning, who seemed to have become even more active with his cameras since these were obviously the last few days of shooting.

By ten, with the sun almost high, this day was becoming warmer than the last few. Jock was beginning to feel the oppression of silence. Beyond the first good morning, Carr had not said a word to him. Only listened, nodded, moved, took his cue, reacted, did his silent best till the word "Cut!" He did not react to Jock's praise, which had been extremely lavish this morning, so much so that it had become embarrassing.

Manning seemed to sense it, for Jock became aware that this morning, more than ever before, Manning was losing no chance to get him and Carr in close, intimate candid shots, of which Jock was always aware only a moment or two too late. Between Carr's silence, and Manning's pursuit, Jock was beginning to feel irritable, even angry. He was working with more and more impatience. Soon he was snapping at his assistant about how much time it was taking to change setups. What was the crew doing, adopting a slowdown because these were the last few days? Were they trying to squeeze out an extra week's work? After months? That's gratitude!

But the assistant, who was used to the moods and vagaries of directors, as well as crews, knew that they were all working at good speed. By comparing elapsed hours to feet of film in the can, they were doing better than average for a big feature. Any faster and they would be shooting at almost TV tempo.

When the word reached Jock that there was a radio call, he refused to take it. When it came in again, he was told that it was Mary. He got into his Ferrari, raced back to camp, leaving a trail of desert dust behind him which hung for minutes in the hot sunlight.

Expecting any kind of emergency, even a catastrophe with yesterday's precious footage, he took the phone from the radio man's hand and asked in anger, "Damn it, Mary! Don't you know I'm shooting!"

In a small voice, and hurt, Mary said, "I thought you wouldn't mind being interrupted for this."

"What?"

418

"I sneaked a look at yesterday's footage before they flew it out of here."

"Yeah?" Jock asked cautiously.

"It's the greatest take I've ever seen," she said softly, none of the exclamation points which are included in standard Hollywood praise for mediocre everyday rushes. Hers was a simple statement, almost in a whisper, but with great sincerity. "How did you ever get it?"

"How do you ever get anything good in this business? You sweat, you bleed. At least it came out, it was worth it. Thanks, sweetheart."

Unexpected, totally disconnected from anything she had said to him in several years, Mary suddenly said, "I still love you." Then she cut off the conversation. Touched, blushing for the first time in his recent memory, Jock handed the phone back to the radio man, who had heard it all.

Exhilarated by what he had just heard about the take, Jock drove back to the battleground, continued taking the multitude of bits and pieces of Preston Carr's performance they still needed. But all the while he was waiting. Just before it would normally be time to break for lunch, the copter could be seen landing back at the camp. Jock, a man who had drawn an ace face down in a card game, said nothing till the lunch break. Then casually he invited Carr, Daisy, and Manning to see the rushes of the big scene.

The three rode back in a jeep. Jock drove alone, in his own Ferrari, even though the union rule was that a paid driver and car must be standing by for his use at all times. They crowded into the projection trailer. The lights went out. The scene came up on the small screen, looking no bigger than a good-sized TV picture. But the color and photography were superb.

It started. From the moment when Carr was waiting for his cue, to the sound of Jock's voice calling, "Action" through the moves they laid out, which Carr had done so expertly, the scene played itself out. The tense, tight battle, which Jock had hoped for. Then there was that moment, the one which would be remarked on by critics in a dozen different languages, that moment of decision when Carr's character, Linc, had to assess his chances of success, his moment in which to decide whether to go on or not, whether he could conquer this animal or not, a moment for which Jock Finley would be lauded for the rest of his career by the truly "in" critics, for its conception, its execution, for extracting such a moment of subtlety from Preston Carr, who would forever be deemed to have reached his maturity, his highest estate as an actor in this moment in this film.

When that moment hit the screen, the composition was fantastic. The beast was rearing up, every muscle of its hindquarters standing out sharply. In mid-screen, Preston Carr, stripped to the waist, tanned, his muscles tense under the strain, his face showing that moment of hesitation, when it seemed he might quit, but actually when he discovered the treachery that Jock Finley had inflicted on him.

At that moment, Jock's eyes flicked to the side to study Carr's face. He found Carr looking not at the screen but at him. In that instant in that dark room, with the colors and lights reflecting on their faces, Preston Carr and Jock Finley exchanged the most honest, frank opinions and hatred of each other they ever would.

Carr's look fiercely accused Jock. Jock answered back, his eyes firm and defiant even in the dark. Go on, they said, hate me! I fooled you, tricked you, conned you, lied to you, did everything in the world you hate! But damn it, I got the scene! I made you the King again! I did it!

When the scene was over, none of them said a word. Carr got up, nodded, left the trailer with Daisy following alongside, saying, "Darling, it was marvelous. Marvelous!" But her words were cut short by the sound of the trailer door as Carr slammed it.

As the projectionist started to rewind, Jock said, "Let me see it again." Manning had not moved, did not move, through the entire replay. When it was over, Jock was satisfied. Silent but satisfied.

"Strange thing," Manning observed. "That moment when he hesitates and decides . . . "

Jock turned on him fiercely, "What about it?"

"I caught that, too. I couldn't quite understand it when I got it. But in the context of the scene it's very clear. Though, in all the

420

discussion about the scene, I never heard you mention that moment."

"Call it luck, if you want," Jock said, improvising a shield of modesty.

"It's more than luck. It meant something to him. Carr, I mean. I could feel it just now when he was watching it. What do you think happened?"

"My art isn't much different from yours," Jock said. "What do you look for when you shoot? The unexpectedly real things that people do, or react to, that reveal what they are. A good picture director does the same. He creates as much of a real-life situation as he can, throws the actor into it, hopes his reaction will be interesting, arresting, genuine, above and beyond acting."

Manning nodded, a gesture of respect, of admiration. Jock knew that his statement was one of those that would show up in the text of the *Life* piece.

"They're crazy about what they've got in New York so far," Manning said, imparting a secret.

"Oh?" Jock reacted. "Good!"

"'Birth of a Classic,' that's the title. And it *is* going to be the cover story. Unless there's an assassination, or a war."

"Great!" Jock exclaimed.

"They were going to use my shot of that first battle scene, Carr against the mustang. But I think I'll call them, ask them to hold up till they see my shot of that moment of decision. My composition is even better than Joe's. And the color, that golden animal, the red mountains, Carr's brown body and his face. Those eyes. Unless I miss my guess, that's the one." Manning was still thoughtful as he left the projection trailer.

On his way to lunch, Jock took a detour to the radiophone. He put in a call to Marty. He caught him in his Rolls, en route to Fox, to have lunch with Dick Zanuck, on a combined film-TV deal. After the usual pleasantries, and a dirty story which the Owl heard last night at a benefit champagne supper for poverty marchers at Jack Lemmon's house, Marty asked, "Okay, kid, what's up? Problems?"

"No problems, Marty. Just wanted to fill you in. *Life*. We're getting a cover story. Titled 'Birth of a Classic.'"

"'Classic'? From *Life*? That's great!" Marty said.

421

"Now I'll tell you what I want you to do. Call the studio to-morrow. Tell them to ship to me, and charge to the picture, fifty bottles of Dom Perignon. Ten pounds of the best gray Beluga. And the best buffet spread from Chasen's."

"When do you want it there?" the Owl asked.

"Thursday. That's when I want to wrap. Thursday, when the sun fades slowly into the west, we are going to fade slowly back to our camp, have one hell of a blast, and blow this place!"

"Okay, kid," the Owl promised. "Anything else?"

"Yeah. I want you to figure what we should ask for our next picture, after that spread in *Life*."

"There's no limit, kid, no limit!" Marty enthused. Jock could already see the eyes behind those thick lenses. If eyes could drool, the Owl's did.

For the last shot of the picture, Jock saved that moment when Preston Carr, as Linc, climbed up outside the truck, looked long at the imprisoned mustang and out at the wide spaces from which he had snatched this noble animal, and then decided that he could not imprison it without suffering some loss of his own freedom as well. It was his final rebellion against the world, the system that enslaved all things, animal and man. It was his farewell to a way of life in which he had bought his own freedom at the expense of these last free beings in the great Southwest.

It was symbolic, too, of the fact that he was turning free this young girl, too young for him, so she could make a good life with a younger, more suitable man.

Emotionally, it was the pivotal point in the picture. The more an audience might resent Linc's capture and conquest of the animal, the more they would love him, and Preston Carr, for this moment in the film. And since this was the last view they would have of him in the film, they would love Linc, and Preston Carr, forever.

Jock shot the moment from a giant Chapman crane looking down into the truck. The noble beast imprisoned there in fore-ground. Just behind it, Preston Carr climbed up into view, using the slats of the side of the truck as a ladder. Now he was as tall as the animal, and to one side of it, looking into camera. The crane moved in and down during the final action, coming to a close two-shot near the end.

As they rehearsed it, Preston Carr reached out to pat the mustang on the neck, then looked off into the distance, the free, wild distance of desert, mountains, arroyos, grazing land. And now we could see the thought come alive in Carr's mind and on his face, how wrong it was to imprison such a noble beast. So, after a moment of hesitation, he reached out, yanked at the rope that governed the slatted tailgate, and raised it. He slapped the animal on the flank and the beast hurtled from the truck, leaping beyond the gangplank to the desert floor and racing toward distant freedom.

Now the camera moved in tight on Preston Carr, for a close shot of his burned, brown, lined face as he watched with the slightest smile of satisfaction coming alive on his face finally.

They held on that. Almost too long. For Jock was reluctant to call "Cut!" This was the end of shooting, the end of a great adventure with a great star.

Jock leaped from the crane into the truck to shake Preston Carr's hand, calling, "Great, just great!"

Modestly or not, Carr did not answer. Jock turned to the crew.

"This is one of those moments I hate. It's like a company that's been together in a great hit on Broadway. But closing night comes, as it does to even the greatest of hits. You have to say good-bye to people you've lived with, loved, hated, admired, and respected. And you never know how to say it.

"Yet this is even tougher. Because we haven't yet had our reviews, our success, our hit. We have to exist on what we know and feel in our guts. On our confidence in each other and what we've done. We have to know, deep down, what we have in the can, how it's going to look and sound. Well, I do know. This is a great picture!

"Thanks to all of you. Especially, thanks to a great actor, a great star, the King! But most important of all, a great man, a great gentleman. In his honor, I'm giving a party tonight. In the commissary. You're all invited."

Jock turned to Carr, expecting he would say something. The

423

usual. About the picture. About the pleasure of working with Jock. At least about the crew. The cooperation. But Preston Carr said nothing. He merely smiled perfunctorily, leaped to the ground.

So it was over, like a badly conceived scene. Some realized no more would be said and began to drift away. Others waited awkwardly and only then started away. It was not the way any director would have ended the scene if he had his choice.

Carr and Daisy started away, deliberately avoiding Jock. When they were gone, Jock realized that he was left alone, except for Manning, who had just finished taking a shot of Daisy and Carr, from the rear, walking away from the final take of the film.

They were holding hands. Actually Daisy was holding Carr's hand, by three fingers, more a child holding her father's hand than a woman holding her lover's. There was something about that moment which made Jock know that Manning had an instinctive sensitivity which, in its way, exceeded all the carefully planned and realized art of the film director.

That shot, that moment, of the little-girl Queen clasping the hand of the King would be the one that would ultimately be the final picture in the *Life* spread some five weeks later.

The party was less than a success. The men and the few women who comprised the crew, while impressed by caviar and champagne, appreciated the excellence of neither. Preston Carr and Daisy did not arrive till very late in the evening, after it seemed sure they would not appear at all.

Joe Goldenberg, pleading fatigue, had a half glass of champagne, no caviar. He retired to his trailer, ostensibly to pack. Manning and Axel, after the formalities of a toast or two, disappeared, one at a time and were not seen again.

When Preston Carr and Daisy did appear, the party was almost over. There was still considerable Dom Perignon left, the crew reverting to bourbon early in the evening. The caviar, surrounded by watery ice now, still abounded, three of the blue fourteen-ounce tins remained unopened. Carr and Daisy drank a polite glass of champagne, exchanged words with some of the crew, then excused

424

themselves on the pretext that they would be rising early to drive to Carr's ranch.

When they stopped in the doorway on their way out, Carr turned back to smile and wave to the crew. Spontaneous applause broke out, a tribute to a fine actor and a very good man. Carr seemed embarrassed. Daisy smiled, looked up at him, and tears started in her eyes.

Whether it was the applause or her tears, Carr was suddenly impelled to announce, "Tomorrow . . . at my place . . . we're getting married!" There was a surge of shouts, applause, outcries of congratulations. The whole company moved to the door to shake Carr's hand, to shake Daisy's hand or kiss her.

Jock waited till last. His director's instinct told him that in moments like this you either started the scene or ended it. The one thing you didn't do was get caught in the mob.

Jock waited at the door as if he were the father of the bride, or the best man, letting the others pay their tribute, wish their wishes. When they had all had their moment, Jock shook hands with Carr, who accepted it casually. Jock kissed Daisy, circumspectly, on the cheek. He whispered, "Good luck. You deserve it!" But he was close enough to breathe in that perfume, to renew the deep longing for her. To feel in his groin that in another moment or two he would be fully aroused and it would be difficult to let her go.

Whether she felt it, or only suspected it, Daisy allowed herself to be kissed, spoken to, but remained aloof, stiff, unyielding.

They were gone. Jock turned back to the party. But he realized there was no one to talk to. He had no interest in anyone there. What was more, no one there had any interest in him. A few of the old-timers, sentimental by virtue of age, came up to him, said nice things about the entire experience, made extravagant predictions for the picture, recalled some of the old times, other places, other pictures with Preston Carr. But it was all polite, empty, meaningless. They felt impelled to talk, as he felt impelled to listen. None of them was truly interested.

Little by little, earlier than Jock expected, they drifted out and were gone. It was not even ten o'clock when Jock was left alone in the large commissary, larger now because the tables had been pushed back for the buffet. He stood in the center of the room, looked around, at deserted glasses, a few empty, most of them half-filled. At abandoned plates, piled with uneaten caviar and potato salad. That's a combination, he said bitterly to himself. Give gray Beluga to pigs. Or Dom Perignon to men who prefer bourbon or cheap rye.

Jock felt around in the icy water of the huge aluminum cooking pot which had become an improvised champagne cooler. Near the bottom he found several unopened bottles. He took one. He snatched a clean champagne glass off the table and started out.

He was sitting alone in his trailer. Half the bottle was gone. It was only just past midnight. If it didn't involve waking the radio man, if there were a phone on the little table, instead of a bottle, he would be calling people in New York or LA or London. Telephones are the antidote for loneliness for men like Jock Finley, who cannot stand to be alone, unless they have work to do. As impatient as they are at the intrusion of other people when they are working, once they are done, they are equally impatient for a human voice, a human touch, any sign that they are not alone in this world.

For himself, Jock invented excuses, motives. He had been too long deprived, sexually. He was edgy, uptight, raunchy from having been away too long from women. It was the first time in years that he had been involved in making a picture, or being out on the road with a play, that he was not shacking up with some girl in the cast. Usually, during the early days of casting, he would select one girl, for some minor part, who would be intended for just that purpose.

Now, tonight, after the last shot was in the can, after the picture was over, the girl he had secretly intended to be for his own private use was in Preston Carr's trailer.

Jock Finley was alone and had been for almost four weeks. He needed a woman, almost any woman.

There was a moment when he was tempted to consider coptering to Vegas to avail himself of Tony's regal hospitality again. But he had no appetite for that girl. Who knew where her mouth had been since he last saw her almost a week ago? And how do you

426

let a girl make love to you, when you keep seeing the image of a little kid, with his mouth half open, trying to breathe in spite of bad tonsils? Or was it adenoids that made kids keep their mouths open that way? Whatever, it was not an appealing sex image, the whole damn thing.

Tomorrow. Tomorrow night. Louise. He could wait that long. He poured himself more champagne. Now he found the taste too delicate, too effete. Some things in life were just too damn good, were intended only for experts and connoisseurs. Dom Perignon. You drank it, you knew it was good, you knew it was the best there was. Then you realized you would rather have Scotch. In that way Jock was an electrician, a grip, or a stagehand. There was a wide stripe in him that was common man. Perhaps that was why he knew what made audiences react, why he could read a script and know they would like it. Or see an actress and know the difference between what he liked and appreciated and what *they* would like.

He switched from Dom Perignon to Scotch, Preston Carr's private brand, which Jock had ordered by the case to flatter him. He had a few belts. But it did not change his personal climate. He was still alone. With no phone to resort to. He would not take a sleeping pill. Certain weaknesses he would never succumb to. Pills were one. If you couldn't sleep, you read, walked, thought, stayed awake. But you did not take pills. It was a confession of weakness.

He was finishing off the last of his drink when there was a knock on his door. It was hurried, furtive, anxious. He got up quickly, felt a little unsteady, instinctively blaming it on the mix of champagne and Scotch. He opened the door. Daisy was there, a robe pulled hastily around her; her hair in unmade blond wisps made her most attractive. Feeling as he did, his mind, his entire being involved in sexual fantasies, he opened the door wide, smiled.

"I can't find Axel," she said, breathless.

Still smiling, Jock said, "There's a damn good reason why you can't. Come in, honey—"

She interrupted, "I need help! Something's happened. Pres! Pres!" She broke down, started to cry. He put his arms around her. He had seen her through crying fits before, through hysteria,

427

times when he dared leave her only at dawn, hoping to God she wouldn't do anything rash or dangerous to herself. Then he would call her again and again, after he got home, till she woke up and answered. But he had not seen her cry this way before. He shepherded her down the steps, across the compound, to Carr's trailer.

When he entered, he could hear it. Carr's stifled sound as he gasped for air, as he tried to overcome the pain which kept him from drawing a deep breath. When Jock looked down at him, he could see the agony, the sweat on Carr's face, his chest, damp, heaving desperately to achieve one good long intake of breath but never accomplishing it.

Jock knew the symptoms well. He knew, too, that the first thing was oxygen. He turned from Carr's bedside, leaped the four steps to the desert earth, raced toward Axel's trailer, calling his assistant as he ran, "Lester! Les! Somebody find me Lester Ansell!"

By the time he had invaded Axel's quarters, found the portable oxygen tank and mask, and was returning to Carr's place, there were four men out there in the light bleeding from now-opened trailer doors. But his assistant was not one of them.

"Find me Lester Ansell!" he shouted, racing toward Carr's trailer.

Inside the trailer, he fixed the mask over Carr's face, opened the valve, heard the sound of the oxygen. He could not tell, but he thought that the oxygen was helping. Carr still felt cold, damp under his hand, and his tan seemed to have an undercoating of pale yellow, giving him a strange, almost Oriental coloration.

The gasping was more regular now, but the breathing was still not deep. The pain was quite obvious. And Carr had not yet said a word. He opened his eyes from time to time, staring up at Jock past the mask, but he did not speak, nor did he try. Hovering over them was Daisy, weeping, whispering over and over, "My fault . . . all my fault . . . " in an almost absent way. "All my fault . . . "

Now Jock's assistant arrived, looking strange, almost unfamiliar, for it was the first time Jock had ever seen him without his glasses.

"Get on the phone! Call the state police! I want the nearest doctor around! The nearest hospital! Then get hold of *his* doctor!"

428

The assistant stared down, obviously frightened.

"Don't stand there! Move your ass!" Jock called out fiercely, as much out of guilt as anger. The assistant left. Now Jock could notice that people had begun to gather outside Carr's trailer, the steps were surrounded by faces, staring, morose, curious, fearful.

Jock said brusquely to Daisy, "Shut that door!" She interrupted her crying to do it. Jock turned back to Carr. He fed the oxygen slowly with one hand, while the other hand reached blindly, finally finding Carr's pulse.

It was too weak, too irregular to follow. It was not like any pulse Jock had ever felt before. It frightened him. He had a man's life, or death, under his hand and there was nothing he could do. Daisy stood across from Carr, staring down, weeping, still blaming herself.

The assistant was back. He had reached the state highway patrol, who raised a doctor, and on a patched-in three-way conversation, he had been told the best thing to do was leave the patient alone, make him comfortable, give him oxygen if it was available. The police would rush the doctor there as soon as they could. They had tried to find Carr's own doctor in LA but he did not answer and his service could promise nothing.

It was almost an hour later. From far in the distance, through the desert night, could be heard the sound of a police siren. Jock left Carr's side long enough to go to the door, open it, stare out. A revolving red light in the distance was drawing closer. The sound of the siren carried promise, if not comfort. Jock hurried to Carr's side. Daisy had stopped weeping. Her eyes were dry, but staring. She kept searching Jock's face for some sign, some hope, some reassurance. The siren brought the doctor almost to the door of the trailer. The car pulled up sharply, a rasp of tires on desert earth. The trailer door opened, a trooper leaned in to give way to the doctor, who was a small, elderly man, with age-moistened eyes behind silver-framed glasses on a creased, ruddy face.

"Where's the . . . " but he spied the patient, went to him. He removed the mask, handed it to Jock. The doctor looked into the patient's eyes, and only then realized it was Preston Carr.

"Good God!" the doctor said turning to Jock.

429

"Don't ask for his autograph! Save him!" Jock said fiercely.

Resentful, the doctor turned back to Carr, made his routine check of vital signs. His reactions were not hopeful. Forcing open Carr's lids, he looked into his eyes. He found his pulse, took it, used his stethoscope as he watched the irregular, tortured breathing. Without a word, he opened his medical bag, filled a hypo, gave Carr an injection.

"Ease the pain, anyhow," was all he said. He looked around, as though searching for next of kin, or anyone who might give him a history. When he saw Daisy, he was about to exclaim again. But Jock's angry face alongside hers killed that impulse. Instead the doctor asked, "This his first?"

"I . . . I don't think so," Jock said. "Figure he had one before, about seven, eight years ago."

"Seven years?" the doctor asked. It had great significance for him. "Hmm! Seven years . . . well . . ."

"What does that mean?" Jock demanded.

"We better get him to a hospital," the little doctor said, turning to the trooper.

"It'll take an hour by car. Can he make it?" the young trooper asked.

"We have a copter!" Jock said. "We can fly him anywhere!"

"Copter? Good!" the trooper said instantly, only thinking to ask the doctor a moment later, "Is that okay?"

"Better than leaving him here," the doctor said. His opinion gave no cause for hope.

With the help of three crewmen and his assistant, Jock supervised the removal of Preston Carr from the trailer to the copter. Wrapped in two blankets, he left little room in the bubble. So it was decided that only the doctor could go along, in the event emergency treatment was required en route. Jock, Daisy, and the others were left standing at the pad, staring, as the machine whipped the air, rose slowly, turned in the direction of a glow of light that was a town eighty-five miles away.

Daisy clutched Jock's arm as they watched the copter move off into the night, its running lights blinking. It was almost out of sight when Axel pushed his way alongside them to ask, breathless and fearful, "What happened?"

430

You fucking fag, if you were here instead of off with your pretty boy friend, you'd know what happened! Where were you when he needed you? Jock thought that, but he said only, "It's a little late to be asking that!"

Manning moved in alongside Axel, protectively. It was strange, because Manning by all visual indications seemed the more feminine of the two. In answer to Jock's tone and attitude, which accused Axel, Manning protected him by his look, which accused Jock. Finally it was Jock who was forced to break off the encounter. He used Daisy as this excuse.

"Come! I'll drive you to the hospital."

Manning asked, "Mind if I go along?"

"It's a Ferrari. Only seats two," Jock said. Then, indicating Axel, he added with a bitter smile. "He can drive you."

If Manning blushed, Jock could not see it in the darkness. But there was no mistaking the anger in the homosexual's eyes.

Jock was doing a hundred and five miles an hour along the dark, empty, flat desert road. With the top down, speed turned the cool air into a chilling wind. Daisy did not seem to feel it. She talked, soberly, explosively, without tears.

"My fault . . . it was my fault . . ." she kept saying. "I shouldn't have let him! Not tonight! Not till we got married!"

So that was how it happened. "You can't blame yourself," Jock said, because there was little else to say.

"Somehow if I . . . if he'd been able to rest . . . if we'd waited . . . but he wanted me so much . . . and it didn't matter to me . . . so I . . . I let him . . . I even helped him . . . I . . . it's wrong . . . you can't start a marriage that way . . . it was a punishment . . . that's what it was . . ."

"You mustn't believe that!"

"You sound like some of the doctors now. Doctors are always saying, you can't blame yourself, you can't have guilt all the time. But you do. You do," she said sadly.

He glanced at her. She was staring straight ahead, her face whiter in the moonlight than usual. Her mink coat was pulled tight around her but the hood was off her head. Her hair was being

431

whipped back. Her profile, its even features exposed to the wind and the darkness, might be a face on some ancient carving seen in the Aegean night.

"There *is* sin. And God. And people pay for what they do. I pay for every time I have been to bed with a man. Even though there is no joy in it. I only allow them. That's all it is. Not loving, not joining, just letting.

"Sometimes I look up, I feel a man doing what he is doing and feel it take hold of him so that it is the only thing in the whole world that matters. I want to stop him, whoever he is, right then and ask, Why? What is it you find in it, or in me, that drives you so? I never ask. Because I think it will spoil it for them. But I would like to know, before I die, what it is.

"Do you know?" she asked suddenly.

"Nobody knows," Jock answered, sensing that to enter this conversation with her would be to open a strange door to a strange room which there would be no closing.

"That's why I didn't ever go to bed with any man I felt I wanted to marry. If it's going to be a disappointment to me, and to him, I don't want to know it till afterward. I don't want him to know it. I would like to find a man who can love me without that. All my husbands . . . I left them, ran away. Like I run away from pictures sometimes. But they know before I leave . . . that it failed . . . I failed. I keep getting married because I am searching. But I don't find it. Then I get frightened they'll leave me. So before they can, I leave them. But they've left me a long time before that . . . a long time. Then I start looking again.

"One doctor said to me, that's why I'm glamorous. A sex symbol. Because I give every man in the world the feeling that I am searching just for him. And I am, he said. I spent a weekend with him once, that doctor. He said he wanted to know firsthand, by personal experience, what my problem really was. He never did tell me. But a short time afterward I stopped going to see him. He kept calling me for weeks, months. To make dates with me. I don't know why. It didn't seem to work any better with him than with any other man. Only he talked more. Before. And after. During, he never said a word, or made a sound. But afterward,

432

he never stopped talking to me, about me. As though I was a whore, and he was paying me the only way he knew.

"He was right about that one thing. I am searching. And if that's what comes through on the screen, I guess that's why I'm what I am. Isn't that strange? That someone should get a million dollars a picture because she is never going to find what she is looking for?

"You're the same, aren't you?" she asked.

Jock was defenseless in face of her suddenness. "Same as what?"

"Searching. All the time . . . Every time that you were at me, I had the feeling, he's searching, needing something from me. It's the picture, I thought sometimes. He's doing this because he wants me to do his damn picture. Then I thought, no, he wants me. Because it will make him feel like a big man, an important man . . . to fuck Daisy Donnell."

Her use of the word, coming as it did from the mouth of a lost little girl, offended him. He had heard many women use it, frequently, aggressively. He was quite accustomed to it. But coming from her it offended him, he who thought he was beyond offending by anything.

"'But,' I said, 'he's had other stars. He's known for it. That's how he got his name. Jock-Sock Finley. Then what is it? What does he want with me? What does he want to prove, that he can make an actress out of me? Or does he want to compare notes with other men to see who finally aroused Daisy Donnell?' I never knew. I don't know now. I don't even care.

"One good thing. My way, I don't have any fond memories. I think except for my first husband there isn't any man I would want to go back to and do it over with, hoping it might be different, or better. To me, men are like places I've been that I never want to go back to. The next man will be the right . . . God, do you think he's going to die?" she asked suddenly, frightened.

"They do wonders these days in those hospitals. With pacemakers, electrical gadgets. Transplants. All kinds of ways of beating heart attacks," Jock lied, wondering what this would do to the picture.

"I'm not asking that he be perfectly okay. I mean, I would be

willing to take care of him the rest of his life. No matter what.
I wouldn't even mind if they said he couldn't ... I've heard some
men say ... I had an agent once ... an older man ... he said having sex was like running up six flights of stairs. A man who'd had
a bad heart attack wasn't allowed ... ever ... to do it again. So
I won't mind ... If I can just take care of him, that would be
enough. I love him. I really do. And if I could just be sure he'd
live, I wouldn't mind if I never had another man the rest of my life.
I wouldn't!"

Jock knew any sound from him would silence her completely.
So he waited, eyes fixed on the concrete desert road, which seemed
white in the strong clear moonlight.

"I ... had this story ... made up this story. I used it once in
that profile in *The New Yorker*. The woman seemed to like it. She
used it in her article. People talked about it. About how I was
raped when I was a little girl. By a foster father. That never
happened. I made it up. How would it look if it ever came out that
the sex symbol of this world didn't care. Just ... just let it happen
to her ... hated it, really. So I made up this story. I thought, if it
ever does come out, people'll say, poor kid, no wonder she feels
that way. Then I told it to the doctor. Not the same one on that
weekend. But another one. An older one. He said it didn't matter
if it was made up or not. It was important that I even thought of
something like that.

"He was the one made me say fuck, out loud. In his office. Every
time I tried to use another word for it, he made me say it. Once he
made me just keep saying it, fuck, fuck, fuck, fuck, for five straight
minutes, till I got over my inhibitions.

"Then one time he made me say it and right in the middle of it
he tried to make me say suck. Fuck, fuck, fuck, suck, suck, suck.
He tried to convince me that's what I really wanted to do but I was
afraid or ashamed to let myself think it or say it or do it. And I
told him right then and there, I'd done it and didn't like it any
better than any other way. He seemed terribly disappointed. I
always thought it was pretty rotten of him to make me say those
things, a man past sixty and a doctor.

"It was funny, though, in a way. Him saying fuck with his
Viennese accent. It almost sounded cute.

434

"He isn't going to die!" she exclaimed suddenly. "They won't let him die!" She was silent the rest of the trip.

They were coming to a stretch of road lit up by the street lights of the small town. Only when he began to pass the dark store fronts, the dark houses, did Jock realize how fast he had been going and that he didn't even know where the hospital was. He slowed down so precipitously he almost threw the powerful car into a skid on dry pavement, the layer of desert dust acting like oil slick. Slowly, he prowled the street looking for the sign he knew must be coming up soon. At one corner he found it. An arrow pointing left, bearing the words DESERT GENERAL HOSPITAL.

As they approached the long, low, one-story modern building, Daisy grew tense, quite small, pale. She pulled her coat closer about her. The nearness of truth made her go cold, colder than she had been while racing through the night air at more than a hundred miles an hour.

Jock pulled up in front of the hospital, to the lighted glass door of the entrance. She reached out to take his hand, again only three fingers of his hand. They entered the hospital.

Beyond the admissions desk, at the end of the long, quiet corridor, they could see the state trooper, writing up his report, using the wall for a desk. They started down the hall. She was still holding Jock's hand. He could feel the ice in her fingers.

They reached the door, saw the neat lettering there. INTENSIVE CARE, VISITORS FORBIDDEN. She seemed almost relieved to be shut out.

The trooper volunteered, "Three doctors in there with him."

Jock nodded, thought a moment, then slipped the door open softly. He could see little, three doctors and two nurses obscuring all view of Carr. But he could tell they had Carr on the stretcher on which he had been wheeled into the room. It was not a good sign, that they dared not move him to a regular bed. They became aware of him now. One of them called, "Shut that door!"

Jock backed out, letting the door close quietly on its new plastic bumpers. Before it closed, he could hear one doctor say, "Give him some. What can we lose?"

435

He hoped that Daisy hadn't heard that. She hadn't. She was leaning against the opposite wall, her head touching it, needing it for support. She was turned away from the door, staring down the corridor, at the end of which, nurses and an orderly had gathered to stare as people stare only at movie stars.

Her blond head was pressed against the pale green wall. Her white face drained of color, the mink hood slipped back from her head, she was a pathetic, lost child, whose father was dying. She did not know what to say, or how to act, or what to do.

There are some events, some experiences for which one never has sufficient preparation. She became aware of the nurses staring. She turned away, toward his door, which seemed the worse alternative. Jock moved to her, put his arms around her. She was relieved to hide her face in his shoulder.

"They won't let him . . . " she said. "He won't."

The trooper suggested softly, "I could get her a drink." Jock shook his head. "Coffee?" the young man volunteered. To get rid of him, Jock nodded. The trooper started down the corridor toward the nurses.

The door to Intensive Care opened. Jock turned to greet the doctor. Daisy would not lift her head or uncover her face. Jock's look asked the question, at the same time that his eyes pleaded, take it easy in front of her. The doctor understood, nodded.

"We've got it under control," he said, adding for Jock's benefit, "We'll know more in twelve hours. If there are no recurrences."

Jock nodded. He lifted her face, "It's okay. It's okay." He looked across at the doctor, who resented being flagrantly misquoted. Daisy nodded. Though she had been exposed to it all, she heard only what she could accept.

"Can we go in?" she asked.

Jock looked toward the doctor who shook his head.

"We better wait," Jock said softly.

"The visitor's room is down the hall, near the entrance," the doctor suggested.

Almost an hour had gone by. They sat in the waiting room. Daisy, silent, staring. Jock watching her. Thinking. Wondering.

436

If Carr died, what would it mean? To the picture, to him. If the story ever came out, if Tex ever talked, what would that mean? To the studio. To the insurance company. To the studio because of the insurance company. And finally, to Jock Finley because of the studio because of the insurance company.

A man is never so pious as before an accusation he knows to be true. Never so penitent as when events have reached an irreversible course. So, he was telling himself, if anything did happen to Carr, he would take care of Daisy, would marry her, would never touch her, would protect and adore her, have separate bedrooms if she wanted them. He would do anything . . . if only . . . if only the whole story never came out, if the whole thing didn't explode in full view of the entire world.

Studios were funny, he reminded himself. Remember Ingrid Bergman, and how no studio in this country would touch her for years after the Rosselini affair. They had built her into a worldwide symbol of sexuality and love, then shunned her because she had proved that in real life she possessed the very attributes which all studios sought in all their stars. So these same studios, which in such cases moved with the unanimity of cartels, might revenge themselves on Jock Finley. It was the way of all mass media, which depend on public favor.

Television networks, their respected owners and board chairmen, would reap every dishonest dollar from any kind of program, violent, unethical, rigged, or crooked. Then when it became public scandal, the executives performed acts of contrition by firing the men who had made the money for them. Underlings always got fired. Men at the top went right on, hiring new men to do new shows. Or new pictures. Till they were fired.

In this case, the president, the studio head, could claim, and prove, they had had no knowledge of Tex's failure to sedate that last mustang. So, clearly deceived, they wouldn't hesitate to destroy Jock in their self-righteous wrath.

Of course, he could go back to Europe. He could make pictures there. But he had just returned from Europe. He was a refugee in his own country. Of course, that was London. He could go to Italy. Or Yugoslavia. Lots of pictures were being made in Yugoslavia these days. And in Rome there was Ponti. They had met at a cocktail party at the Dorchester during Jock's last week in London. And Ponti had said, "Baby, we got to make a picture together some day."

But hell, they were always saying that. That was always Tony's opening remark and his closing remark in almost every conversation. He was even reputed to have said that once to a wisecracking cabdriver in New York, and then actually had used the guy in a film.

But the fact was, nobody made a picture with anybody till somebody else put up the money. That was Rule Number One in picture-making. Or any other production.

Right now, Jock had a sick feeling that if the word got around about what he had done, people like Tony would mark him lousy. Then go try to get a star! And without a star, no story in the world would raise a quarter. So talent didn't matter, scripts didn't matter, the whole goddamn business depended on stars, stars, stars!

If he got a reputation as a star-killer, that could be the end.

Almost half an hour had gone now. There was no further word from Intensive Care. No doctor had come by the visitor's lounge. Only one nurse had appeared to offer coffee or a sedative to Daisy. Now there was a stir down the hall at the entrance. Jock left Daisy's side to investigate. It sounded like what he had been fearing. The news media must have the word. Photographers, perhaps even TV cameras, would be intruding here, probing, rooting, looking, spying.

But when he stared down the corridor toward the entrance, he could see it was a carload from location. Axel was in the lead, Manning hurrying to keep up with him, Joe Goldenberg was on his other side, but unable to keep pace. Behind them was Jock's assistant. And one more man, tall, very lean, face burned to a permanent reddish tan. Tex.

The rest, yes, Jock said to himself. But Tex, what was he doing here? Jock started down the hall to meet them. He made broad gestures with both hands to enforce absolute quiet. When they met, he whispered to them, "He's in Intensive Care. He seems okay. So quiet. Everybody. And wait in there."

They started for the waiting room, their boots and rubber-soled

438

shoes making hissing sounds on the new vinyl tile. Jock allowed them to pass him, all except his assistant. He subtly seized Les's sleeve. When the others had gone in, he asked, "What the hell is *he* doing here?" indicating Tex.

"He drove. He's the only one knew the way."

Relieved, Jock started for the waiting room. He discovered Manning in the process of shooting Daisy. She was completely oblivious, completely naked to his probing lens, unaware of the sounds of his Minox, which he handled with surgical precision and speed. Defenseless, stunned, her face withheld nothing. The feelings ran out of her like the stuffing out of a ruptured cloth doll.

Jock moved between her and Manning, spoiling his shot, saying in a harsh whisper. "God damn it! Not now!" But Manning, who had shot many things in many forbidden places in this world, moved quickly and deftly around Jock to get the shot he wanted. Jock seized him by the shoulder of his zipper jacket, spun him around with one hand, holding him so tight, his toes barely touched the floor. Then Jock felt a strong hand on his shoulder, pressing against the complex of flesh, nerve, and muscle in a spot so tender and responsive that he not only released Manning but almost sagged to the floor. He looked around and up. It was Axel, who from that angle seemed a giant.

"You fag sonofabitch!" Jock whispered fiercely.

Axel exerted an extra, vicious measure of pressure till Jock gasped in pain. Then Axel released him. All the while Manning went on shooting, shot after shot of Daisy, whose eyes were now staring but moist, moist but not weeping. Tears hung on her lids, not daring to flow.

Suddenly, with no warning, though it must have been in his mind for some minutes, Manning turned on Jock and took one, two, three, four, five, six shots in rapid succession. Close, tight, almost with the speed of a motion picture camera. So that when they were laid side by side one would read Jock's mind through his eyes and his reactions, that he was being photographed, that he resented it, that he felt guilty about something, that he hated the photographer, that he was about to attack him, that he was lunging.

Manning's camera did not show that it was Axel who inter-

439

vened. Jock turned away from him, from Manning, went to sit beside Daisy. Days later Marty White would compliment Jock on that move, that inspiration. Because, out of it all, one of the most famous photographs of the year would be Manning's shot of director and star waiting loyally together, both almost weeping, not far from the door of the King's hospital room.

Daisy would not relax or even take a sedative till they let her see him. It was Jock who finally convinced the doctors. Jock took her to the door, stopped, and only she was permitted in. She took off her shoes, so as not to make the slightest sound. On stockinged feet, she tiptoed into the room.

Carr was surrounded by an oxygen tent. On each side of his bed stood a nurse and a doctor. Above the bed a battery of green-tinted screens gave a running account of his vital signs, with blips that traced and raced across the right side of the screen and off, only to reappear at the left end and start again. There was solace in knowing that every measurable fact of importance which would determine his life and death was at least exposed to the doctors' view. There were no secrets here, but one. Would there be another attack?

Daisy did not realize that. So she was reassured that he was alive, breathing, his heart working. But she did not realize that it was not working well, hints of fibrilation already were in evidence.

The doctor turned to see her, smiled, nodded. Daisy smiled back. Now the tears started. Whether it was relief, or the sight of seeing Pres there, surrounded, invaded, and exposed by all the equipment, or the failure of the doctor to inspire confidence, it was his smile that made her cry. As she turned away, the nurse put her arm around her and took her out.

Daisy was sedated, settled in a room two doors from Intensive Care. When she had dozed off, Jock left her side. He stepped out into the hall, noticing at the far end of the corridor, through the front entrance, that the first pink rays of desert dawn were coloring the chrome door frame. He started down the hall, passed the waiting room, did not look in.

Now Joe Goldenberg reached his side.

"Well?" Joe asked.

440

"Still the same."

"I hope to God . . . " Joe started to say, then he stopped. "For your sake, I hope he makes it." There was something vindictive, accusatory, scathing, in this mild little man's prayer.

Jock turned fiercely, defensively, but the little man held his ground, face to face with Jock, defiant, almost daring Jock to take physical action against him. Jock reached out, seized Joe's corduroy jacket. But the little man, with a strength one would not suspect, brushed Jock's hand aside.

"You going to try to quiet everybody that way?" Joe asked. "Too many people saw it. Watched it, day after day. You hounded that man, drove him. I begged you not to. But you whipped him with pride. You drove him with the memory of his past greatness. You crucified him with his own youth. Anybody else in the world lives as a young man only in the memory of other people. But a picture star, he can go back and see it over and over, what he did, how he looked, how he moved, smiled, kissed girls, rode horses, scaled fences, climbed walls, did scenes as a prizefighter. He can see it all, over and over in the projection room. And then die trying to imitate himself."

It was the first time Jock knew this. It showed on his face.

"That's right," Joe went on. "That's what he did. Before he came out to do this picture he ran that stuff, over and over. He asked me to run it with him. I . . . I begged him not to do this picture . . . I begged him. But you with your talk about a new Preston Carr! A last great picture! A chance to do a part of depth and substance! He never minded being a star. But he never got over not being considered a fine actor. You found his weakness, and you killed him!"

"He isn't dead," Jock said. "He won't die." He slipped out of Joe's grasp, moved toward the door, toward daylight, toward fresh air.

The morning air in the desert was so dry it reached into his nostrils, puckered the inner lining of his nose. There was no wind, no breeze. Only still, clean, dry air which, after the processed, conditioned air of the hospital, seemed artificial. Then Jock became aware of the sweet strong scents and smells of the desert, and he knew this was the real air.

He breathed deeply. Unaware, till moments later, that Tex was sitting at the wheel of the command car that had brought them all down from the compound. And Tex was watching him. Jock considered for a moment walking over, talking to his chief wrangler but decided against it. The less said, the less would be open to misinterpretation later. But Tex got out of the car, started toward him. Now, Jock knew, it could not be avoided.

"Anything new?" Tex asked, reaching for the cigarettes in his shirt pocket. Jock shook his head. Tex lit up, "You don't have to worry. It'll be like we agreed. If he doesn't say anything, I won't."

Jock knew it was treacherous to answer, so he merely nodded, a thoughtful, understanding, we-have-just-made-a-gentleman's-agreement kind of nod. One that you couldn't quote. Or misconstrue in retrospect. Tex had said everything, Jock had said nothing, so there would be nothing to explain or deny or retract.

But there was only small, temporary reassurance in it. Who knew when, drunk or sober, on a long trip to location, or during bad-weather days on some other picture, when stories of past glory were being told, or inside secrets exposed, Tex would tell the whole story? It defies accounting, the things that show people tell other show people during the long waits between takes or nights on location or on long plane trips or car trips to locations or back. No story personal, vicious, or untrue is immune to repetition.

But for the moment, Tex had given his assurance.

Jock looked down the street, first one way then the other. A neon sign, still lit against the night, proclaimed in red, DINER. Jock looked at it a moment, then asked, "Coffee?"

"Had some," Tex said, going back to the car. Jock started down the street alone. Tall, lean, sun-browned face, this young man from Brooklyn looked native to the desert. As he walked, catching a glimpse of himself in the window of the closed dry-cleaning shop, he wondered, How the hell did I get here? What am I doing, walking down the street of this little desert town, wondering if the biggest picture star in all the world is going to live or die? And not only that, but I made it happen. I did! Me! Jacob Finestock. Jock Finley. And if I don't watch out, if something in this

442

very tricky situation goes wrong, it can all explode around me, and I can be back East again, walking down Broadway, hungry for a good script to direct, if someone can get the money, if someone can get the star, and no star wants to work with Jock Finley ever again.

He reached the diner. His hand was on the door knob when he realized that Manning was at the counter, having coffee with Axel.

Jock was about to turn away, but Manning had seen him. There was that moment of contact of eyes that lets each know the other has seen him. So Jock went in. Instead of the counter, he went to a booth, sat on a vinyl-covered bench, at a vinyl-topped table, both a shade of light, ugly marbleized yellow and white, resembling loosely scrambled eggs.

The man behind the counter called, "Coffee? Sweet roll?" Jock nodded. The man drew coffee into a plastic cup, put yesterday's dry sweet roll on a plastic plate, and brought them over. As he set them down, Jock noticed a word pass between Manning and Axel. Axel got up, left, stopping only to buy a pack of cigarettes from the machine at the door.

Jock stirred his coffee, added a little cream from the small, scratched, plastic pitcher, with a retractable top, which was no longer retractable because of the stale cream encrusting it. He picked up the sweet roll, but the icing looked dry, fake as plastic. So he let it drop back onto the plate.

Manning came over.

"Mind?"

"Uh-uh," Jock said.

Manning sat down, easily, gracefully. He said nothing, just stared. Jock lifted his cup, sipped. The coffee was too hot.

"Coffee is always either too hot or too cold," Jock observed, uneasy, waiting.

"One thing I couldn't understand," Manning said, "One shot I got. Bothered me when I saw it. Been bothering me ever since. Bothers Axel, too."

This last was said defiantly. Manning expected that Jock would react, possibly even say something hostile, vulgar, distasteful. But Jock kept sipping coffee.

443

"Axel knows him well. Known him a long time. Even Axel couldn't understand it when I showed it to him."

Manning reached into his shirt pocket, took out a small, flat object, protected by two sheets of cellophane. It was a photograph. He laid it down facing Jock.

It was a shot of Preston Carr, in action, at the moment when Carr had discovered that this animal, this king among mustangs, had not been doctored or sedated. That it was powerful raw brute against man, with no aids, no holds barred. The moment when Preston Carr had realized that someone, Jock Finley, had done to him the one thing, the only thing he had ever violently objected to in the course of the entire picture, had caught him by surprise in front of a camera. The moment in which Preston Carr weighed, however briefly, the possibility of aborting the take, turning on Jock Finley, exposing him before the entire company.

Manning had caught that moment entirely by chance. The expression on Carr's grim, agonized face was as explicit as if it were a caption under a photograph, not in it.

"What do you think that was?" Manning asked.

Jock shook his head, negative. "What do *you* think it was?" he asked evasively.

"I think . . . " Manning said, "I think he felt something in himself that made him hesitate, made him wonder if he could do it. Maybe that was the first pain. He had pains he never let on to anybody, except Axel. Even his doctor. Axel thinks this could have been his first real, strong pain, and he was trying to decide whether to quit or not."

Jock nodded, "Possible. Fact, the more you look at it, the more possible it seems."

"That's what Axel thinks," Manning said, making it quite clear that there were other schools of thought on the subject. Jock was tempted to look up and across the table into the green eyes of the homosexual, who was subtly but quite clearly accusing him. Jock shoved the picture back toward Manning.

"I think . . . " Manning said, "I think that what he felt wasn't in himself. It was in that animal. That mustang didn't act, or react, like any of the others . . . "

"It was bigger, stronger," Jock said.

444

"It was bigger, stronger. And it was something else, too. Was that animal sedated with the dose Carr asked for?"

"Why, you sonofabitch, you fag sonofabitch! Just because I found out about you and Axel, you're going to try to cover that up by making diversionary accusations against me!"

The counterman, who had been cutting up vegetables for the day's stew, came out of the kitchen, staring, frightened, as both Jock and Manning rose up. Reaching across the table, Jock suddenly grabbed Manning by the jacket and shouted, "You fucking fag, you try to smear me, and I'll sue you and your god-damned magazine for fifty million dollars! I'll expose you! I'll tell them where you were and what you were doing when Axel should have been there, taking care of him!"

It would have made Jock feel better if Manning had gone pale or red or exhibited some fear of lawsuits involving millions of dollars. But Manning stood there, almost casual, cramped as he was with the bench at his knees, the table in his gut, and Jock's angry grip on his leather jacket. Manning neither resisted nor pulled away.

Finally Jock released him. Not even troubling to take back the photograph, Manning slipped out of the booth, out of the restaurant. Jock looked down at the picture, dared finally to pick it up. He shoved it into his pocket, started for the door when he noticed the counterman still staring.

"Some day, you may have to testify about all this! How that fag . . . that's what he is . . . he and that other guy that were in here! That fag was trying to blackmail me! Because I know about them!" Jock realized suddenly he was sounding too melodramatic. If there was any truth to what he said, about this counterman having to be a witness, he should use the episode to make a better record. "Full of degenerates like that, our business. They're treacherous. Dangerous. They only like their own kind! They hate everybody else! Try to destroy everybody else. Sorry about the blow-up!"

"S'okay," the counterman said. "You think he's going to make it? Mr. Carr, I mean?"

"So far, so good," Jock said, holding up two crossed fingers. He dropped a dollar on the counter and started out.

As he looked down the street he saw in the distance a car come hurtling off the desert road and into town at high speed. Followed by another car, and another. Then herding them all, a red-eyed patrol car. Jock knew the news was out. They would be here in droves now. Every newspaper, magazine, syndicate, and network would have men here in a matter of hours now.

Jock started back to the hospital. When he reached the door, the cars were already unloading their reporters and photographers. They invaded the small hospital the way Russians invade a satellite country, in overwhelming numbers, all at once and with all-encompassing effectiveness. Corridor, waiting room, admitting room office, door of Intensive Care, they seemed to be everywhere. It was amazing to the doctors, how much the reporters knew of the vital indications, dangers, and prognosis of heart attacks.

Jock, Axel, Manning, Joe, it took all of them to herd the press into the little waiting room so that the matter could be handled in the form of a press conference.

With the advent of television, all disasters, public and private, great and small, seemed to be handled by press conference as if all of life was merely an event arranged for its ultimate destiny, television.

Jock explained to the press that Preston Carr had become ill after the party marking the end of shooting of the picture. It had been looked upon at first as an indisposition due to too much champagne or food. He was taken to the hospital as a precaution. It was discovered here that he had, in fact, had a minor heart attack.

With that as prelude, Jock introduced the chief of the medical staff. A dour man in his mid-fifties, he was confronted by the press for the first time in his career. The doctor made it very clear at the outset that he was battling valiantly to save a gravely stricken man. As he had seen done on television, the doctor comported himself with an outward display of great professional calm and honesty, while discussing in detail the EKGs, the vital signs, and all other matters, which used to be deemed, not many years ago, to be personal and private matters, and which by medical ethics every doctor was forbidden to discuss with anyone save the patient's family. But the probing eye of the television camera plus the

446

resulting hunger for recognition in doctors had changed all that.

Once the doctor had established the gravity of the situation and the detailed condition of the patient at the moment, the conference was thrown open to questions, mainly about the intimate functions of the patient's various organs. All of which the doctor proceeded to answer, accented by, but never interrupted by, the continual flashes and flares of blinding photo bulbs. In the absence of photographs of famous patients, photos of their doctors seemed to satisfy audiences these days.

If Jock felt any distaste for this display of organized and vulgar curiosity, he had no time to indulge it. For a nurse was at his side, touching his arm, signaling him to step outside. He did. He feared word from Intensive Care. Instead it was the phone, several calls, all at once. All three lines of the hospital were holding for him.

He went to the supervisor's office. From there, through the glass window, he could see the switchboard and the operator on duty there. He picked up the phone, caught a familiar voice in mid-sentence "... and I have a right! Mr. Finley isn't sick! You got to let him get on the phone! He's my client..."

Jock calmed the Owl's frustrated anger with, "Marty ... I'm on."

"Well, it's about time!" the little, bald, round man said. "Okay, now what happened?"

"His heart. And it looks bad."

"Shut up!" the Owl counseled. "Don't say that. You're not a doctor. You don't know. Keep a good face on this, till it's no longer possible. Now, tell me, were you finished shooting?"

"Everything. Every last foot."

He could hear the relief in Marty White's voice. Reassured, the Owl could now luxuriate in details, "How did it happen?"

"He was getting laid. And pow!"

"Laid? By her? Boy, how many guys I heard say in my life, 'Fucking her could kill you, but what a way to go.' And it actually happened, actually happened," the Owl was saying. His moment of philosophic reflection indulged, he spoke rapidly, "Look, laddie, keep your mouth shut! Be the silent hero. Suffer. Sadly. But don't say a goddamn word. Till the right time. Then you'll have a public statement, a public tribute."

447

The last word made Jock ask, "Marty, what do you know about his condition?"

"His LA doctor called the hospital. About an hour and a half ago. Got the real word. He's bad. Very bad. If they can keep him alive forty-eight hours, he has a chance. That's the most optimistic estimate. A chance."

"They didn't tell me," Jock said.

"Look! Shut up! Don't say a word! If I hear anything, I'll get back to you!"

Marty hung up. The next call was from the studio head who was in New York with the president, on his way back to the Coast from Madrid. They were on a bridge phone, both spoke at once.

"Kid! Can you hear me?" the president was asking.

"Look, Finley, where the hell have you been? You should be calling us, not us looking all over Nevada for you!" The studio head was doubly indignant, on his own behalf, as well as on behalf of his president.

"Okay! I'm here. At the hospital!" Jock said angrily.

"Now, what happened?" the president demanded. Jock recited the story, omitting the specific details of exactly where Preston Carr was, and what he was doing at the moment of the attack. When Jock was through, the president, appearing as casual and disinterested as a highly tense, nervous president can, asked, "What about . . . well, did you finish shooting, kid?"

"Why else would I have been giving a party?"

"True, true." Meaning, good, good, and thank God. Because insurance or no, it was very difficult to explain to stockholders even such natural occurrences as heart attacks. Stockholders were a ruthless breed. Greatly gifted with hindsight, they sought men gifted only with foresight.

As with Marty, this conversation was far less tense, far less probing, once it was established that the shooting was completed.

The last thing the president said, "Congers will handle the press. He's on his way. So don't say anything."

"Just what the hell do you think there is to say?" Jock exploded.

"Easy, kid, easy. I know how attached you've become to the Old Man. All I'm saying is, don't do anything or say anything

448

in a moment of stress that might be subject to misinterpretation later on," the president counseled and consoled.

"Such as?" Jock persisted.

"Kid, you got the footage in the can? Sit on it. If it's great, like we hear, and this *is* his last picture, it could be of great value. I mean, it could boost the box office like say, ten million, domestic. I mean, if he dies it is top-of-the-show news on every network coast-to-coast. Even worldwide!"

"Thanks," Jock said, with the proper degree of bitterness.

"Kid, you're an artist. You were his friend, but businessmen like me have to account. To banks. To stockholders. Exhibitors. We have to think of all the sordid details. Do you think I like it? But that's my end of the business, and I'm stuck with it. So all I say, you got an artistic triumph, let it stand. Don't do anything . . . foolish . . . emotional. Don't say anything. You know?"

Allowing himself to be assuaged, Jock finally conceded, "I understand. Just that I've been working with this man, I know him, I respect him, I love him. That's right. Love him. He's the greatest. And to see him like this . . . it's not easy . . ."

"We understand, kid. We understand. When can we see the rough cut?"

"I don't know. I won't leave here till he's on his way to recovery."

"Sure, kid, sure," the president said. "Talk to you later."

The forty-eight hours had passed. Carr's condition did not improve. But neither did it worsen, which was a small victory.

By the end of the second day, disappointed that the big news had not peaked quickly, the press and TV began to depart. If they arrived in an air of tension, expectation, and excitement, they left dispirited, deceived, resentful. Preston Carr had let them down. Having been so stricken, he was bound, as by a debt of honor, to die, because they were there to cover it.

The hospital settled down, the town settled down. Daisy, her life having been filled mostly with young men, had never had a husband or a lover who had to be tended through any illness more severe than a hangover or a bout with the flu. For the first time in her life she could wait devotedly, smiling, serving, holding his hand, smiling, offering him a sip of cold fluid through a glass straw, smiling, helping the nurse to bathe him, and smiling. Doing all the things in a matter of hours and days that she had hoped to do for him, or some man, during a lifetime.

No other visitor was allowed to see Carr. Not Jock. Or even Joe Goldenberg. On the third day, assured that Carr's illness was under control and no serious worsening of his condition was anticipated, Joe decided to return to LA. When Daisy told Pres, he asked to see Joe. Reluctantly the doctor permitted it. Five minutes. No more. And only one person at a time. So that Joe saw Pres Carr alone.

When Joe came out, Jock was waiting, "How is he? How did he look? He say anything?"

"Only that he's tired."

"That's all he said? In five minutes?"

"He said some other things."

"Like?" Jock asked quickly.

"How he enjoyed working with me again. I should come out to the ranch some time, after he gets back. Things like that."

Relieved that he had not been the subject of conversation, Jock indulged in some optimism, "At least he sounds hopeful. The doctor said attitude is very important in cases like this."

"Yeah?" Joe asked skeptically. "I'll *shenk* you attitude. Give me a good EKG 'in cases like this.'" Then Joe added, "*Shenk* . . . that's a Yiddish word. It means—"

"I know what it means," Jock interrupted.

"Oh, yes. Sure. I forgot." And the fact of Jock's Jewishness seemed to sadden Joe.

"Look, Joe, thanks for everything. See you back in LA?" When Joe did not respond to the invitation, Jock added, "We'll work together again soon. I'll ask for you on my next picture. I hope you'll be available."

"Don't bother," Joe said with brisk sadness, and some irritation. "When will you young bastards ever learn! The greatness of another man does not diminish you. If he was a great picture actor, did that make you less a director? You should have appreciated him, gloried in his talent, loved him for it. Not hated him.

450

"But these days," Joe said angrily, "you young directors, you young actors, with you, brutality is a way of life! You use pictures as weapons, to express your own hostility. And I guess as long as the critics are as sick as you are, and pander to your sickness, you will be considered great.

"Well, not by me! I am old-fashioned! I like gentility. I like decent people. I like respect. I like pride, not arrogance. I believe that if a man has talent, that imposes an obligation on him. No privilege, no immunity from decency attaches to talent. Why you should think your talent gives you the right to be an unmitigated bastard, I don't know.

"I know one thing. I do not want to make pictures any more. Not with savages like you. This one was my last. And I'm glad it's over. Because I feel I've been a witness to a murder."

Joe started down the corridor toward the daylight, carrying his little bag of personal things and looking more like a tailor on his way to work than one of the world's finest cinematographers on his way back to his three-hundred-thousand-dollar home and his two-million-dollar art collection in Beverly Hills.

451

CHAPTER

16

THREE times that day Jock phoned Mary. What about the rough cut? When could he see it? And he did not want anyone else, not even her assistant, to see it till he did. Especially not the studio head, who had been back in LA for two days now. In her quiet, understated, undemonstrative way, Mary assured Jock that everything was coming along fine. A roughest of rough cuts would be available in about five days. The last bits and pieces, the reaction shots, the close-ups of Preston Carr were all very good, very much in character. In fact when you looked at them, knowing what the world knew now, about how ill he was, they took on added significance and impact. You could, in fact, look for and find the impending illness lurking in his eyes and in every line in his handsome, tired face.

Mary warned Jock that the multi-image opticals would be tricky, would take weeks. But all the necessary bits and pieces were there, and in her imagination she could cut the whole sequence together. It was always reassuring to talk to Mary. She never lied, never overstated an advantage, never underestimated a difficulty.

If things went well here at the hospital for another twenty-four hours, Jock decided he would leave for LA. But he would like to talk to Pres Carr before he did. More than like to, he wanted to very much. Had to! But the doctor kept saying no.

So, that afternoon, tired of hanging around the small, modern, chrome and plastic hospital in the small, dusty, plastic, desert town, Jock got into his Ferrari and drove back to the location. On the way, he did a leisurely eight-five, enjoying the wind against his face, the sense of movement, of being thrust forward, free and clear of huge worries for the moment. And, as usual, it was only when he was free of the pressures and concerns of a production that he began to realize how tired he was.

Tired in Jock Finley's world was two things. It was tired from lack of sleep, as he had been in the past four days. Waiting on word, spending most of his time in the hospital, taking Daisy out for coffee, for lunch, for dinner. Talking to her, keeping her thinking and feeling strong, affirmative. Not making love to her, though he did spend two whole nights with her. Somehow, after the things she had said that night in his car speeding toward the hospital, he could not have anything sexual to do with her. To know she didn't welcome it, like it, want it, was not even interested in it, that she did it, not for any satisfaction of her own, would now make sex with her seem to be masturbation.

For two nights she had lain curled up in his arms, because she could not fall asleep alone, even with the pills. So he held that precious body in his arms, that body most desired in the world, and had never even had an erection.

But driving alone, away from her, free, he could feel a deep, strong liveness in his groin. What a challenge it seemed, to marry her, or have a long wonderful affair with her and thus change her whole outlook on sex, life, men, everything. To rescue her from the strange world in which she lived, haunted by fame, inadequate to the enormous responsibilities thrust on her, seeking something she would never find, which was to be like every other woman, though every other woman was seeking to be like her.

The best thing, of course, would be for Carr to recover soon, marry her, and spend the rest of his life taking care of her. If she were able to have once, just once, a father who loved her, cared for her, wanted her, if that need were fulfilled, maybe that would cure her finally. Then she would not have to go to lecherous psychiatric fakes who abused her more than other men had ever done. So Jock told himself.

454

He had reached the place where he should turn off the highway and start over unpaved desert, over the road tracked by vehicles of the production caravan. The sign they had once posted as a marker for supply trucks and visitors was gone. As he drew close to the camp he could see why.

It was almost completely disassembled. Generator trucks, valuable and charged to a picture by the day, were gone. So were the equipment trucks with booms, dollies, huge cranes, camera track, reflectors, cable, and the million other pieces of equipment, simple and complex, that it took to shoot a picture. All that remained were a commissary truck to feed the dismantling crew, and a few personal trailers. His, Carr's, Daisy's.

The commissary, designed and built elsewhere but assembled here, was being disassembled now. A small crane and two fork-lifts took it apart, panel by panel, and loaded them on trucks. In another eight hours all trace of it would be gone too.

That was the way pictures were made. You built cities to make them. You disassembled cities when it was over. There was a sense of power in it, and much sadness too.

Jock walked over the earth which he had trod for weeks now, or was it months, years? Every picture, every production was the only thing in the world to him while it was going on. And it seemed to go on forever, till it was over suddenly. As this one was now over. Yes, there would be the editing, the arguments over music, over sound. There would be endless viewing and reviewing of the film, foot by tortured foot. Even more in this film than most others because of the multi-image effect, plus the fact that the studio had named this its "big" picture for the year. So they would spend millions just to advertise and publicize it, and they would be overbearingly careful, proprietary, and domineering at every finishing stage of the production. After the first cut of the film, a studio could, by contract, take the picture away from the director, could recut it or change it any damned way it pleased.

In effect, the last time this picture had really belonged to Jock Finley was the day, the last moment when he called out "Cut" on the last shot of Preston Carr, the day of the night of his heart attack.

Jock was overcome by a great empty longing as he walked the

tracked earth of the compound. There the projection trailer used to stand where he saw his dailies. And here the radio truck, where all those damned phone calls came in. The crew had slept there, the makeup people over there.

He exchanged greetings with a workman or a crew hand, and they asked how "he" was. Jock told them "he" was getting along fine and "he" was going to be okay. They were happy to hear it and went back to their work.

Jock climbed the steps into his own trailer. He emptied the drawers, throwing his things into several bags. He collected the various versions of the script, the many bundles of revised pages of different colors. Each bag, each bundle, he tagged either "home" or "studio" and left them all to be shipped back by the crew. He came out of his trailer for the last time, hopped into his red Ferrari, without opening the door, pulled away slowly. But at the last moment instead of making for the tracked road to the highway, he made a wide right turn, drove out toward the battleground to take one last look.

It was almost impossible to find the place. If it were not for the post holes of the temporary corral, there would be no sign at all. Be it the wind or the work of a meticulous work crew, all traces were gone. Where camera track had been laid and had made grooves in the ground, there was no longer any mark. Where hooves of frantic trapped mustangs had cut scars into the crusty earth, there was only desert dust. In some places, small red and purple flowers had sprung up, meaning there must have been rain sometime during the past four days.

He walked closer to the place where the corral had stood. The post holes were already filling up, being covered over and would soon be gone. The proud animals, captured, tethered there against their wild will, were all gone. Back to the foothills, Jock supposed. Suddenly, he was reminded about his promise to Carr, that one last mustang, the one he wanted when the picture was over. What had ever happened to that one? Did someone remember to keep it captive? Had it been sent, as promised, to the Carr ranch? Jock made a resolve to pursue that, to find out. But he never would. Promises made too late are never kept.

Jock took one last slow look around the battleground. This was

456

where a man had lived and, for all real purposes, died, working his heart out, giving all the strength, every talent he possessed to put on film something that would outlast him by a hundred years. Something which would excite, grip, amuse, and entertain millions of people. For a long time, Jock stared, wondering if it had been worth it. Then he leaped into his Ferrari and was about to accelerate, but instead he leaped out. This time he opened the door and got in. He slammed the door, started away.

When he arrived at the hospital, there had been no change. Carr was still conscious, feeling better, sleeping less, still on liquids, still exhibiting, with continued regularity, an irregular EKG. He was living through that first five days of a heart attack when the best thing that could happen was nothing.

The doctors thought it desirable that everyone except Daisy leave, so that hospital and patient could settle down. For even though no one except Daisy was allowed to see Carr, there was an unsettled air that in some invisible way transmitted itself to the patient. He was aware, alert to it.

Jock had only one request to make of the doctor. He would like, if it would not endanger the patient, to see Carr before he left. The doctor thought a moment, and with that new air of gravity which he had learned in those two days of press conferences, he finally answered, "Considering his condition, vital signs, attitude of increased interest, I would say yes. You can see him. But briefly. Do not say or do anything to increase his anxiety. That is most important."

"Naturally," Jock said. He went to the door, pushed it open quietly. The nurse made a sign from the bedside, the patient was asleep. Jock looked up at the battery of electronic graphs and oscilloscopes which were working in a reassuringly persistent and monotonous way, bouncing and moving across the screen. Then he withdrew.

As he backed out of the door, Daisy rushed to his side, seized his arm, asked desperately, "What happened? What's wrong?"

"Nothing, honey. The doctor gave me permission to see him before I go. That's a good sign."

457

She nodded. Any comfort was huge comfort after five days of waiting, hoping.

"Is there anything I can do for you back in LA? Anything I can send, anyone I can call?"

She shook her head. She was too fearful to need anything or to ask for anything, except that he recover.

"If there is, call me. And don't worry. He'll be okay. In fact, we'll make a date now, I'll come out to the ranch after you two are married and settled down. We'll talk about this as if it were old times. You'll see," he promised, hoping that his baby-blues were really selling now, because the look on her face was one of fear, great fear. "Do something for me. Once, before I go, smile? Please?"

She tried. When she smiled, her white face, untouched by make-up, framed by her carelessly naturally curly blond hair, was lovely. But the smile could not hold together for long. The tears started. He had to put his arms around her, hold her very tight. She pressed against him. He could feel the gasps surge through her body, even though he could not hear them. He was holding her thus when he became aware that Manning was only a few feet away, using his Minox with his usual swift agility. Jock glared at him, angrily, but for Manning that only provided the opportunity for another shot and yet another.

The nurse came out now. Mr. Carr was awake. They could go in to see him. One at a time. Very quietly. For very brief visits. Daisy asked Jock to go in first. She had to recover, remove all trace of tears, give him the smiling, bright, white face, the clear happy eyes that he liked to see. Jock released her and started into the room.

He entered with meticulous care, sliding rather than stepping lest he make any disturbing sound, till one shoe scraped the vinyl floor, causing Preston Carr to open his eyes. He spied Jock, stared for a moment, closed his eyes again, as if too tired to show any interest or emotion.

Jock studied Carr's face. Strange how old a man could become in five days of illness. His hair was beginning to betray streaks of gray, which had been carefully concealed before. The beard was growing in white in contrast to the black of his thin, dyed moustache. The white stubble accented his jowls, which the tan skin had somehow camouflaged.

This was no movie star, no King. This was an old man.

Carr opened his eyes again. Jock spoke the first word, "Pres? Hi. How do you feel?" Carr nodded, indicating satisfactory. "Good. Good!" Jock exclaimed in a strong whisper.

Carr closed his eyes again.

"You're coming along fine. Daisy, too. So I'm going back to LA. I think it's just great the way you two found each other, because you need each other so much. It's going to be great. Great!"

Helpless, guilty, Jock was at a loss for words, all words except the cheapest coinage of movie talk—"great." "Great" was the cement that held most conversations together. Nothing was less than great. It meant yes. It meant maybe. It meant don't bother me. It meant the picture, the weather, see you at dinner, meet you in bed, at my place or yours.

If it began to sound not quite sincere enough, you changed occasionally from "great" to "terrific." But it was really the same empty word.

Jock could feel the word stick to his tongue as if it were a fish hook embedded there. He couldn't shake it or dislodge it. He had great news from LA. The almost-finished rough cut was great. The studio head sent his regards, delighted to hear Pres was doing great. Jock had been out to the location, great how those guys took a whole city apart in a few days. It was the kind of nimble-footed, counterfeit, and thoroughly uneasy conversation in which if someone suddenly told you World War III had just started, you would automatically have said, "Great!"

All the while Carr's eyes remained shut. Jock leaned in, saw his slight breathing, thought perhaps Carr was asleep. But as soon as he stopped talking, Carr opened his eyes. A signal to go on.

"Pres, you'll love this. Mary, my cutter? Spoke to her yesterday. With all the pieces assembled, she says the right opticals are going to make that multi-image sequence great! Terrific! Sensational!"

Jock paused. Carr opened his eyes.

"New York called. The president said they're voting a four-million-dollar advertising and exploitation budget. Remember

459

when you could make eight pictures for that kind of money?"
Jock asked, smiling too ingratiatingly.

Pres looked at him, unsmiling, challenging, as if asking, who
invited you into my old days, when pictures were made far, far
differently from now?

If it was what Carr intended, or only what he read into it, Jock
could not know. All he did know was that as long as Carr kept his
eyes open he had to keep talking. About anything, everything. If
only the man would say something, or give some clear sign. But
he lay quietly, listening. And breathing. Suddenly, Jock found
himself improvising.

"Oh, Mary said that one big take works sensationally! Even in
the rough cut! She said it is even twice as powerful coming after
the buildup than it was just by itself. And you know how powerful
that was!"

When he told this first lie, Jock realized suddenly that he had
arrived at his own prognosis. Preston Carr would never recover.
He might go on breathing, for hours, days, weeks, but he would
never recover. He was too old, too tired, too damaged by the
severe strain of recent weeks to survive. You tell a dying man anything, because you never have to deliver. So one lie could follow
another.

"Oh, by the way, Pres, that mustang! We've got it ready and
waiting for your shipping instructions." Carr tried to nod. It was
the first thing Jock had said which seemed to elicit approval. It
forced Jock to talk on, to say whatever thing might come into his
mind that he thought would please, stimulate, or interest Preston
Carr. The best thing Jock could do would be to get out. And he
knew it. Yet somehow he couldn't.

Nor was it enough for Jock to talk. He must hear the man talk
before he left. He needed something from him. Some word, some
sign of acceptance. Approval. Comradeship. During all the days
when he drove him, challenged him, seduced, bullied, lied to him,
tried to demean him, he had never once felt equal to him.

Had it been that Carr was King and Jock Finley felt a strong
need, as any young, proud director might, to feel superior to
the King? Or to any star? Was that what it was all about?
Right or wrong, if you were a director, it was necessary, vital, to

460

dominate everything you saw, every person with whom you came in contact.

Stars, presidents, studio heads, critics, audiences! By one means or another, by guile, threat, sham, or playing the game, you must dominate them by making them do what you wanted, see what you wanted, respond as you wanted, and love you, laud you, and pay for it.

Why, then, after having accomplished all that, so that now studios would risk millions of dollars on his talent, why did the estimation, the regard of one tired, old, dying man . . . yes, dying . . . man mean so much? But it did! If Carr were not dying it would not have been a matter of such desperate urgency for Jock to get the word from him now.

Jock Finley needed, needed desperately, what only Preston Carr could bestow. Acceptance, equality, regard, affection.

That was what Jock Finley wanted now. From Preston Carr. A word, or even a smile, or a nod of the head that said, You're good, you're okay, kid, as good as we ever were. You have my permission to be one of the greats.

The legends of our youth never leave us. We grow up, we may even outdo them, but we only think less of our achievements so that we need not measure ourselves against them. The past is hallowed. The heroes of our past are giants, casting shadows over us the rest of our lives. Even while we do those things which will cast shadows over our sons, we are looking back at the past, at the giants, wanting to be as large and as good.

We scoff at them, but we need them, need their approbation, their consent to go on and be greater.

Jock needed that now. He needed more, too. Needed to explain, if explanations could help, about that scene, that animal, that surprise. If he could not justify it now, he would never be able to justify it.

He had run out of meaningless things to say. He had been unduly happy about Daisy's strength in this time of trial. About the doctor's estimate of Pres's prognosis. About the studio's prognosis for the picture. Now all those things were out of the way, all "great"-ed and gone.

But there was yet one last thing to talk about.

461

Carr, his eyes closed, was breathing shallowly. Jock heard himself saying with sudden urgency and more voice, "Pres . . ."

Carr opened his eyes as though rescued from the absentmindedness of aged drowsing. He looked up, eyes turning slowly to find Jock.

"Pres . . . about that scene. I want to explain! It was as much for your sake as mine. I didn't want you to spend the rest of your life saying to yourself, 'I could have done it better if I'd had the chance, if he'd made me do it again.'

"You know that empty futile feeling in your gut when you leave a projection room and say, 'Damn, we could have done that better.' At the previews you know it, only more so. Finally, at the premiere, when everyone else is applauding politely, you feel that bitter taste in your mouth and say to yourself, 'Fools, if only they'd seen it the way we could have done it, should have done it, they'd be up out of their seats screaming their applause.' You know what I mean, don't you?"

There was no sign from Carr, no smile, no reaction, except that his eyes closed now.

"So I thought, I'll give him the chance. I won't ask him. I won't let him think about it. He's a great man, with great instincts. I'll let him face it suddenly and react. If it's too much for him, he'll know it and abort the scene. Otherwise, he'll rise to it with that greatness he has. He'll put on film for all time a scene that'll stand like a . . ."

In his earnestness, he had gone too far and too fast, for suddenly the word was out ". . . like a monument . . . to his career."

Carr opened his eyes. They turned quickly toward Jock. Those eyes which had been able to transmit so much to so many millions of people revealed little to Jock now. Neither hostility nor forgiveness, neither understanding nor condemnation. If it was anger, it was not clear. If it was condemnation, it was too tired. Then the eyes looked away, up at the ceiling, and closed.

"That moment when you hesitated, Pres, what were you thinking? Was it only whether to go on with the scene? Was it anger? Or was it . . . was it hatred for me? I would like to know!"

There was no answer.

"Even if it was hatred, I have to say now, I would do it again.

That's right, Pres, to me that is more important than anything or anybody in the world. Make it live, get it on film! And everything else in the world is second! Everything!"

Pres turned his head slightly in Jock's direction. The black eyes glanced at him, a quick glance, sharp, direct, like a short, sudden straight left at a boxer who didn't expect it. Jock stopped, hardly completing the last syllable of that last word. If Preston Carr was going to talk, he wanted neither to inhibit nor interrupt him. But Carr did not speak. He just looked, waited, breathing in small, economical inhalations.

"Would you have wanted me to be content with less?" Carr did not answer. "You'd want it to be right. The best! Wouldn't you?

"I know you said never to surprise you. Not with the camera rolling. Still, that one scene had to work that way. Because the fact that you didn't know gave it the suspense, that real sense of life-and-death danger which, once you capture it, lives on and on. I had to do it that way! And because I did, you have a scene now that is a classic.

"That's right, a classic! That's what *Life* is going to say on its cover. With a big shot of you. 'Birth of a Classic!' That should make up for everything, should explain everything.

"Or is that small consolation? Maybe I should have left you the way I found you. Preston Carr, retired star, ranchman, horse breeder, oilman, investor, bachelor, lover, living on the most of the best in this whole wide world. After all, you were entitled to that. You earned it. You went out and fought for it, won it. Won it bigger and better than anyone ever did in pictures! Maybe I resented that. Maybe I said to myself, that smug, rich, comfortable bastard, with the best the entire world has to offer in food, drink, women, and security! I'll shake him loose! I'll stir him up! I'll prove something to him!

"Or maybe part of it was the way you handled me. I resented being the smart-ass young director who knew every angle, who gave you the big sell. Except that all the while you were expecting me and knew all about it. So when I left I felt like a damn fool and swore I'd even the score.

"I don't know. Maybe it was just as simple as what it started to be. I needed you to get this picture made. So I set out to get

463

you, and you had nothing to do with it. Once I got you, I decided that I was going to use you to the very best and most of your talent, so that when it was over they'd say, 'Finley got things out of Preston Carr that no one ever suspected were there.' If it was all those things,. or none of them, I knew I had to drive you, challenge you, use you to get a performance and a film that everyone would respect and remember long after . . . after we're both gone.

"One day in acting class in New York, the teacher, one of the most respected in the world, said, 'An actor lives to be challenged. Challenge him correctly and he will perform miracles he never knew he had within him. Surprise him and he becomes great in a flash, an instant! He will die trying, rather than admit that anything is beyond him. An actor *acting* an emergency can be technically great. An actor *in* an emergency in which his own identity and being as an actor are challenged will be really great, truly great. What he is will make him do what he must. Which is why some fine actors, and even some bad ones, have done a scene while very ill, made their exit, and dropped dead not three feet out of view of the audience.

"'An actor will do anything except appear weak, ill, or inept in front of an audience. That is the stuff of actors, and all of them have it, to a greater degree, or a lesser, depending on their talent. The need to *seem* to be is greater even that the need to *be*. That is the secret of all great acting and all great actors.'

"That was the only thing of value about acting I have ever heard in many classes and from many teachers. Yes, Pres, I started out to be an actor. God, how terrified I was. And how bad. My last teacher said it best, 'Finestock,' he said, 'you are a terrible actor. But anybody with such great desire for theater and so little talent for acting should make a good director.' I hope he was right. But it was by being an actor, or wanting to, that I got my understanding of how actors feel and why, and how they can be manipulated and used.

"Maybe that kind of power should never be put into the hands of men, young men. Young men like me. Because there comes a time . . . I can say this now . . . remember that first night, I told you about Muni and directing him. Well, I didn't quite tell it all.

"Oh, it happened. Just the way I told you. But I left one thing

464

out. When I chose Muni, it wasn't only because he could give such a great performance in the role. There was one thing more. He had a name and a reputation that were great, so that by sheer association and reflection of his glory a kid like me would gain stature. So that someday, somewhere, in some tight corner, when I desperately needed a star for some project, I could let it drop that I had directed Muni! I used that great man and his love for acting as a calling card, as a reference. That was a pretty cheap thing to do with a great man's talent and reputation.

"And yet, Pres, you're as much to blame for that as I am! Admit it! That day, when I told you about Muni, it did impress you. It changed your mind about working with me. I was no longer a kid you'd vaguely heard about. Suddenly I became a real director in your eyes, an important director. So you see, Pres, we all play the same game. Don't we?" Jock pleaded earnestly. "Don't we?"

There was no answer. Out of hostility or contempt or sheer exhaustion, Preston Carr was not going to answer. And Jock Finley finally knew that. He turned away, but couldn't bring himself to leave.

"I could have let you go easy, Pres. Then, and now. But I feel I have to be honest with you. It's the least I owe a man like Preston Carr. I did it to you. I gave Tex the order. No sedation for that horse! I even lied about it. I told him *you* wanted it that way. Now you can curse me, hate me, call me a no-good, deceitful, dangerous bastard, call me anything you want. But I will tell you, I would do it again, to get you as great as you were in that scene and have it forever, on film!

"And as long as we're being honest, there is one thing you can do for me. You can say you understand. That you think that I did the right thing for the picture. And for Preston Carr. You can do what Muni did, you can say, 'God bless you.' Pres?"

Having finished, Jock did not turn back to Carr. He waited for some sign, some sound. There was none. Perhaps the man was making a gesture. Jock turned to see. But instead Jock saw clear and plain, the blips were gone from the screen. Now the door opened, the nurse burst into the room, "The monitors! They stopped . . . they . . ." She looked down at Carr, turned to call down the hall, "Doctor, Doctor!"

The nurse's cry brought Daisy in before the doctor. One look, and she knew that it was too late. She burst into tears and would have collapsed, but Jock held her tightly, pressing her against him. She tried to bury her head in his chest. He stared down at Preston Carr, wondering if he had heard. All of it? Any of it? Had he heard enough to understand or to forgive before he died?

Now the doctor was here. And Manning with his prying, persistent Minox. Manning had it all, a complete, precious exclusive on the death of Preston Carr, the bereavement of Daisy Donnell, the look on Jock Finley's face as he consoled Daisy while staring down stunned, at Preston Carr's lifeless body.

CHAPTER

17

Five weeks had gone by. The editing was taking longer than Jock liked. And the calls from New York, frantic and frequent, had not helped. But there was merger talk in New York. A conglomerate company, which originally made air-conditioners, and which had since gathered under its wing a tool-and-die plant, an auto rental company, a manufacturer of female-hygiene products, and an agricultural chemical company, was seeking to acquire a film company.

And the president was seeking some corporate cyclone cellar to protect him from the persistent pressure by stockholders, and seeking as well, of course, a new stock-option deal.

Negotiations were pretty far along. One factor in setting the ultimate price was how big a picture *Mustang!* promised to be, box-office-wise. So the president called almost every day. The head of the studio dropped into Jock's editing room, when he walked between his office and the commissary, both before and after lunch.

The potential of *Mustang!* could mean the difference between the company's stock being exchanged at sixty-six dollars a share or an even seventy. With more than eight million shares involved, *Mustang!* might literally be worth its weight in gold on that basis alone.

But that did not help or facilitate the editing. Nothing can speed or take the place of the process of endless cutting, splicing, and running, recutting, resplicing, and rerunning. Nothing can avoid the tyranny of the Moviola, in which, on a small screen no more than a dozen inches wide, a man can see his ambitions, his hopes, his accomplishments, and his blunders, over and over, and be powerless to change them. Modify them, yes. Change them, no.

There had been times when Jock Finley found editing to present a challenge and an excitement all its own. For there was as much skill, ingenuity, and creativity in taking footage which was deficient in some way because it was less than you had imagined during shooting, and skillfully rendering it so close to what you had wanted as to achieve the effect, despite its shortcomings.

But this time, for Jock, editing had become a grind. Perhaps it was the face of Preston Carr, seen endlessly, the same scene over and over, cut, recut, and re-recut a dozen times or more. Carr smiling, Carr frowning, Carr looking lovingly, Carr resenting, Carr kissing, Carr hating, Carr loving, Carr roping, Carr in combat, Carr under tension, Carr thoughtful, Carr concerned, Carr resigned, Carr stripped to the waist, Carr in battered old hat, Carr rope in hand, Carr planted firm, Carr rolling on the ground, Carr in pain, Carr bloodied, Carr joking, Carr sweating, Carr grimacing, Carr seizing a lariat, Carr tossing a lariat, Carr kissing Daisy's naked breast, Carr being kissed, Carr imprisoning that mustang, Carr setting it free, Carr hesitating, Carr deciding to continue combat, Carr, Carr, Carr!

Jock blamed the pressure from New York, the stupid, urgent need for speed. So he worked fourteen, fifteen hours a day. Mary was with him all the time. In truth, his drive was not due to New York at all. It was the need, simply, to have the editing over with!

The need to be free of the need to have to look at Preston Carr's face hour after endless hour on that damned Moviola.

Jock would admit many things, would blame many people, but he would never admit that. So at night, after long, long hours at editing he had no particular need for a woman, any woman. He had seen Louise half a dozen times since he returned. They had dinner together, they talked, they went to see other films. They had even had sex a few times. But something was missing. He blamed that other guy, who it turned out was an attorney with a big real-estate firm in Beverly Hills and wanted to marry her. But since Louise was not involved with him in a sexual way, it shouldn't have changed or inhibited the sex she shared with Jock.

Yet there was no denying, it was not the same any more. She knew it. He knew it. Nothing was the same any more.

Of course, there was Daisy. But the two times he had seen her since the week after the funeral, those last two times, they did not have sex. It was a reaction to the seven days and nights of mourning when he was with her in bed almost constantly. As though her tenuous hold on sanity had depended on his stiff prick. The pills could not do it. Nor the liquor. Only he, only that part of him, had been able to soothe her sufficiently to let her slip exhaustedly into a few hours of sleep during those days and nights.

It had not been easy for him. Perhaps it was that night ride to the hospital, the things she had said. Or being compelled to make love to her from the sheer terror of what might happen if he didn't. But those seven days and seven nights in that bed with her had left a mark on him comparable to the scars he would always bear from Julie West.

There would never be the same sock to the old Jock again. He had hoped that when he returned to Louise it would be different. That it would go back to being the same wonderful, easy, carefree sex again. Sex that never palled, never tired, never waned, never needed gymnastics or innovations or indulgence in the personal aberrations of the other partner. Just straight, simple, clean, healthy sex. Fun and excitement, almost every time. And release. Pleasure. Contentment. When the biggest complication was who was going to get up and go make the drinks or get a fresh pack of cigarettes.

But that was old times, laddie, old times.

There was a film to edit. And Daisy had been settled down for a while with a new analyst, a new regimen of permanent sedation. It seemed she would not be overdoing anything soon, even by miscalculation.

469

So Jock was not called on to deliver or make good on those promises he had made to himself about her during the days of Preston Carr's final illness.

Aside from the night he had made himself exceedingly drunk at Mary's apartment, and slept with her, he had done little else but edit, edit, edit. And keep looking at that face, Carr's face.

And answer or avoid phone calls from New York.

During the last day of the fourth week, while Jock was working on the opening moments of the big battle scene, the phone rang. It was Congers, from New York, head of all company publicity and public relations. He was talking from the office of the president, who took over the phone now.

"Kid! You'll never believe it! Sixteen pages *and* the cover! Congers just brought in the advance copy. Sixteen pages!"

"Sixteen pages of what?" Jock demanded.

"Of *Life! Life!* Sixteen pages and the cover! It's the biggest spread for a picture in *Life*'s history! I bet you this boosts the stock five dollars a share at the market opening! The merger is in the bag! Did you buy that stock like I told you last month? Kid?"

With little jubilation, Jock asked, "What's the cover? What did they use?"

"Carr naturally. That shot of him alone, where he's just about to move into his final attack on that mustang. Great shot! The look on Carr's face is like a painting . . . a painting, kid!"

"Yeah, yeah, I know."

"Look, I'm having Congers put two copies in the evening pouch. They'll be on the plane tonight, in the studio in the morning."

"Great."

"Great? The greatest! Greatest publicity I've ever seen for a picture, kid! You can be real proud!"

"Yeah. Great."

"Call me soon as you see it. Okay? Kid?"

"Yeah," Jock said.

"Good . . . good."

470

"Oh, by the way, what title did they put on it?"

"'Birth of a Classic'. Sensational, huh?" the president gloried.

"Oh, great. Great."

The next morning Jock was at the studio, in his office, at eight o'clock. When eight-thirty arrived and the copy of *Life* did not, he began calling the mail room. Within fifteen minutes he had the envelope in his hands. But instead of reading it at once, he left, went down to the parking lot, got into his Ferrari, and drove up into the hills, high and away from studios, LA, smog.

Higher and higher, up into the scarred yellow hills of Hollywood the red Ferrari climbed. The road twisted, turned, hairpinned, higher and higher, leaving behind the close-packed houses, eventually the solitary ones, finally all signs of all the vulgar architecture that defaces the arid but noble California earth.

When he was above the city, when he could see the festering cloud below him, he stopped the car. Removing his sunglasses, he settled down to rip open the envelope and read the article in *Life*.

"Birth of a Classic" by Manning. Who was himself a star, needing only his last name to identify him to the world.

The cover was Preston Carr in hesitation. It was a huge, bold shot, with all the color and rough texture of the desert, with the red hills against the blue sky in counterpoint. Carr was to the left of the frame and the mustang, rearing, was to the right. Carr was staring up at the beast, but plain on his face, in his stance, was the hesitation which preceded his final joining of battle.

Inside, sixteen pages were devoted to *Mustang!*, including the centerfold, which was a huge shot of Carr and Daisy in the most intimate moment of their love scene with Daisy nude from the waist up. But shots of the action within the film were only a small part of the layout.

Most of the sixteen pages was given over to photos of Preston Carr, the star. Some of Manning's shots were uncanny in their ability to catch clearly on Carr's face his inner turmoil and resentment. The sense of a man aware every moment that he was dealing with precious currency, his own life. And that he was expending it at too fast a rate.

There were shots of Carr alone. Carr in Makeup, Carr and Daisy. Carr and Joe Goldenberg, Carr selecting a mustang, Carr and Jock Finley. One of Carr and Finley in which there was no secret of Carr's anger. There was the Carr of the cruel muscle cramp, writhing on the ground. Carr exhausted by combat, slipping down the back of the truck to collapse. There was Tex giving an animal a shot of sedative before a battle scene. There was a shot of Jock Finley, watching the final battle over Joe's shoulder.

It could have been the arrangement of the pictures, or the few subtle suggestions in the text, but without any statement to that effect, the article said clearly, and for all to know, that this story was about a star who would rather die than fail, of a star who had given all he had to prove to the new critics, the new generation, the New Wave directors of the world, that the old stars were really the great ones.

About the cover shot there was a whole paragraph in the text, explaining the difficulty of the scene, the need for it in the film, the need for it as a single continuous take, with the strongest of the mustangs. Here Manning permitted himself the editorial speculation as to what chance of fate brought Preston Carr up against this particular beast for the greatest, and as it turned out, last effort of his life. Had Preston Carr, in choosing this animal as he had done, decided to go out in a blaze of glory? Or had it been simply an unwise, foolhardy, or unfortunate choice?

Read it as Jock would, one big fact emerged. Step by step, bit by bit, with photos to prove it, Manning had made it quite clear, without ever saying it, that to satisfy his ego, or to avenge himself on Preston Carr because of Daisy Donnell, or to make the classic Western, Jock Finley had killed a great star.

If there was any doubt, Manning's final sentence said it all, "Thus, I witnessed it, the birth of a classic, the death of a star!"

That fag, that fucking fag, Jock was saying to himself as he dropped his sunglasses down over his eyes, started the Ferrari, and pulled away. He headed down again, toward the cloud of smog and the shadowy city that hid under it.

In a rage which prevented him from remembering later exactly

472

how he had been able to get back without having an accident, Jock arrived at the studio. He slammed into his office, picked up his private line, dialed Marty White on his private line so that the Owl himself picked up the phone.

"Laddie, I've been waiting for you to call! Some spread! Sixteen pages! From now on, no matter what you do, or how you do it, you are a big name. Worldwide! Nothing unimportant is ever going to happen to you again! This'll do for you what Taylor did for Burton!"

"Marty, I want to keep this issue from hitting the stands!"

"Laddie?"

"I want to sue that bastard and that magazine!"

"Are you crazy?" Marty exploded.

"I'm on my way down to a lawyer right now, Marty! Right now!"

"Laddie! Laddie, listen to me! You wait right there! I'll be right over! Okay?"

Jock slammed down the phone.

Little Marty White sat in his high, fan-back, black patent leather swivel chair, his fingers still on the phone, playing nervously. The studio head? Or the president? Or his own lawyer? Which one to call first? The studio head really didn't count. The president? Why send out an alarm when there wasn't even a fire yet? His lawyer! That was the answer. Marty dialed. Held on. Waited. Then heard the attorney's voice.

"Murph? Marty. You going to be in your office a while? Good. I'll be over. Something I want to show you. I want your opinion."

Within the hour two advance copies of *Life* were lying on two different attorneys' desks in two different air-conditioned offices within a few blocks of each other on Wilshire Boulevard.

In the office of Edward Grant, partner in Grant, Harris, Mendelson, & Grant, Jock Finley paced as Edward Grant, Senior, turned the sixteen pages of *Life* slowly, dwelling on the text, then studying the photographs, then going on to the next page and the next.

473

Jock paced, but glanced frequently at Grant's face in an effort to find there a fraction of the indignation and seething anger he himself felt. Grant was a man in his early sixties, with an excellent reputation for fighting and winning large plagiarism and defamation suits against the major studios. It was said in Beverly Hills that if Edward Grant took your case, it was already half won, since the studios were afraid of him.

When Grant was through, he thought a moment, looked up, and asked, "Just what is the nature of your complaint, Mr. Finley?"

"What is the nature . . . ?" Jock exploded. "That goddamn fag is saying that I killed Preston Carr! He's trying to destroy me! Trying to make sure that no other star will work with me! That's slander, isn't it? Attacking a man that way?"

"Well," Grant said, speaking more softly and slowly than normal, as he generally did when confronted by an emotional client, "in the first place, if he did what you say, it is not slander but libel."

"That's even worse, isn't it?" Jock demanded.

"Yes. And in a magazine with such a large circulation, it is quite serious. If, indeed, it did happen."

Disappointed that he had not found an immediate champion, Jock unconsciously began to turn his hostility on Grant.

"*If? If?* What is that right there on your desk? He's calling me a murderer!"

"Well, not exactly," Grant said, picking up the magazine again.

"Not exactly? You mean that most people reading that article, seeing those pictures, won't come away with the conclusion that I killed Carr? That I forced him to overwork even though I knew he had a heart condition?" Jock demanded.

Grant looked up from the magazine at Jock then he asked, again slowly, softly, "Mr. Finley, take this yellow pad and this pen and list for me precisely what's happened to you as a result of this article."

"What's happened?" Jock asked, confused.

"What damage you've suffered. After all, that would be the basis of our case. Damage."

"Damage? How do I know? It isn't even out yet! Nobody's seen it except a few guys at the studio and Marty White."

474

"So there's no damage?" Grant seemed to contemplate.

"I'm here to prevent them from damaging me! I'm asking you to get an injunction, a court order, something to keep them from destroying my reputation!" Jock was beginning to shout from indignant frustration.

"Mr. Finley, do you know what's involved in getting an injunction? Even a temporary injunction? We'd have to go to court. Make our case. Which is not the best case I've ever seen. And post a bond of some three or four hundred thousand dollars, possibly more. That's what it would cost to stop an issue of *Life*. Because if we're wrong, if we lose this case, they'd be the injured party, and they'd have to be protected."

"I'm willing to post a bond!"

"And there's my fee. I couldn't touch a case as involved and chancy as this one for less than a twenty-five-thousand-dollar retainer."

"I didn't ask what it would cost, did I?" Jock demanded.

"No," Grant admitted, though unimpressed.

"Well?" Jock waited.

Grant thought a few minutes, then glanced at the magazine again, mainly at the last four pages. Then he closed the copy, gently pushed it across the desk and said, "No, Mr. Finley. I don't think so."

"What do you mean, you don't think so?"

"I don't think I'd like to handle this case."

"My reputation is involved here! I'm entitled to legal representation!"

"Of course, Mr. Finley, but not necessarily by me. There are plenty of good lawyers in Beverly Hills."

"I want you!" Jock insisted, being denied having made him more insistent.

"I'm afraid that won't be possible," Grant said softly, but with unmistakable finality.

With anger that now bordered on contempt, Jock snatched the copy of *Life* from the desk, "Boy, no wonder you've got a good reputation. You only take cases you're sure you'll win."

"Young man, if you want to know why I won't take your case,

I'll tell you. But I don't want to discuss it with you. And I won't stand for rudeness or arrogance in my office."

Jock's silence was as much of an apology as he was capable of making. It was enough for Grant.

"In the first place, I don't think most people would consider this article libelous. What I got from it was that you are a bright, highly capable, young director. Difficult, driving, overbearing, disliked, hated perhaps, but capable. So that from a professional point of view this article may not be damaging at all. Not exactly ideal grounds for a libel suit."

"He as much as says that I killed Carr!"

"Yes . . ." Grant admitted reluctantly, "I suppose one could get that impression. But that's all it is, an impression. My advice, though, would be to forget it!"

"I won't stand for being called a murderer!"

"Oh, I know that," Grant said. "That's why I suggested you go see another lawyer. But as for me, sorry."

Jock turned angrily, dismissing Grant in that one swift gesture. He was at the door, when Grant said, "There's one piece of advice you can have for free, Finley."

Jock turned back, glared angrily.

"Aside from my strong caution not to sue, there's one other thing. If I were you I wouldn't talk to anybody while I'm as angry as you are. You're liable to say things you'll be sorry for, things that'll prejudice your case. For example, there's not a word or hint in that article about Carr having had a previous heart attack. I took a second look to make sure.

"*Did* you know Carr had had a previous heart attack? Don't tell me. I don't want to know. I just want to point out to you the danger of talking when you're overemotional. Good day, Finley."

In the offices of Murphy, Rose, Engles, & Moscow, on Wilshire Boulevard, Marty White was just concluding his conference with Dennis Murphy, senior partner.

"What do you think, Murph?"

"He's crazy if he sues."

"But does he have a case? If he goes to a lawyer, will he take it?"

476

"For a good fee, he'll find a lawyer. He won't win, but he'll create quite a stink before he loses," Murphy said.

"And hurt the picture?" Marty asked.

"It's lousy publicity, Marty."

"So the trick is to keep him from suing?"

"That's the trick. But I don't have to tell you what some of these crazy, talented young bastards can do when they get angry," Murphy said regretfully.

"No, Murph, you don't." Marty took the copy of *Life* off Murphy's desk.

It was evening. Jock Finley was mixing himself another drink at the bar, out back near the pool. It was his fourth. No, his fifth. Scotch and soda. And the Scotch was Preston Carr's brand, of which he still had two cases.

He had followed Grant's advice, though he resented it. He had not gone to see another lawyer that day, but he had arranged an appointment for the next morning, with an attorney famous for handling the complicated matrimonial affairs of movie stars. Since making that appointment by phone, he had been drinking. Steadily. Good stiff angry drinks, where the Scotch rose up over the five cubes of ice and there was hardly enough room for soda.

The more he drank, the angrier he became. That goddamn fag! That bastard Manning! He wouldn't get away with it! He wouldn't!

By the time Louise arrived, he was vicious, cruel. This time when she stripped and dove into the pool it was to avoid him, avoid his foul words and angry threats against Manning and *Life*.

But he was in the pool after her, naked, brown, alive, tense, erect. Erect as only anger could make him. When she allowed him to come close to her, to embrace her, to enter her, it was more to let the anger burst out of him than to derive any satisfaction. When he was done with her, and released her, letting her slip away, she sank into the water and made her way along the bottom coming up at the farthest end from him.

Low in the water, her lips just above the surface, so that her soft voice carried, she said, "Jock, you're razor blades all over.

477

What's happened to you?" He didn't answer, just turned over on his back, then angled down into the water and came up close to her, ready to make love again. She turned away, eluding him.

"No, Jock. Please?" He glared at her, angry, fierce. "If it would help you to hit me, go ahead. But don't make love to me. Please?"

He turned away. He reached the steps, climbed out. He crossed to the chaise with the phone resting on it. He hesitated, then picked up the phone, dialed the operator, and asked to put through a call to Manning at *Life* in New York.

When the operator inquired for Mr. Manning's first name, Jock answered sharply, "He hasn't got a first name! If they have any trouble identifying him, tell them I want the Manning who's a fag!"

"Jock, please!" Louise said, coming from the pool, wet, naked, and wanting to take away the phone. But he tore it from her reaching hand, turned away, blocking her with his broad back.

Manning was not at the office, it being past nine o'clock, New York time. But after Jock's insistence, the switchboard operator was willing to patch in the call to Manning's apartment, without disclosing his number.

Louise had pulled a robe around herself. She was putting one across Jock's shoulders when the call was finally put through.

"Manning? Finley! Jock Finley! Just saw an advance copy of your article."

"Oh? Good. They're very high on it here, you know. Your studio and *Life*."

"Oh, are they? Well, Mr. Manning, I am not high on it! I am bringing suit tomorrow to have this issue of *Life* banned! That's right! Banned! For criminal libel!"

"Finley . . . Jock. Listen to me . . ."

"I am suing *Life* and you! For five million dollars! What are you trying to do? Get even with me? Because I found out about you and Axel Steenstrup? Is that it? Well, this'll only make the whole thing a big public scandal! You try to destroy me, I'll destroy you! That's right! You say I murdered Carr, I say that if Axel had been where he was supposed to be, taking care of Carr,

478

instead of out screwing with you, we might have saved his life! Yeah! We might have saved Carr's life."

Riding a tide of drunken, self-righteous indignation, and with a feeling of having destroyed Manning completely, Jock asked, "What do you say to that, Queenie?"

Louise made another move to take the phone away, but Jock turned again, not only eluding her but hurting her in the process.

"Finley, can you hear me?" Manning was saying, his voice cool, hurt, and quite tense.

"I can hear you!"

"Finley, I know how you feel about me. I've known it from the very first time we talked, out on location. When I looked into your eyes. I saw that you knew instantly not only what I am. But how I could have come to feel about you."

"You bet your sweet ass, to quote a phrase from Freud," Jock said viciously.

"I didn't resent your antagonism toward me. I didn't even mind too much your finding out about Ax. It didn't keep me from respecting your work. I understood you. I even understood your disliking me. Because I think you're afraid of me, and people like me. As though something about us might rub off on you. Believe me, I understand that. After all . . ."

Here Manning paused, debating whether to continue or not.

"After all, the thing men like you never remember, or perhaps never even think about, is that some time, yesterday, or long ago, I had to find out for myself that I am what you hate so much. And when I did find out, I hated me just as much as you do. More. So I know how you feel about me.

"And I think maybe that's why you're so upset now. That I'm the one who did the story. I held you up for the world to see, for yourself to see. You're saying, what right does a fag have to criticize me? I'm better than he is! More a man than he is! To be criticized by a fag, yes, that could hurt.

"Or is it that my camera is your conscience? That it shows you what you are, and you don't like it. Any more than I particularly like what I am. There is one difference between us, though. I have made peace with what I am. I accept myself, finally. You don't. You still have to wrestle with your conscience. I don't.

479

"So I'm better off than you. Not better, mind you, just better off."

"I'm still going to sue!" Jock said, but with less venom, less voice, now.

"I can't stop you," Manning said. "And it will be a mess. But I can't back down. And *Life* certainly won't."

"We'll see!" Jock threatened.

"I'm sorry you feel that way, Jock. I would have liked to be your friend."

"I'll bet you would! And that's not all!"

"No," Manning said softly, sadly. "No, that's not all." And he hung up.

When Louise tried to take the phone from his hands, this time Jock let her.

As soon as she hung up, it rang. This time it was Marty. He insisted on talking to Jock. But Jock would not answer. So he left word with Louise.

There was to be a meeting tomorrow, at one o'clock, at the studio. Jock had better be there! Louise hung up, gave Jock the message. But Jock glared at the phone and called out, "Fuck you, Marty White! Fuck you, laddie!"

The red Ferrari pulled into the executive parking lot and was expected, for the uniformed guard directed Jock to a space reserved between Marty's big white Rolls and the president's limousine. Jock turned off the ignition. His hand still on the key in the switch, he looked up at the administration building across the way.

Oh, you bastards, so you're all waiting up there! And you're going to try to talk me out of it! Well, I've got a surprise for all you pricks!

He got out of the car. But instead of crossing the street to administration, he waited at the entrance to the lot. In a few minutes another car pulled in, a blue Mercedes 300 sedan. There was a moment when the guard refused to grant it parking space. But Jock said, "Mike, if my lawyer isn't allowed to park here, there won't be any meeting." Jock accented the point by referring to the president's limousine. The guard yielded instantly.

480

Jock Finley, client, and Marvin Mossberg, attorney, went up the steps of administration, past the rigorously guarded front desk, up the elevator to the topmost floor and down the long hall to the office of the head of the studio. The receptionist, who seemed to have been smiling stiffly from the moment the guard in the parking lot called to announce that Finley and his lawyer were on the way, trilled nervously, "Oh, Mr. Finley, good afternoon! I believe they're waiting for you."

As she swung open the door to the small executive conference room, Jock could see in quick succession, revealed as in a pan shot, the president at the head of the table, the studio head alongside him, Joe Moscowitz, chief counsel from New York, Harris Congers, head of all public relations, and Abel Neustadt, whom Jock recognized from photographs which he had seen in newspapers and magazines in connection with many famous, well-publicized legal trials.

Marty White sat at the far end of the table, and by virtue of geography occupied a seemingly neutral position, midway between both sides and opposite the president. The near side of the conference table was unoccupied.

The president was on his feet, smiling, extending his hand. "Jock! Hiya, kid!" As they shook hands, the president seemed aware of Mossberg for the first time. As though there had been no warning from the guard and no warning from the receptionist, the president acted surprised.

"Marvin Mossberg, my attorney," Jock introduced.

"Attorney? Between friends, kid?" the president asked, deeply and much too obviously hurt. But he shook hands with Mossberg and introduced him. Mossberg knew Marty White, the studio head, and Moscowitz, chief counsel.

When Mossberg was introduced to Abel Neustadt, his questioning, suspicious look caused the president to explain.

"Mr. Neustadt is here in his capacity as counsel to the Motion Picture Producers Association. We consider this situation and its implications important to the entire industry."

Mossberg only nodded and gestured to Jock to be seated. They were ready for the opening of the meeting.

"Gentlemen, let's be honest with each other. Let's be frank,"

481

the president began. "We're all friends in this room. Our interests are the same. We have nothing to hide from each other. From the company's side, we think we're in a very fortunate position.

"We have a wonderful picture, a big picture, a roadshow, hard-ticket picture! We have the last and best performance of Preston Carr. With ... I add ... with the magic chemistry of Daisy Donnell. And the debut, as a producer-director of big, big pictures, of a young man who I am proud to say is the most brilliant young director in America! Maybe the world!"

Screw you, Mr. President, Jock was saying to himself.

"Now, this young man is highly sensitive. As he must be, as he should be. How else is a man going to be such a creative director unless he is sensitive? But there is such a thing as being supersensitive. For example, his sensitivity has, unfortunately, made him react in very distressing fashion to an article in *Life*. Due, I might add, not to what the article says. But due to his interpretation of it. No one else, I repeat, no one else has put this same interpretation on this same article."

Half rising out of his chair, Jock exploded, "No one else, I repeat, no one else has been libeled either!" Mossberg reached out to restrain Jock, who continued, "So stop trying to turn this meeting into a trial. Because nothing is going to be decided here! I am not going to change my mind!"

Mossberg's tight grip on his forearm forced Jock back into his chair and into momentary silence.

"Now, it would be better for all concerned," the president continued, "for our young director, for the picture, for the company, if we didn't go looking for trouble. The word is out about the picture, and it is excellent. The *Life* article is sensational. So why look for lawsuits?

"To show you how fair and open-minded I have tried to be about this, despite the fact that I am an attorney, and despite the feeling of our house counsel and vice-president, Mr. Moscowitz, I have taken the *Life* spread to outside counsel for their opinion. You know what they said? Absolutely, definitely, it is not libelous!

"But not satisfied with that, Amco Industries, in view of the pending merger, has consulted their own counsel about the matter.

482

Same answer! Not libelous! We can't *all* be wrong, can we?" the president pleaded.

Brushing aside Mossberg's restraining hand, Jock was up on his feet. "Oh, what a big ball game *this* has turned out to be! You're going to hem me in with your counsel, and Amco's counsel, and the slick, sharp, famous, overly publicized bastard sitting right there representing the MPPA. And why? Because it's the merger you're worried about! Well, screw you and your merger! My reputation is more valuable to me than all your stock deals and all your mergers!"

The president smiled, gently, indulgently, as one does toward the too-young and the too-sensitive. "What do you think you're going to accomplish with a suit and trial? I'll tell you. Those people who never read the *Life* article will learn about it. And those people who read it and forgot it will be reminded of it. You'll do more to make that article famous by suing than by forgetting. If you really think it's libelous, don't call attention to it. Bury it! A lawsuit won't do that."

Turning to Mossberg, the president asked, "Do you think you're protecting your client's reputation and his professional future, by bringing suit? Speaking frankly, and among friends, can you see anything to be achieved for him by lawsuits and bad publicity?"

As Mossberg was about to answer, the door opened silently. One of Congers's young assistants from publicity slipped into the room, placed a single-sheet memo face down before Congers, and departed.

During Mossberg's answer, Congers pulled the memo forward, and like a poker player with a hole card, lifted it just enough to read the brief message typed there. Then he passed it, face down, to the president, and so it went from one to another on the company's side of the table, all through Mossberg's answer.

"I am here, gentlemen, because my client, after due consideration, feels that the *Life* article, good as it may be for the picture, is highly damaging to his career, his public image. The article accuses him, by strong and direct inference, of a heinous moral crime. Hence, it is libelous and damaging to him, both professionally and personally. So papers demanding an injunction *pendente*

483

lite are being drawn at this moment and will be served within the next twenty-four hours. Against *Life*. And against a photographer-writer named Russell Manning."

"We think it would be terrible mistake!" the president warned.

"And we don't think so," Mossberg said simply, but quite firmly.

"And there is nothing we can do to change your client's mind?"

"Nothing!" Jock exploded.

"Nothing," Mossberg repeated in more judicial tone. "Unless you can convince *Life* to withdraw the issue."

By this time the face-down memo had been passed to Neustadt. The short, dark man, who seemed one half head, one half body, leaned forward for the first time. He picked up the memo, glanced at it, folded it. Marty White, who would have been next in line, could barely restrain himself from asking to see it.

"We can't persuade *Life* to kill an issue," the president said. "No one can!" Mossberg made a gesture indicating, then, how helpless he was to reverse the decision to sue. "Too bad," the president said. "This will ruin all our plans! Everything!"

Jock couldn't resist saying bitterly, "I'm sorry about your merger!"

"Oh, that," the president belittled. "I meant we were about to offer you a three-picture deal. You and Marty White. Two properties to be mutually agreed upon, each with a budget of five million, and the third with a budget not to exceed ten million. A really big picture! That property also subject to mutual agreement."

The amount of preparation that had gone into this meeting was suddenly quite clear to Jock Finley. They had been through every phase of it, Marty and the president, right down to the details of the deal. So it was a buy-out, a bribe! Anything to keep Jock Finley's mouth shut, tight! And Marty was part of it!

Mossberg, in a cool professional way, asked, "Is that an offer? And if it is, is it conditioned upon my client's agreement not to sue?"

Jock waited for the answer. What did one call a bribe when one didn't want to call it a bribe?

"It is an offer," the president said with meticulous enunciation. "Without any strings. We have such high regard for this young man, and his talent, that we want him to make pictures for us, no matter what!" Then he added, quite significantly, "Regardless of lawsuits or magazine articles or what anybody says. Even if he considers it libelous, we don't."

Aware of the legal noose the president had thrown around Jock Finley, Mossberg said only, "We'll take it under advisement."

"Good! Good!" the president said. He looked to Neustadt, seeking his next cue. Neustadt was folding the single-sheet memo yet another time, to a razor-sharp edge. He paused, giving himself a long moment of silence before he spoke.

"Mr. Mossberg . . . Mr. Finley . . ." and Neustadt turned to Marty to add, "Mr. White . . ." to give fabric to the fiction that Marty had not been part of the plan till now. "No doubt you are all wondering what I am doing here. Aside from my capacity as counsel to the MPPA. I will make no secret of it. Your president asked me to attend, as a sort of mediator, as a third party, to help to resolve this very sticky, very distasteful problem.

"I wouldn't be fair and honest if I didn't tell you, in advance, that as counsel to the association, I would always rather see a compromise than a lawsuit, with all the expense, hard feeling, and bad personal publicity. We are one big industry, one big family, and constantly in the public eye. Not always a friendly public eye, I might add. For everybody's sake, I think that in all cases it is better to settle in private than to litigate in public. So I admit I start out being prejudiced in favor of settlement.

"But aside from that, it's as much to my interest as yours, Mr. Mossberg, to see that Jock Finley, as a member of this industry, is protected. That he is not libeled. Or victimized in any way. So when I hear the recitation of the facts, when I study the article that is the basis of this potential lawsuit, I have to ask, as one good lawyer to another, suppose you sue and suppose your case is not thrown out on motion, and you finally get to a jury, how are you going to prove damages?"

It was obvious to Jock that Mossberg did not intend to enter such a discussion with Neustadt. Even Neustadt did not expect that Mossberg would. So he continued.

"Money damages? How can you prove that? When I, and a

number of other reliable witnesses"—and here Neustadt made a small but quite clear gesture indicating one of the reasons there were so many men at this table—"sat here and heard one of the largest studios in the industry, well aware of the *Life* article, make a bonafide offer of a three-picture deal to your client, on terms as good as it is possible to get. In the face of that, how can you prove damage?"

Even without a lawyer's knowledge of the fine points, Jock knew. He had that same cold feeling in his groin that he had had in the moment when Preston Carr was suddenly thrown and almost trampled by that mustang. He knew the trickery involved here. He knew Marty's part in it.

Now Mossberg realized that he could no longer delay or evade.

"Mr. Neustadt, I pride myself on being a pretty good lawyer. But when it comes to libel and slander, you are the expert."

Jock could see from the way Mossberg said it, and the way Neustadt reacted to it, reddening somewhat in restrained anger, that it was a remark that hung on the slender edge between flattery and insult. But Mossberg continued.

"But there are, after all, other kinds of damage to a man besides crass dollars. There is damage to his standing in the community. There is his public image. There is what people think of him in his chosen profession. A man is entitled to walk down the street without the world pointing to him as a murderer. Reputation, gentlemen, Mr. Finley's reputation is what is at stake here!"

Neustadt, who had seemed to listen to Mossberg with meticulous attention, glanced at the president. Now Neustadt smiled warmly, indulgently, and said, "It would have been nicer if it came as a surprise. But I suppose you have to tell him now."

Jock stole a glance at Mossberg, who was as openly and obviously puzzled as he was.

"In view of the fact that Preston Carr, the King, made his last picture for this studio," the president said, "and that he died of a heart attack, our board of directors felt the least we could do was help to fight this deadly disease. So last evening, we voted a one-hundred-thousand-dollar grant to establish a Preston Carr Annual Memorial Medal. To be given each year by the American Heart Fund for outstanding service to humanity!"

486

Jock waited, not daring to breathe. Then he heard it.

"The first recipient of the Preston Carr Medal will be his friend, his admirer, and coworker, the distinguished American film director, Jock Finley!"

"That's . . . that's . . . very nice . ..." Jock said, turning to Mossberg. Before Mossberg could say a word, Congers intruded.

"Tell him about the world premiere!"

"Oh yes," the president continued. "The presentation will be made the night of the Heart Fund Benefit at Lincoln Center. Which will be the world premiere of *Mustang!*"

"The Heart Fund?" Mossberg asked. "They accepted? They agreed to all this?"

Neustadt strained to lean across the table and spread the memo face up. It was a Xeroxed copy of a teletype message.

> HEART FUND AGREES TO ACCEPT DONATION
> ANNUAL MEDAL. FINLEY AND PREMIERE
> OKAYED FOR JAN. 20TH. DETAILS UPCOMING.

Without smiling, and in a grave tone, Neustadt said, "Now, one couldn't very well say that Mr. Finley's reputation has been damaged, could one?"

Brushing aside Mossberg's restraining hand, rising so precipitously that his chair was hurled against the wall, Jock shouted, "You're not going to shut me up that way! I don't have to accept any deal or any medal!"

"Fortunately, that doesn't matter," Neustadt said. "You see, libel is dependent upon what *other* people think of you. Your reputation is not based on what *you* feel but on what *they* feel. They've offered you the deal, the medal, knowing full well what's in *Life*. So, obviously, in the opinion of other people your reputation has not been damaged, professionally or otherwise. Your own counsel will tell you that."

Jock did not even turn to Mossberg. He knew. He knew the truth of it, the inevitable, irreversible, dishonest truth of it. They had him boxed in. No lawsuit could succeed now.

When men are fighting for huge rewards there are no holds

487

barred, not bribery, blackmail, violence, certainly not honors, rewards, or whatever it takes to still any disturbing voice.

With the neatness and dispatch of men experienced at this kind of corporate surgery they had cut off his balls and sewn them up in his mouth at the same time, so that he could not even cry out in pain.

Jock Finley did not wait for his attorney, but started out of the room. The last thing he heard was the president saying to Mossberg, "Counselor, we don't feel it's fair for you to suffer due to this unexpected turn of events. The studio stands ready to pay your fee, whatever it would have been."

It was evening. Dusk. The sun was gone. The last red glow was going. The vapor trails of the New York-bound jets were gray now, not pink. On one of those jets, the president and Abel Neustadt were relaxing over their first cocktail after a very good, highly satisfactory day's work.

Jock Finley lay fully clothed on the chaise out back by his unlighted pool. He turned his gaze from the sky and a jet heading East toward the dark pool before him. It would be a cool evening, for even now steam was beginning to rise from the heated water.

He had been here alone for some hours, though he knew there was editing still to be done. The phone had rung many times. It must have been Mary from the editing room. Or possibly Louise. It didn't matter. He had not answered.

Now the soft sound of a motor car pulled into the driveway. It stopped, the engine was turned off. A car door opened and closed with expensive, luxurious solidity. The fence door that led from the driveway to the pool area opened a bit squeakily and swung closed.

Jock did not turn. Nor was he surprised when it was Marty's voice.

"Laddie. It's me. I called half a dozen times. You didn't answer. I sent my chauffeur to see. He reported your Ferrari was in the driveway. So I came over."

488

It was dark now. No lights were on. Nor did Jock move to put them on. The short, plump man with the shiny bald head, the heavy black eyeglass frames, sat down on the other chaise and waited. But Jock did not turn to him. After minutes of silence, the round little Owl talked.

"Laddie, what do you think is bugging you? Manning's accusation that you killed Preston Carr? Oh, no. What's eating you is the fact that you *did* kill Preston Carr."

Marty expected the young man would face him now. But he didn't.

"They were loaded for you, kid. Yes! If you hadn't walked out when you did, they were ready with a written statement from your chief wrangler. From Tex."

Now Jock did turn.

"That's right, laddie. They had it all. Because as you yourself said, it's a big ball game. The World Series! Millions are involved. Hundreds of millions! No one, certainly no thirty-one-year-old kid, is going to be allowed to stand in the way.

"What's the moral of the story? There isn't any. And there is no judgment. No justice. They didn't do anything different than you did. They didn't spare you. You didn't spare Preston Carr. You're even. So you have no right to complain or feel aggrieved about them or *Life* or Manning.

"But you don't like that. You'd like to be free to do whatever comes into your head. Only you don't want to grant the other guy the same right. That's what's so strange about you young cannibals today. You'd like to devour us all! Well, you found out that the other guys, the older guys, are not going to take it lying down.

"You found out something else, too. You're not as free as you'd like to think. The tough young man is a boy scout underneath. You have a conscience, a soft spot. You're sensitive inside. Cocky, proud, superior, ruthless! And soft on the inside. So you don't know how to handle it. Well, take a little advice from an old-timer."

Jock moved quickly to reach for a cigarette. Marty misunderstood it as anger.

"I know. After all, I'm an agent. A flesh-peddler. A dirty old man who indulges his tastes in ways you don't approve. So who am

I to give you advice? Every community has its Shylock, someone to call names, to make jokes about. Out here it's agents. But I ask you, think back and decide for yourself, did I do less for you than I should have, or could have? If I did, then you can call me names.

"Sure I used you in order to become an executive producer. Right? But in the process I made you an important producer-director. So where's the loss? Haven't I at least earned the right to have you listen to me?"

Jock lit up a cigarette, did not answer. But silence would do for Marty.

"Laddie . . . what makes you think you're so different from anyone else? What makes you think that when Morris Weiss came out here he didn't feel the same way you did? Yes, this fat, sometimes foolish, self-indulgent, past middle-aged man, who can't sleep for scheming, was like you once. Even though your youthful vanity won't let you think so. But I was.

"Till I learned one thing. Out here, or anywhere in this wide world, in our system or any system, there are winners, and there are losers. But no heroes. Life does not allow for heroes. All of us do terrible things in our time, and feel justified when we do them.

"You did a terrible thing to Preston Carr! Yes! And you can go around the rest of your life looking for punishment. But you shouldn't. Because there isn't any. Except the punishment you make for yourself.

"I say, don't become a loser just to punish yourself. After all, what leads you to believe that losers have more ethics and more piety than winners? That's a lie. Made up by losers.

"If you feel guilty, and you should, learn something from it. How to be a decent human being. Put a limit, an outside boundary, on your ambition. On what you'll do to make a picture, get a shot, achieve an effect. You'll be important from now on. You'll be in a position now to use people, desperate people, vain people, frightened people, hungry, unsatisfied, ambitious people. That's a power that's almost godlike. Use it well. That's what you can do to ease your conscience.

"In other words, be a *mensch*," the little man said intensely. Then he spoke more softly.

490

"Now, you'll finish editing the picture. You'll have it scored and dubbed and ready for the premiere. Then you'll go to New York, accept that award, and make a nice speech. And we'll start looking for the next property for our next picture. Better advice I couldn't give my own son."

Marty White rose, waited. Jock did not turn to face him. He was silent a long time, motionless a long time. Then, finally, he nodded his head without facing the older man. Marty was gratified, and he suggested softly, "There's a girl named Louise. . ."

Jock turned quickly, curious and resentful.

"Yes, she called me. Who else is she going to talk to? You?" Marty asked. "She's worried. Very worried. She sounds like a nice, sensible girl. You should call her."

Marty started away. By the squeak of the fence door, Jock knew Marty was gone. He heard the car door, the motor, the Rolls backing out of the driveway. He was alone again. In the dark.

He turned back to the huge house, considered for a moment turning on some lights. Instead he picked up the phone, dialed, waited. It rang at the other end. Finally it was answered. She sounded breathless, as though she had to leave the shower to answer, or had just been unlocking the front door when he rang.

"Hello?"

"Louise?"

"Oh . . . Jock."

"Busy tonight?"

"I have a date."

"With him?"

"Uh-huh."

"Could you break it?"

"Jock, he's a terribly nice guy. He doesn't deserve that kind of treatment."

"I have to talk to someone." There was a pause and no answer. "I need you, Louise."

"I'll . . . I'll call him," she said finally, but not without regret.

Before she could hang up, he said quickly, "Lulu!"

"Yes, Jock?"

"In . . . in January, I have to go to New York. To get some kind of award. It'll be the premiere, too. Would you come with me?"

491

"We'll see . . ."

"I . . . I can't go alone. Say you'll come. Please?"

"Jock, I have to call if I want to catch him before he leaves his office."

"Sure . . . sure. Pick you up in an hour."

THE AMERICAN HEART FUND

cordially invites you to attend
its Annual Benefit Film Festival
at Philharmonic Hall, Lincoln Center
for the Performing Arts.

January 20, 1971

This event will also mark the
First Annual Award for Distinguished Service
to Humanity of the
PRESTON CARR-AMERICAN HEART FUND MEDAL.

This year's honored recipient
will be the famed American Producer-Director
JOCK FINLEY whose film MUSTANG!
will have its world premiere
performance as our festival film.
All proceeds from this performance
will go to the benefit of the fund.

Presentation 8 P.M.   *Black Tie Requested*
Performance 8:35   *Price per person $50*

(Ticket $5 Contribution $45)

Jock Finley, in his velvet-collared dinner jacket, tailored in London, stood on the stage of the Philharmonic Hall of Lincoln

492

Center for the Performing Arts, and, to great applause, was presented with a solid gold medallion in a royal blue leather case. The medal bore, in relief, the fine, strong profile of Preston Carr.

Jock spoke briefly, thanked the Heart Fund for selecting *Mustang!* for their benefit and for awarding him the first Preston Carr-Heart Fund award. He ended, saying, "The man who really deserves this award is only here in spirit tonight. A great man, a great actor, who was the victim of the disease we are all dedicated to fight tonight. I am sure Preston Carr would have wanted it just this way."

There was more applause. Jock Finley made his way back to his seat, fifth row on the aisle, just behind the president, the head of the studio, and Abel Neustadt, all of whom applauded loudly and looked up and smiled warmly as Jock passed them.

The lights came down. The first bold music shook the hall. The first shot of *Mustang!* burst onto the screen. Jock whispered to the striking blond girl beside him, "Let's get the hell out of here!"

They started up the dark aisle, Jock with the leather case in hand, leading the way. Louise hurried to keep up with him. Applause exploded all around them each time another credit flashed onto the screen. When they reached the auditorium door, they heard the greatest burst of applause. Jock and Louise turned to see.

On the screen, superimposed over a great wide helicopter shot of the Nevada mountains, in brilliant color, was the name and legend PRODUCED AND DIRECTED BY JOCK FINLEY.

Louise started to applaud now, too.

"Don't!" Jock said, seizing her hand.

He shouldered his way through the door, still holding her hand. And they were gone.

HENRY DENKER is best known as a writer for stage, screen, and television. For Broadway he wrote *Time Limit*; *A Far Country*, a dramatic biography of Sigmund Freud; and the prize-winning *A Case of Libel*, an adaptation of Louis Nizer's *My Life in Court*.

For ten years, he was producer-director of *The Greatest Story Ever Told* on radio, for which he won the first Emmy ever awarded. He has written for such television programs as *The Hallmark Hall of Fame*, *Studio One* and the Alcoa and Philco playhouses.